This companion volume to the complete PS Publishing edition of *The Inhabitant of the Lake and Other Unwelcome Tenants* collects all of Ramsey Campbell's remaining Lovecraftian stories that are of less than novel length. It begins with the first tale Campbell wrote immediately after that first Arkham House book, and comes up to date with the novella *The Last Revelation of Gla'aki*, his recent return to his own Lovecraftian territory, where he rediscovers Lovecraft's first principles and strips away the accretions of the mythos that developed after Lovecraft's death.

The book includes the first drafts of "Cold Print" and "The Franklyn Paragraphs", and offers the bonus of "Mushrooms from Merseyside", all his Lovecraftian tales inhumanly transmuted into limericks. The book also collects his Lovecraftian non-fiction, not least his transcription of an English correspondent's letters to Lovecraft and a close reading of three Lovecraft tales.

Like the companion volume, this book is superbly illustrated by Randy Broecker in the great tradition of *Weird Tales*.

VISIONS *from* BRICHESTER

VISIONS *from*
BRICHESTER

RAMSEY CAMPBELL

Illustrated by
RANDY BROECKER

PS Publishing Ltd | Grosvenor House | 1 New Road
Hornsea, HU18 1PG | United Kingdom

editor@pspublishing.co.uk | www.pspublishing.co.uk

Contents

Appendices

VISIONS *from* BRICHESTER

to Isaac, with love—
read on, young man!

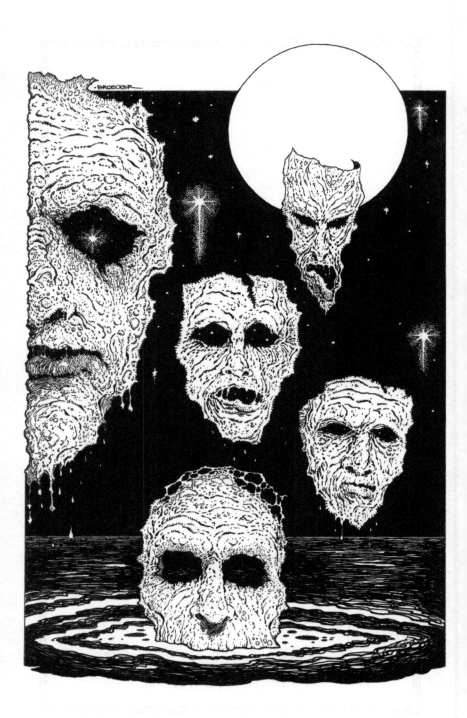

THE STONE ON THE ISLAND

ARRIVING HOME THAT NIGHT, MICHAEL NASH THOUGHT AT first that his father was asleep.

Dr Stanley Nash, his father, was lying back in an armchair in the living-room. On the table beside him stood an empty glass, propping up a sealed envelope, and near these lay a library book. It was all quite ordinary, and Michael only glanced at him before entering the kitchen in search of coffee. Fifteen minutes later he tried to wake his father, and realised what the contents of the glass must have been.

Nash sensed the events of the next few days with numbed nerves. While he realised that any further evidence he might give would be disbelieved, he heard the words "suicide while the balance of the mind was disturbed" with a feeling of guilt; he fingered that envelope in his pocket, but forced himself to keep it there. After that arrived those people who saw their admiration of Nash's medical ability as a pretext for taking a half-day off work; then the largely incomprehensible funeral service, the rattle of earth on wood, and the faster journey home.

Various duties prevented Michael Nash from examining his father's papers until 27 October 1962. He might not have plunged into even then, but for the explicit injunction in his father's final note. Thus it was that as the sun flamed redly on the windows of Gladstone Place, Nash sat in the study of No 6, with the envelope

open before him on the desk and the enclosed sheet spread out for
reading.

"My recent research" (Michael read) "has pried into regions
whose danger I did not realise. You know enough of these hidden
forces which I have attempted to destroy to see that, in certain cases,
death is the only way out. Something has fastened itself upon me,
but I will suicide before its highest pitch of potency is reached. It has
to do with the island beyond Severnford, and my notes and diary
will furnish more details that I have time to give. If you want to
carry on my work, confine yourself to other powers—and take my
case as a warning not to go too far."

That was all; and no doubt many people would have torn up the
letter. But Michael Nash knew enough of the basis of his father's
beliefs not to treat them lightly; indeed, he held the same creeds.
From an early age he had read his father's secret library of rare
books, and from these had acquired an awareness which the
majority of people never possess. Even in the modern office building
where he worked or in the crowded streets of central Brichester, he
could sense things drifting invisibly whose existence the crowd never
suspected; and he knew very well of the hidden forces which clustered about a house in Victoria Road, a demolished wall at the
bottom of Mercy Hill, and such towns as Clotton, Temphill and
Goatswood. So he did not scoff at his father's last note, but only
turned to the private papers kept in the study.

In the desk drawer he found the relevant documents, inside a file
cover covertly removed from his office building. The file contained
a photograph of the island beyond Severnford by daylight, snapped
from the Severn bank and hence undetailed; another photograph,
taken by a member of the Society for Psychical Research, of the
island with dim white ovals floating above it, more likely reflections
on the camera lens than psychic manifestations, but inexplicable
enough to be reported in the *Brichester Weekly News;* and several
sheets of notepaper inscribed in varicoloured inks. To these pages
Michael turned.

The writing consisted of a description of the island and a
chronology of various events connected with it. "Approx. 200 ft
across, roughly circular. Little vegetation except short grass. Ruins of
Roman temple to unnamed deity at centre of island (top of slight
hill). Opp. side of hill from Severnford, about 35 ft down, artificial
hollow extending back 10ft and containing stone.

"Island continuously site of place of worship. Poss. pre-Roman nature deity (stone predates Roman occupation); then Roman temple built. In medieval times witch supposed to live on island. In 17th cent. witch-cult met there and invoked water elementals. *In all cases stone avoided.* Circa 1790 witch-cult disbanded, but stray believers continued to visit.

"1803: Joseph Norton to island to worship. Found soon after in Severnford, mutilated and raving about 'going too near to stone'. Died same day.

"1804: Recurring stories of pale object floating over island. Vaguely globular and inexplicably disturbing.

"1827: Nevill Rayner, clergyman at Severnford, to island ('I must rid my flock of this evil'). Found in church the day after, alive but mutilated.

"1856: Attempt by unknown tramp to steal boat and spend night on island. Returns frantically to Severnford, but will only say that something had 'fluttered at him' as he grounded the boat.

"1866: Prostitute strangled and dumped on island, but regains consciousness. Taken off by party of dockside workers and transported to Brichester Central Hospital. Two days later found horribly mutilated in hospital ward. Attacker never discovered.

"1870: onward: Recrudescence of rumours about pale globes on island.

"1890: Alan Thorpe, investigating local customs, visits island. Removes stone and takes it to London. Three days later is found wounded horribly—and stone is back on island.

"1930: Brichester University students visit island. One is stranded by others as joke. Taken off in morning in hysterical condition over something he has seen. Four days later runs screaming from Mercy Hill Hospital, and is run over. Mutilations not all accounted for by car accident.

"To date no more visits to island—generally shunned."

So much for the historical data; now Nash hunted for the diary to clarify this synopsis. But the diary was not to be found in the study, nor indeed in the house, and he had learned very little about the island. But what he had learned did not seem particularly frightening. After all, perhaps his father had 'gone too near the s tone', whatever that meant, which he was not going to do; further, he would take some of the five-pointed stones from the study cupboard; and there was always the Saaamaaa Ritual if things got too dangerous. He most certainly must go, for this thing on the island had driven his father to poison himself, and might do worse if not stopped. It was dark now, and he did not intend to make a nocturnal trip; but tomorrow, Sunday, he would hire a boat and visit the island.

On the edge of the docks next day he found a small hut ("Hire a boat and see the Severn at its best!") where he paid 7/6 and was helped into a rather wet, rather unpainted motor-boat. He spun the wheel and hissed through the water. Upriver the island climbed into view and rushed at him. At the top of its hill stood an isolated fragment of temple wall, but otherwise it was only a green dome round which water rippled, with faint connotations of a woman in the bath. He twisted the wheel and the island hurried to one side. The boat rounded the verdant tip; he switched off the motor, pulled the boat inshore and grounded it; he looked up, and there, glimmering faintly from the shadowy hollow, was the stone.

It was carved of some white rock, in the shape of a globe supported by a small pillar. Nash noticed at once its vaguely luminous quality; it seemed to flicker dimly, almost as if continually appearing and vanishing. And it looked very harmless and purposeless. Further up the hill he momentarily thought something pale wavered; but his sharp glance caught nothing.

His hand closed on the five-pointed star he carried, but he did not draw it out. Instead, a sudden feeling engulfed him that he could not approach that stone, that he was physically incapable of doing so. He could not move his foot—but, with a great effort, he managed to lift it and take a step forward. He forced himself toward the stone, and succeeded in pushing himself within a foot of it. However, while he might have reached it, he was unable to touch it. His hand could not reach out—but he strained it out trembling, and one finger poked the hard surface. A shiver of cold ran up his arm, and that was all.

Immediately he knew that he had done the wrong thing. The whole place seemed to grow dark and cold, and somewhere there was a faint shifting noise. Without knowing why, Nash threw himself back from the stone and stumbled down the hill to the boat. He started the motor, slammed the wheel left and cut away through the water—and not until the island had dropped out of sight did he begin to approach the bank.

———

"You didn't have to come back to work so soon, you know."

"I know," Nash said, "but I think I'll feel better here," and he crossed to his desk. The post had mounted up, he noted disgustedly, though there were few enough pieces to suggest that someone had tried to help him out—Gloria, probably. He began to sort the bits of paper into order; Ambrose Dickens, F. M. Donnelly, H. Dyck, Ernest Earl—and having married the post with the relevant files, he sat down again. The first one only required issue of a form, but one of which he had no stock.

"Baal," he remarked to some perverse deity, and immediately afterwards discovered that Gloria also lacked the form. A search around the office gained him five or six, but these would not last long.

"I think this calls for a trip downstairs," he remarked to Gloria.

"Not today," she informed him. "Since you've . . . been away, they've brought in a new arrangement—everybody makes out a list of what they want, and on Wednesdays one person goes down and gets the lot. The rest of the time the storeroom is locked."

"Great," said Nash resignedly, "so we have to hang on for three days . . . What else has happened?"

"Well, you've noticed the new arrival over there—her name's Jackie—and there's someone new on the third floor too. Don't know his name, but he likes foreign films, so John got talking to him at once, of course . . . "

"Jackie—" he mused. ". . . . Oh hell, that reminds me! I'm supposed to be calling on Jack Purvis today where he works in Camside, to collect some money he owes me!"

"Well, what are you going to do?"

"Take the afternoon off, maybe—" and he began to fill in his leave sheet. He passed the new girl's desk, where John was unsuccessfully attempting to discover any interest in Continental films ('No, Ing*mar*') and continued to a slight argument with Mr Faber over his projected leave, finally granted because of his recent bereavement.

That afternoon he collected the debt in Camside and caught the bus home. It was dark by the time the vehicle drew up at the bottom of Mercy Hill, and the streets were almost deserted. As he climbed the hill his footsteps clattered back from the three-storey walls, and he slipped on the frost which was beginning to glisten in the pavement's pores. Lunar sickles echoed from Gladstone Place's windows and slid from the panes of the front door as he opened it. He hung up his coat, gathered the envelopes from the doormat and, peeling one open, entered the living-room and switched on the light.

He saw immediately the face watching him between the curtains.

For a minute Nash considered the courses open to him. He could turn and run from the house, but the intruder would then be free in the building—and besides, he did not like to turn his back. The telephone was in the study, and hence inaccessible. He saw the one remaining course in detail, came out of his trance and, grabbing a poker from the fireplace, slowly approached the curtains, staring into the other's eyes.

"Come out," he said, "or I'll split your head with this. I mean that."

The eyes watched him unmoving, and there was no motion under the curtain.

"If you don't come out now—" Nash warned again.

He waited for some movement, then swung the poker at the point behind the curtain where he judged the man's stomach to be. There was no response from the face, but a tinkle of glass sounded. Confused, Nash poised the poker again and, with his other hand, wrenched the curtains apart.

Then he screamed.

The face hung there for a moment, then fluttered out through the broken pane.

Next morning, after a sleepless and hermetic night, Nash decided to go to the office.

On the bus, after a jolt of memory caused by the conductor's pale reflection, he could not avoid thoughts of last night's events. That they were connected with the island beyond Severnford he did not doubt; he had acted unwisely there, but now he knew to be wary. He must take every precaution, and that was why he was working today; to barricade his sanity against the interloper. He carried a five-pointed star in his pocket, and clutched it as he left the bus.

The lift caught him up and raised him to the fourth floor. He returned greetings automatically as he passed desks, but his face stiffened any attempted smile, and he was sure that everybody wondered 'What's wrong with Mike this morning?' Hanging up his coat, he glanced at the teapot, and remembered that he and Gloria were to make it that week.

Many of the files on his desk, he saw bitterly, related to cases needing that elusive form. He wandered down to the third floor, borrowed a few copies, and on the way out noticed someone's back view which seemed unfamiliar—the new arrival, he realised, and headed for the lift.

"Well," Gloria broke in some time later, "I'd better collect the cups."

Nash collected the teapot and followed her out. In a room at the end of the passage water bubbled in a heater, and the room's doorway gaped lightlessly. His thoughts turned to his pocket as he switched on the light. They filled up the pot and transferred the tea to the cups.

"I'll take our end of the office," he remarked, and balanced the tray into the office.

Two faces were pressed against the window, staring in at him.

He managed to save the tray, but one cup toppled and inundated Mr Faber's desk. "Sorry—I'm sorry—here, let me mop it up, quick," he said hurriedly, and the faces rippled horribly in a stray breeze. Thinking in a muddled way of the things outside the window, the pentacle in his pocket, and the disgust of Mr Faber's client on receiving teastained correspondence, he splashed the tray to the remaining desks and positioned his and Gloria's cups atop their beermats.

He glared for a minute into the bizarrely-set eyes beyond the pane, noticed a pigeon perched on the opposite roof, and turned to Gloria. "What's wrong with that pigeon?" he inquired, pointing with an unsteady finger. The faces must block any view of the bird from her desk.

"What, that one over there? I don't see anything wrong with it," she replied, looking straight through the faces.

"Oh, I . . . just thought it was injured," answered Nash, unable to frame any further remark *(Am I going mad or what?)*—and the telephone rang. Gloria glanced at him questioningly, then lifted the receiver. "Good morning, can I help you?" she asked, and scribbled on a scrap of paper. "And your initials? Yes, hold on a minute, please . . . G. F. E. Dickman's one of yours, isn't it, Mike?"

"What? . . . Oh, yes," and he extracted the file and, one eye on the silent watchers outside, returned to his desk. (For God's sake, they're only looking—not *doing* anything!) "Hello—Mr Dickman?"

". . . My . . . married recently . . . " filtered through office murmur and client's mumble.

"Would you like to speak up, please? I'm afraid I can't hear you."
The faces wavered towards the point where his gaze was resolutely
fixed.

"My son Da—. . . "

"Could you repeat your son's name, please?" The faces followed
his fugitive glance.

"What d'ya say?"

"Could you *repeat* that, please!" (Leave me alone, you bastards!)

"My son *David,* I said! If I'd known this was all I'd get, I'd of
come round meself!"

"Well, I might suggest that the next time you call, you take a few
elocution lessons first!—Hello?". . . He let the receiver click back
listlessly, and the faces were caught by the wind and flapped away
over the rooftops.

Gloria said "Oh, Mike, what did you do?"

The rest of the morning passed quickly and unpleasantly. Mr
Faber became emphatic over the correct way to treat clients, and
several other people stopped in passing to remark that they wished
they had the courage to answer calls that way ("Everyone seems to
have forgotten about your father," said Gloria.) But one o'clock
arrived at last, and Nash left for the canteen. He still looked round
sharply at every reflection in a plate-glass window, but managed to
forget temporarily in a search around the bookshops for the new
Lawrence Durrell, with the awareness of his pocket's contents
comforting him.

At two o'clock he returned to the office. At three he managed to
transport the tray without mishap; at four, unknown to Nash, a still
enraged G. F. E. Dickman arrived, and at four-thirty left, a little
mollified. A few minutes later came a phone message from Mr
Miller.

"Well, Mr Nash," said Mr Miller, sitting back in his chair, "I
believe you had a little trouble this morning. With a Mr Dickman,
I think. I hear you got a bit impatient with him."

"I'm afraid that's true," Nash agreed. "You see, he was mumbling
so much I couldn't make it out, and he got disagreeable when I
asked him to speak up."

"Ah . . . yes, I know," Mr Miller interrupted, "but I think you said
a little more to him than that. Er—abusive language. Well, now, I
know I feel myself like saying a few things to some of the people
who phone, but I feel this isn't the way . . . Is something the

matter?" He followed Nash's gaze to the window and turned back to him. "Anything wrong?"

"No . . . no, nothing at all." *(Three* now? God, how many of them are there?)

"Well, as I was saying, there's a right and a wrong way to handle clients. I know 'the customer is always right' is a stock phrase—it often isn't true here anyway, as you know—but we must try and avoid any direct offence. That only leads to ill feeling, and that won't do anybody any good. Now, I had Mr Dickman round here this afternoon, and I found it quite hard to smooth him down. I hope I won't have to do it again."

"Yes, I realise how you feel," Nash answered, peering frantically at the window, "but you must understand my situation."

"What situation is that?"

"Well, since my father died . . . That is, the way he died—"

"Oh, of course I realise that, but really you can't make it the excuse for everything."

"Well, if that's your shitty opinion—!"

Mr Miller looked up, but said nothing.

"All right," Nash said wearily. "I'm sorry, but— you know—"

"Of course," Mr Miller replied coldly. "But I would ask you to use a little more tact in future."

Something white bobbed outside the pane and disappeared in the distance.

That night, despite the strain of the day, Nash slept. He woke frequently from odd dreams of the stone and of his father with some mutilation he could never remember on waking. But when he boarded the bus the next day he felt few qualms when he remembered the haunters; he was more disturbed by the tensions he was building up in the office. After all, if the faces were confining themselves to mental torture, he was growing almost used to them by now. Their alienness repulsed him, but he could bear to look at them; and if they could attack him physically, surely they would already have done so.

The lift hummed sixty feet. Nash reached his desk via the cloakroom, found the Dickman file still lying before him and slung it viciously out of his way. He stared at the heap of files awaiting forms to be issued, then involuntarily glanced out of the window.

"Never mind," Gloria remarked, her back to the radiator. "You'll be able to stock up on those forms today."

At ten o'clock Mr Faber looked up over the tea-tray: 'I wonder if you'd mind going down for the stock today?'

At 10:10, after spending ten minutes over his own cup, Nash rose with a wry grin at Gloria and sank in the lift. The storeroom seemed deserted, brooding silently, but as the door was open he entered and began to search for items on the list. He dragged a stepladder into one of the aisles and climbed to reach stocks of the elusive forms. He leaned over, looked down, and saw the fourth face staring up at him from the darkness of the other aisle.

He withdrew his hand from the shelf and stared at the pale visage. For a moment there was total silence—then the thing's lips twitched and the mouth began to open.

He knew he would not be able to bear the thing's voice—and what it might say. He drew back his foot and kicked the watcher in the eye, drew it back and kicked again. The face fell out of the orifice and Nash heard a thud on the other side of the shelves.

A faint unease overtook Nash. He clattered down the ladder, turned into the next aisle and pulled the hanging light cord. For a moment he glared at the man's body lying on the floor, at the burst eyeball and the general appearance which too late he vaguely recognised, and remembered Gloria's remark: "There's somebody new on the third floor"'—and then he fled. He threw open the door at the far end of the room, reeled down the back stairs and out the rear entrance, and jumped aboard the first bus out of Brichester. He should have hidden the body—he realised that as soon as he had paid his fare, for someone (please, not Gloria!) would soon go to the storeroom in search of Nash or the other, and make a discovery— but it was too late now. All he could do was get out at the terminus and hide there. He looked back as if to glimpse the situation in the office building, and saw the four faces straggling whitely after him over the metal bus-roofs.

The bus, he realised on reaching the terminus, went as far as Severnford.

Though it lost him all sharp outlines, he removed his spectacles and strolled with stiff facial muscles for some time. On the theory that anything in plain sight is invisible to the searcher, he explored bookshops and at twelve o'clock headed for the Harrison Hotel at the edge of dockland. Three-and-a-half hours went quickly by, broken only by a near-argument with a darts-player seeking a partner and unable to understand Nash's inability to see the board. Nash reminded himself not to draw attention in any circumstances, and left.

A cinema across the road caught his eye, and he fumbled with his wallet. It should be safe to don his glasses now, he thought, put them on—and threw himself back out of sight of the policeman talking at the paybox.

Where was there left to hide? (And what about tomorrow...?) He hurried away from the cinema and searched for another bookshop, a library even—and two streets away discovered a grimy library, entered and browsed ticketless. How long, he wondered, before the librarian approached with a "can I be of any assistance?" and acquired an impression which he might later transmit to the police? But five-thirty arrived and no help had been offered; even though he had a grim few minutes as he passed the librarian who, seeing him leave with no book apparent, might have suspected him of removing a volume under cover of his coat.

He continued his journey in the same direction, and the lampposts moved further apart, the streets narrowed and the roadways grew rougher. Nearby ships blared out of the night, and somewhere above him a child was crying. Nobody passed him, though occasionally someone peered languidly from a doorway or street-corner.

The houses clustered closer, more narrow arched passages appeared between them, more lampposts were twisted or lightless, and still he went on—until he realised with a start, on reaching a hill and viewing the way ahead, that the streets soon gave out. He could not bring himself to cross open country at night just yet, and turned to an alley on the left—and was confronted with red-glowing miniature fires and dull black-leather shadows. No, that was not the way. He struck off through another alley, past two high-set gas lamps, and was suddenly on the bank of the Severn.

A wind blew icily over the water, rippling it and stirring the weeds. A light went out somewhere behind him, the water splashed nearby, and five faces rose from the river.

They fluttered towards him on a glacial breeze. He stood and watched as they approached, spreading in a semicircle, a circle, closing the circle, rustling pallidly. He threw out his arms to ward them off, and touched one with his left hand. It was cold and wet— the sensations of the grave. He screamed and hit out, but the faces still approached, one settling over his face, the others following, and a clammy film choked his mouth and nose so that he had no chance to scream, even to breathe until they had finished.

When the Severnford police found him, he could do nothing but scream. They did not connect him at first with the murderer for whom the Brichester constabulary were searching; and when the latter identified him he could not of course be prosecuted.

"I've never seen anything like it," said Inspector Daniels from Brichester.

"Well, we try to keep these dockside gangs under control," said Inspector Blackwood of Severnford, "but people get beaten up now and then—nothing like this though . . . But you can be sure we'll find the attacker, even so."

They have not yet found the attacker. Inspector Blackwood suspected homicidal mania at first, but there was no similar crime. But he does not like to think that even Severnford's gangs would be capable of such a crime. It would, he contends, take a very confirmed and accomplished sadist to remove, cleanly in one piece, the skin of a man's face.

BEFORE THE STORM

ABOVE THE TOWN THE SUN STRAINED BEHIND GREY blankness; thunder rumbled wakefully on the horizon. Along Walton Street the flocking crowds escaped into the open to catch their breaths, tried vainly to avoid their own throbbing heat. A blinding stasis held the buildings.

He knew suddenly that before the storm broke, the heat would release the life which even now he felt stirring in the darkness. Where could he hide? Not beyond the plodding shoppers, whose lightest touch released a twist of pain in him; but then how could he leave the burning street? He turned to stare at the blurred buildings, and managed to focus an entrance to the left. He plunged, kicking the tin of money to spill across the newspapers, through a low vestibule, into an elevator on the right.

The walls were featureless except for a row of buttons before his face. Instinctively he pressed the highest, with a finger through which pain blazed. The doors met and the lift jerked upwards, and the man's hands moved unoccupied at his sides. His streaming eyes bent the ceiling; he thought something small and round ran up against the roof. He was crawling through a cavern whose roof pressed down less than a foot above him. The place was lightless, but somehow he could see the spiders which swarmed overhead, covering the entire roof, at intervals falling softly on him. Then the end of the cave appeared: a pitted wall from floor to ceiling, cutting

off all escape. There came a vast rustling. He turned on his back and saw the globular bodies dropping, rushing across the cavern towards him, biting. He hit out in black despair as they prised their way into his mouth.

His flailing hand struck the opening elevator door. He fell out into an empty vestibule. Windows shone ahead of him, but at least the sun's rays turned down beyond the panes. A pointing finger with, to him, illegible words above it on the wall directed him. This was better than the street—there was even the suggestion of a breeze through one open window. He obeyed the finger and limped down a short passage, at whose end he followed a second digital instruction. The latter brought him into what seemed to be a waiting-room. A door faced him, on his right a second invited. A partition slammed left of him, and a face bobbed in the opening. Was there any shelter in that direction? No, the opening was too high for access, and he turned, a coil of vertigo twisting up, and stumbled through the right-hand doorway.

He had no clear picture of the room beyond, nor did he care. He had an impression of cabinets close to him, a long high room, at a great distance a murmur as of conversation, muted. There was only one thing of importance: the chair ahead of him, by a table. He staggered sickly forward and painfully lowered himself into the chair. Then he closed his eyes. He remembered at once and snapped them open; yet in that instant he had been sucked downward to a pitted plain of crumbling spires, out of which groped tentative hands. Feverish heat burned through him. He blinked about him in despair and discovered a young man seated nearby at a desk, perhaps the closest of many. He called out as best he could, and saw the young man look enquiringly towards him, stand up slowly, approach, emerging gradually from the liquid haze.

"Who's that? Oh, sorry," Joan added as she realised Bob was answering the phone. He confirmed something and replaced the receiver, signalled to her that he was open to remarks. "It's just that someone odd seems to want an interview," she said. "Down by the interviewing table. He looks really ill."

"Yes, the switchboard told me. Seems he ignored the girl at the enquiry window and came straight in. Sounds like a difficult taxpayer. Better not be one of mine. If he is, I'm not taking the interview."

"Well, you can't expect me to do this one! Anyway," she pointed out, "it looks as if he's roped in Bernie."

This was going to be difficult and unpleasant, thought Bernard
Cohen as he sat down across the table. At least that was a barrier
between him and the man opposite. Bernard had seen him come in;
it would have been impossible not to notice the arrival, with his
boots awkwardly thumping the floor in a ridiculously bowlegged
walk. Up close, Bernard's dislike hardened. There were unshaven
men scattered across the town, but surely more shaven than this; the
newcomer's coat was filthy; his whole form was pale and greasily
swollen, with almost the fatness of a drowned corpse, and the
bulging eyes were cracked by crimson veins. He seemed in the last
stages of some foul disease.

"Do you have a query about your income tax?" enquired Bernard.

And he saw that the interview would be worse than he had anticipated. The man's hand came up and flapped loosely at his nearer
ear; the mouth opened and hung that way. Bernard wondered with
a shock of revulsion whether the other was mentally defective. Then
the mouth moved and loud petulant sounds issued from it. Down
the office people looked up or around. "Wa-uh . . . eer," throbbed
through the office, and Bernard did not understand.

He tried again. "Would you like to give me your name? That'd be
a help."

But now the corners of the mouth turned downwards and the
hands fluttered flabbily, wildly. The sounds came again, thick, more
petulant. Bernard cleared his throat. "Excuse me," he said, and
hurried away down the room.

Alone again, isolated by walls of optical fog, the man rested his
chin on his hands; even this action pricked his elbows. His clothes
had shrunk to a second skin, and pulled free stickily whenever he
moved. He looked about, straining at the vagueness. Ahead of him,
on the left, was the recently vacated form-strewn desk, beside which
closed curtains hung wearily. His head wavered right; his eyes
managed to isolate a metal cabinet with high double doors. High
double doors—like those in that house . . .

He had believed when first he had been drawn into the Society,
one night in a pub; all scepticism vanished when, outside one of the
small nearby towns, they led him down steps into a pit; by the time
he came up from that pit, from the touch and the whispers of
unseen inhabitants of black pools down there, he was insulated from
any kind of mundane knowledge. So when he walked down South
Street that night and came to the house beyond the road, he

accepted as truth the tales hinted by the local people, of vast faces that peered from the windows of that house, of shapes seen on the roof by moonlight—for this had been the residence of a witch, a witch who had run screaming from it one night decades ago, screaming and clawing at the shapes that swarmed on her body as she vanished into the nearby woods. But if he had gone with doubts in his mind, such doubts would have disappeared at the sight of the house. The distortedly peaked roof and tottering chimney loomed against the blackened sky, the front door leaned open on twisted hinges, the windows peered at the sky; all bespoke the gateway the building was.

He entered under an oddly carved overhang, and it was as if he had turned over a stone in some dark moist place; he felt things come alive and retreat into the dark. He was engulfed by a fear overcome only by knowledge of the bargain he was here to make. The place was alive—he sensed that life pulsed and watched from every unlit room. As he passed the iron balustrade of the stair, something moved above him in the filtered moonlight, and he thought he saw an object like the tail of something huge drawn quickly round the bend of the staircase. The doors in the hall beyond the balustrade were closed; perhaps they had only just been closed, for from one room there came a flapping as of wings straining for release. The door of the last room gaped lightlessly; he hastened past it, but could not avoid glimpsing a bed in the depths of the room and a pale motionless figure propped up in that bed. Now he was facing the high double doors at the end of the hall. He hesitated, and as he did so, he heard something heavy begin to rumble down the stairs. He pulled open the doors and plunged beyond.

He fell into total darkness, screamed as his foot went down to avoid a tumble and found no floor to hold it. He fell until it seemed he would never stop, vainly trying to catch his breath as unseen gusts howled over him, down tunnels lined with a soft substance whose nature he did not care to consider. But he hit bottom at last: a circular area of some rubbery material, away from which he crawled down a passage, feeling shapes in the dark which throbbed and recoiled from his hands. He emerged in a great vault with an arched ceiling; countless passages entered the vault and converged on a dark well in the floor. He went cold at the sight of that well, and while he yet wavered he saw the bobbing white things stream out of the passages to the cavern rim and felt those which pushed him from his refuge. Then came pale movement in the well, and something clambered up from the dark—a bloated blanched oval supported on myriad fleshless legs. Eyes formed in the gelatinous oval and stared at him. And he prostrated himself as he had been told, and called the horror's name—Eihort—and under the arched roof amid the nighted tunnels, the bargain was sealed.

He became aware once more of the table before him, the seat under him, the voices that ebbed and the heat that pricked—and as suddenly all these retreated. He tried to hold on, but this was no memory like the well and the tunnels—this was *real*.

He was clawing his way up a spiral ramp of some gleaming metal, to what end he did not know. He levered himself to the edge, his body responding with unfamiliar movements, and looked over for one vertiginous second. The ramp climbed the interior of a tower which extended downwards and upwards further than he could see. At the limit of his downward vision, a shape was rushing with appalling speed around the spiral, gaining on him as he watched. He pulled himself upwards in blind terror. No window broke the walls, and he was somehow glad not to see what lay outside, for in his flight he passed murals depicting a city of towers which rose from a marsh—a city in whose streets walked tall skeletal figures whose faces were always obscured. A faint hope pushed him again to the edge to peer upwards, but the roof was not in sight, and as he turned back, the climbing ramp reflected both what he was and what now stood one step behind him. He shrieked.

Bernard looked up from complaining to Joan and Robert. "We've got a nut on our hands."

Mr Weedall hurried over to them. "What on earth is wrong with that fellow? Who's dealing with him?"

"I was, but I found him impossible to deal with," Bernard said.

"Well, somebody must be able to deal with him! My God!" Mr Weedall hissed. "What must the taxpayers at the other interview table think? Whose taxpayer is he anyway?"

"I didn't even find that out—or rather, I couldn't—"

"Surely you've been in the department long enough to master that much procedure. Very well, I'll conduct the interview." He strode on down the room, glancing back until the group dispersed, and reached the table. But the eyes of the seated man were glazed and did not fill with awareness. This was a very sick man, Mr Weedall decided, and touched the other's wrist to recall him—but he drew back his hand in dismay, for the man's skin throbbed as though all the nerves and muscles had come alive.

The night sky was not that of Earth. The black city around him was ruined; its pillars lay on stone stairways, its walls with their minute windows were jagged against the glacial void. Whatever his mission had been, he should not have entered these labyrinthine streets; for the more dead a city the more life it conceals. Something peered around a pillar; there was a rustle of debris behind him, and he whirled to see a hooded ragged figure in pursuit. While he stood helpless it skimmed nearer, the hood half open and revealing a head of flying cobwebs. He had no chance to scream as the head pressed into his face.

The hand on his wrist created the table and chair. Opposite him a figure swam on his vision; it enquired something of him. It was not like his earlier questioner; its manner was purposefully official. It leaned closer and asked in a whisper that sliced through him "What seems to be the trouble, please?"

Could this be a minion of Eihort or perhaps a member of some cult? If so, it might turn him out of his shade into the sun—he must play for time. Explain. But his throat had thickened and no word bubbled up. He twisted dizzily in the chair and found a desk, scraps of paper, scattered ballpoint pens. With a hand that twinged like a plucked tooth he groped at them, so desperately that eventually they were placed in front of him.

His flesh was crawling, but he dared not scratch. Sensation in his hand had subsided into a pounding ache. He fumbled with the pen and tried to think, to select items from his memory that would help describe his plight. But other images crowded in, things he had seen, places he had visited: the colossi guarding black canals on Yuggoth—the whistling heads—the horn-notes which pursued through the forests of Tond—the giant eye which peered between trees—the face which mouthed in the gulf beyond the rim—the dead things in orbit around the worlds beyond Shaggai—the shuttered storehouses hidden in a dockland town—the last revelation by the lake of Gla'aki—the sun-bleached buildings of a forgotten city whose walls throbbed a word T R A K and in whose comers white shapes shifted feebly—

Mr Weedall was uncomprehendingly disturbed. The man before him would begin to write, his face twisted with exertion—then his eyes would dim and he would stiffen with panic. This became almost a rhythm as the pen struggled over the paper, slowly forming words:

> *Made bargein with Eihort God of the Labyrinth Gave me other lives Life selling papers didnt matter because i could go into other bodies leave mine behind to sell papers But people told me i didnt know all about the bargein Nobody made it any more and when they did years after Hed use them to send His children into the world Now i cant control places i go When His servants die they come into my body and make me go into thiers and die in thier place Got no control His children will come through if you dont let me stay*

The pen faltered; there was nothing more to be said, and the swollen hand laid it down on the table. Mr Weedall reread the tottering letters, which dimmed under the onrushing storm outside, and found no sense among them. He was sure that the man was both physically and mentally in need of medical attention, and that he should be escorted from the office, one way or another, in early course. He leaned down and said "I think I understand now. Hold on, and I'll contact someone who can help you."

So he *was* one of the servants of Eihort, and calling others to close in for the breakthrough. The man lurched to his feet, feeling as if pain were slashing open his limbs. He must escape, find another shelter. The room was growing darker, as though something was engulfing the walls. He reeled to the door and threw it open, swayed sickly through the waiting-room, into the vestibule. A voice called behind him. Which way? The lifts would take time to respond. He saw a door on the right, rushed at it, his legs leaden and boiling.

"Not that way!" Mr Weedall shouted.

Emerging from the office with a file, Robert saw what happened. He did not faint, but threw himself back into the waiting-room and wrenched open the office door. Joan was on her way out, but he pushed her back and somehow managed to persuade her and the rest not to approach the door. At last Mr Weedall appeared, very pale, attempting calmness as he told them he had called an ambulance. He would let nobody leave the room.

But before long he motioned Robert outside and suggested vaguely that they search the open rooms, staircases and halls of the building for something he did not specify. Strings of rain writhed on the windows as they searched; the storm exploded triumphantly overhead. They found nothing. Nevertheless, Mr Weedall arranged himself a transfer to another office, and Robert persuaded him to obtain transfers for himself and Joan. For the others in the office, who had not even glimpsed the object from which the ambulance men turned their eyes as they lifted it from the vestibule floor, nothing could be done. Robert does not like to think of what may threaten those working in that high office building, especially after dark.

For the crippled visitor had swung open the door despite Mr Weedall's warning—and been confronted by the roofs beyond the fire escape. Stagnant air pressed in through the opening, and a last pure ray of sunlight had struck in, so accurate in its aim as to seem deliberate. It caught the man, who let out a dreadful glutinous howl and staggered round to confront them, his head shaking insanely. Then Mr Weedall went sick, and Robert fled back to sanity and what he had once accepted as the everyday.

Perhaps he had not seen what he spent the rest of his life trying to forget: the man's face tearing, a rent appearing from temple to jaw, opening the cheek to hang revealed; for there had been no blood—only something pale as things that had never seen the sun, something that poured down the man's body, which collapsed like a balloon. Surely Robert could not have had time to see the flood separate into moving objects that rolled away down the stairs into the depths of the building, but that was the memory he always shrank from focusing; for some instinct told him that if he ever remembered clearly what he had seen, it would be something even worse than a swarm of enormous fat white spiders.

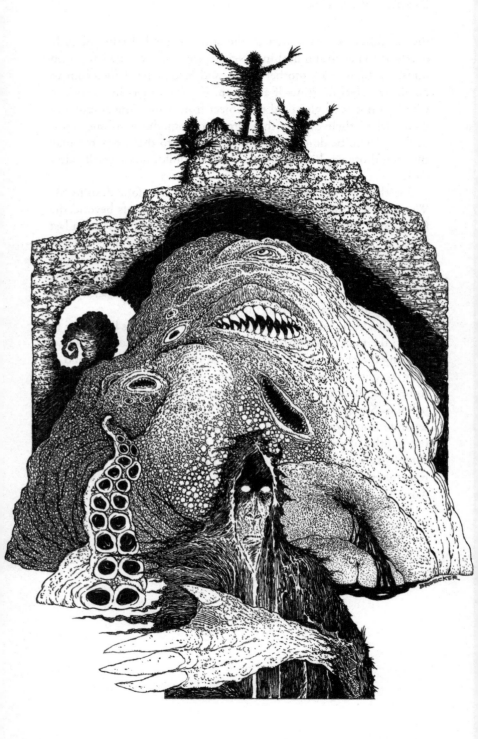

COLD PRINT

"... for even the minions of Cthulhu dare not speak of
Y'golonac; yet the time will come when Y'golonac strides
forth from the loneliness of aeons to walk once more
among men ... "

Revelations of Glaaki, vol.12

SAM STRUTT LICKED HIS FINGERS AND WIPED THEM ON
his handkerchief; his fingertips were grey with snow from the
pole on the bus platform. Then he coaxed his book out of the polythene bag on the seat beside him, withdrew the bus-ticket from
between the pages, held it against the cover to protect the latter
from his fingers, and began to read. As often happened the
conductor assumed that the ticket authorised Strutt's present
journey; Strutt did not enlighten him. Outside, the snow whirled
down the side streets and slipped beneath the wheels of cautious
cars.

The slush splashed into his boots as he stepped down outside
Brichester Central and, snuggling the bag beneath his coat for extra
safety, pushed his way towards the bookstall, treading on the settling
snowflakes. The glass panels of the stall were not quite closed; snow
had filtered through and dulled the glossy paperbacks. "Look at
that!" Strutt complained to a young man who stood next to him
and anxiously surveyed the crowd, drawing his neck down inside
his collar like a tortoise. "Isn't that disgusting? These people just
don't care!" The young man, still searching the wet faces, agreed

27

abstractedly. Strutt strode to the other counter of the stall, where the
assistant was handing out newspapers. "I say!" called Strutt. The
assistant, sorting change for a customer, gestured him to wait. Over
the paperbacks, through the streaming glass, Strutt watched the
young man rush forward and embrace a girl, then gently dry her face
with a handkerchief. Strutt glanced at the newspaper held by the
man awaiting change. *Brutal Murder in Ruined Church,* he read;
the previous night a body had been found inside the roofless walls of
a church in Lower Brichester; when the snow had been cleared from
this marble image, frightful mutilations had been revealed covering
the corpse, oval mutilations which resembled—The man took the
paper and his change away into the station. The assistant turned to
Strutt with a smile: "Sorry to keep you waiting." "Yes," said Strutt.
"Do you realise those books are getting snowed on? People may
want to buy them, you know." "Do *you?*" the assistant replied.
Strutt tightened his lips and turned back into the snow-filled gusts.
Behind him he heard the ring of glass pane meeting pane.

Good Books on The Highway provided shelter; he closed out the
lashing sleet and stood taking stock. On the shelves the current titles
showed their faces while the others turned their backs. Girls were
giggling over comic Christmas cards; an unshaven man was swept in
on a flake-edged blast and halted, staring around uneasily. Strutt
clucked his tongue; tramps shouldn't be allowed in bookshops to
soil the books. Glancing sideways to observe whether the man
would bend back the covers or break the spines, Strutt moved
among the shelves, but could not find what he sought. Chatting
with the cashier, however, was the assistant who had praised *Last
Exit to Brooklyn* to him when he had bought it last week, and had
listened patiently to a list of Strutt's recent reading, though he had
not seemed to recognise the titles. Strutt approached him and
enquired "Hello—any more exciting books this week?"

The man faced him, puzzled. "Any more—?"

"You know, books like this?" Strutt held up his polythene bag to
show the grey Ultimate Press cover of *The Caning-Master* by
Hector Q.

"Ah, no. I don't think we have." He tapped his lip. "Except—
Jean Genet?"

"Who? Oh, you mean *Jennet.* No, thanks, he's dull as dishwater."

"Well, I'm sorry, sir, I'm afraid I can't help you."

"Oh." Strutt felt rebuffed. The man seemed not to recognise him,

or perhaps he was pretending. Strutt had met his kind before and
had them mutely patronise his reading. He scanned the shelves
again, but no cover caught his eye. At the door he furtively unbut-
toned his shirt to protect his book still further, and a hand fell on his
arm. Lined with grime, the hand slid down to his and touched his
bag. Strutt shook it off angrily and confronted the tramp.

"Wait a minute!" the man hissed. "Are you after more books like
that? I know where we can get some."

This approach offended Strutt's self-righteous sense of reading
books which had no right to be suppressed. He snatched the bag out
of the fingers closing on it. "So you like them too, do you?"

"Oh, yes, I've got lots."

Strutt sprang his trap. "Such as?"

"Oh, *Adam and Evan, Take Me How You Like,* all the Harrison
adventures, you know, there's lots."

Strutt grudgingly admitted that the man's offer seemed genuine.
The assistant at the cash-desk was eyeing them; Strutt stared back.
"All right," he said. "Where's this place you're talking about?"

The other took his arm and pulled him eagerly into the slanting
snow. Clutching shut their collars, pedestrians were slipping
between cars as they waited for a skidded bus ahead to be removed;
flakes were crushed into the comers of the windscreens by the
wipers. The man dragged Strutt amid the horns which brayed and
honked, then between two store windows from which girls watched
smugly as they dressed headless figures, and down an alley. Strutt
recognised the area as one which he vainly combed for back-street
bookshops; disappointing alcoves of men's magazines, occasional
hot pungent breaths from kitchens, cars fitted with caps of snow,
loud pubs warm against the weather. Strutt's guide dodged into the
doorway of a public bar to shake his coat; the white glaze cracked
and fell from him. Strutt joined the man and adjusted the book in
its bag, snuggled beneath his shirt. He stamped the crust loose from
his boots, stopping when the other followed suit; he did not wish to
be connected with the man even by such a trivial action. He looked
with distaste at his companion, at his swollen nose through which he
was now snorting back snot, at the stubble shifting on the cheeks as
they inflated and the man blew on his trembling hands. Strutt had a
horror of touching anyone who was not fastidious. Beyond the
doorway flakes were already obscuring their footprints, and the man
said "I get terrible thirsty walking fast like this."

"So that's the game, is it?" But the bookshop lay ahead. Strutt led the way into the bar and bought two pints from a colossal barmaid, her bosom bristling with ruffles, who billowed back and forth with glasses and worked the pumps with gusto. Old men sucked at pipes in vague alcoves, a radio blared marches, men clutching tankards aimed with jovial inaccuracy at dart-board or spittoon. Strutt flapped his overcoat and hung it next to him; the other retained his and stared into his beer. Determined not to talk, Strutt surveyed the murky mirrors which reflected gesticulating parties around littered tables not directly visible. But he was gradually surprised by the taciturnity of his table-mate; surely these people (he thought) were remarkably loquacious, in fact virtually impossible to silence? This was intolerable; sitting idly in an airless backstreet bar when he could be on the move or reading—something must be done. He gulped down his beer and thumped the glass upon its mat. The other started. Then, visibly abashed, he began to sip, seeming oddly nervous. At last it was obvious that he was dawdling over the froth, and he set down his glass and stared at it. "It looks as if it's time to go," said Strutt.

The man looked up; fear widened his eyes. "Christ, I'm wet," he muttered. "I'll take you again when the snow goes off."

"That's the game, is it?" Strutt shouted. In the mirrors, eyes sought him. "You don't get that drink out of me for nothing! I haven't come this far—!!"

The man swung round and back, trapped. "All right, all right, only maybe I won't find it in this weather."

Strutt found this remark too inane to comment. He rose and, buttoning his coat, strode into the arcs of snow, glaring behind to ensure he was followed.

The last few shop-fronts, behind them pyramids of tins marked with misspelt placards, were cast out by lines of furtively curtained windows set in unrelieved vistas of red brick; behind the panes Christmas decorations hung like wreaths. Across the road, framed in a bedroom window, a middle-aged woman drew the curtains and hid the teenage boy at her shoulder. "Hel-*lo*, there they go," Strutt did not say; he felt he could control the figure ahead without speaking to him, and indeed had no desire to speak to the man as he halted trembling, no doubt from the cold, and hurried onward as Strutt, an inch taller than his five-and-a-half feet and better built, loomed behind him. For an instant, as a body of snow drove

towards him down the street, flakes overexposing the landscape and
cutting his cheeks like transitory razors of ice, Strutt yearned to
speak, to tell of nights when he lay awake in his room, hearing the
landlady's daughter being beaten by her father in the attic bedroom
above, straining to catch muffled sounds through the creak of bed-
springs, perhaps from the couple below. But the moment passed,
swept away by the snow; the end of the street had opened, split by a
traffic-island into two roads thickly draped with snow, one curling
away to hide between the houses, the other short, attached to a
roundabout. Now Strutt knew where he was. From a bus earlier in
the week he had noticed the *Keep Left* sign lying helpless on its
back on the traffic island, its face kicked in.

They crossed the roundabout, negotiated the crumbling lips of
ruts full of deceptively glazed pools collecting behind the bulldozer
treads of a redevelopment scheme, and onward through the whirling
white to a patch of waste ground where a lone fireplace drank the
snow. Strutt's guide scuttled into an alley and Strutt followed, intent
on keeping close to the other as he knocked powdered snow from
dustbin lids and flinched from backyard doors at which dogs clawed
and snarled. The man dodged left, then right, between the close
labyrinthine walls, among houses whose cruel edges of jagged
windowpanes and thrusting askew doors even the snow, kinder to
buildings than to their occupants, could not soften. A last turning,
and the man slithered onto a pavement beside the remnants of a
store, its front gaping emptily to frame wine-bottles abandoned
beneath a *Hein 57 Variet* poster. A dollop of snow fell from the
awning's skeleton to be swallowed by the drift below. The man
shook, but as Strutt confronted him, pointed fearfully to the opposite pavement: "That's it. I've brought you here."

The tracks of slush splashed up Strutt's trouser legs as he ran
across, checking mentally that while the man had tried to disorient
him he had deduced which main road lay some five hundred yards
away, then read the inscription over the shop: *American Books
Bought and Sold.* He touched a railing which protected an opaque
window below street level, wet rust gritting beneath his nails, and
surveyed the display in the window facing him: *History of the
Rod*—a book he had found monotonous—thrusting out its shoulders among science-fiction novels by Aldiss, Tubb and Harrison,
which hid shamefacedly hind lurid covers; *Le Sadisme au Cinema;*
Robbie-Grillet's *Voyeur* looking lost; *The Naked Lunch*—nothing

worth his journey there, Strutt thought. "All right, it's about time
we went in," he urged the man inside, and with a glance up the
eroded red brick at the first-floor window, the back of a dressing-
table mirror shoved against it to replace one pane, entered also. The
other had halted again, and for an unpleasant second Strutt's fingers
brushed the man's musty overcoat. "Come on, where's the books?"
he demanded, shoving past into the shop.

The yellow daylight was made murkier by the window display
and the pin-up magazines hanging on the inside of the glass-
panelled door; dust hung lazily in the stray beams. Strutt stopped to
read the covers of paperbacks stuffed into cardboard boxes on one
table, but the boxes contained only Westerns, fantasies and
American erotica, selling at half price. Grimacing at the books which
stretched wide their comers like flowering petals, Strutt bypassed the
hardcovers and squinted behind the counter, slightly preoccupied;
as he had closed the door beneath its tongueless bell, he had imagined he had heard a cry somewhere near, quickly cut off. No doubt
round here you heard that sort of thing all the time, he thought, and
turned on the other. "Well, I don't see what I came for. Doesn't
anybody work in this place?"

Wide-eyed, the man gazed past Strutt's shoulder; Strutt looked
back and saw the frosted glass panel of a door, one corner of the glass
repaired with cardboard, black against a dim yellow light which
filtered through the panel. The bookseller's office, presumably—
had he heard Strutt's remark? Strutt confronted the door, ready to
face impertinence. Then the man pushed by him, searching distractedly behind the counter, fumbling open a glass-fronted bookcase
full of volumes in brown paper jackets and finally extracting a parcel
in grey paper from its hiding-place in one comer of a shelf. He
thrust it at Strutt, muttering "This is one, this is one," and watched,
the skin beneath his eyes twitching, as Strutt tore off the paper.

The Secret Life of Wackford Squeers—"Ah, that's fine," Strutt
approved, forgetting himself momentarily, and reached for his
wallet; but greasy fingers clawed at his wrist. "Pay next time," the
man pleaded. Strutt hesitated; could he get away with the book
without paying? At that moment, a shadow rippled across the
frosted glass: a headless man dragging something heavy. Decapitated
by the frosted glass and by his hunched position, Strutt decided,
then realised that the shopkeeper must be in contact with Ultimate
Press; he must not prejudice this contact by stealing a book. He

knocked away the frantic fingers and counted out two pounds; but the other backed away, stretching out his fingers in stark fear, and crouched against the office door, from whose pane the silhouette had disappeared, before flinching almost into Strutt's arms. Strutt pushed him back and laid the notes in the space left on the shelf by *Wackford Squeers,* then turned on him. "Don't you intend to wrap it up? No, on second thoughts I'll do it myself."

The roller on the counter rumbled forth a streamer of brown paper; Strutt sought an undiscoloured stretch. As he parcelled the book, disentangling his feet from the rejected coil, something crashed to the floor. The other had retreated towards the street door until one dangling cuff-button had hooked the comer of a carton full of paperbacks; he froze above the scattered books, mouth and hands gaping wide, one foot atop an open novel like a broken moth, and around him motes floated into beams of light mottled by the sifting snow. Somewhere a lock clicked. Strutt breathed hard, taped the package and, circling the man in distaste, opened the door. The cold attacked his legs. He began to mount the steps and the other flurried in pursuit. The man's foot was on the doorstep when a heavy tread approached across the boards. The man spun about and below Strutt the door slammed. Strutt waited; then it occurred to him that he could hurry and shake off his guide. He reached the street and a powdered breeze pecked at his cheeks, cleaning away the stale dust of the shop. He turned away his face and, kicking the rind of snow from the headline of a sodden newspaper, made for the main road which he knew to pass close by.

Strutt woke shivering. The neon sign outside the window of his flat, a cliché but relentless as toothache, was garishly defined against the night every five seconds, and by this and the shafts of cold Strutt knew that it was early morning. He closed his eyes again, but though his lids were hot and heavy his mind would not be lulled. Beyond the limits of his memory lurked the dream which had awoken him; he moved uneasily. For some reason he thought of a passage from the previous evening's reading: 'As Adam reached the door he felt Evan's hand grip his, twisting his arm behind his back, forcing him to the floor—' His eyes opened and sought the bookcase as if for reassurance; yes, there was the book, secure within its covers, carefully aligned with its fellows. He recalled returning home one

evening to find *Miss Whippe, Old-Style Governess,* thrust inside
Prefects and Fags, straddled by *Prefects and Fags;* the landlady had
explained that she must have replaced them wrongly after dusting,
but Strutt knew that she had damaged them vindictively. He had
bought a case that locked, and when she asked him for the key had
replied "Thanks, I think I can do them justice." You couldn't make
friends nowadays. He closed his eyes again; the room and bookcase,
created in five seconds by the neon and destroyed with equal regu-
larity, filled him with their emptiness, reminding him that weeks lay
ahead before the beginning of next term, when he would confront
the first class of the morning and add "You know me by now" to his
usual introduction "You play fair with me and I'll play fair with
you," a warning which somebody would be sure to test, and Strutt
would have him; he saw the expanse of white gymshorts seat
stretched tight down on which he would bring a gym-shoe with
satisfying force—Strutt relaxed; soothed by an overwhelming echo
of the pounding feet on the wooden gymnasium floor, the fevered
shaking of the wallbars as the boys swarmed ceilingwards and he
stared up from below, he slept.

Panting, he drove himself through his morning exercises, then
tossed off the fruit juice which was always his first call on the tray
brought up by the landlady's daughter. Viciously he banged the
glass back on the tray; the glass splintered (he'd say it was an accident; he paid enough rent to cover, he might as well get a little
satisfaction for his money). "Bet you have a fab Christmas," the girl
had said, surveying the room. He'd made to grab her round the
waist and curb her pert femininity—but she'd already gone, her
skirt's pleats whirling, leaving his stomach hotly knotted in anticipation.

Later he trudged to the supermarket. From several front gardens
came the teeth-grinding scrape of spades clearing snow; these faded
and were answered by the crushed squeak of snow engulfing boots.
When he emerged from the supermarket clutching an armful of cans,
a snowball whipped by his face to thud against the window, a
translucent beard spreading down the pane like that fluid from the
noses of those boys who felt Strutt's wrath most often, for he was
determined to beat this ugliness, this revoltingness out of them.
Strutt glared about him for the marksman—a seven-year-old,
boarding his tricycle for a quick retreat; Strutt moved involuntarily
as if to pull the boy across his knee. But the street was not deserted;

even now the child's mother, in slacks and curlers peeking from beneath a headscarf, was slapping her son's hand. "I've told you, *don't* do that. —Sorry," she called to Strutt. "Yes, I'm sure," he snarled, and tramped back to his flat. His heart pumped uncontrollably. He wished fervently that he could talk to someone as he had talked to the bookseller on the edge of Goatswood who had shared his urges; when the man had died earlier that year Strutt had felt abandoned in a tacitly conspiring, hostile world. Perhaps the new shop's owner might prove similarly sympathetic? Strutt hoped that the man who had conducted him there yesterday would not be in attendance, but if he were, surely he could be got rid of—a bookseller dealing with Ultimate Press must be a man after Strutt's own heart, who would be as opposed as he to that other's presence while they were talking frankly. As well as this discussion, Strutt needed books to read over Christmas, and *Squeers* would not last him long; the shop would scarcely be closed on Christmas Eve. Thus reassured, he unloaded the cans on the kitchen table and ran downstairs.

Strutt stepped from the bus into silence; the engine's throb was quickly muffled among the laden houses. The piled snow waited for some sound. He splashed through the tracks of cars to the pavement, its dull coat depressed by countless overlapping footprints. The road twisted slyly; as soon as the main road was out of sight the side street revealed its real character. The snow laid over the housefronts became threadbare; rusty protrusions poked through. One or two windows showed Christmas trees, their ageing needles falling out, their branches tipped with luridly sputtering lights. Strutt, however, had no eye for this but kept his gaze on the pavement, seeking to avoid stains circled by dogs' pawmarks. Once he met the gaze of an old woman staring down at a point below her window which was perhaps the extent of her outside world. Momentarily chilled, he hurried on, pursued by a woman who, on the evidence within her pram, had given birth to a litter of newspapers, and halted before the shop.

Though the orange sky could scarcely have illuminated the interior, no electric gleam was visible through the magazines, and the torn notice hanging behind the grime might read CLOSED. Slowly Strutt descended the steps. The pram squealed by, the latest flakes spreading across the newspapers. Strutt stared at its inquisitive proprietor, turned and almost fell into sudden darkness. The door had opened and a figure blocked the doorway.

"You're not shut, surely?" Strutt's tongue tangled.

"Perhaps not. Can I help you?"

"I was here yesterday. Ultimate Press book," Strutt replied to the face level with his own and uncomfortably close.

"Of course you were, yes, I recall." The other swayed incessantly like an athlete limbering up, and his voice wavered constantly from bass to falsetto, dismaying Strutt. "Well, come in before the snow gets to you," the other said and slammed the door behind them, evoking a note from the ghost of the bell's tongue.

The bookseller—this was he, Strutt presumed—loomed behind him, a head taller; down in the half-light, among the vague vindictive corners of the tables, Strutt felt an obscure compulsion to assert himself somehow, and remarked "I hope you found the money for the book. Your man didn't seem to want me to pay. Some people would have taken him at his word."

"He's not with us today." The bookseller switched on the light inside his office. As his lined pouched face was lit up it seemed to grow; the eyes were sunk in sagging stars of wrinkles; the cheeks and forehead bulged from furrows; the head floated like a half-inflated balloon above the stuffed tweed suit. Beneath the unshaded bulb the walls pressed close, surrounding a battered desk from which overflowed fingerprinted copies of *The Bookseller* thrust aside by a black typewriter clogged with dirt, beside which lay a stub of sealing-wax and an open box of matches. Two chairs faced each other across the desk, and behind it was a closed door. Strutt seated himself before the desk, brushing dust to the floor. The bookseller paced round him and suddenly, as if struck by the question, demanded "Tell me, why d'you read these books?"

This was a question often aimed at Strutt by the English master in the staffroom until he had ceased to read his novels in the breaks. Its sudden reappearance caught him off guard, and he could only call on his old riposte. "How d'you mean, why? Why not?"

"I wasn't being critical," the other hurried on, moving restlessly around the desk. "I'm genuinely interested. I was going to make the point that don't you want what you read about to happen, in a sense?"

"Well, maybe." Strutt was suspicious of the trend of this discussion, and wished that he could dominate; his words seemed to plunge into the snow-cloaked silence inside the dusty walls to vanish immediately, leaving no impression.

"I mean this: when you read a book don't you make it happen before you, in your mind? Particularly if you consciously attempt to visualise, but that's not essential. You might cast the book away from you, of course. I knew a bookseller who worked on this theory; you don't get much time to be yourself in this sort of area, but when he could he worked on it, though he never quite formulated—Wait a minute, I'll show you something."

He leapt away from the desk and into the shop. Strutt wondered what was beyond the door behind the desk. He half-rose but, peering back, saw the bookseller already returning through the drifting shadows with a volume extracted from among the Lovecrafts and Derleths.

"This ties in with your Ultimate Press books, really," the other said, banging the office door to as he entered. "They're publishing a book by Johannes Henricus Pott next year, so we hear, and that's concerned with forbidden lore as well, like this one; you'll no doubt be amazed to hear that they think they may have to leave some of Pott in the original Latin. This here should interest you, though; the only copy. You probably won't know the *Revelations of Glaaki;* it's a sort of Bible written under supernatural guidance. There were only eleven volumes—but this is the twelfth, written by a man at the top of Mercy Hill guided through his dreams." His voice grew unsteadier as he continued. "I don't know how it got out; I suppose the man's family may have found it in some attic after his death and thought it worth a few coppers, who knows? My bookseller—well, he knew of the *Revelations,* and he realised this was priceless; but he didn't want the seller to realise he had a find and perhaps take it to the library or the University, so he took it off his hands as part of a job lot and said he might use it for scribbling. When he read it— Well, there was one passage that for testing his theory looked like a godsend. Look."

The bookseller circled Strutt again and placed the book in his lap, his arms resting on Strutt's shoulders. Strutt compressed his lips and glanced up at the other's face; but some strength weakened, refusing to support his disapproval, and he opened the book. It was an old ledger, its hinges cracking, its yellowed pages covered by irregular lines of scrawny handwriting. Through the introductory monologue Strutt had been baffled; now the book was before him, it vaguely recalled those bundles of duplicated typewritten sheets which had been passed around the toilets in his adolescence. 'Revelations' suggested the forbidden. Thus intrigued, he read at random. Up here in Lower Brichester the bare bulb defined each scrap of flaking paint on the door opposite, and hands moved on his shoulders, but somewhere down below he would be pursued through darkness by vast soft footsteps; when he turned to look a swollen glowing figure was upon him—What was all this about? A hand gripped his left shoulder and the right hand turned pages; finally one finger underlined a phrase:

Beyond a gulf in the subterranean night a passage leads to a wall of massive bricks, and beyond the wall rises Y'golonac to be served by the tattered eyeless figures of the dark. Long has he slept beyond the wall, and those which crawl over the bricks scuttle across his body never knowing it to be Y'golonac; but when his name is spoken or read he comes forth to be worshipped or to feed and take on the shape and soul of those he feeds upon. For those who read of evil and search for its form within their minds call forth evil, and so may Y'golonac return to walk among men and await that time when the earth is cleared off and Cthulhu rises from his tomb among the weeds, Gla'aki thrusts open the crystal trapdoor, the brood of Eihort are born into daylight, Shub-Niggurath strides forth to smash the moon-lens, Byatis bursts forth from his prison, Daoloth tears away illusion to expose the reality concealed behind.'

The hands on his shoulders shifted constantly, slackening and tightening. The voice fluctuated. "What did you think of that?"

Strutt thought it was rubbish, but somewhere his courage had slipped; he replied unevenly "Well, it's—not the sort of thing you see on sale."

"You mean you found it interesting?" The voice was deepening; now it was an overwhelming bass. The other swung round behind the desk; he seemed taller—his head struck the bulb, setting shadows peering from the corners and withdrawing, and peering again. "You're interested?" His expression was intense, as far as it could be made out; for the light moved darkness in the hollows of his face, as if the bone structure were melting visibly.

In the murk of Strutt's mind appeared a suspicion; had he not heard from his dear dead friend the Goatswood bookseller that a black magic cult existed in Brichester, a circle of young men dominated by somebody Franklin or Franklyn? Was he being interviewed for this? "I wouldn't say that," he countered.

"Listen. There was a bookseller who read this, and I told him you may be the high priest of Y'golonac. You will call down the shapes of night to worship him at the times of year; you will prostrate yourself before him and in return you will survive when the earth is cleared off for the Great Old Ones; you will go beyond the rim to what stirs out of the light . . . "

Before he could consider Strutt blurted. "Are you talking about me?" He had realised he was alone in a room with a madman.

"No, no, I meant the bookseller. But the offer now is for you."

"Well, I'm sorry, I've got things to do." Strutt prepared to stand up.

"He refused also." The timbre of the voice grated in Strutt's ears. "I had to kill him."

Strutt froze. How did one treat the insane? Pacify them. "Now, now, hold on a minute . . . "

"How can it benefit you to doubt? I have more proof at my disposal than you could bear. You will be my high priest, or you will never leave this room."

For the first time in his life, as the shadows between the harsh oppressive walls moved slower as if anticipating, Strutt battled to control an emotion; he subdued his mingled fear and ire with calm. "If you don't mind, I've got to meet somebody."

"Not when your fulfilment lies here between these walls." The voice was thickening. "You know I killed the bookseller—it was in your papers. He fled into the ruined church, but I caught him with my hands . . . Then I left the book in the shop to be read, but the only one who picked it up by mistake was the man who brought you here . . . Fool! He went mad and cowered in the corner when he saw the mouths! I kept him because I thought he might bring some of his friends who wallow in physical taboos and lose the true experiences, those places forbidden to the spirit. But he only contacted you and brought you here while I was feeding. There is food occasionally; young boys who come here for books in secret; they make sure nobody knows what they read!—and can be persuaded to look at the *Revelations*. Imbecile! He can no longer betray me with his fumbling—but I knew you would return. Now you will be mine."

Strutt's teeth ground together silently until he thought his jaws would break; he stood up, nodding, and handed the volume of the *Revelations* towards the figure; he was poised, and when the hand closed on the ledger he would dart for the office door.

"You can't get out, you know; it's locked." The bookseller rocked on his feet, but did not start towards him; the shadows now were mercilessly clear and dust hung in the silence. "You're not afraid—you look too calculating. Is it possible that you still do not believe? All right—" he laid his hand on the doorknob behind the desk: "—do you want to see what is left of my food?"

A door opened in Strutt's mind, and he recoiled from what might lie beyond. "No! No!" he shrieked. Fury followed his involuntary display of fear; he wished he had a cane to subjugate the figure taunting him. Judging by the face, he thought, the bulges filling the tweed suit must be of fat; if they should struggle, Strutt would win. "Let's get this clear," he shouted, "we've played games long enough! You'll let me out of here or I—" but he found himself glaring about for a weapon. Suddenly he thought of the book still in his hand. He snatched the matchbox from the desk, behind which the figure watched, ominously impassive. Strutt struck a match, then pinched the boards between finger and thumb and shook out the pages. "I'll burn this book!" he threatened.

The figure tensed, and Strutt went cold with fear of his next move. He touched the flame to paper, and the pages curled and were consumed so swiftly that Strutt had only the impression of bright fire and shadows growing unsteadily massive on the walls before he was shaking ashes to the floor. For a moment they faced each other, immobile. After the flames a darkness had rushed into Strutt's eyes. Through it he saw the tweed tear loudly as the figure expanded.

Strutt threw himself against the office door, which resisted. He drew back his fist, and watched with an odd timeless detachment as it shattered the frosted glass; the act seemed to isolate him, as if suspending all action outside himself. Through the knives of glass, on which gleamed drops of blood, he saw the snowflakes settle through the amber light, infinitely far; too far to call for help. A horror filled him of being overpowered from behind. From the back of the office came a sound; Strutt spun and as he did so closed his eyes, terrified to face the source of such a sound—but when he opened them he saw why the shadow on the frosted pane yesterday had been headless, and he screamed. As the desk was thrust aside by the towering naked figure, on whose surface still hung rags of the tweed suit, Strutt's last thought was an unbelieving conviction that this was happening because he had read the *Revelations;* somewhere, someone had *wanted* this to happen to him. It wasn't playing fair, he hadn't done anything to deserve this—but before he could scream out his protest his breath was cut off, as the hands descended on his face and the wet red mouths opened in their palms.

THE FRANKLYN PARAGRAPHS

THE DISAPPEARANCE OF ERROL UNDERCLIFFE IN 1967 from his flat in Lower Brichester was not widely reported. The little speculation provoked by the mystery was soon resolved by the belief that Undercliffe had "disappeared" in search of publicity. While he has not reappeared, his public seems still to be waiting for him to produce himself out of a hat. At the time I hinted in print that I could supply evidence of something more sinister, but I fear that the general branding of Undercliffe as charlatan was sufficiently persuasive to dissuade me from publishing evidence in case Undercliffe reappeared and objected to my making public letters written privately to me. By now, however, I should be more than pleased if Undercliffe declared both his absence and his last letter a hoax.

Undercliffe first wrote to me in 1965, when my first book had just become available from Brichester Central Library. Typically, he enclosed a cutting from the letter-column of the *Brichester Herald*; under the heading "Can Ghost Stories Be Libellous?" one "Countryman" had written: "I have recently perused a book of ghost stories by a Mr J. Ramsey Campbell, mainly located in Brichester. Mr Campbell seems to look upon the citizens of our town as either witches, warlocks, or illiterate 'country folks'. The advertising for the book makes much of the fact that the author is still an infant; since this is obvious from the contents, I would scarcely have thought it necessary to advertise the fact. I would suggest that before he writes another such book Mr Campbell should (1) visit Brichester, where he has clearly never set foot, and (2) grow up." And so on. I could have replied that on the basis of my several visits to Brichester I didn't consider it the sort of town where I'd care to spend a night; but I find this kind of letter-column duel a little childish, and didn't feel disposed to join swords or even pens. For the record, these days Brichester has an impressively mundane surface, but I still sense that it may crack. When I and Kirby McCauley passed through the area in 1965, a month or so before Undercliffe's first letter, I was disturbed to be unable to find the turn-off to Severnford and Brichester, and the groups of youths inert in the sun outside a shack-like cinema in Berkeley (showing, oddly enough, Jerry Lewis' one horror film) proved less than helpful. Hours later, after dark, we were directed by a roundabout policeman, but without conferring we sneaked around the round- about—only to find ourselves somehow on the road originally indicated and to stay at an inn whose sign we discovered in the dawn to be that of a goat!

However, I digress. I quote the letter from the *Herald* at length because it seems to me to demonstrate some aspects of Undercliffe's character; not that he wrote it (at least I shouldn't think so), but he did enclose it with his first letter to me, though it is hardly the sort of enclosure most of us would choose when initiating a correspon- dence. However, Undercliffe's sense of humour was wry—some might call it cynical or cruel. I'm inclined to believe it was the product of a basic insecurity, from what little I know of his life. I never visited him, and his letters were rarely self-revelatory (though the first of the batch here published is more so than he might have wished). Most of them were first drafts of stories, signed and dated; he kept a copy of every letter he wrote—these were carefully filed in his flat—and several of the incidents which he described to me in the two years of our correspondence turned up virtually verbatim in his short stories. In particular the description of the disused station in "The Through Train" was lifted bodily from his letter to me of 20 November 1966.

If this says little about the man himself, I can only maintain that for the rest of us Errol Undercliffe was the Mr Arkadin of the horror-story world. "Errol Undercliffe" was almost certainly not his christened name. His refusal to provide biographical detail was not as notorious as J. D. Salinger's, but it was fully as obsessive. He seems to have been educated in or near Brichester (see the first letter here) but I cannot trace his school, nor the friend whose engagement party he describes. I never saw a photograph of him. Perhaps he thought the aura of mystery with which he surrounded himself carried over to his stories; perhaps, again, he was bent on preserving his own isolation. If so, he served himself ill as far as his final ordeal was concerned; he had nobody to whom he could turn.

When I went down to Undercliffe's flat on hearing that he'd disappeared, I was less surprised than saddened by the experience. The Lower Brichester area, as I've mentioned elsewhere, is the sort of miniature cosmopolis one finds in most major English towns: three-storey houses full of errant lodgers, curtains as varied as flags at a conference but more faded, the occasional smashed pane, the frequent furtive watchers. Somebody was tuning a motorcycle in Pitt Street, and the fumes drifted into Undercliffe's flat through a crack in the pane and clouded the page in his typewriter. The landlady was making ready to dispose of this, together with Undercliffe's books and other possessions, as soon as the rent gave out at the end of the month. I finally persuaded her to let me handle the disposal, after a good deal of wrangling and invocation of August Derleth (who'd never published Undercliffe), the Arts Council (who'd never heard of him, I imagine) and others. Having ushered her out at last, well aware that she'd be prepared to search me before I left the house, I examined the flat. The wardrobe and chest-of-drawers contained two suits, some shirts and so forth, none of which could have looked particularly stylish at an engagement party. The bed commanded a fine view of an arachnidial crack in the ceiling (clearly that crack which "suddenly, with a horrid lethargy, detached itself from the plaster and fell on Peter's upturned face" in "The Man Who Feared to Sleep"). The wallpaper had a Charlotte Perkins Gilman look; once Undercliffe complained that "such an absurd story should have used up an inspiration which I could work into one of my best tales". The window looked out on the fuming motorcycle, now stuck stubbornly in first gear, and its fuming owner; at night I suppose Undercliffe, seated at his typewriter before the window, might have waved to the girl slipping off her slip in the flat across the street, and I carried on his neighbourly gesture, though without much success. On the sill outside his window cigarette-stubs had collected like bird-droppings; he tended to cast these into the night, disliking the sight of a brimming ashtray. He'd go through a packet per thousand words, he once told me; he'd tried chewing-gum once, but this drew his fillings, and he was terrified of the dentist (cf. "The Drill"). All this, of course, is trivial, but I needed—still need—distraction. I'd already followed Undercliffe's search through the first three letters printed here, and that page still in the typewriter—a letter to me, probably the last thing he wrote— told of what he found. I removed it, unwillingly enough, and left; the landlady let it go. Later I arranged for transportation of the contents of the flat. The books—which seemed to be Undercliffe's treasured possessions, books of horror stories bought with the profits from his horror stories, a sad and lonely vicious circle—are now held in trust by the British Science Fiction Association library; the rest is in storage. I wish more than ever that Undercliffe would come forward to claim them.

Undercliffe's first letter to me (15 October 1965) contains a passage which in retrospect seems informed by a macabre irony. "The implicit theme of your story 'The Insects from Shaggai'," he writes, "is interesting, but you never come to grips with the true point of the plot: the horror-story author who is skeptical of the supernatural and finally is faced with overwhelming evidence of its reality. What would be his reaction? Certainly not to write of 'the lurid glow which shines on the razor lying on the table before me'! This is as unlikely as the ending of 'The Yellow Wallpaper'. I'd be interested to hear whether you yourself believe in what you write. For myself, I think the fact that I take great pains to check material on the supernatural here in our Central Library is eloquent enough. By the way, have you come across Roland Franklyn's *We Pass from View?* The author is a local man who has some quite arresting theories about reincarnation and the like."

Which brings us to Franklyn and *We Pass from View*, in themselves as mysterious as the fate of Undercliffe; but I suspect that the two mysteries are interdependent, that one explains the other—if indeed one wishes to probe for explanation. Before discussing Franklyn, however, I'd like to note some of Undercliffe's work; I feel obliged to bring it to the notice of a wider public. His favourites of his own work were "The Drains" (the blood of a bygone murder drips from the cold tap), "The Carved Desk" (the runes carved on what was once a Druid tree call up something which claws at the ankles of anyone foolish enough to sit down to write), and "The

Drifting Face" (never published: originally intended for the ill-fated second issue of *Alien Worlds*, it now cannot be traced). I favour his more personal, less popular work: "The Window in the Fog" (in which the narrator's glimpses of a girl across the street mount to an obsessive pitch until he accosts her one night and rebuffed, murders her), "The Steeple on the Hill" (where a writer fond of lonely walks is followed by the members of a cult, is eventually drawn within their circle and becomes the incarnation of their god), and "The Man Who Feared to Sleep", which lent its title (*Peur de Sommeil* in France) to Undercliffe's best collection, under the imprint of that excellent publisher who rediscovered such writers as Pursewarden and Sebastian Knight and made again available Robert Blake's legendary collection *The Stairs in the Crypt*. It is amusing to note that the entire contents of Undercliffe's collection—including the title story, which is surely a study of insanity—was listed under "Supernatural Phenomena" in the H. W. Wilson *Short Story Index* (in an earlier volume than that which placed my own "Church in High Street" under "Church Entertainments", making it sound like a parish farce or a Britten mystery play). Undercliffe was latterly working on a script for Delta Film Productions, but producer Harry Nadler reports that this was never completed; nor was his story "Through the Zone of the Colossi", a metaphysical piece based on a reference in my "Mine on Yuggoth" coupled with material from *We Pass from View*.

Which brings me back to the necessity of discussing Franklyn's book, a duty which I fear I've been avoiding. I've never seen the book, but I have little desire to do so. I refrained from consulting Brichester Central Library's copy when I went to Undercliffe's flat; I suppose I could obtain this through the National Central Library, though I suspect that in fact the copy (like all others, apparently) has mysteriously disappeared.

Although, as Undercliffe points out, *We Pass from View* displays marked affinities with the Cthulhu Mythos in certain passages, such Lovecraft scholars as Derleth, Lin Carter, Timothy d'Arch Smith and J. Vernon Shea can supply no information on the book. I understand that it was published in 1964 by the "True Light Press", Brichester; references in Undercliffe's letters suggest that it was a duplicated publication, originally circulated in card covers but probably bound by libraries taking copies. I have not been able to discover where, if anywhere, it was on sale. An odd rumour reached

me recently that almost the entire edition was stolen from the "True
Light Press"—actually the house of Roland Franklyn—and has not
been heard of since; perhaps destroyed, but by whom?

Here is the little information I've obtained from various sources.
The British National Bibliography gives the following entry:

> 129.4—Incarnation and reincarnation
> FRANKLYN, Roland
> We pass from View. Brichester, True Light Press, 9/6. Jan 1964.
> 126 p. 22 cm.

However, the Cumulative Book Index, which lists all books
published in English, does not acknowledge the book; at least,
neither I nor the staff of Liverpool's Picton Library can trace the
reference.

While correlating notes I was surprised to turn up in my
commonplace book the following review, which might have been
copied from the *Times Literary Supplement*.

PSEUDOPODDITIES

The last few decades have seen the emergence of many
disturbing pseudo-philosophies, but *We Pass from View* must
rank lowest. The author, Roland Franklyn, has less idea of style
than most of his kind; however, the ideas behind the writing
are expressed with less ambiguity than one might wish. His
basic thesis seems to be that the number of souls in the universe
is limited, by some illegitimate application of the conservation
of energy principle, and that humanity must therefore
acknowledge an infinite number of simultaneous incarnations.
The last chapter, "Toward the True Self", is a sort of reductio
ad absurdum of the theory, concluding that the "true self" is to
be found "outside space", and that each human being is merely
a facet of his "self", which is itself able to experience all its
incarnations simultaneously but unable to control them. There
is a suggestion of Beckett here (particularly *L'Innomable*), and
Mr Franklyn has infused enough unconscious humour into
many passages to cause hilarity when the book was read aloud
at a party. But a book which advocates the use of drugs to

achieve fulfilment of black-magic rites is worth attention not so much as humour (and certainly not as it was intended) as a sociological phenomenon.

Laughter at a party, indeed! I still find that remark rather frightening. What copy was being read aloud? The *TLS* review copy, perhaps, but in that case what happened to it? Like so much in this affair, the end fades into mystery. I doubt that many indignant letters replied to the review; those that were written probably weren't printable. In 1966, I heard vaguely of a book called *How I Discovered my Infinite Self* by "An Initiate", but whether it was ever published I don't know.

Undercliffe quoted several passages from *We Pass from View* which, though I find them faintly distasteful, I had better include. I still have all of Undercliffe's letters; some day I may edit them into a memorial article for *The Arkham Collector*, but it seems in rather bad taste to write a memoir of a man who may still be alive somewhere. The letters printed here are, I think, essential.

In his letter of 2 November 1965 Undercliffe wrote: "Here's a bizarre passage which might set you off on a short story. From the first page of *We Pass from View*: 'The novice must remind himself always that the Self is infinite and that he is but one part of his Self, not yet aware of his other bodies and lives. REMIND YOURSELF on sleeping. REMIND YOURSELF on waking. *Above all, REMIND YOURSELF* when entering the First Stage of Initiation.' As for this first stage, I've traced references later in the text, but nothing very lucid. Franklyn keeps mentioning 'the aids' which seem to be drugs of some sort, usually taken under supervision of an 'initiate' who chants invocations ('Ag'lak Sauron, Daoloth asgu'i, Eihort phul'aag'—that ought to ring a bell with you) and attempts to tap the novice's subconscious knowledge of his other incarnations. Not that I necessarily believe what Franklyn says, but it certainly gives you that sense of instability which all good horror stories should provide. I can't discover much about Franklyn. He seems in the last year or two to have drawn together a circle of young men who, from what I hear, visit Goatswood, Clotton, Temphill, the island beyond Severnford, and other places in which you're no doubt as interested as I am. I'd like to get in on the act."

I replied that he surely didn't need drugs for inspiration and that, warnings from Dennis Wheatley aside, I didn't feel it was advisable to become involved in black magic. "Experience makes the writer," Undercliffe retorted. Subsequently he avoided direct quotation, but I gathered he had not joined Franklyn's circle; his own decision, I think. Then, in September 1966, when he was writing "The Crawling in the Attic" (I'd just started library work and sent him the manuscript of "The Stocking" to read, which he didn't like—"elaborately pointless"), he quoted the following:

"Today's psychologists are wrong about dreams coming from the subconscious mind. Dreams are the links between us and the experiences of our other incarnations. *We must be receptive to them.* TELL YOURSELF BEFORE YOU SLEEP THAT YOU WILL SEE BEYOND YOUR FACET. The initiate known as Yokh'khim, his name on Tond, came to me describing a dream of long tunnels in which he was pursued but could not see his body. After several sessions, he managed to see himself as a ball of hair rolling through the tunnel away from the Trunks in the Ooze. The ball was known on Tond as Yokh'khim. He has now attained the stage of Black Initiate and spends his time beyond his facet, having set aside all but the minimum of his life on Earth."

I hadn't much to say to that except to suggest that Franklyn had plagiarized the "Tond" reference, provoking Undercliffe to reply: "Surely Franklyn has undermined your complacency enough to make complaints about copyright a little trivial. Anyway, no doubt he'd point out that you knew of Tond through your dreams." I couldn't decide whether his tongue was in his cheek; I passed over his comment, and our correspondence fell off somewhat.

In February 1967 he quoted a passage which is significant indeed. "What about a story of a writer who haunts his own books?" he suggested. "Franklyn has a paragraph on ghosts: 'The death of a body does not mean that the soul will leave it. This depends on whether there is an incarnation for it to pass into. If not, the body continues to be inhabited until it is destroyed. The initiate knows that Edgar Allan Poe's fear of premature burial was well-founded. If the death is violent, then it is more difficult than ever for the soul to leave. FOR HIS OWN SAFETY, THE INITIATE MUST INSIST ON CREMATION. Otherwise he will be hopelessly attracted back to Earth, and the burrowers of the core may drag off his body from the grave with him still in it to the feast of Eihort.'"

Interesting, I said somewhat wearily. I was rather tired of this sort of verbal delirium. On 5 July 1967 Undercliffe reported that the

Brichester Herald had noted Franklyn's death. This meant little to me at the time. Then came the final sequence of letters.

7 Pitt Street : Lower Brichester, Glos : 14 July 1967 : 1.03 a.m.:
slightly intoxicated

Dear JRC:
  Always this point at a party where the beer tastes like vomit. Pretty putrid party, actually. Friend of mine from school who got engaged and sent me an invite. Can't think why, I'd just about forgotten him myself, but I wanted to meet him again. Didn't get near. Great fat bluebottle of a woman he got engaged to pawing over him all evening and wanting to be kissed, messily at that, whenever he tried to act the host. Good luck say I. So I had to make my own way round the conversations. I just don't know where he got them from. All bow ties and "God, Bernard, surely you realise the novel is absolutely *dead*" and banging down tankards of ale which they'd bought to be all boys together, sloshing them over and making little lakes down these trestle tables in the Co-op Hall (another blow for the old town and the Brichester folks—our engaged friend kept patting his bluebottle and bellowing "I had a wonderful childhood in Brichester, absolutely wonderful, they're fine people", no Palm Court for *him*.) Whole place murky with smoke and some tin band playing in the fog. Hundreds of ashtrays surrounded by those pieces of ash like dead flies. Finally our friend fell to his feet to give thanks for "all the superb presents", which didn't make me feel any more accepted, since I hadn't known it was done to bring one. I feel a little
  Better. Repartee: the morning after. Beg pardon, I shouldn't have mentioned engagements and fiancées. Still, I'm sure you're better off. Writers always bloom better with elbow room. I have your letter by me. You're right, your last argument with your girlfriend in Lime Street Station cafeteria with bare tables, balls of cellophane and someone next to you trying not to listen—it'd never come off in print, even though it happened to you they'd be sure to scream Graham Greene was here first. And then her calling down "I love you" through the rain before her mother dragged her back from her window—yes, it's very poignant, but you'll have to rewrite before you can print. More on our wavelength, what you say about this

other girl running out of your haunted Hornby Library in panic certainly sounds promising. You going to lock yourself in there overnight? I'd give a lot for a genuine supernatural experience.

There was this idiot at the party wanting to know what I did. Horror stories I said. Should have seen him blanch. "Why do you write those things?" he asked as if he'd caught me picking my nose. "For the money," I said. A young couple sliding down the wall behind us laughed. Great, an audience I thought. No doubt if I'd said I wasn't joking they'd have laughed harder. "No, but seriously" said this poor man's F. R. Leavis (you couldn't write for anything as base as money, you see) "would you not agree that the writer is a sort of Christ figure who suffers in order to cohere his suffering for the reader's benefit?" The extent of his suffering was his bank manager calling him on his overdraft, I'll bet. "And don't you think the horror story coheres (I wasn't cohering myself by that time) an experience?" "Are you telling me you believe in what you write?" he demanded as if it'd been *Mein Kampf.* "You don't think I'd write something in which I didn't believe?" I retorted, carefully placing the preposition. The young couple left; the show was over. He stalked off to tell Bernard about me.

At least the streets were clean and empty. Remarkable girl in the flat across the street. You should come down. Anyway, to bed. Tomorrow to work on "Through the Zone of the Colossi" and check the library.

Best,

EU

Pitt of Hell : Lowest Brichester, Glos : 14 July 1967 : later!

Dear JRC:

I don't normally write twice in a day. Today's events, however, are too important to let fade. I have had my experience. It will unquestionably form into a short story, so forgive me this first draft. I trust you not to use it.

Today, as anticipated, I visited the library. After last night/this morning, I felt somewhat sick, but that's the penance. On the bus I was trying to cohere "Zone of the Colossi", but they wouldn't let me; you must know how it is. Half the passengers were ducking and screaming beneath the flight of a wasp, and the other half were sitting stoically pouring forth clouds of tobacco-smoke, which curled in the hot air. I sat next to some whistling fool and my thoughts kept getting sidetracked into a search for the lyrics in order to fit them to his tune and be rid of it. Not an auspicious start, but "Zones of the Colossi" was forgotten when I left the library. I couldn't find *We Pass from View* on the shelf in the Religion section; mind you, some cretin in an aged mac was pottering round the shelves and sampling books and replacing them at whatever position he'd pottered to, earning himself glares from the staff. Someone else had erected a fortress of books on one of the tables and behind it was completing his football coupon. He cursed me visibly when I examined his barricade; I've rarely felt so self-conscious as then, his gaze on my canted head. But there it was: *We Pass from View* beneath *The Mass in Slow Motion* and *The Catholic Marriage Manual* and Graham Fisher's *Identity and Awareness*. I pulled out the foundation, but the wall held.

The book was bound in bright blue. The table-top was pastel green. The room was warm and sunny, if a little stifling. At the further end behind a creamy desk, one of the staff was recounting his adventures in a branch library, how he'd been plagued by old ladies pleading for what he call "cheap novelettes"; I could tell he looked upon all fiction as the poor relation of non-fiction, like all academic librarians—so much for our writing. You couldn't get further from a Lovecraft setting, but then this was the real thing.

I turned back the cover; it slapped the table-top. Silence fell. A blade of sunlight moved along the floor, intensifying cracks. Then the pages of *We Pass from View* began to turn of their own accord.

At first I thought it must be a draught. When you're sitting in a bright new library among books and people you don't think of the possibility of the supernatural. When the book exhibits traces of its readership (chewing-gum on one page, a dead fly on another) it's difficult to view it as haunted. And yet I couldn't take my eyes from those moving pages. They turned up the dedication ("to my faithful friends") and for a second, as though my vision were failing, I saw lines of some other print waver as if superimposed on the text. The page turned to the next, a blank leaf. I put out my hand, but I couldn't quite bring myself to touch the book. As I hesitated, lines of print appeared on the blank paper.

HELP ME

It stood out starkly on the paper, next to the fingerprint of some unclean reader. HELP ME. The letters held for several seconds: great black capitals which seemed to burn my eyeballs as I stared at them. And I was overwhelmed by the sense of an appeal, of someone trying desperately to contact me. Then they blurred and faded.

FEEL SOMEONE READING MUST BE

That flashed and disappeared; I read it in a second. The room seemed airless; I was sweating, my ribs were closing on my lungs. I could see only the book open on the table and feel a terrible, tortuous strain, as of a mind in torment trying to communicate its suffering.

SHE HAD ME BURIED   HER REVENGE   TOLD HER CREMATE   BITCH   WOMEN   CANT TRUST   HELP ME

That HELP ME was molten.

FEEL THEM COMING   SLOWLY BURROWING   WANT ME TO SUFFER   CANT MOVE   GET ME OUT   SAVE ME SOMEWHERE IN BRICHESTER   HELP ME

And the page, which had been lifted trembling, fell back. I waited. The room assembled round me in the merciless sunlight. The page remained blank. I don't know how long I waited. At last it occurred to me that the setting was wrong; back in my room I might be able to re-establish contact. I picked up the book—holding it rather gingerly; somehow I expected to feel it move, struggle between my fingers—and carried it to the desk and back into mundanity.

"I'm afraid this is a reference copy only," said the girl at the desk, flashing a smile and her engagement ring at me.

I told her that it seemed to be their only copy and that there were various of my books in the fiction section and that I knew the chief librarian (well, I'd glimpsed him enthroned in his office as someone bore in his coffee the day I was invited by his secretary to sign my books). I could have told her that I felt the book throbbing in my hand. But she replied "Well, *personally* I know we can trust you with it and if it were up to me I'd let you have it, but—" and much more of the I'm-only-doing-my-job speech. I set the book down on the desk in order to wave my hands about and she handed it to a girl who was replacing books on the shelves, belatedly asking "You didn't want it again, did you?"

I saw it carried away on the toppling pile; already the transcendental was being erased by the mundane; Franklyn would be filed carefully and forgotten. And that showed me what I must do. Of course I knew that it was Franklyn whose paragraphs I had been reading from beyond the grave, indeed, from in the grave. But I didn't know how to find him. The *Brichester Herald* had given neither his address nor where he was buried. "Do you know anything about Roland Franklyn himself?" I enquired.

"Yes, he used to come in quite often . . ." but she obviously didn't want to talk about it. "Eric, don't let Mary do all the clearing," she said to her companion at the desk, who was building a house of holiday postcards.

"Franklyn, the little queer in the cloak?" he addressed me. "You're not a friend of his, are you? Good job. Used to come in here with a whole crowd of them, the Twelve Disciples we used to call them. One of them came up to the desk one day because we were talking about his master and waved his great emaciated fist at us—you could see the drugs running out of his eyes. Why are you interested in that queer? Can't think what attracted them all, what with that moth-eaten cloak and that huge bald head—he'd probably pulled out the last few hairs to stick on that spidery beard. He had a wife too, I think—must've been before he came to the crossroads. What's the matter, Mary, you want me to rupture myself?"

"Do you know where he lived?" I stayed him.

"Bottom of Mercy Hill. House looked like Satan was in residence. You can't miss it." He knocked down the house of cards and walked away, and so, feeling rather adrift, did I.

I suppose I could have tried to find Franklyn today, but I wanted to crystallise the experience, to preserve it before it lost its form. I came home and set this down; I think it needs rewriting. Reality always does; I suppose we have to give it some form, even while paying the price of distortion. I keep thinking of Franklyn in his coffin, aware of something tunnelling toward him, unable to move a muscle but still capable of feelings. But it's dark now; I couldn't find him in the dark. Tomorrow, more. Goodbye, girl in the window.

EU

a fixed point : 15 July 1967

Dear JRC:

Today has been disturbing.

I knew Franklyn lived on Mercy Hill, but the Hill covers a lot of ground; I couldn't search it for his house. Finally I thought of the

street directory—odd I didn't think of that before—and called at
the library today to check. There was only one R. Franklyn on
Mercy Hill. I did return to the Religion section, but they couldn't
find *We Pass from View*; I suppose they're classifying me as one of
their regular cranks.

I caught a bus to Mercy Hill. High sun, slight breeze; a bluebottle
was patting its reflexion on the window, trying to escape. In the
streets couples were taking their ice-creams for a walk; toward the
Hill tennis-balls were punctuating their pauses, girls were leaping,
bowls were clicking, and from the houses behind a procession was
bearing trays of cakes to the pavilion. It was one of those days when
if anything is to happen you have to make it happen; or for me to
complete the next episode of my short story.

I dismounted at the foot of the Hill and climbed the piled
terraces. At one corner they were erecting a new school; workmen
were sunning themselves on girders. Two levels further up I came
into Dee Terrace, and at once saw Franklyn's house.

It was unmistakeable. The personality which gave that house its
final form was not the architect's. One chimney had been built into
a frustum of white stone; an extra room had been added on the left,
and its window had been blocked with newer brick; all the curtains,
except those of one ground-floor window draped in green, were
black. The house looked deserted, the more so for its garden, which
could not have been tended in years; grass and weeds grew knee-
high. I brushed through, imagining things crawling into my shoes.
A bustling cloud of flies rose from something to one side. I reached
the front door and saw the green curtain move; a face peered and
drew back. I knocked. There was silence for a moment. Then inside
a woman's voice screamed: "Oh, lie down with you!" Before I could
ponder on that, the door was open.

The woman was certainly not in mourning—which was encouraging, for I hadn't known quite what approach to make. She wore a
red dress, which looked pale against the crimson wallpaper of the
hall. She was heavily, if inaccurately, made up, and her hair was
rather arbitrarily bleached. She waited.

"Would you be Mrs. Franklyn?"

She looked suspicious, as if I'd intended a threat. "Roland
Franklyn was my husband," she admitted ungraciously. "Who are
you?"

Who indeed. It didn't seem as though I'd get far by declaring the supernatural nature of my quest. "I'm a writer," I compromised. "I've read your husband's book several times. I was shocked to hear of his death," I added to get it over with.

"Well, you don't have to be. Come in, anyway," she said. She looked round the hall and grimaced. "Look at this. Would you live with this? Not likely. Getting them in the right mood—half of them didn't know what they were being got in the mood for. Nice boys, some of them, to begin with." She kicked the crimson wall and ushered me into a room on the right.

I wasn't prepared—I couldn't have been. A ground-floor room with wardrobe, dressing-table complete with cobwebbed mirror, a bed beneath the window, piles of women's magazines, some thick with dust, and a cat chained to the leg of a chair in the middle of the floor; it wasn't a sense of evil or fear that choked me, it was a sense of something locked away, forgotten and gone bad. The cat padded up to meet me; its chain gave it freedom of the room, but it couldn't quite reach the door.

"Pussy likes you," said Mrs Franklyn, closing the door and sinking into a chair amid a haze of dust; her dress drew up her thighs, but she didn't pull it down. "That could be a good sign, but don't they say only effeminate men can make friends with cats? Why are you looking at me like that?" I hadn't realised I was looking like anything in particular; I was carrying the cat, chain and all, to the chair I took opposite her. "Don't like the chain, is that it? But me and my cat, we're all we've got—I'm not letting her out so they can carry her off and sacrifice her. They would, you know, on their nights. I take her in the garden, that's all; wouldn't trust them further than that." I remembered the flies. "What do you write?" she demanded.

In this context it seemed a little pale to say "Stories of the supernatural."

"Stories, eh? Yes, we all like stories," she mused. "Anything's better than the real thing. Do you want some tea? I'm afraid that's about all I have to offer."

"It's all right, thank you," I refused; I could see cracked cups in the kitchen behind her head. She caught my eye; she was always doing that, damn her.

"Oh, I can't blame you for thinking," she said. "But it gets you down after a while. After he took the house over—you didn't know that, did you?—yes, he did, he married me and then he encroached on every room, keeping things I wouldn't touch all over the house, until I took this room and the kitchen and I told him if you try anything in my rooms *I'll kill you!*" She thumped the chair-arm and dust flew out.

"But why did you put up with it?" I had to ask.

"Why? *Because I married him!*" The cat fled, knocked over a pile of magazines, sneezed and jumped back; she reeled it in and fondled it. "Now, pussy's not scared of mummy," she soothed and put it down. It began to scratch at her shoe. "Lie down with you, for God's sake," she hissed. It came to me for comfort.

"When I married him," she returned to me, "he promised I'd have all this house to entertain, to do all the things I never could. I believed him. Then I found out how he really was. So I waited. Every day I wished him dead so I'd have my house, what was left of my life. I haven't spoken to him for years, did you know that?— hardly even seen him. I used to leave his meals outside his room on a tray; if he didn't eat them that was up to him. But when he didn't touch them for three days I went into his room. No, I didn't go in— all those filthy statues and lights and books—but I could see he wasn't there. He was in his stupid little printing press room. He was dead all right. There was a book—he must have been going to copy something—but I didn't read it; the way his face looked was enough. I threw it in the bin. Didn't touch him, though—oh, no, they're not going to say I killed him after all the years I've suffered."

"But how did you stand it?" Of course the answer was—she didn't.

"Oh, he made me long ago. We met when we were students—I was impressionable then, I thought he was a good man, the best— and later we got married. I ought to have known; there was a rumour he'd been expelled from the University even then, but when he swore he hadn't I trusted him. Then his parents died and left him this house and we got married. My husband—" Her face contorted as if she'd put her hand in something foul. "He took me down to Temphill and made me watch those things dancing on the graves. I didn't want to but he said it was for a book he was writing. He held my hand, then. And later we went down the steps below Clotton— oh, you may write, but you'd never dare to write about . . . I don't want to think about it. But it hardened me. It made me tough when he began his mummery back here, trying to stop me destroying all his muck . . . "

That sounded like a cue. "If you haven't thrown away all his books do you think I could look them over? Purely from a writer's viewpoint," I tacked on, why I'm not sure.

"But you're a nice young man, you don't want to become another of his," she said, and sat down on the bed; her dress rose again like a curtain. She began to clear piles of magazines festooned with dust away from the bed; atop one was a vase of dandelions—"Just a touch of colour, what's it matter what they are, no-one ever comes," she explained, though the petals had curled and dulled in the flecked light. "Did you ever write from experience? How could you, you've never had what I've had to put up with. The things he's doing even now to hinder me— Only yesterday I picked up one of his books to throw it out and it went sticky and soft things started pushing between my fingers—God!" She wiped her hands down her dress. "I used to lie awake listening to him going to the bathroom and wishing he was dead—and last night I heard him flopping round his room, beating on the walls. And this morning I woke early, I thought the sun was coming up—but it was his face floating over the rooftops . . . It came to the windows, filled them, it followed me from room to room, mouthing at me—God! You'd never write about it, you'd never write about anything again. But he can't get me down, and he knows it. He was always scared of me. That's why he kept me here, to keep me quiet. But he can't have left many of his little tricks behind him. He knows I'll win. But you don't want to get mixed up with the wrong things. You're a nice young man." She swung her legs up and lay back on the pillow, where I could see imprints of hair-dye.

For some time now I'd had the impression that my short story was taking over its own writing; now we seemed to be building to a climax I hadn't foreseen. I had to be direct. "Your husband was buried, wasn't he?" I asked. "Didn't he want to be cremated?"

She seemed to take an age to sit up; her eyes were on me all the while. "How did you know that?" she demanded softly. "You gave yourself away there, didn't you? You are one of his! I knew it before you got to the door! Yes, he's buried, where you all should be. Go on, go up and be with him, I'm sure he'd like you to be. He must be able to feel them coming by now—I hope he can. Yes, he was always on about his Eihort, but he doesn't like it when they come for him. You go and look after him, you—"

I didn't know what she might be capable of; I retreated hastily,

seeing her watching in the mirror and sneering when she caught my
eye. Somehow I dislodged a heap of magazines and buried the cat,
which fought its way out and tangled my feet in its chain. "Don't
you touch my cat!" she screamed. "She's worth a million of you!
What is it, darling, come to mummy—" and I escaped, running
down the hall, an inflamed intestine, and through the grass, careless
of what I might tread in unseen.

Suddenly I was on solid pavement. Down the street an ice-cream
van was playing "Greensleeves." This time the intrusion of
mundanity didn't seem so tasteless. I walked home.

By the time I reached the typewriter I'd glimpsed the paradox.
Even the supernatural-story writer who believes what he writes (and
I'm not saying I don't) isn't prepared for an actual confrontation.
Quite the reverse, for every time he fabricates the supernatural in a
story (unless based on experience) he clinches his skepticism; he
knows such things can't be, because he wrote them. Thus for him a
confrontation would be doubly upsetting. It would at least force
him to re-think all his works. Is this desirable? From the self-
completion angle I suppose it is. At any rate, I'm going. "Go up and
be with him" she said—it must be the cemetery on Mercy Hill.

Tomorrow.

EU

(Undated, unaddressed)

I don't know what

(Foregoing deleted, does not appear on carbon; page apparently
withdrawn, carbon attached, reinserted into typewriter) Nonsense.
Of course I can write about it. The very fact that I can write proves
that I'm still functioning.

I took the bus up Mercy Hill at the height of the day. Few things
moved; flies and pedestrians crawled, and the workmen climbed
sluggishly on the skeletal school. At the intersection with Dee
Terrace I saw the house; it seemed swallowed up by grass, forever
isolated from its surroundings.

I want to get this over. The caretaker directed me down an
avenue, and when I reached—No. Description of graveyard. Why
write as if this were my last page? Willows, their branches glowing
stippled curves, were spaced carefully toward the Hill out of which
the cemetery was carved; in the Hill itself were catacombs, black
behind ivy or railings, and above stood the hospital, a grey reminder

of hope or despair. What awful irony juxtaposed hospital and grave-yard? The avenues were guarded by broken-nosed angels yearning heavenward; one showed a leprous patch where her left eye and cheek had sloughed away. Urns stood here and there like empty glasses at a sick-bed, and a young woman was kneeling with a wreath at a shining memorial; I wonder how long before she shakes him off? And then, toward the catacombs, I saw the new headstone and its bed of pebbles. They gleamed beneath the high sun. I read Franklyn's name and the framing dates, and waited.

It eventually occurred to me that I didn't quite know what I was waiting for; not in that sunlight. Yet the air had hushed. I paced around the grave, and the pebbles shifted. My shadow had moved them. I'm still capable of an anticlimax! My God. I thought: Franklyn is alive down there—or perhaps no longer. Then I saw a possibility. I looked back down the perspective. The young mourner was passing through the gates. I lay down on the grass and put my ear to the pebbles. They ground together, then there was nothing. I felt vilely uncomfortable. Suddenly I realised that I was visible all the way down the avenue to the gates. I went hot all over and scrambled to my feet.

And on the way up I heard something. Something. If only I knew. It'd be better if I had something to confront, anything but this uncertainty which sucks the confidence from me. It could have been the foreman at that school calling over the noise of riveting. Or it could—yes, must write—it could have been someone imprisoned, paralyzed, summoning a last muscular spasm, screaming thickly for help and beating his fists in the dark as he was dragged downward, downward . . .

I couldn't run; it was too hot. I walked. When I reached the school the girders were rippling in the heat-haze, as if they were alive. I wish I hadn't seen that. No longer could I trust the surface of the world. It was as though it had been instantaneously revealed to me that there were countless forces awake in everything, invisible, things lurking in daylight, shifting, planning—What had they built into the school? What would stalk unseen among the children?

I walked. Of course I was visualizing too much, but I could imagine, I could feel the pavement thin as ice, ready to engulf me in a world where life crawled. I sat in the parks. It was no good; I didn't know what watched from the trees; I didn't know how many of the passers-by might be masked, agents not of this world, preparing the way for—*what?* Who had Franklyn left behind? The peril of the writer: he can't stop thinking. He may survive by writing, but he doesn't really survive. Why am I no—mustn't give in—I wandered until dark, found a cafe, I don't remember. I was in a deserted street of shops with one red window lit above a darkened store. I don't know why, it seemed evil. Franklyn's hall, I suppose.

So I came back and typed this. The street is empty; only the shadow of the streetlamp seems to move. The window opposite is dark. What may be there, waiting?

I can't turn round. I stare at the reflexion of the room behind me. The reflexion—like a framed photograph about to be split open by something climbing forth. When I've written this I shall turn round.

"I don't dare," I have just said aloud.

Where can I go where I don't sense movement behind the scenes?

(Unsigned)

A MADNESS FROM THE VAULTS

BENEATH THE CITY OF DERD ON THE PLANET OF TOND LIES a labyrinth of vaults, whose origins remain obscure. The yarkdao who built the city could intuit no explanation for their presence, nor were they encouraged to explore by the fragmentary legends of well-nigh endless passages, linked in a manner that defied mapping. The yarkdao assumed that the vaults had served some hermetic function in the lives of the unknown citizens of that ruined pyramid-city on whose foundations Derd was to be built, and neglected further thought. In the heyday of Derd, some yarkdao elected to be entombed in the vaults rather than suffer abandonment on the peak of Liota above the city, but such rebels were uncommon. The openings from the vaults which occasionally gaped on the streets of Derd were avoided by the multitude, deterred by the legend that on certain nights the corpses preserved below would stalk forth from their alcoves and emerging, their faces turned to the dead and ashen sun of Baalblo, would parade through the streets.

At the end of its life, Derd lay beneath the tyranny of its last governor, Opojollac, whose law for any crime required the culprit to be cast into the vaults. The poorer quarters of the city were laden with the corpses of those whose taxes had enriched his robes with glimmering black charms, while the richer yarkdao could only weep as their mansions crumbled beneath the ever-rising crystal serpents

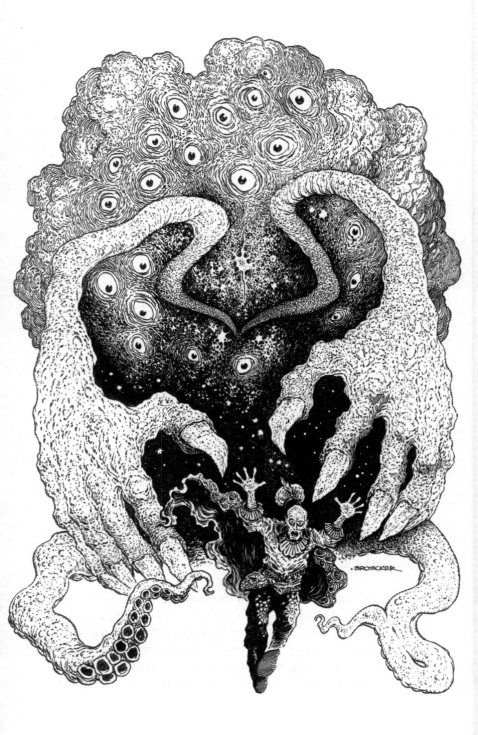

with which Opojollac's palace was spired. In Derd the names of the newborn were no longer the outcome of a day-long christening ritual but were subject to the whim of Opojollac, who thus ensured that none could boast a name so sonorous as his and by that token hold sway over his city. Certain words, phrases, and syntactical modes were the property of Opojollac alone, for on Tond language is power. There were rumours that he might order a temple built to himself, and none dared meditate on the eventual fate of those virgins who were summoned to his palace: although some said that at such times the crystal serpents would rise redly gorged against the green sun, and some, indeed, that they would preen their scales lethargically.

So Opojollac ruled through myth, and decadence simpered in Derd with lips painted with the blood of torture: and with decadence came apathy. Nonetheless, at the rising of a day, as Opojollac dined beneath the translucent roof formed of a shell found in the desert, a servitor fought free of the curtains of mauve skin which veiled the entrance to the dining-hall and presented himself, bowing backwards towards Opojollac through his legs.

"O omnisapient and benevolent Opojollac," he moaned. "O omnipotent—"

"Your praises, however fulsome and gratifying," pronounced Opojollac, "represent an interruption of my meal. Cease, and justify your presence. But first show me your tongue—yes, it appears tender, and if it cannot provide a satisfactory explanation I may well transfer it to my plate."

"Amen, O gracious Opojollac," responded the servitor, shuddering. "A yarkdao waits outside, saying that he must speak to you immediately of some danger to your glorious self."

"I imagined I heard a participle," mused Opojollac in a voice hoarse with mirthless laughter. "Guard your syntax. Let the yarkdao enter, reminding him the while that he may not behold me otherwise than inverted. As to your tongue—perhaps I may benefit from allowing it to mature a little."

Almost immediately, a yarkdao in tattered robes appeared, bowing once without grace. "O governor," he said, "there is a yarkdao dead in the Streets of Pleasure—"

But Opojollac laughed without humour. "I am alive," he cried, "and it follows that such deaths cannot affect me. Since the pleasure-givers do not trouble me, their methods of extracting payment are no concern of mine. Servitor, have this intruder shorn of all but the last syllable of his name and cast him to the vaults."

The servitor, skilled in the ways of Opojollac's palace, managed while yet bowing to capture the miscreant, and Opojollac returned to his meal. But coincidence dictated that Beav Lanpbeav, Opojollac's chief administrator, should that day be collecting taxes in the Streets of Pleasure: and presently, while Opojollac was trifling with his collection of musical instruments, Beav Lanpbeav craved audience. "Play to me," Opojollac commanded, "and tell me your tale."

The administrator took up a lute tuned in quarter-tones, shuddering at the stains which marked its frame and remembering how Opojollac had acquired the instrument. But it was the governor's favourite toy, and Beav Lanpbeav had so ingratiated himself with Opojollac by his art that he was not required to bow: so, while the dissonances of the lute touched the petrified trees which were the pillars of the hall, he spoke.

"O beneficence, I had made my way through the Streets of Pleasure and was about to quit them by the northward egress, when in my path I encountered a crowd of the tenants of the street. I called upon them in your name to move aside, which, of course, was done with dispatch; yet I observed that they huddled into the hives on that side of the thoroughfare farthest from an entrance to the vaults. Beneath the green rays of Yifne that entrance seemed instinct with movement of a kind I could not distinguish. When I approached, I saw tracks of a nature unknown to me, as if something that possessed an ill-matched number of limbs had emerged from, and returned to, the vault. I turned then to that which lay in the street, but for a space could make little of it. It appeared to be a black and pitted mass trampled into the earth, more than the height of a yarkdao in span, and acrawl with insects. 'What droppings is this?' I shouted in your name. 'Who has befouled the street?' But from beyond one of the barred doors, a voice cried that the mass in the street had but recently been the husband of one of them."

"Doubtless a sorcerer's revenge," Opojollac mused, but he frowned. "Nevertheless, I and no other hold power in Derd. Go now, send forth spies and be quick to bring me any further such tales."

Days passed, and Opojollac kept to the hall of music, where he tried to coax from his instruments the tunes which the embalmed songsters suspended among the trees had sung in life. But always he failed, and each day brought new tales of the unknown peril that stalked the city. At last Beav Lanpbeav took up the lute once more and told Opojollac of his findings.

"O kindly tyrant, it seems clear that a forgotten monster has come forth from the vaults. Many have spoken of a shape which rears forth from the entrances and leaps on its prey from the shadows. You must know that those entrances from which it preys draw ever nearer to your palace and that there is an entrance situated near your portal. There is but one course to take: to ask counsel of the protectors of our world, the Globes of Hakkthu."

"For once your wisdom is equal to my own," Opojollac said. "Go then and seek counsel."

"Not I, for pity," Beav Lanpbeav cried, paling, "for they would scarcely grant indulgence to my poor tales. Me they would crush; you have the language to converse with them."

It troubled Opojollac that his dealings with the city of Derd might find little favour with the implacable Globes; yet he admitted grudgingly that his administrator might prove less equal to the task. So he made ready, donning a robe like a skin of mirrors for the desert, and took his leave. Glancing back, he saw Beav Lanpbeav musing among the black branches and pale silent songsters within the hall.

Slowly Opojollac passed among the low mansions which were dazzled by his palace, and between the brown hives of the poorer quarter. Few yarkdao were to be seen, nor were caravans or traders to be heard; and everywhere, it seemed, gaped the entrances to the vaults. At last, close to the rim of the city, Opojollac approached one of the entrances. Within, the dark rough walls stretched away beyond his sight and beads of moisture gleamed from the shadows. At the edge of total darkness Opojollac saw an image set in an alcove; he distinguished a limbless torso surmounted by a pitted malformed head, flat like a serpent's, whose wide mouth and deep-set eyes were frozen in a vapid smile. Vague memories stirred of tales told at the birth of Derd, but Opojollac shrugged quickly and hurried out into the desert.

Already, against the dazzling white sand, he could see the broken totem-pillars which marked the tip of the path to Hakkthu. He gained this path, which was formed of cracked and treacherous fused sand, and, as he hurried on, the blinding desert coated his eyes. Soon he found it difficult to distinguish his surroundings or to reassure himself of the reality of what he saw. Once he imagined that from a shattered amber dome on the horizon, thin tattered figures pranced forth and beckoned hungrily to him, and some immeasurable time later that he glimpsed a huge toothed head struggling to raise its body from the sand.

At last the path began to dip, and he knew that he was approaching Hakkthu. He paused to brush the paste of dust and sweat from his face, and the mirrors flashed intolerably on his arms. After a while he made out in the omnipresent whiteness a gigantic cloud of dust which puffed up incessantly from a hollow of the desert. Opojollac drew all the power of his language to him and hastened down the unsteady track to stand at the lip of the hollow.

Within the restless cloud of sand, which loomed more mightily than his palace, he thought that he perceived the rolling of great rusted surfaces and heard a low unceasing rumble, like the musings of a metal colossus. He threw himself down and, crying out the ritual invocation, began to address the Globes.

"O ageless Globes, who have moved since the beginning of Tond and who, before the birth of my poor world, were pleased to roll through the unimaginable depths of space, the greatest and wisest of planets, hear my supplication! Know that a monster has risen from the vaults beneath Derd and craves power on this world, which is thine alone!"

Minutes of silence passed, so that Opojollac dared glance towards Hakkthu. Then he threw himself supine again, for he had glimpsed a gigantic rusted mouth yawning above him through the dust. For a moment only the dust whispered, and then a voice like the grinding of ponderous gears boomed out above Opojollac.

"It was well done to bring this intelligence to Hakkthu. Listen well to our command. We, the Globes, had the labyrinth beneath the pyramids constructed to pen the avatar of Azathoth who lurks below. Yet we knew that he who festers there must one day learn the labyrinth, though it were the work of aeons, and emerge to bring chaos to Tond. Thus we caused a further protection to be constructed. Go now to the vaults, touching the walls at the span of your arm, and a light will guard you and protect you. Above the pit in the deepest vault, a lever stands from the wall which touched, contains once more the avatar of Azathoth. Go now, and fear not."

When Opojollac raised his head again, only the dust rolled; and so he made his way back across the dimming waste to Derd. The silence of the desert lay upon the city, and Opojollac encountered no citizen in the streets. The entrances of the hives and mansions stood unguarded, and Opojollac saw that his city had been abandoned.

As a wind from the desert sang thinly in the shells which roofed his palace, Opojollac cursed the traitorous citizens and thought to flee. Then a vision mocked him of his palace ruined and inhabited by the creatures of the surrounding waste. An entrance to the vaults gaped close by. Opojollac strode to it and, stretching forth an unsteady hand, touched the wall within the entrance. As he did so, a line of light sprang forth beneath his fingers and sped along the wall into darkness. It was a warm light, like the glow of fires at midnight in the desert; and so Opojollac gave himself into its protection and passed into the vaults.

For hours, it seemed, he walked. The walls were pocked like ancient flesh, down which black sweat rolled. At times the floor descended sharply, and he slid beyond the path of the light beneath the low looming roof of black stone. Often the passage broadened into a junction whose limits the light could not distinguish, where the shadows crowded and nodded towards him as the luminous path rushed on. Once, far down a transverse passage, he saw a great flat stain amid which seemed to glimmer the face of a criminal he had consigned to the vaults. Sometimes the light threaded the eyes of cadavers standing like grim servitors in niches; sometimes it startled clusters of round pale shapes which withdrew hastily into the walls; sometimes it leapt across the mouths of other passages, faintly illuminating dank choked depths, and Opojollac, panicking, fled in its wake.

Long after Opojollac had ceased to count the branching passages, he halted at a junction. But for the stumbling of his feet, there was silence in the vaults; yet for a moment he was sure that he had heard, filtering distorted down the corridors at whose rendezvous he stood, a long stertorous hollow inhalation. His whole body pumped like a stranded fish in fear. The sound was not repeated, however, and after a while he hurried in pursuit of the guiding tip of light.

Minutes later he heard the sound again, breathing down an unlighted corridor on his left. Now it was louder, and Opojollac stared in terror into the indistinguishable depths, where condensation dripped unseen from the ceiling. Once again he hastened in the path of the light, which curved ever beyond his vision. Vertigo spun within him; he felt that he was running into a spiral of claustrophobic stone, like the interior of a gigantic subterranean shell. He ran, his head swimming, and all at once light burst intensified upon his eyes. He had reached the centre of the labyrinth.

Beyond the termination of the corridor, the light had encircled a domed chamber. A mixture of dust and moisture coursed down the walls, and drops hung trembling beneath the dome. Within the loop of light lay a circular well, its rim cracked and encrusted with mud, and beyond the well, opposite the entrance in which stood Opojollac, a rusty lever protruded from the wall.

After hesitating, Opojollac entered the chamber. The path around the rim was more than wide enough to permit him to gain the lever, yet he could not bring himself to look down into the well. Indeed, his eyes half-closed protectively as he came within reach of the lever and dragged it down.

For a moment there came no sound, nor any indication that the lever had done its work. Then, from far down the well, rose a vast bubbling breath.

Opojollac looked down. Deep in the grey encrusted well a figure stood. In the dim light he took it to be a colossal version of the image which guarded the entrance to the vaults, a limbless trunk on which was set a flat head like a reptile's whose stretched mouth smiled senselessly. Beads of mud trickled over its face, and cobwebs hung from its lips. Opojollac peered closer, distinguishing that globes of dull moisture had fallen on the eyelids of the image. Then he saw that this was not so: that the eyes had opened and were glaring up at him.

He cried out in horror and, pressing his hands against the wall behind him, began to edge back towards the entrance. As he did so he saw grey buds form at the shoulders of the shape in the well. While he was yet some paces from the entrance, the buds bloated and long knobbed fingers sprang from them. As Opojollac reached the passage, huge unequal hands broke free of the shoulders and rose towards him through the well on boneless arms.

Shrieking, stumbling, falling against the walls, Opojollac fled the vaults. He emerged from the central spiral and blundered onwards, drawn outwards by the unwavering light. No sounds pursued him, but in parallel corridors he glimpsed dim grey forms which seemed to match his pace.

Eventually he halted, choking. From the junction at which he stood, several passages plunged into subterranean blackness; but the thread of light was there to guide him. He leaned against a wall to allow himself to cohere, and his mirrors rattled dully about him. Then, in the dim corridor opposite him, he saw a movement like the swift unfurling of a pale fungus. He turned to flee, and in the passage from which he had recently emerged he saw the light extinguished and a grey scrabbling hand reach forth for him. As he backed away, the hand traced the line of light into the junction and doused it like slime. Opojollac's being was turned inside out, for he glimpsed the two hands groping through the junction with no body intervening, and their arms stretched back into darkness; but he cried out and fled.

At last he fell out into the city of Derd. For a moment he turned to his palace; then he began to run towards the desert through the twilit green-tinged streets. But he perceived that some odd quality was shared by the light and by the silence; and, gazing upwards, he saw the cause. The Globes of Hakkthu had not betrayed their trust. The action of the lever had indeed contained the avatar of Azathoth; for a great translucent dome covered the entire city of Derd.

Opojollac beat on the dome with his fists, crying out curses against his people, against the Globes of Hakkthu, against the abomination from the vaults. But the dome did not respond to his pleas; and while he yet threw his body against the translucent surface, two vast unequal shadows of hands rose up against the dome and descended towards him.

Such is the tale which the Globes of Hakkthu, to whom the protection of the planet Tond was entrusted, are wont to intone at the nadir of the night.

AMONG THE PICTURES ARE THESE:

A VOID. AGAINST IT STAND SEVERAL CUT-OUT FIGURES, representing men. One feels they give a glimpse of an infinite series. They are completely featureless except for a small slit in the region of the heart. Below them, half obscuring the undivided legs of one, is a small figure, formed of dust; it is impossible to discern its slit. Above, a hand protrudes from a cylinder and manipulates a puppet, which wears a crude crown and brandishes a stick tipped with a pointed stone or jewel. Near the hobbling unequal feet of the puppet, a mouth hangs in the void. Within it a record-player balances on the lower lip.

An undistinguished stone landscape. A single tuft of grass sprouts from a rock, a river rushes by. Against a lone cloud stretched to a point, a landed spaceship smokes. A rubber simulacrum of a tree bears a single apple, and a naked man with abnormally short legs, perhaps the pilot of the spaceship, reaches for the fruit.

A cave. Several creatures—a one-eyed chinless humanoid with one arm considerably longer than the other, a figure with a long thin head and eyes on stalks, a small snarling pot-bellied dinosaur, a disquieted lizard—regard a fragment tied to the wall of the cave. The fragment depicts a spaceship which has crashed among rocks. A man wearing a jacket and shrunken checked trousers, and with rudimentary hands and gun, steps forward from it. One foot rests on the floor of the cave.

A title page: *Ye Anciente Marinere.* Web envelops the capital letters. A one-eyed grinning snake with bared fangs curls about the margin. Above a bow and arrow floats a contented skull. A bird with horns, bat-wings and a small penis stands on a rock in the sea. A zephyr who has lost one eye rests his head on the skull of an animal and blows in unison with a furious dog-headed creature with webbed feet. The sea's crest of foam contains three skulls.

A crossroads at midnight, deserted except for a faceless witch kneeling in a pentagram. From the flames in the pot before her rises the head of a demon, its face rather like that of a sleepy cat. One word is visible on the signpost: EXHAM.

A plain. In the middle stands a thumb-shaped rock, seen through (or contained in) a drinking-glass. A head like a malformed potato grips the top joint of the thumb with eleven spidery legs. The head glares skyward with its one eye and bares a single fang. Below, tiny figures kneel and worship, and one stands with a fuming cup in its hand. Outside the glass, more distant, another head unattended by worshippers clings to its rock and gazes sadly at the sky.

A landscape of high thin peaks and spears of rock. A comet with the face of a skull rushes over the horizon. Nearer and higher, a second comet drifts. Its neck and shoulders solidify into the head, whose face is that of a blind horse with long eyelashes, while from the shoulders hang claws on arms like fragile pipes. In the fore-ground a grimoire is held open by two long-fingered hands, clearly not those of one person. From the pages fumes a flattened cloud, containing a plain broken by mountains and, above the plain, a snarling bat-winged demon with fangs, horns, and moustache. Behind the cloud hovers a figure with a single webbed wing and the stump of another. It has the face of a grasshopper, and its proboscis reaches down to the tips of its pendulous breasts. From its waist curls a thin trail of dust.

Night under a full moon, outside the mouth of a cave. On the ground two figures copulate. The female lies in an attitude of submission, her arms splayed limply. Her face and pointed ears are huge, and her upper lip is extremely prominent. Her mouth gapes, showing pointed teeth, and her glazed eyes gaze upwards; she may be hypnotised or dead. The male's head is smaller, but his ears cover most of the side of his head. His jaw opens wide enough to touch his throat, and he bites into the female's armpit, drawing streams of blood. His arms appear to be boneless; one curls around his mate's body, while his other hand is poised above his head, its pointed fingers aimed at her face. Within the cave, a shadow with a conical head frowns down.

A void. Nearest, a lugubrious face whose mouth has grown down into the chin on the left side. The backs of two hands with pointed nails beat a tuned drum. Beneath a bed a naked man lies smirking; against the bed rests a large wheel with a cutting edge. A living bust with a terrified face floats above the footboard, staring at a vibrating stick thrust into a plank. Outside an askew window, a disembodied face stares in from the night. The cross-pieces of the window obscure both the eyes and the mouth of the face completely.

An avenue of wild bare trees on a plain. Several display raw stumps. Some way down the avenue, six figures join hands and dance around a corpse. From their midst rises a wraith, passing across the moon with pointed arm outstretched. At the near end of the avenue stands a figure; one breast, the chin, an ear and the other side of the face have melted. A hand reaches toward it, its nails liquefying.

A title page: *Alethia Phrikodes*. Webbed capitals. A cross formed of tentacles stands gesturing at the foot of a hill. From the tower of a melted church a tree waves, and above it a globe is veined by black lightning.

A finger beckons, pointing to a figure with malformed fragile arms, almost nude except for a loincloth. The face is covered by a hood of sacking, and only the pointed chin is visible. Pan-pipes shriek a discord, and behind them appears an eye and a mouth overhung by a blood-tipped fang. A hand, within whose insubstantial wrist can be seen the silhouette of a hanging, points to a gibbet. From the gibbet swings a skeleton. The skull is oval; the teeth protrude, and the lower jaw is missing.

A naked man with abnormally short legs climbs a rock face. Legless birds with flattened heads and long beaks torment him. There is a large open wound beneath his left shoulder blade. At the top of the rock face lies a corpse wearing a jacket or sweater. Its limp fingers hang over the edge, and from near them falls a rock. Further along the edge stands a tree like a flash of lightning stylized in wood.

An explosion in an abyss. Portions of wall fly out of the smoke, some framing shattered windows. An arm is hurled out, and more distant, a tattered torso still bearing its head and one arm. Highest against the fish-shaped clouds rise a leg and, still calmly smoking, a chimney.

Caption: "Once I beheld . . . a thing I saw not clearly, yet from glimpsing, fled." A man wearing a short jacket and trousers stares horrified at a slab before a cave. Behind him a hand with four digits gropes from a pool. On the slab a chinless head, tufted like a pineapple, grips the stone with eleven short legs and stares at the sky with a look of dismayed resignation. Beside it hover three faceless bats. A shadow kneels before the slab.

A mountainous landscape. Against the moon hangs the askew silhouette of a horned man with bat-wings. Nearer, on a rock, another stands. He has long hair and a pugnacious Neanderthal face. His wings rise from his shoulders; he has no arms, and instead of buttocks a wistful face with a snub nose surmounts his thighs. His toes grip the rock. Ropes and claws of dust drift past him, across the sky.

An operating theatre. From beneath a sheet protrudes the head and arm of an unconscious man. The sheet is drawn so tight that it appears there is no body beneath it; in any case, the table is by no means long enough to accommodate a body in proportion to the head. Within a stain on the sheet can be seen disembodied eyes and a sneering face with a cowl pulled down over its eyes. A surgeon, his eyes masked, stares away from the table. His eyes and mouth are rudimentary, and he holds a knife perhaps a foot long. About him drift clouds containing affrighted faces, one with a knife in its throat; a huge shadowy skull; a howling fanged mouth with flaring nostrils, thrusting out a hand which holds a glass globe; the head of a man on the table, pouring blood, with a disembodied arm flourishing a dagger above it, and beside it a sorrowful naked figure with a chinless phallic head, kneeling and declaiming.

A plain. A few gravestones stand or lean. Against one sits a skeleton, one hand caressing its pelvis. From its mouth drifts the legless body of a vampire, her mouth and shroud daubed with blood. Nearby a figure holds a bone to its fanged mouth, its stance reminiscent both of gnawing and of playing a flute. Its pointed head rises straight from its chest through the V of its jacket, emerging only from the ears upwards. Above a single sketchy tree on the horizon, a dismayed face floats. Its hair is plastered blackly to its long head, and its eyes are drawn vertically into thin rectangles. Its arms and shoulders withdraw to huddle behind the head, and together with the rest of it are stretched to a ragged ectoplasmic point above the tree. As it gazes down, its whole attitude recalls that of a distressed priest.

A plateau broken by erect clubs of rock. A figure wearing a loin-cloth stands with one hand on a cracked skull. Its hair is long and its nose hooked; its breasts are rudimentary, but although the loincloth has slipped it is impossible to determine the figure's sex. One foot presses on a small snake with an eye missing. The figure's right hand holds a book, one finger marking a place. From that page streams a sparkling mist, forming into a head and arms with long hands. The conical reptilian face frowns, and one hand displays a globe containing a silhouette of a gibbet. Near the skull a shattered hour-glass drifts, while in the sky oval bat-winged heads flutter.

A mountainous area. Narrow veils of a distorting mist rise from the ground. On a short length of railway line stands an engine. Its boiler is tilted far to the left, and from the tilted funnel flies an animal's skull. A face with fangs, lacking ears and one eye, grimaces from within the circle of the front of the boiler. A figure dressed in sacking, malformed by decay and the mist, stretches out an unde-cayed hand towards the engine. Skulls hover or streak skyward. Near one, a broken crystal ball contains a bedstead. A huge gun shoots liquid at the engine. Above the gun, a crescent moon lies on its back, sliced by the mist and imperfectly reassembled, and beside the moon appears a great eye set in dust.

Caption: 'All this he bade—but my soul . . . fled without aim or knowledge, shrieking in silence through the gibbering deeps.' An inverted mountain landscape hangs over a void. A head with upswept hair clings to the mountains with eight thick tufted legs. The head has one eye, two fangs and a cleft chin. A watery hand points away across the void, while beneath it two hands whose wrists trail off into dust cover a terrified face.

An extinguished candle smoulders. Behind it, a slightly taller figure is completely hooded, and the hood rises to a high point at the back of the head. Closer, a woman fingers one of her breasts, which press together on the left side of her body. Beneath her hair, her face is a shadow containing one eye, the socket of another, and a painted mouth. A figure, whose head may be hooded or faceless, stands with hands on hips; its arms appear to be sewn to the body. A man wearing a hat and cape leaps from a pinnacle into the sea. A door opens, revealing a shadow. Near the top half of a corpse lying in a pool of blood hangs a dripping knife, while above the corpse hovers a cluster of terrified masks. Several of the masks, however, are smiling.

> *In 1973 I came across some notebooks full of drawings I'd made twelve years previously. Their technique was minimal, but their effect on me was too disconcerting not to share. Influences on them include Lovecraft as well as surrealism and* Weird Tales *covers. I've tried to describe what's here as objectively as possible.*

THE TUGGING

I

WHEN INGELS AWOKE HE KNEW AT ONCE HE'D BEEN dreaming again. There was an image, a memory clamouring faintly but urgently at the edge of his mind; he snatched at it, but it was gone. He swung himself off the crumpled bed. Hilary must have gone to do her research in the library hours ago, leaving him a cold breakfast. Outside hung a chill glazed blue sky, and frost was fading from the window pane.

The dream continued to nag at his mind. He let it pluck at him, hoping that the nagging would turn by itself into memory. He slowed himself down, dressing slowly, eating slowly, to allow the memory to catch up. But there was only the insistence, like a distant recollection of a plucked tooth. Through the wall he could hear a radio announcer's voice in the next flat, a blurred cadence rising as if to leap a barrier that obscured its words completely. It buzzed at his mind, bumbling. He washed up quickly, irritably, and hurried out.

And found that he couldn't look up at the sky.

The feeling seized his neck like a violent cramp, forcing his head down. Around him women were wheeling prams in which babies and groceries fought for space, dogs were playing together in the alleys, buses quaked at bus stops, farting. But on Ingels, pressing down from a clear rather watery blue expanse to which he couldn't

even raise his eyes, weighed a sense of intolerable stress, as if the calm sky were stretched to splitting: as if it were about to split and to let his unformed fear through at him.

A bus braked, a long tortured scraping squeal. When Ingels recovered from his heart-clutching start he'd jolted off the fear. He ran for the bus as the last of the queue shuffled on. Scared of the sky indeed, he thought. I've got to get more sleep. Pill myself to sleep if I have to. His eyes felt as if floating in quicklime.

He sat among the coughing shoppers. Across the aisle a man shook his head at the tobacco-smoke, snorting like a horse. A woman threw herself and three carrier bags onto a seat, patting them reassuringly, and slammed her predecessor's open window. Ingels rummaged in his briefcase. He'd left one notebook at his own flat, he discovered, muttering. He flicked through the notes for his column, holding them flat on his briefcase. Wonder if the fellow whose knee I'm fighting recognises my style. World's champion egotist, he rebuked himself, hiding the notes with his forearm. Don't worry, he won't steal the copyright, he scoffed, pulling his arm back. He put the notes away. They looked as bleary as he felt.

He gazed around the bus, at the flat stagnant smoke, at the ranks of heads like wig-blocks, and settled on headlines over the shoulder in front of him:

IS THE SOLAR SYSTEM ON TOW?
Six months ago an amateur astronomer wrote to us, warning
that a planet might pass dangerously close to Earth.

THE ASTRONOMER ROYAL'S COMMENT:
'UTTER TWADDLE'.
Now the world's leading astronomers have agreed to let us
have the facts.

TODAY WE TELL ALL.
In an exclusive interview

But he'd turned over, to the smaller print of the story. Ingels sat back again, remembering how the *Herald* had received a copy of that letter six months ago. They hadn't published it, and the letters editor had gazed at Ingels pityingly when he'd suggested they might at least follow it up. "I suppose you arts people need imagination,"

he'd said. Ingels grimaced wryly, wondering how they would handle
the story in tonight's edition. He leaned forward, but the man had
reached the editorial comment: "Even if his aim was to prevent
panic, are we paying the Astronomer Royal to tell us what too many
people are now suggesting was a lie?"

Ingels glanced out of the window. Offices flashed past, glazed
displays of figures at desks, the abrupt flight of perspective down
alleys with a shock like a fall in a dream, more displays. The offices
thinned out and aged as the bus gathered speed towards the edge of
Brichester. Nearly there, Ingels thought, then realised with a leap
from his seat that he'd passed the *Herald* building three stops back.
For a second he knew where he'd been heading. So what? he
thought savagely, the rims of his eyes rusty and burning, as he clattered downstairs. But once he was on the street he wished that he'd
thought to remember: now he couldn't imagine where he could
have been going in that direction.

BRICHESTER HERALD: BRICHESTER'S EVENING
VOICE. The iron poem (two-thirds of a haiku, he'd thought until
he grew used to it) clung to the bricks above him. The foyer was
quiet. He wondered how long it would be before the presses began
to thump heartily, disproving the soundproofing. Not long, and he
had to write his column.

His mind felt flat and empty as the lift. He drifted numbly
through the hundred-yard open-plan office, past the glancing heads
behind glass personalised in plastic. Some looked away quickly,
some stared, some smiled. My God, I don't even know his name,
Ingels thought of several. "Hello, Moira," he said. "How's it going,
Bert." Telephones shrilled, were answered, their calls leapt prank-
ishly across the floor. Reporters sidestepped through the aisles.
Smells of deodorant and sweat, tang of ink, brandished paper, scurrying typewriters, hasty agitated conferences.

Bert had been following him to his desk. "Don't wait for your
personal bulletin," Bert said, throwing a telex sheet on the desk.
"The latest on your wandering planet."

"Don't tell me I've convinced you at last."

"No chance," Bert said, retreating. "Just so you don't start
turning the place upside down for it."

Ingels read the sheet, thinking: I could have told them this six
months ago. The Americans had admitted that an unmanned probe
was well on its way to photograph the wanderer. He rested his elbow

on the desk and covered his eyes. Against the restless patches of light he almost glimpsed what he'd dreamed. He started, bewildered; the noise of the newspaper poured into him. Enough, he thought, sorting out his notes.

He typed the television review—a good play from Birmingham, when are we going to see a studio in Brichester—and passed it to Bert. Then he pawed desultorily at the day's accumulation on his desk. Must go and see my folks this week. Might drain my tension a little. He turned over a brown envelope. A press ticket, elaborately pretty lettering: exhibition of associational painting—the new primitivism and surrealism. Ugh, he thought, and whatever you say to surrealists. Private view this afternoon. Which means now. "You can have a local arts review tomorrow," he said, showing the ticket to Bert, and went out.

Once out of the building his mind teetered like a dislocated compass. Again the sky seemed brittle glass, ready to crack, and when he moved to shake off the obsession he found himself urged towards the edge of Brichester. A woman flinched from him as he snarled himself to a halt. "Sorry," he called after her. Whatever's in that direction, it isn't the show I've been invited to. But there must be something there. Maybe I went there when I was young. Have a look when I can. Before I sleepwalk there.

Although he could have taken a bus into Lower Brichester, where the exhibition was, he walked. Clear my head, perhaps, if I don't get high on petrol first. The sky was thin and blue; nothing more, now. He swung his briefcase. Haven't heard of these artists before. Who knows, they could be good.

He hadn't been through Lower Brichester for months, and was taken aback by its dereliction. Dogs scrabbled clattering in gouged shop-fronts, an uprooted streetlamp lay across a road, humped earth was scattered with disembowelled mattresses, their entrails fluttering feebly. He passed houses where one window was blinded with brick, the next still open and filmy with a drooping curtain. He examined his ticket. Believe it or not, I'm on the right track.

Soon whole streets were derelict. There was nothing but Ingels, the gaping houses and uneven pavements, the discreet sky, his footsteps alone; the rush of the city was subdued, quiescent. The houses went by, shoulder to shoulder, ribs open to the sky, red-brick fronts revealing their jumble of shattered walls and staircases. Ingels felt a lurking sympathy for the area in its abandonment, its indifference to time. He slowed down, strolling. Let myself go a bit. The private view's open for hours yet. Relax. He did, and felt an irrational impulse pleading with him.

And why not, he thought. He glanced about: nobody. Then he began to lope through the deserted streets, arms hanging, fingers almost touching the road. Unga bunga, he thought. One way to prepare myself for the primitives, I suppose.

He found his behaviour touched a memory; perhaps the memory was its source. A figure running crouched through ruins, somewhere nearby. A kind of proof of virility. But they hadn't been deserted city streets, he thought, loping. Just flat blocks of black rock in which square windows gaped. Abandoned long before but hardly affected by time. A figure running along a narrow path through the stone, not looking at the windows.

Clouds were creeping into the sky; darkness was suffusing the streets around him. Ingels ran, not looking at the houses, allowing them to merge with the memory they touched. It was coming clearer. You had to run all the way along one of the stone paths. Any path at all, for there were no intersections, just a straight unbroken run. You had to run fast, before something within the windows became aware of you, rather as a carnivorous plant becomes aware of a fly. The last part of the run was the worst, because you knew that at any moment something would appear in all the windows at once: things that, although they had mouths, were not faces—

Ingels stumbled wildly as he halted, glaring up at the empty windows of the houses. What on earth was that? he thought distractedly. Like one of those dreams I used to have, the ones that were so vivid. Of course, that's what it must have been. These streets reminded me of one of them. Though the memory felt much older, somehow. From the womb, no doubt, he shouted angrily at his pounding heart.

When he reached the exhibition he walked straight past it. Returning, he peered at the address on the ticket. My God, this is it. Two of a street of dingy but tenanted terraced houses had been run together; on the front door of one, in lettering he'd taken for graffiti, were the words LOWER BRICHESTER ARTS LAB. He recalled how, when it had opened last year, the invitations to the opening had arrived two days later. The project he'd described after a hurried telephone interview hadn't looked at all like this. Oh well, he thought, and went in.

In the hall, by the reception desk, two clowns were crawling about with children on their backs. One of the children ran behind the desk and gazed up at Ingels. "Do you know where the exhibition is?" he said. "Up your arse," she said, giggling. "First floor up," said one of the clowns, who Ingels now realised was a made-up local poet, and chased the children into a playroom full of inflatables.

The first floor was a maze of plywood partitions in metal frames. On the partitions hung paintings and sketches. As Ingels entered, half-a-dozen people converged on him, all the artists save one, who was trying to relight a refractory cone of incense. Feeling outnumbered, Ingels wished he'd made it to the maze. "You've just missed the guy from Radio Brichester," one said. "Are you going to talk to all of us, like him?" another asked. "Do you like modem art?" "Do you want coffee?"

"Now leave him be," said Annabel Pringle, as Ingels recognised her from her picture on the cover of the catalogue. "They're new to exhibiting, you see, you can't blame them. I mean, this whole show is my idea but their enthusiasm. Now, I can explain the principles as you go round if you like, or you can read them in the catalogue."

"The latter, thanks." Ingels hurried into the maze, opening the typed catalogue. A baby with an ear-trumpet, which was 2: Untitled. 3 was a man throwing his nose into a wastebasket, and Untitled. 4: Untitled. 5, 6, 7 -Well, their paintings are certainly better than their prose, Ingels thought. The incense unravelled ahead of him. A child playing half-submerged in a lake. A blackened green-tinged city shouldering up from the sea. A winged top hat gliding over a jungle. Suddenly Ingels stopped short and turned back to the previous painting. He was sure he had seen it before.

22: Atlantis. But it wasn't like any Atlantis he'd seen pictured. The technique was crude and rather banal, obviously one of the primitives, yet Ingels found that it touched images buried somewhere in him. Its leaning slabs of rock felt vast, the sea poured from its surfaces as if it had just exploded triumphantly into sight. Drawn closer, Ingels peered into the darkness within a slab of rock, beyond what might be an open doorway. If there were the outline of a pale face staring featurelessly up from within the rock, its owner must be immense. If there were, Ingels thought, withdrawing: but why should he feel there ought to be?

When he'd hurried around the rest of the exhibition he tried to ask about the painting, but Annabel Pringle headed him off.

"You understand what we mean by associational painting?" she demanded. "Let me tell you. We select an initial idea by aleatory means."

"Eh?" Ingels said, scribbling.

"Based on chance. We use the I Ching, like John Cage. The American composer, he originated it. Once we have the idea we silently associate from it until each of us has an idea they feel they must communicate. This exhibition is based on six initial ideas. You can see the diversity."

"Indeed," Ingels said. "When I said eh I was being an average reader of our paper, you understand. Listen, the one that particularly interested me was number 22. I'd like to know how that came about."

"That's mine," one young man said, leaping up as if it were House.

"The point of our method," Annabel Pringle said, gazing at the painter, "is to erase all the associational steps from your mind, leaving only the image you paint. Of course Clive here wouldn't remember what led up to that painting."

"No, of course," Ingels said numbly. "It doesn't matter. Thank you. Thanks all very much." He hurried downstairs, past a sodden clown, and into the street. In fact it didn't matter. A memory had torn its way through his insomnia. For the second time that day he realised why something had looked familiar, but this time more disturbingly. Decades ago he had himself dreamed the city in the painting.

II

Ingels switched off the television. As the point of light dwindled into darkness it touched off the image in him of a gleam shooting away into space. Then he saw that the light hadn't sunk into darkness but into Hilary's reflection, leaning forward from the cane rocking-chair next to him, about to speak. "Give me fifteen minutes," he said, scribbling notes for his review.

The programme had shown the perturbations which the wandering planet had caused in the orbits of Pluto, Neptune and Uranus, and had begun and ended by pointing out that the planet was now swinging away from the Solar System; its effect on Earth's orbit would be negligible. Photographs from the space-probe were promised within days. Despite its cold scientific clarity (Ingels wrote) and perhaps without meaning to, the programme managed to communicate a sense of foreboding, of the intrusion into and interference with our familiar skies. "Not to me it didn't," Hilary said, reading over his shoulder.

"That's sad," he said. "I was going to tell you about my dreams."

"Don't if I wouldn't understand them either. Aren't I allowed to criticise now?"

"Sorry. Let's start again. Just let me tell you a few of the things that have happened to me. I was thinking of them all today. Some of them even you'll have to admit are strange. Make some coffee and I'll tell you about them."

When she'd brought the coffee he waited until she sat forward, ready to be engrossed, long soft black hooks of hair angling for her jawbone. "I used to dream a lot when I was young," he said. "Not your average childhood dream, if there is such a thing. There was one I remember, about these enormous clouds of matter floating in outer space, forming very slowly into something. I mean *very* slowly . . . I woke up long before they got there, yet while I was dreaming I knew whatever it was would have a face, and that made me very anxious to wake up. Then there was another where I was being carried through a kind of network of light, on and on across intersections for what felt like days, until I ended up on the edge of this gigantic web of paths of light. And I was fighting to stop myself going in, because I knew that hiding behind the light there was something old and dark and shapeless, something dried-up and evil that I couldn't make out. I could hear it rustling like an old dry spider. You know what I suddenly realised that web was? My brain, I'd been chasing along my nervous system to my brain. Well, leave that one to the psychologists. But there were odd things about these dreams—I mean, apart from all that. They always used to begin the same way, and always about the same time of the month."

"The night of the full moon?" Hilary said, slurping coffee.

"Funnily enough, yes. Don't worry, I didn't sprout midnight shadow or anything. But some people are sensitive to the full moon, that's well enough documented. And I always used to begin by dreaming I could see the full moon over the sea, way out in the middle of the ocean. I could see the reflection resting on the water, and after a while I'd always find myself thinking it wasn't the moon at all but a great pale face peering up out of the ocean, and I'd panic. Then I wouldn't be able to move and I'd know that the full moon was pulling at something deep in the ocean, waking it up. I'd feel my panic swelling up in me, and all of a sudden it would burst and I'd be in the next dream. That's how it happened, every time."

"Didn't your parents know? Didn't they try to find out what was wrong?"

"I don't know what you mean by wrong. But yes, they knew eventually, when I told them. That was after I had the idea my father might be able to explain. I was eleven then and I'd had strange feelings sometimes, intuitions and premonitions and so forth, and sometimes I'd discovered they'd been my father's feelings too."

"I know all about your father's feelings," Hilary said. "More than he knows about mine."

Soon after they'd met, Ingels had taken her to see his parents. She'd felt his father had been too stiffly polite to her, and when she'd cross-examined Ingels he'd eventually admitted that his father had felt she was wrong for him, unsympathetic to him. "You were going to let me tell you about my dreams," he said. "I told my father about the sea dream and I could see there was something he wasn't saying. My mother had to make him tell me. Her attitude to the whole thing was rather what yours would have been, but she told him to get it over with, he'd have to tell me sometime. So he told me he'd sometimes shared his father's dreams without either of them ever knowing why. And he'd had several of my dreams when he'd been young, until one night in the mid-twenties—early 1925, I think he said. Then he'd dreamed a city had risen out of the sea. After that he'd never dreamed again. Well, maybe hearing that was some kind of release for me, because the next time I dreamed of the city too."

"You dreamed of a city," Hilary said.

"The same one. I told him about it next morning, details of it he hadn't told me, that were the same in both our dreams. I was watching the sea, the same place as always. Don't ask me how I knew it was always the same. I knew. One moment I was watching the moon on the water, then I saw it was trembling. The next moment an island rose out of the ocean with a roaring like a water-fall, louder than that, louder than anything I've ever heard while awake; I could actually feel my ears bursting. There was a city on the island, all huge greenish blocks with sea and seaweed pouring off them. And the mud was boiling with stranded creatures, panting and bursting. Right in front of me and above me and below me there was a door. Mud was trickling down from it, and I knew that the great pale face I was terrified of was behind the door, getting ready to come out, opening its eyes in the dark. I woke up then, and that was the end of the dreams. Say they were only dreams if you like. You might find it easiest to believe my father and I were sharing them by telepathy."

"You know perfectly well," Hilary said, "that I'd find nothing of the sort."

"No? Then try this," he said sharply. "At the exhibition I visited today there was a painting of our dream. And not by either of us."

"So what does that mean?" she cried. "What on earth is that supposed to mean?"

"Well, a dream I can recall so vividly after all this time is worth a thought. And that painting suggests it's a good deal more objectively real."

"So your father read about the island in a story," she said. "So did you, so did the painter. What else can you possibly be suggesting?"

"Nothing," he said at last.

"So what were the other strange things you were going to tell me?"

"That's all," he said. "Just the painting. Nothing else. Really." She was looking miserable, a little ashamed. "Don't you believe me?" he said. "Come here."

As the sheepskin rug joined their caresses she said "I don't really need to be psychic for you, do I?" "No," he said, probing her ear with his tongue, triggering her ready. Switching off the goosenecked steel lamps as she went, she led him through the flat as if wheeling a basket behind her; they began laughing as a car's beam shone up from Mercy Hill and seized for a moment on her hand, his handle. They reached the crisp bed and suddenly, urgently, couldn't prolong their play. She was all around him, working to draw him deeper and out, he was lapped softly, thrusting roughly at her grip on him to urge it to return redoubled. They were rising above everything but each other, gasping. He felt himself rushing to a height, and closed his eyes.

And was falling into a maelstrom of flesh, in a vast almost lightless cave whose roof seemed as far above him as the sky. He had a long way still to fall, and beneath him he could make out the movements of huge bubbles and ropes of flesh, of eyes swelling and splitting the flesh, of gigantic dark green masses climbing sluggishly over one another. "No, Christ no," he cried, gripped helpless.

He slumped on Hilary. "Oh God," she said. "What is it now?"

He lay beside her. Above them the ceiling shivered with reflected light. It looked as he felt. He closed his eyes and found dark calm, but couldn't bear to keep them closed for long. "All right," he said. "There's more I haven't told you. I know you've been worried about how I've looked lately. I told you it was lack of sleep, and so it is, but it's because I've begun dreaming again. It started about nine months ago, just before I met you, and it's becoming more frequent, once or twice a week now. Only this time I can never remember what it is, perhaps because I haven't dreamed for so long. I think it has something to do with the sky, maybe this planet we've been hearing about. The last time was this morning, after you went to the library. For some reason I don't have them when I'm with you."

"Of course if you want to go back to your place, go ahead," Hilary said, gazing at the ceiling.

"In one way I don't," he said. "That's just the trouble. Whenever I try to dream I find I don't want to sleep, as if I'm fighting the dream. But today I'm tired enough just to drift off and have it anyway. I've been getting hallucinations all day that I think are coming from the dream. And it feels more urgent, somehow. I've got to have it. I knew it was important before, but that painting's made me sure it's more than a dream. I wish you could understand this. It's not easy for me."

"Suppose I did believe you?" she said. "What on earth would you do then? Stand on the street warning people? Or would you try to sell it to your paper? I don't want to believe you, how can you think they would?"

"That's exactly the sort of thing I don't need to hear," Ingels said. "I want to talk to my father about it. I think he may be able to help. Maybe you wouldn't mind not coming with me."

"I wouldn't want to," she said. "You go and have your dream and your chat with your father if you want. But as far as I'm concerned that means you don't want me."

Ingels walked to his flat, further up Mercy Hill. Newspapers clung to bushes, flapping; cars hissed through nearby streets, luminous waves. Only the houses stood between him and the sky, their walls seeming low and thin. Even in the pools of lamplight he felt the night gaping overhead.

The building where he lived was silent. The stereo that usually thumped like an electronic heart was quiet. Ingels climbed to the third floor, his footsteps dropping wooden blocks into the silence, nudging him awake. He fumbled in his entrance hall for the coat hook on the back of the door, which wasn't where Hilary kept hers. Beneath the window in the main room he saw her desk spread with her syndicated cartoon strip—except that when he switched on the light it was his own desk, scattered with television schedules. He peered blearily at the rumpled bed. Around him the room felt and moved like muddy water. He sagged on the bed and was asleep at once.

The darkness drew him out, coaxing him forward, swimming softly through his eyes. A great silent darkness surrounded him. He sailed through it, sleeping yet aware. He sensed energy flowering far out in the darkness, vast soundless explosions that cooled and congealed. He sensed immense weights slowly rolling at the edge of his blindness.

Then he could see, though the darkness persisted almost unchanged. Across its furthest distances a few points of light shone like tiny flaws. He began to sail towards them, faster. They parted and fled to the edge of his vision as he approached. He was rushing between them, towards others that now swooped minutely out of the boundless night, carrying cooler grains of congealed dust around them. They were multiplying, his vision was filling with sprinkled light and its attendant parasites. He was turning, imprinting each silently blazing vista on his mind. His mind felt enormous. He felt it take each pattern of light and store it easily as it returned alert for the next.

It was so long before he came to rest he had no conscious memory of starting out. Somehow the path he'd followed had brought him back to his point of origin. Now he sailed in equilibrium with the entire system of light and dust that surrounded him, boundless. His mind locked on everything he'd seen.

He found that part of his mind had fastened telescopically on details of the worlds he'd passed: cities of globes acrawl with black winged insects; mountains carved or otherwise formed into heads within whose hollow sockets worshippers squirmed; a sea from whose depths rose a jointed arm, reaching miles inland with a filmy web of skin to net itself food. One tiny world in particular seemed to teem with life that was aware of him.

Deep in one of its seas a city slept, and he shared the dreams of its sleepers: of an infancy spent in a vast almost lightless cave, tended by a thin rustling shape so tall its head was lost to sight; of flight to this minute but fecund planet; of dancing hugely and clumsily beneath the light of a fragment they'd torn free of this world and flung into space; of dormancy in the submarine basalt tombs. Dormant, they waited and shared the lives of other similar beings active on the surface; for a moment he was the inhabitant of a black city deserted by its builders, coming alert and groping lazily forth as a pale grub fled along a path between the buildings.

Later, as the active ones on the surface had to hide from the multiplying grubs, those in the submarine city stilled, waiting. Ingels felt their thoughts searching sleepily, ranging the surface, touching and sampling the minds of the grubs, vastly patient and purposeful. He felt the womb of the sea lapping his cell. His huge flesh quivered, anticipating rebirth.

Without warning he was in a room, gazing through a telescope at the sky. He seemed to have been gazing for hours; his eyes burned. He was referring to a chart, adjusting the mounting of the telescope. A pool of light from an oil-lamp roved, snatching at books in cases against the walls, spilling over the charts at his feet. Then he was outside the room, hurrying through a darkened theatre; cowls of darkness peered down from the boxes. Outside the theatre he glanced up towards the speckled sky, towards the roof, where he knew one slate hid the upturned telescope. He hurried away through the gas-lit streets, out of Ingels' dream.

He awoke and knew at once where the theatre was: at the edge of Brichester, where his mind had been tugging him all day.

III

He rose at dawn, feeling purged and refreshed. He washed, shaved, dressed, made himself breakfast. In his lightened state the preamble of his dream seemed not to matter: he had had his inclination towards the edge of Brichester explained, the rest seemed external to him, perhaps elaborately symbolic. He knew Hilary regarded his dreams as symptoms of disturbance, and perhaps she was right. Maybe, he thought, they all meant the theatre was trying to get up through my mind. A lot of fuss, but that's what dreams are like. Especially when they're having to fight their way, no doubt. Can't wait to see what the theatre means to me.

When he went out the dawn clutched him as if he hadn't shaken off his dreams. The dull laden light settled about him, ambiguous shapes hurried by. The air felt suffocated by imminence, not keen as the cold should make it. That'll teach me to get up at cock-crow, he thought. Feels like insomnia. Can't imagine what they find to crow about. The queues of commuters moved forward like the tickings of doom.

Someone had left a sheet from the telex on his desk. Photographs from the space probe were expected any hour. He wrote his reviews hurriedly, glancing up to dispel a sense that the floor was alive with pale grubs, teeming through the aisles. Must have needed more sleep than I thought. Maybe catch a nap later.

Although his dream had reverted the streets, replacing the electric lamps with gas, he knew exactly where the theatre should be. He hurried along the edge of Lower Brichester, past champing steam-shovels, roaring skeletons of burning houses. He strode straight to the street of his dream.

One side was razed, a jagged strip of brown earth extending cracks into the pavement and into the fields beyond. But the theatre was on the other side. Ingels hurried past the red-brick houses, past the wind-whipped gardens and broken flowers, towards the patched gouge in the road where he knew a gas-lamp had used to guard the theatre. He stood arrested on it, cars sweeping past, and stared at the houses before him, safe from his glare in their sameness. The theatre was not there.

Only the shout of an overtaking car roused him. He wandered along, feeling sheepish and absurd. He remembered vaguely having walked this way with his parents once, on the way to a picnic. The gas-lamp had been standing then; he'd gazed at it and at the theatre, which by then was possessed by a cinema, until they'd coaxed him away. Which explained the dream, the insomnia, everything. And I never used to be convinced by *Citizen Kane*. Rosebud to me too, with knobs on. In fact he'd even mistaken the location of the lamp; there it was, a hundred yards ahead of him. Suddenly he began to run. Already he could see the theatre, now renamed as a furniture warehouse.

He was almost through the double doors and into the first aisle of suites when he realised that he didn't know what he was going to say.

Excuse me, I'd like to look under your rafters. Sorry to bother you, but I believe you have a secret room here. For God's sake, he said, blushing, hurrying down the steps as a salesman came forward to open the doors for him. I know what the dream was now. I've made sure I won't have it again. Forget the rest.

He threw himself down at his desk. Now sit there and behave. What a piddling reason for falling out with Hilary. At least I can admit that to her. Call her now. He was reaching for the telephone when Bert tramped up, waving Ingels' review of the astronomical television programme. "I know you'd like to rewrite this," he said.

"Sorry about that."

"We'll call off the men in white this time. Thought you'd gone the same way as this fellow," Bert said, throwing a cutting on the desk.

"Just lack of sleep," Ingels said, not looking. "As our Methuselah, tell me something. When the warehouse on Fieldview was a theatre, what was it called?"

"The Variety, you mean?" Bert said, dashing for his phone. "Remind me to tell you about the time I saw Beaumont and Fletcher performing there. Great double act."

Ingels turned the cutting over, smiling half at Bert, half at himself for the way he had still not let go of his dream. Go on, look through the files in your lunch-hour, he told himself satirically. Bet the Variety never made a headline in its life.

LSD CAUSES ATTEMPTED SUICIDE, said the cutting. American student claims that in LSD 'vision' he was told that the planet now passing through our solar system heralded the rising of Atlantis. Threw himself from second-storey window. Insists that the rising of Atlantis means the end of humanity. Says the Atlanteans are ready to awaken. Ingels gazed at the cutting; the sounds of the newspaper surged against his ears like blood. Suddenly he thrust back his chair and ran upstairs, to the morgue of the *Herald*.

Beneath the ceiling pressed low by the roof, a fluorescent tube fluttered and buzzed. Ingels hugged the bound newspapers to his chest, each volume an armful, and hefted them to a table, where they puffed out dust. 1900 was the first that came to hand. The streets would have been gas-lit then. Dust trickled into his nostrils and frowned over him, the phone next to Hilary was mute, his television review plucked at his mind, anxious to be rewritten. Scanning and blinking, he tried to shake them off with his doubts.

But it didn't take him long, though his gaze was tired of ranging up and down, up and down, by the time he saw the headline:

ATTEMPTED THEFT AT 'THE VARIETY.'
TRADESMEN IN THE DOCK.

Francis Wareing, a draper pursuing his trade in Brichester, Donald Norden, a butcher [and so on, Ingels snarled, sweeping past impatiently] were charged before the Brichester stipendiary magistrates with forcibly entering 'The Variety' theatre, on Fieldview, in attempted commission of robbery. Mr. Radcliffe, the owner and manager of this establishment

It looked good, Ingels thought wearily, abandoning the report, tearing onward. But two issues later the sequel's headline stopped him short:

ACCUSATION AND COUNTER-ACCUSATION IN
COURT. A BLASPHEMOUS CULT REVEALED.

And there it was, halfway down the column:

Examined by Mr. Kirby for the prosecution, Mr. Radcliffe affirmed that he had been busily engaged in preparing his accounts when, overhearing sounds of stealth outside his office, he summoned his courage and ventured forth. In the auditorium he beheld several men

Get on with it, Ingels urged, and saw that there had been impatience in the court too:

Mr. Radcliffe's narrative was rudely interrupted by Wareing, who accused him of having let a room in his theatre to the accused four. This privilege having been summarily withdrawn, Wareing alleged, the four had entered the building in a bid to reclaim such possessions as were rightfully theirs. He pursued:

'Mr. Radcliffe is aware of this. He has been one of our number for years, and still would be, if he had the courage.'

Mr. Radcliffe replied: 'That is a wicked untruth. However, I am not surprised by the depths of your iniquity. I have evidence of it here.'

So saying, he produced for the Court's inspection a notebook containing, as he said, matter of a blasphemous and sacrilegious nature. This which he had found beneath a seat in his theatre, he indicated to be the prize sought by the unsuccessful robbers. The book, which Mr. Radcliffe described as 'the journal of a cult dedicated to preparing themselves for a blasphemous travesty of the Second Coming,' was handed to Mr. Poole, the magistrate, who swiftly pronounced it to conform to this description.

Mr. Kirby adduced as evidence of the corruption which this cult wrought, its bringing of four respectable tradesmen to the state of common robbers. Had they not felt the shame of the beliefs they professed, he continued, they had but to petition Mr. Radcliffe for the return of their mislaid property.

But what beliefs? Ingels demanded. He riffled onward, crumbling yellow fragments from the pages. The tube buzzed like a bright trapped insect. He almost missed the page.

FOILED ROBBERS AT 'THE VARIETY'.
FIFTH MAN YIELDS HIMSELF TO JUSTICE.

What fifth man? Ingels searched:

Mr. Poole condemned the cult of which the accused were adherents as conclusive proof of the iniquity of those religions which presume to rival Christianity. He described the cult as 'unworthy of the lowest breed of mulatto.'

At this juncture a commotion ensued, as a man entered precipitately and begged leave to address the Court. Some few minutes later Mr. Radcliffe also entered, wearing a resolute expression. When he saw the latecomer, however, he appeared to relinquish his purpose, and took a place in the gallery. The man, meanwhile, sought to throw himself on the Court's mercy, declaring himself to be the fifth of the robbers. He had been prompted to confess, he affirmed, by a sense of his injustice in allowing his friends to take full blame. His name, he said, was Joseph Ingels

Who had received a lighter sentence in acknowledgement of his gesture, Ingels saw in a blur at the foot of the column. He hardly noticed. He was still staring at his grandfather's name.

"Nice of you to come," his father said ambiguously. They'd finished decorating, Ingels saw; the flowers on the hall wallpaper had grown and turned bright orange. But the light was still dim, and the walls settled about his eyes like night around a feeble lamp. Next to the coat rack he saw the mirror in which he'd made sure of himself before teenage dates, the crack in one corner where he'd driven his fist, caged by fury and by their incomprehension of his adolescent restlessness. An ugly socket of plaster gaped through the wallpaper next to the supporting nail's less treacherous home. "I could have hung the mirror for you," Ingels said, not meaning to disparage his father, who frowned and said "No need." They went into the dining-room, where his mother was setting out the best tablecloth and cutlery. "Wash hands," she said. "Tea's nearly ready."

They ate and talked. Ingels watched the conversation as if it were a pocket maze into which he had to slip a ball when the opening tilted towards him. "How's your girlfriend?" his mother said. Don't you know her name? Ingels didn't say. "Fine," he said. They didn't mention Hilary again. His mother produced infant photographs of him they'd discovered in the sideboard drawer. "You were a lovely little boy," she said. "Speaking of memories," Ingels said, "do you remember the old Variety theatre?"

His father was moving his shirt along the fireguard to give himself a glimpse of the fire, his back to Ingels. "The old Variety," his mother said. "We wanted to take you to a pantomime there once. But," she glanced at her husband's back, "when your father got there all the tickets were sold. Then there was the Gaiety," and she produced a list of theatres and anecdotes.

Ingels sat opposite his father, whose pipe-smoke was pouring up the chimney. "I was looking through our old newspapers," he said. "I came across a case that involved the Variety."

"Don't you ever work at that paper?" his father said.

"This was research. It seems there was a robbery at the theatre. Before you were born, it was, but I wonder if you remember hearing about it."

"Now, we aren't all as clever as you," his mother said. "We don't remember what we heard in our cradle."

Ingels laughed, tightening inside; the opening was turning away from him. "You might have heard about it when you were older," he told his father. "Your father was involved."

"No," his father said. "He was not."

"He was in the paper."

"His name was," he father said, facing Ingels with a blank stare in his eyes. "It was another man. Your grandfather took years to live that down. The newspapers wouldn't publish an apology or say it wasn't him. And you wonder why we didn't want you to work for a paper. You wouldn't be a decent shopkeeper, you let our shop go out of the family, and now here you are, raking up old dirt and lies. That's what you chose for yourself."

"I didn't mean to be offensive," Ingels said, holding himself down. "But it was an interesting case, that's all. I'm going to follow it up tomorrow, at the theatre."

"If you go there you'll be rubbing our name in the dirt. Don't bother coming here again."

"Now hold on," Ingels said. "If your father wasn't involved you can't very well mean that. My God," he cried, flooded with a memory, "you do know something! You told me about it once, when I was a child! I'd just started dreaming and you told it to me so I wouldn't be frightened, to show me you had these dreams too. You were in a room with a telescope, waiting to see something. You told me because I'd dreamed it too! That's the second time I've had that dream! It's the room at the Variety, it has to be!"

"I don't know what you mean," his father said. "I never dreamed that."

"You told me you had."

"I must have told you that to calm you down. Go on, say I shouldn't have lied to you. It must have been for your own good."

He'd blanked out his eyes with an unblinking stare. Ingels gazed at him and knew at once there was more behind the blank than the lie about his childhood. "You've been dreaming again," he said. "You've been having the dream I had last night, I know you have. And I think you know what it means."

The stare shifted almost imperceptibly, then returned strengthened. "What do you know?" his father said. "You live in the same town as us and visit us once a week, if that. Yet you know I've been dreaming? Sometimes we wonder if you even know we're here!"

"I know. I'm sorry," Ingels said. "But these dreams—you used to have them. The ones we used to share, remember?"

"We shared everything when you were a little boy. But that's over," his father said. "Dreams and all."

"That's nothing to do with it!" Ingels shouted. "You still have the ability! I know you must have been having these dreams! It's been in your eyes for months!" He trailed off, trying to remember whether that was true. He turned to his mother, pleading. "Hasn't he been dreaming?"

"What do I know about it?" she said. "It's nothing to do with me." She was clearing the table in the dim rationed light beyond the fire, not looking at either of them. Suddenly Ingels saw her as he never had before: bewildered by her husband's dreams and intuitions, further excluded from the disturbingly incomprehensible bond between him and her son. All at once Ingels knew why he'd always felt she had been happy to see him leave home: it was only then that she'd been able to start reclaiming her husband. He took his coat from the hall and looked into the dining-room. They hadn't moved: his father was staring at the fire, his mother at the table. "I'll see you," he said, but the only sound was the crinkling of the fire as it crumbled, breaking open pinkish embers.

IV

He watched television. Movement of light and colours, forming shapes. Outside the window the sky drew his gaze, stretched taut, heavily imminent as thunder. He wrote words.

Later, he was sailing through enormous darkness; glinting globes turned slowly around him, one wearing an attenuated band of light; ahead, the darkness was scattered with dust and chunks of rock. A piece of metal was circling him like a timid needle, poking towards him, now spitting flame and swinging away. He felt a contempt so profound it was simply vast indifference. He closed his eyes as he might have blinked away a speck of dust.

In the morning he wrote his review at the flat. He knew he wouldn't be able to bear the teeming aisles for long. Blindly shouldering his way across the floor, he found Bert. He had to gaze at him for a minute or so; he couldn't remember immediately what he should look like. "That rewrite you did on the TV review wasn't your best," Bert said. "Ah well," Ingels said, snatching his copy of last night's *Herald* automatically from his desk, and hurried for the door.

He'd nearly reached it when he heard the news editor shouting into the telephone. "But it can't affect Saturn and Jupiter! I mean, it can't change its mass, can it? . . . I'm sorry, sir. Obviously I didn't mean to imply I knew more about your field than you. But is it possible for its mass to change? . . . What, trajectory as well?" Ingels grinned at the crowd around the editor's desk, at their rapt expressions. They'd be more rapt when he returned. He strode out.

Through the writhing crowds, up the steps, into a vista of beds and dressing-tables like a street of cramped bedrooms whose walls had been tricked away. "Can I speak to the manager, please," he said to the man who stepped forward. *"Brichester Herald."*

The manager was a young man in a pale streamlined suit, longish clipped hair, a smile which he held forward as if for inspection. "I'm following a story," Ingels said, displaying his press card. "It seems that when your warehouse was a theatre a room was leased to an astronomical group. We think their records are still here, and if they can be found they're of enormous historical interest."

"That's interesting," the manager said. "Where are they supposed to be?"

"In a room at the top of the building somewhere."

"I'd like to help, of course." Four men passed, carrying pieces of a dismembered bed to a van. "There were some offices at the top of the building once, I believe. But we don't use them now, they're boarded up. It would be a good deal of trouble to open them now. If you'd phoned I might have been able to free some men."

"I've been out of town," Ingels said, improvising hastily now his plans were going awry. "Found this story on my desk when I got back. I tried to phone earlier but couldn't get through. Must be a tribute to the business you're doing." An old man, one of the loaders, was sitting on a chair nearby, listening; Ingels wished he would move, he couldn't bear an audience as well. "These records really would be important,' he said wildly. 'Great historical value."

"In any case I can't think they'd still be here. If they were in one of the top rooms they would have been cleared out long ago."

"I think you're a bit wrong there," the old man said from his chair.

"Have you nothing to do?" the manager demanded.

"We've done loading," the man said. "Driver's not here yet. Mother's sick. It's not for me to say you're wrong, but I remember when they were mending the roof after the war. Men who were doing it said they could see a room full of books, they looked like, all covered up. But we couldn't find it from down here and nobody wanted to break their necks trying to get in from the roof. Must be there still, though."

"That has to be the one," Ingels said. "Whereabouts was it?"

"Round about there," the old man said, pointing above a Scandinavian four-poster. "Behind one of the offices, we used to reckon."

"Could you help find it?" Ingels said. "Maybe your workmates could give you a hand while they're waiting. That's of course if this gentleman doesn't mind. We'd make a point of your cooperation," he told the manager. "Might even be able to give you a special advertising rate, if you wanted to run an ad on that day."

The five of them climbed a rusty spiral staircase, tastefully screened by a partition, to the first floor. The manager, still frowning, had left one loader watching for the driver. "Call us as soon as he comes," he said. "Whatever the reason, time lost loses money." Across the first floor, which was a maze of crated and cartoned furniture, Ingels glimpsed reminiscences of his dream: the outline of theatre boxes in the walls, almost erased by bricks; a hook that had supported a chandelier. They seemed to protrude from the mundane, beckoning him on.

The staircase continued upwards, more rustily. "I'll go first," the manager said, taking the flashlight one of the loaders had brought. "We don't want accidents," and his legs drew up like a tail through a trapdoor. They heard him stamping about, challenging the floor. "All right," he called, and Ingels thrust his face through drifting dust into a bare plank corridor.

"Here, you said?" the manager asked the old man, pointing to some of the boards that formed a wall. "That's it," the old man said, already ripping out nails with his hammer, aided by his workmates. A door peeked dully through. Ingels felt a smile wrenching at his face. He controlled himself. Wait until they've gone.

As soon as they'd prised open the office door he ran forward. A glum green room, a ruined desk in whose splintered innards squatted a dust-furred typewriter. "I'm afraid it's as I thought," the manager said. "There's no way through. You can't expect us to knock down a wall, obviously. Not without a good deal of consultation."

"But there must have been an entrance," Ingels said. "Beyond this other wall. It must have been sealed up before you got the building. Surely we can look for it."

"You won't have to," the old man said. He was kicking at the wall nearest the supposed location of the room. Plaster crumbled along a crack, then they heard the shifting of brick. "Thought as much," he said. "The war did this, shook the building. The boards are all right but the mortar's done for." He kicked again and whipped back his foot. He'd dislodged two bricks, and at once part of the wall collapsed, leaving an opening four feet high.

"That'll be enough!" the manager said. Ingels was stooping, peering through the dust-curtained gap. Bare boards, rafters and slates above, what must be bookcases draped with cloth around the walls, something in the centre of the room wholly covered by a frame hung with heavy material, perhaps velvet. Dust crawled on his hot face, prickling like fever. "If the wall would have collapsed anyway it's a good job you were here when it did," he told the manager. "Now it's done I'm sure you won't object if I have a look around. If I'm injured I promise not to claim. I'll sign a waiver if you like."

"I think you'd better," the manager said, and waited while Ingels struggled with his briefcase, last night's *Herald,* a pen and sheet from his notebook, brushing at his eyebrows where dust and sweat had become a trickle of mud, rubbing his trembling fingers together to clean them. The men had clambered over the heap of bricks and were lifting the velvety frame. Beneath it was a reflector telescope almost a foot long, mounted on a high sturdy stand. One of the men bent to the eyepiece, touching the focus. "Don't!" Ingels screamed. "The setting may be extremely important," he explained, trying to laugh.

The manager was peering at him. "What did you say you do at the *Herald?*" he said.

"Astronomy correspondent," Ingels said, immediately dreading that the man might read the paper regularly. "I don't get too much work," he blundered on. "This is a scoop. If I could I'd like to spend a few hours looking at the books."

He heard them descending the spiral staircase. Squirm away, he thought. He lifted the covers from the bookcases gingerly, anxious to keep dust away from the telescope, as the velvety cover had for decades. Suddenly he hurried back to the corridor. Its walls bobbed about him as the flashlight swung. He selected a plank and, hefting it over the bricks, poked it at the rafters above the telescope, shielding the latter with his arm. After a minute the slate above slid away, and a moment later he heard a distant crash.

He squatted down to look through the eyepiece. No doubt a chair had been provided once. All he could see was a blurred twilit sky. Soon be night, he thought, and turned the flashlight on the books. He remembered the light from the oil-lamp lapping at his feet in the dream.

Much of the material was devoted to astronomy. As many of the books and charts were astrological, he found, some in Oriental script. But there were others, on shelves in the corner furthest from the sealed-off door: *The Story of Atlantis and the Lost Lemuria, Image du Monde, Liber Investigationis, Revelations of Glaaki*. There were nine volumes of the last. He pulled them out, curious, and dust rose about his face like clouds of sleep.

Voices trickled tinily up the staircase, selling beds. In the close room dimmed by the dust that crowded at the hole in the roof, towards which the telescope patiently gazed, Ingels felt as if he were sinking back into his dream. Cracked fragments of the pages clung beneath his nails. He read; the words flowed on like an incantation, like voices muttering in sleep, melting into another style, jerking clumsily into another. Sketches and paintings were tipped into the books, some childishly crude, some startlingly detailed: M'nagalah, a tentacled mass of what looked like bloated raw entrails and eyes; Gla'aki, a half-submerged spongy face peering stalk-eyed from a lake; R'lyeh, an island city towering triumphant above the sea, a vast door ajar. This he recognised, calmly accepting the information. He felt now as if he could never have had reason to doubt his dream.

The early winter night had blocked up the hole in the roof. Ingels stooped to the eyepiece again. Now there was only darkness through the telescope. It felt blurred by distance; he felt the distance drawing him vertiginously down the tube of darkness, out into a boundless emptiness no amount of matter could fill. Not yet, he thought, withdrawing swiftly. Soon.

Someone was staring at him. A girl. She was frowning up at the hole in the roof. A saleswoman. "We're closing soon," she said.

"All right," Ingels said, returning to the book, lying face upwards in the splayed light. It had settled into a more comfortable position, revealing a new page to him, and an underlined phrase: "when the stars are right." He stared at it, trying to connect. It should mean something. The dim books hemmed him in. He shook his head and turned the pages swiftly, searching for underlining. Here it was repeated in the next volume, no, augmented: "when the stars are right again." He glanced sharply at the insistent gap of night above him. In a minute, he snarled. Here was a whole passage underlined:

"Though the universe may feign the semblance of fickleness, its soul has always known its masters. The sleep of its masters is but the largest cycle of all life, for as the defiance and forgetfulness of winter is rendered vain by summer, so the defiance and forgetfulness of man, and of those others who have assumed stewardship, shall be cast aside by the reawakened masters. When these hibernal times are over, and the time for reawakening is near, the universe itself shall send forth the Harbinger and Maker, Ghroth. Who shall urge the stars and worlds to rightness. Who shall raise the sleeping masters from their burrows and drowned tombs; who shall raise the tombs themselves. Who shall be attentive to those worlds where worshippers presume themselves stewards. Who shall bring those worlds under sway, until all acknowledge their presumption, and bow down."

Ghroth, Ingels thought, gazing up at the gap in the roof. They even had a name for it then, despite the superstitious language. Not that that was so surprising, he thought. Man used to look upon comets that way, this is the same sort of thing. An omen that becomes almost a god.

But an omen of what? he thought suddenly. What exactly was supposed to happen when the stars were right again? He knelt in the dust and flurried through the books. No more underlining. He rushed back to the telescope. His thighs twinged as he squatted. Something had entered the field of view.

It was the outer edge of the wandering planet, creeping into the telescope's field. As it came it blurred, occasionally sharpening

almost into focus for a moment. Ingels felt as if the void were
making sudden feeble snatches at him. Now the planet was only a
spreading reddish smudge. He reached for the focus, altering it
minutely. "We're closing now," said the manager behind him.

"I won't be long," Ingels said, feeling the focus sharpen,
sharpen—

"We're waiting to close the doors," the manager said. "And I'm
afraid I'm in a hurry."

"Not long!" Ingels screamed, tearing his gaze from the eyepiece to
glare.

When the man had gone Ingels switched off the flashlight. Now
he could see nothing but the tiny dim gap in the roof. He let the
room settle on his eyes. At last he made out the immobile uplifted
telescope. He groped towards it and squatted down.

As soon as he touched the eyepiece the night rushed through the
telescope and clutched him. He was sailing through the void, yet he
was motionless; everything moved with him. Through the vast
silence he heard the ring of a lifted telephone, a voice saying "Give
me the chief editor of the *Herald,* please," back there across the
void. He could hear the pale grubs squeaking tinnily, back all that
way. He remembered the way they moved, soft, uncarapaced.
Before him, suspended in the dark and facing him, was Ghroth.

It was red as rust, featureless except for bulbous protrusions like
hills. Except that of course they weren't hills if he could see them at
that distance; they must be immense. A rusty globe covered with
lumps, then. That was all, but that couldn't explain why he felt as if
the whole of him were magnetised to it through his eyes. It seemed
to hang ponderously, communicating a thunderous sense of imminence, of power. But that was just its unfamiliarity, Ingels thought,
struggling against the suction of boundless space; just the sense of its
intrusion. It's only a planet, after all. Pain was blazing along his
thighs. Just a red warty globe.

Then it moved.

Ingels was trying to remember how to move his body to get his
face away from the eyepiece; he was throwing his weight against the
telescope mounting to sweep away what he could see. It was blur-
ring, that was it, although it was a cold windless day air movements
must be causing the image to blur, the surface of a planet doesn't
move, it's only a planet, the surface of a planet doesn't crack, it
doesn't roll back like that, it doesn't peel back for thousands of miles

so you can see what's underneath, pale and glistening. When he tried to scream air whooped into his lungs as if space had exploded a vacuum within him.

He'd tripped over the bricks, fallen agonisingly down the stairs, smashed the manager out of the way with his shoulder and was at the *Herald* building before he knew that was where he intended to go. He couldn't speak, only make the whooping sound as he sucked in air; he threw his briefcase and last night's paper on his desk and sat there clutching himself, shaking. The floor seemed to have been in turmoil before he arrived, but they were crowding around him, asking him impatiently what was wrong.

But he was staring at the headline in his last night's newspaper: SURFACE ACTIVITY ON WANDERER 'MORE APPARENT THAN REAL' SAY SCIENTISTS. Photographs of the planet from the space-probe: one showing an area like a great round pale glistening sea, the next circuit recording only mountains and rock plains. "Don't you see?" Ingels shouted at Bert among the packed faces. 'It closed its eye when it saw us coming!'

Hilary came at once when they telephoned her, and took Ingels back to her flat. But he wouldn't sleep, laughed at the doctor and the tranquillisers, though he swallowed the tablets indifferently enough. Hilary unplugged the television, went out as little as possible, bought no newspapers, threw away her contributor's copies unopened, talked to him while she worked, stroked him soothingly, slept with him. Neither of them felt the earth begin to shift.

THE FACES AT PINE DUNES

I

WHEN HIS PARENTS BEGAN ARGUING MICHAEL WENT outside. He could still hear them through the thin wall of the caravan. "We needn't stop yet," his mother was pleading.

But why should she want to leave here? Michael gazed about the Pine Dunes Caravanserai. The metal village of caravans surrounded him, cold and bright in the November afternoon. Beyond the dunes ahead he heard the dozing of the sea. On the three remaining sides a forest stood: remnants of autumn, ghosts of colour, were scattered over the trees; distant branches displayed a last golden mist of leaves. He inhaled the calm. Already he felt at home.

His mother was persisting. "You're still young," she told his father.

She's kidding! Michael thought. Perhaps she was trying flattery. "There are places we haven't seen," she said wistfully.

"We don't need to. We need to be here."

The slowness of the argument, the voices muffled by the metal wall, frustrated Michael; he wanted to be sure that he was staying here. He hurried into the caravan. "I want to stay here. Why do we have to keep moving all the time?"

"Don't come in here talking to your mother like that," his father shouted.

He should have stayed out. The argument seemed to cramp the already crowded space within the caravan; it made his father's presence yet more overwhelming. The man's enormous wheezing body sat plumped on the couch, which sagged beneath his weight; his small frail wife was perched on what little of the couch was unoccupied, as though she'd been squeezed tiny to fit. Gazing at them, Michael felt suffocated. "I'm going out," he said.

"Don't go out," his mother said anxiously; he couldn't see why. "We won't argue any more. You stay in and do something. Study."

"Let him be. The sooner he meets people here, the better."

Michael resented the implication that by going out he was obeying his father. "I'm just going out for a walk," he said. The reassurance might help her; he knew how it felt to be overborne by the man.

At the door he glanced back. His mother had opened her mouth, but his father said "We're staying. I've made my decision." And he'd lie in it, Michael thought, still resentful. All the man could do was lie there, he thought spitefully; that was all he was fat for. He went out, sniggering. The way his father had gained weight during the past year, his coming to rest in this caravan park reminded Michael of an elephant's arrival at its graveyard.

It was colder now. Michael turned up the hood of his anorak. Curtains were closing and glowing. Trees stood, intricately precise, against a sky like translucent papery jade. He began to climb the dunes towards the sea. But over there the sky was blackened; a sea dark as mud tossed nervously and flopped across the bleak beach. He turned toward the forest. Behind him sand hissed through grass.

The forest shifted in the wind. Shoals of leaves swam in the air, at the tips of webs of twigs. He followed a path which led from the Caravanserai's approach road. Shortly the diversity of trees gave way to thousands of pines. Pine cones lay like wattled eggs on beds of fallen needles. The spread of needles glowed deep orange in the early evening, an orange tapestry displaying rank upon rank of slender pines, dwindling into twilight.

The path led him on. The pines were shouldered out by stouter trees, which reached overhead, tangling. Beyond the tangle the blue of the sky grew deeper; a crescent moon slid from branch to branch. Bushes massed among the trunks; they grew higher and closer as he pushed through. The curve of the path would take him back toward the road.

The ground was turning softer underfoot. It sucked his feet in the dark. The shrubs had closed over him now; he could hardly see. He struggled between them, pursuing the curve. Leaves rubbed together rustling at his ear, like desiccated lips; their dry dead tongues rattled. All at once the roof of the wooden tunnel dropped sharply. To go further he would have to crawl.

He turned with difficulty. On both sides thorns caught his sleeves; his dark was hemmed in by two ranks of dim captors. It was as though midnight had already fallen here, beneath the tangled arches; but the dark was solid and clawed. Overhead, netted fragments of night sky illuminated the tunnel hardly at all.

He managed to extricate himself, and hurried back. But he had taken only a few steps when his way was blocked by hulking spiky darkness. He dodged to the left of the shrub, then to the right, trying irritably to calm his heart. But there was no path. He had lost his way in the dark. Around him dimness rustled, chattering.

He began to curse himself. What had possessed him to come in here? Why on earth had he chosen to explore so late in the day? How could the woods be so interminable? He groped for openings between masses of thorns. Sometimes he found them, though often they would not admit his body. The darkness was a maze of false paths.

Eventually he had to return to the mouth of the tunnel and crawl. Unseen moisture welled up from the ground, between his fingers. Shrubs leaned closer as he advanced, poking him with thorns. His skin felt fragile, and nervously unstable; he burned, but his heat often seemed to break, flooding him with the chill of the night.

There was something even less pleasant. As he crawled, the leaning darkness—or part of it—seemed to move beside him. It was as though someone were pacing him, perhaps on all fours, outside the tunnel. When he halted, so did the pacing. It would reach the end of the tunnel just as he did.

Nothing but imagination, helped by the closely looming tree-trunks beyond the shrubs. Apart from the creaking of wood and the rattling sway of leaves, there was no sound beyond the tunnel—certainly none of pacing. He crawled. The cumbersome moist sounds that accompanied the pacing were those of his own progress. But he crawled more slowly, and the darkness imitated him. Wasn't the thorny tunnel dwindling ahead? It would trap him. Suddenly panicking, he began to scrabble backwards.

The thorns hardly hindered his retreat. He must have broken them down. He emerged gasping, glad of the tiny gain in light. Around him shrubs pressed close as ever. He stamped his way back along what he'd thought was his original path. When he reached the hindrance he smashed his way between the shrubs, struggling and snarling, savage with panic, determined not to yield. His hands were torn; he heard cloth rip. Well, the thorns could have that.

When at last he reached an open space his panic sighed loudly out of him. He began to walk as rapidly as seemed safe, towards where he remembered the road to be. Overhead black nets of branches turned, momentarily catching stars. Once, amid the enormous threshing of the woods, he thought he heard a heavy body shoving through the nearby bushes. Good luck to whoever it was. Ahead, in the barred dark, hung little lighted windows. He had found the caravan park, but only by losing his way.

He was home. He hurried into the light, smiling. In the metal alleys pegged shirts hung neck down, dripping; they flapped desperately on the wind. The caravan was dark. In the main room, lying on the couch like someone's abandoned reading, was a note: OUT, BACK LATER. His mother had added DON'T GO TO BED TOO LATE.

He'd been looking forward to companionship. Now the caravan seemed too brightly lit, and false: a furnished tin can. He made himself coffee, leafed desultorily through his floppy paperbacks, opened and closed a pocket chess set. He poked through his box of souvenirs: shells, smooth stones; a minute Bible; a globe of synthetic snow within which a huge vague figure, presumably meant to be a snowman, loomed outside a house; a dead flashlight fitted with a set of clip-on Halloween faces; a dull grey ring whose metal swelled into a bulge over which colours crawled slowly, changing. The cardboard box was full of memories: the Severn valley, the Welsh hills, the garishly glittering mile of Blackpool: he couldn't remember where the ring had come from. But the memories were dim tonight, uninvolving.

He wandered into his parents' room. It looked to him like a second-hand store for clothes and toiletries. He found his father's large metal box, but it was locked as usual. Well, Michael didn't want to read his old books anyway. He searched for contraceptives, but as he'd expected, there were none. If he wasn't mistaken, his parents had no need for them. Poor buggers. He'd never been able to imagine how, out of proportion as they seemed to be, they had begot him.

Eventually he went out. The incessant rocking of the caravan, its hollow booming in the wind, had begun to infuriate him. He hurried along the road between the pines; wind sifted through needles. On the main road buses ran to Liverpool. But he'd already been there several times. He caught a bus to the opposite terminus.

The bus was almost empty. A few passengers rattled in their lighted pod over the bumpy country roads. Darkness streamed by, sometimes becoming dim hedges. The scoop of the headlamps set light to moths, and once to a squirrel. Ahead the sky glowed, as if with a localised dawn. Lights began to emerge from behind silhouetted houses; streets opened, brightening.

The bus halted in a square, beside a village cross. The passengers hurried away, snuggling into their collars. Almost at once the street was deserted, the bus extinguished. Folded awnings clattered, tugged by the wind. Perhaps after all he should have gone into the city. He was stranded here for—he read the timetable: God, two hours until the last bus.

He wandered among the grey stone houses. Streetlamps glared silver; the light coated shop windows, behind whose flowering of frost he could see faint ghosts of merchandise. Curtains shone warmly, chimneys smoked. His heels clanked mechanically on the cobbles. Streets, streets, empty streets. Then the streets became crowded, with gleaming parked cars. Ahead, on the wall of a building, was a plaque of coloured light. FOUR IN THE MORNING. A club.

He hesitated, then he descended the steps. Maybe he wouldn't fit in with the brand-new sports car set, but anything was better than wandering the icy streets. At the bottom of the stone flight, a desk stood beside a door to coloured dimness. A broken-nosed man wearing evening dress sat behind the desk. "Are you a member, sir?" he said in an accent that was almost as convincing as his suit.

Inside was worse than Michael had feared. On a dance-floor couples turned lethargically, glittering and changing colour like toy dancers. Clumps of people stood shouting at each other in county accents, swaying and laughing; some stared at him as they laughed. He heard their talk: motor-boats, bloody bolshies, someone's third abortion. He didn't mind meeting new people—he'd had to learn not to mind—but he could tell these people preferred, now they'd stared, to ignore him.

His three pounds' membership fee included a free drink. I should think so too, he thought. He ordered a beer, to the barman's faint contempt. As he carried the tankard to one of the low bare tables he was conscious of his boots, tramping the floorboards. There was nothing wrong with them, he'd wiped them. He sipped, making the drink last, and gazed into the beer's dim glow.

When someone else sat at the table he didn't look at her. He had to glance up at last, because she was staring. What was the matter with her, was he on show? Often in groups he felt alien, but he'd never felt more of a freak than here. His large-boned arms huddled protectively around him, his gawky legs drew up.

But she was smiling. Her stare was wide-eyed, innocent, if somehow odd. "I haven't seen you before," she said. "What's your name?"

"Michael." It sounded like phlegm; he cleared his throat. "Michael. What's yours?"

"June." She made a face as though it tasted like medicine.

"Nothing wrong with that." Her hint of dissatisfaction with herself had emboldened him.

"You haven't moved here, have you? Are you visiting?"

There was something strange about her: about her eyes, about the way she seemed to search for questions. "My parents have a caravan," he said. "We're in the Pine Dunes Caravanserai. We docked just last week."

"Yeah." She drew the word out like a sigh. "Like a ship. That must be fantastic. I wish I had that. Just to be able to see new things all the time, new places. The only way you can see new things here is taking acid. I'm tripping now."

His eyebrows lifted slightly; his faint smile shrugged.

"That's what I mean," she said, smiling. "These people here would be really shocked. They're so provincial. You aren't."

In fact he hadn't been sure how to react. The pupils of her eyes were expanding and contracting rapidly, independently of each other. But her small face was attractive, her small body had large firm breasts.

"I saw the moon dancing before," she said. "I'm beginning to come down now. I thought I'd like to look at people. You wouldn't know I was tripping, would you? I can control it when I want to."

She wasn't really talking to him, he thought; she just wanted an audience to trip to. He'd heard things about LSD. "Aren't you afraid of starting to trip when you don't mean to?"

"Flashbacks, you mean. I never have them. I shouldn't like that."
She gazed at his skepticism. "There's no need to be afraid of drugs,"
she said. "All sorts of people used to trip. Witches used to. Look, it
tells you about it in here."

She fumbled a book out of her handbag; she seemed to have difficulty in wielding her fingers. *Witchcraft in England.* "You can have
that," she said. "Have you got a job?"

It took him a moment to realise that she'd changed the subject.
"No," he said. "I haven't left school long. I had to have extra school
because of all the moving. I'm twenty. I expect I'll get a job soon. I
think we're staying here."

"That could be a good job," she said, pointing at a notice behind
the bar: TRAINEE BARMAN REQUIRED. "I think they want to
get rid of that guy there. People don't like him. I know a lot of
people would come here if they got someone friendly like you."

Was it just her trip talking? Two girls said goodbye to a group,
and came over. "We're going now, June. See you shortly."

"Right. Hey, this is Michael."

"Nice to meet you, Michael."

"Hope we'll see you again."

Perhaps they might. These people didn't seem so bad after all.
He drank his beer and bought another, wincing at the price and
gazing at the job notice. June refused a drink: "It's a downer." They
talked about his travels, her dissatisfactions and her lack of cash to
pay for moving. When he had to leave she said "I'm glad I met you.
I like you." And she called after him "If you got that job I'd come
here."

II

Darkness blinded him. It was heavy on him, and moved. It was
more than darkness: it was flesh. Beneath him and around him
and above him, somnolent bodies crawled blindly. They were huge;
so was he. As they shifted incessantly he heard sounds of mud or
flesh.

He was shifting too. It was more than restlessness. His whole
body felt unstable; he couldn't make out his own form—whenever
he seemed to perceive it, it changed. And his mind; it felt too full, of
alien chunks that ground harshly together. Memories or fantasies

floated vaguely through him. Stone circles. Honeycombed mountains; glimmering faces like a cluster of bubbles in a cave mouth. Enormous dreaming eyes beneath stone and sea. A labyrinth of thorns. His own face. But why was his own face only a memory?

He woke. Dawn suffocated him like grey gas; he lay panting. It was all right. It hadn't been his own face that he'd seemed to remember in the dream. His body hadn't grown huge. His large bones were still lanky. But there was a huge figure, nonetheless. It loomed above him at the window, its spread of face staring down at him.

He woke, and had to grab the dark before he could find the light-switch. He twisted himself to sit on the edge of the couch, legs tangled in the blankets, so as not to fall asleep again. Around him the caravan was flat and bright, and empty. Beyond the ajar door of his parents' room he could see that their bed was smooth and deserted.

He was sure he'd had that dream before—the figure at the window. Somehow he associated it with a windmill, a childhood memory he couldn't locate. Had he been staying with his grandparents? The dream was fading in the light. He glanced at his clock: two in the morning. He didn't want to sleep again until the dream had gone.

He stood outside the caravan. A wind was rising; a loud whisper passed through the forest, unlit caravans rocked and creaked a little at their moorings; behind everything, vast and constant, the sea rushed vaguely. Scraps of cloud slid over the filling moon; light caught at them, but they slipped away. His parents hadn't taken the car. Where had they gone? Irrationally, he felt he knew, if only he could remember. Why did they go out at night so much?

A sound interrupted his musing. The wind carried it to him only to snatch it away. It seemed distant, and therefore must be loud. Did it contain words? Was someone being violently ill, and trying to shout? The moon's light flapped between a procession of dark clouds. A drunk, no doubt, shouting incoherently. Michael gazed at the edge of the forest and wondered about his parents. Light and wind shifted the foliage. Then he shrugged. He ought to be used to his parents' nocturnal behaviour by now.

He slammed the door. His dream was still clinging to him. There had been something odd about the head at the window, besides its size. Something about it had reminded him unpleasantly of a bubble. Hadn't that happened the first time he'd had the dream?

But he was grinning at himself: never mind dreams, or his parents. Think of June.

She had been in the club almost every evening since he'd taken the job, a month ago. He had dithered for a week, then he'd returned and asked about the notice. Frowning, the barman had called the manager—to throw Michael out? But June had told them her parents knew Michael well. "All right. We'll give you six weeks and see how you do." The barman had trained him, always faintly snooty and quick to criticise. But the customers had begun to prefer Michael to serve them. They accepted him, and he found he could be friendly. He'd never felt less like an outsider.

So long as the manager didn't question June's parents. June had invited Michael to the cottage a couple of times. Her parents had been polite, cold, fascinated, contemptuous. He'd tried to fit his lanky legs beneath his chair, so that the flares of his trousers would cover up his boots—and all the while he'd felt superior to these people in some way, if only he could think of it. "They aren't my kind of people either," June had told him, walking to the club. "When can we go to your caravan?"

He didn't know. He hadn't yet told his parents about her; the reaction to the news of his job hadn't been what he'd hoped. His mother had gazed at him sadly, and he'd felt she was holding more of her feelings hidden, as they all had to in the cramped caravan. "Why don't you go to the city? They'll have better jobs there."

"But I feel at home here."

"That's right," his father had said. "That's right." He'd stared at Michael strangely, with a kind of uneasy joy. Michael had felt oppressed, engulfed by the stare. Of course there was nothing wrong, his father had become uneasy on hearing of his son's first job, his first step in the world, that was all.

"Can I borrow the car to get to the club?"

His father had become dogmatic at once; his shell had snapped tight. "Not yet. You'll get the key soon enough."

It hadn't seemed worth arguing. Though his parents rarely used the car at night, Michael was never given the key. Where *did* they go at night? "When you're older" had never seemed much of an explanation. But surely their nocturnal excursions were more frequent now they'd docked at Pine Dunes? And why was his mother so anxious to persuade him to leave?

It didn't matter. Sometimes he was glad that they went out; it gave him a chance to be alone, the caravan seemed less cramped, he could breathe freely. He could relax, safe from the threat of his father's overwhelming presence. And if they hadn't gone out that night he would never have met June.

Because of the wanderings of the caravan he had never had time for close friendships. He had felt more attached to this latest berth than to any person—until he'd met June. She was the first girl to arouse him. Her small slim body, her bright quick eyes, her handfuls of breast—he felt his body stirring as he thought of her.

For years he'd feared he was impotent. Once, in a village school, a boy had shown him an erotic novel. He'd read about the gasps of pleasure, the creaking of the bed. Gradually he'd realised why that troubled him. The walls of the caravan were thin; he could always hear his father snoring or wheezing, like a huge fish stranded on the shore of a dream. But he had never heard his parents copulating.

Their sexual impulse must have faded quickly, soon after he was born—as soon, he thought, as it had served its purpose. Would his own be as feeble? Would it work at all? Yes, he'd gasped over June, the first night her parents were out. "I think it'd be good to make love on acid," she'd said as they lay embraced. "That way you really become one, united together." But he thought he would be terrified to take LSD, even though what she'd said appealed deeply to him.

He wished she were here now. The caravan rocked; his parents' door swung creaking, imitated by the bathroom door, which often sprang open. He slammed them irritably. The dream of the bubbling head at the window—if that had been what was wrong with it—was drifting away. Soon he'd sleep. He picked up *Witchcraft in England*. It looked dull enough to help him sleep. And it was June's.

Naked witches danced about on the cover, and on many of the pages. They danced obscenely. They danced lewdly. They chanted obscenely. And so on. They used poisonous drugs, such as belladonna. No doubt that had interested June. He leafed idly onward; his gaze flickered impatiently.

Suddenly he halted, at a name: Severnford. Now that *was* interesting. We can imagine, the book insisted, the witches rowing out to the island in the middle of the dark river, and committing unspeakable acts before the pallid stone in the moonlight; but Michael couldn't imagine anything of the kind, nor did he intend to try. Witches are still reputed to visit the island, the book told him before he interrupted it and riffled on. But a few pages later his gaze was caught again.

He stared at this new name. Then reluctantly he turned to the index. At once words stood out from the columns, eager to be seen. They slipped into his mind as if their slots had been ready for years. Exham. Whitminster. The Old Horns. Holihaven. Dilham. Severnford. His father had halted the caravan at all of them, and his parents had gone out at night.

He was still staring numbly at the list when the door snapped open. His father glanced sharply at him, then went into the bedroom. "Come on," he told Michael's mother, and sat heavily on the bed, which squealed. To Michael's bewildered mind his father's body seemed to spread as he sat down, like a dropped jelly. His mother sat obediently; her gaze dodged timidly, she looked pale and shrunken—by fear, Michael knew at once. "Go to bed," his father told him, raising one foot effortfully to kick the door shut. Almost until dawn Michael lay in the creaking unstable dark, thinking.

III

"You must have seen all sorts of places," June said.

"We've seen a few," said Michael's mother. Her eyes moved uneasily. She seemed nervously resentful, perhaps at being reminded of something she wanted desperately to forget. At last, as if she'd struggled and found courage, she managed to say "We may see a few more."

"Oh no we won't," her husband said. He sat slumped on the couch, as though his body were a burden he'd had to drop there. Now that there were four people in the caravan he seemed to take up even more room; his presence overwhelmed all the spaces between them.

Michael refused to be overwhelmed. He stared at his father. "What made you choose the places we've lived?" he demanded.

"I had my reasons."

"What reasons?"

"I'll tell you sometime. Not now, son. You don't want us arguing in front of your girlfriend, do you?"

Into the embarrassed silence June said "I really envy you, being able to go everywhere."

"You'd like to, would you?" Michael's mother said.

"Oh yes. I'd love to see the world."

His mother turned from the stove. "You ought to. You're the right age for it. It wouldn't do Michael any harm, either."

For a moment her eyes were less dull. Michael was glad: he'd thought she would approve of June's wanderlust—that was one reason why he'd given in to June's pleas to meet his parents. Then his father was speaking, and his mother dulled again. "Best to stay where you're born," his father told June. "You won't find a better place than here. I know what I'm talking about."

"You should try living where I do. It'd kill your head in no time."

"Mike feels at home here. That's right, isn't it, son? You tell her."

"I like it here," Michael said. Words blocked his throat. "I mean, I met you," he hawked at June.

His mother chopped vegetables: chop, chop, chop—the sound was harsh, trapped within the metal walls. "Can I do anything?" June said.

"No thank you. It's all right," she said indifferently. She hadn't accepted June yet, after all.

"If you're so keen on seeing the world," his father demanded, "what's stopping you?"

"I can't afford it, not yet. I work in a boutique, I'm saving the money I'd have spent on clothes. And then I can't drive. I'd need to go with someone who can."

"Good luck to you. But I don't see Mikey going with you."

Well, ask *me!* Michael shouted at her, gagged (by his unsureness: she mightn't have had him in mind at all). But she only said "When I travel I'm going to have things from everywhere."

"I've got some," he said. "I've kept some things." He carried the cardboard box to her, and displayed his souvenirs. "You can have them if you like," he said impulsively; if she accepted he would be more sure of her. "The flashlight only needs batteries."

But she pushed the plastic faces aside, and picked up the ring. "I like that," she said, turning it so that its colours spilled slowly over one another, merging and separating. She whispered "It's like tripping."

"There you are. I'm giving it to you."

His father stared at the ring, and then a smile spread his mouth. "Yes, you give her that. It's as good as an engagement, that ring."

Michael slid the ring onto her finger before she could change her mind; she had begun to look embarrassed. "It's lovely," she said. "Have we time for Mike to take me for a walk before dinner?"

"You can stay out for an hour if you like," his mother said, then anxiously: "Go down to the beach. You might get lost in the woods, in the fog."

The fog was ambiguous: perhaps thinning, perhaps gathering again. Inside a caravan a radio sang Christmas carols. A sharp-edged bronze sun hung close to the sea. Sea and fog had merged, and might be advancing over the beach. June took Michael's hand as they climbed the slithering dunes. "I just wanted to come out to talk," she explained.

So had he. He wanted to tell her what he'd discovered. That was his main reason for inviting her: he needed her support in confronting his parents, he would be too disturbed to confront them alone—he'd needed it earlier when he'd tried to interrogate his father. But what could he tell her? I've found out my parents are witches? You know that book you lent me—

"No, I didn't really want to talk," she said. "There were just too many bad vibes in there. I'll be all right, we'll go back soon. But they're strange, your parents, aren't they? I didn't realise your father was so heavy."

"He used to be like me. He's been getting fatter for the last few months." After a pause he voiced his worst secret fear. "I hope I never get like him."

"You'll have to get lots of exercise. Let's walk as far as the point."

Ahead along the beach, the grey that lay stretched on the sea was land, not fog. They trudged towards it. Sand splashed from his boots; June slid, and gripped his hand. He strained to tell her what he'd found out, but each phrase he prepared sounded more absurd: his voice echoed hollowly, closed into his mind. He'd tell her—but not today. He relaxed, and felt enormously relieved; he enjoyed her hand small in his. "I like fog," she said. "There are always surprises in it."

The bronze sun paced them, sinking. The sea shifted restlessly, muffled. To their left, above the dunes, trees were a flat mass of prickly fog. They were nearly at the point now. It pulled free of the grey, darkening and sharpening. It looked safe enough for them to climb the path.

But when they reached the top it seemed hardly worth the effort. A drab patch of beach and dunes, an indistinct fragment of sea scattered with glitterings of dull brass, surrounded them in a soft unstable frame of fog. Otherwise the view was featureless, except for a tree growing beside the far dunes. Was it a tree? Its branches seemed too straight, its trunk too thick. Suddenly troubled, Michael picked his way over the point as far as he dared. The fog withdrew a little. It wasn't a tree. It was a windmill.

A windmill by the sea! "My grandparents lived here," he blurted. "Oh, did they?"

"You don't understand. They lived near that windmill. It's the same one, I know it is."

He still wasn't sure whether she felt his confusion. Memories rushed him, as if all at once afloat: he'd been lying on the couch in his grandparents' decrepit caravan, the huge head had loomed at the window, vague with dawn. It must have been a dream then too.

He followed June down the path. Chill fog trailed them, lapping the point. His thoughts drifted, swirling. What did his discovery mean? He couldn't remember his grandparents at all, not even what they'd looked like. They had been his father's parents—why had the man never mentioned them? Why hadn't he remarked that they'd lived here? The sun slid along the rim of the sea, swollen as though with glowing blood. Had his grandparents also been witches?

"Did Mike's grandparents live here, then?" June said.

His mother stared at her. The spoon and saucepan she was holding chattered like nervous teeth. He was sure she was going to scream and throw everything away—the utensils, her self-control, the mask behind which she'd hidden to protect him: for how long? For the whole of his childhood? But she stammered "How did you know that?"

"Mike told me. The windmill just reminded him."

"Is dinner ready?" Michael interrupted. He wanted to think everything out before questioning his father. But June was opening her mouth to continue. The caravan was crowded, suffocating. Shut up! he screamed at her. Get out! "Were they born here, then?" June said.

"No, I don't think so." His mother had turned away and was washing vegetables. June went to hold the dishes. "So why did they come here?" she said.

His mother frowned, turning her back; within her frown she was searching. "To retire," she said abruptly.

His father nodded and smiled to himself, squeezing forward his ruff of chins. "You could retire from the human race here," June said sourly, and he wheezed like a punctured balloon.

As the four ate dinner, their constraint grew. Michael and June made most of the conversation; his parents replied shortly when at all, and watched. His mother observed June uneasily; he read dislike in her eyes, or pity. He felt irritably resentful, her uneasiness made his skin nervous. Night edged closer to the windows, blank-faced.

His father leaned back as if his weight had toppled the chair, which creaked loudly. He patted his quaking stomach. "Just storing it up for the winter," he said, winking at June.

His arms flopped around her shoulders and Michael's. "You two go well together. Don't they, eh?"

But his wife said only "I'm going to bed now. I'm very tired. Perhaps we'll see you again," which sounded like dutiful politeness.

"I hope so," June said.

"I know we will," Michael's father said expansively.

Michael walked June to the bus-stop. "I'll see you at the club," she said through a kiss. Smouldering cones of yellow light led the bus away, and were engulfed. As he walked back, twisted shapes of fog bulked between the trees. Nearby in the dark, something shifted moistly.

He halted. What had it been? Blurred trees creaked with a deadened sound, thin trails of fog reached out for him from branches. He'd heard a shifting, deep in the dark. A vague memory plucked at him. He shivered as if to shake it free, into the chill clinging night. A restless moist shifting. He felt as though the depths of the forest were reaching for his mind with ambiguous tatters of grey. He strode rapidly toward the invisible light. Again he heard the slow moist shifting. Only the sea, he told himself. Only the sea.

IV

As he emerged into the open, the clouds parted and the moon rolled free. The enormous shape in the open space glistened with moonlight. The unstable head turned its crawling face towards him.

The dream trailed him to Liverpool, to the central library, although the space and the head had faded before he could make them out—if indeed he had wanted to. A rush of rain, and the bright lights of the library, washed the dream away. He hurried up the wide green stairs to the Religion and Philosophy section.

He pulled books from the shelves. *Lancashire Witches. North-West Hauntings. Ghostly Lancashire.* The banality of their covers was reassuring; it seemed absurd that his parents could be mixed up in such things. Yet he couldn't quite laugh. Even if they were, what could he do? He slammed the books angrily on a table, startling echoes.

As he read he began to feel safer. Pine Dunes wasn't indexed in *North-West Hauntings.* His attention strayed fascinated into irrelevances. The hanged man's ghost in Everton Library. The poltergeist of the Palace Hotel, Birkdale. Jokey ghost stories in Lancashire dialect, ee lad. Rain and wind shook the windows, fluorescent light lay flat on the tables. Beyond a glass partition people sat studying, library staff clattered up and down open staircases, carrying scraps of paper. Reassured, he turned to *Lancashire Witches.* Pine Dunes. It was there, on three pages.

When he made himself search the pages they didn't say much. Over the centuries, witches had been rumoured to gather in the Pine Dunes forest. Was that surprising? Wouldn't they naturally have done so, for concealment? Besides, these were only rumours; few people would have bothered struggling through the undergrowth. He opened *Ghostly Lancashire,* expecting irrelevances. But the index showed that Pine Dunes covered several pages.

The author had interviewed a group the other books ignored: the travellers. Their stories were unreliable, he warned, but fascinating. Few travellers would walk the Pine Dunes road after dark; they kept their children out of the woods even by day. A superstitious people, the author pointed out. The book had been written thirty years ago, Michael reminded himself. And the travellers gave no reason for their nervousness except vague tales of something unpleasantly large glimpsed moving beyond the most distant trees. Surely distance must have formed the trees into a solid wall; how could anyone have seen beyond?

One traveller, senile and often incoherent, told a story. A long time ago he, or someone else—the author couldn't tell—had wandered back to the travellers' camp, very drunk. The author didn't believe the story, but included it because it was vivid and unusual. Straying from the road, the man had become lost in the forest. Blinded by angry panic, he'd fought his way towards an open space. But it wasn't the camp, as he'd thought. He had lost his footing on the slippery earth and had gone skidding into a pit.

Had it been a pit, or the mouth of a tunnel? As he'd scrabbled, bruised but otherwise unhurt, for a foothold on the mud at the bottom, he'd seen an opening that led deeper into darkness. The darkness had begun moving slowly and enormously towards him, with a sound like that of a huge shifting beneath mud—darkness which had parted loudly, resolving itself into several sluggish forms that glistened dimly as they advanced to surround him. Terror had hurled him in a leap halfway up the pit; his hands had clamped on rock, and he'd wrenched himself up the rest of the way. He'd run blindly. In the morning he'd found himself full of thorns on a sprung bed of undergrowth.

So what did all that prove? Michael argued with himself on the bus to Pine Dunes. The man had been drunk. All right, so there were other tales about Pine Dunes, but nothing very evil. Why shouldn't his parents go out at night? Maybe they were ghost-hunters, witch-hunters. Maybe they were going to write a book about their observations. How else could such books be written? His mind was becoming desperate as he kept remembering his mother's masked fear.

His parents were asleep. His father lay beached on the bed, snoring flabbily; beyond his stomach his wife could hardly be seen. Michael was glad, for he hadn't known what to say to them. He wheeled out the bicycle he'd bought from his first month's wages.

He cycled to the Four in the Morning. His knees protruded on either side of him, jerking up and down. Hedges sailed by slowly; their colours faded and dimmed into twilight. The whirr of his dynamo caught among the leaves. He struggled uphill, standing on the pedals. Dim countryside opened below him, the sea glinted dully. As he poised on the edge of the downhill rush he knew how he could unburden himself, or begin to. Tonight he would tell June everything.

But she didn't come to the club. People crowded in; the lights painted them carelessly monochrome. Discotheque records snarled and thumped, swirls of tobacco-smoke glared red, pink, purple. Michael hurried about, serving. Dim wet discoloured faces jostled to reach him, shouting "Mike! Mike!" Faces rose obsessively to the surface of the jostling: June's, who wasn't there; his mother's, her eyes trying to dodge fear. He was suffocating. His frustration gathered within him; he felt swollen, encumbered. He stared at luridly pink smoke while voices called. "I've got to go home," he told the barman.

"Had enough, have you?"

"My parents aren't well. I'm worried."

"Strange you didn't say so when you came in. Well, I've managed by myself before." He turned away, dismissing Michael. "You'll have to make do with me tonight," he told the shouting.

The last of the lit streets faded behind Michael. The moon was full, but blurred by unkempt fields of cloud; it showed him only a faint windy swaying that surrounded him for miles. When he confronted his father, what would his mother do? Would she break down? If she admitted to witchcraft and said it was time Michael knew, the scene would be easier—if she did. The moon struggled among plump clouds, and was engulfed.

He cycled fast up the Pine Dunes road. Get there, don't delay to reconsider. Gravel ground together squeaking beneath his wheels; his yellow light wobbled, plucking at trees. The depths of the forest creaked; distant treetrunks were pushed apart to let a huge unstable face peer through. He was overtired—of course there was nothing among the far trees but dark. He sped into the Caravanserai; random patches of unlit caravans bobbed up and faded by. His caravan was unlit too.

Perhaps his parents weren't there. He realised furiously that he felt relieved. They were in there all right, they'd be asleep. He would wake his father, the man might betray himself while still half-asleep. He'd dazzle his father awake, like an interrogator. But his parents' bed was empty.

He punched the wall, which rang flatly. His father had outwitted him again. He stared around the room, enraged. His father's huge suits dangled emptily, like sloughed skin; his mother's clothes hid in drawers. His father's metal box of books sat on top of the wardrobe. Michael glanced resentfully at it, then stared. It was unlocked.

He lifted it down and made to sit on his parents' bed. That made him feel uneasy; he carried the box into the main room. Let his father come in and find him reading. Michael hoped he would. He tugged at the lid, which resisted then sprang open with a loud clang.

He remembered that sound. He'd heard it when he was quite young, and his mother's voice, pleading "Let him at least have a normal childhood." After a moment he'd heard the box closed again. "All right. He'll find out when it's time," he'd heard his father say.

The box contained no printed books, but several notebooks. They had been written in by numerous people; the inks in the oldest notebook, whose spine had given way, were brown as old bloodstains. Some of the writing in the latest book was his mother's. Odd pages showed rough maps: The Old Horns, Exham, Whitminster, though none of Pine Dunes. These he recognised; but he couldn't understand a word of the text.

Most of it was in English, but might as well not have been. It consisted largely of quotations copied from books; sometimes the source was indicated—*Necro, Revelations Glaaki, Garimiaz, Vermis, Theobald*, whatever they were. The whole thing reminded him of pamphlets issued by cranky cults—like the people who gave all their worldly goods to a man in America, or the others who'd once lured Michael into a seedy hotel for a personality profile, which they'd lied would be fun. He read, baffled.

After a while he gave up. Even the entries his mother had written made no sense. Some of the words he couldn't even pronounce. Kuthullhoo? Kuthoolhew? And what was supposed to be so Great about it, whatever it was?

He shrugged, sniggering a little. He didn't feel so worried now. If this was all his parents were involved in, it seemed silly but harmless. The fact that they'd concealed it from him so successfully for so long seemed to prove as much. They were so convincingly normal, it couldn't be anything very bad. After all, many businessmen belonged to secret societies with jargon nobody else could understand. Maybe his father had been initiated into this society as part of one of the jobs he'd taken in his wanderings!

One thing still troubled Michael: his mother's fear. He couldn't see what there was to fear in the blurred language of the notebooks. He made a last effort, and let the books fall open where they would—at the pages that had been read most frequently.

What a waste of time! He strained his mind, but the pages became more bewildering still; he began to laugh. What on earth was "the millenial gestation"? Something to do with "the fosterling of the Great Old Ones"? "The hereditary rebirth"? "Each of Its rebirths comes closer to incarnation"? "When the mind opens to all the dimensions will come the incarnation. Upon the incarnation all minds will become one." Ah, that explains it! Michael sniggered wildly. But there was more: "the ingestion," "the mating beyond marriage," "the melting and merging" —

He threw the book angrily into the box. The skin of his eyes crawled hotly; he could hardly keep them open, yet he was wasting his time reading this. The caravan rocked as something huge tugged at it: the wind. The oldest, spineless, notebook began to disintegrate. As he knocked it square, an envelope slipped out.

It was addressed in his father's large handwriting; the last word had had to be cramped. TO MICHAEL: NOT TO BE OPENED UNTIL AFTER I AM GONE. He turned it over and began to tear, but his hand faltered. He'd been unreasonable enough to his father for one day. After a moment he put the envelope unopened in his pocket, feeling sly and ashamed. He replaced the box, and then he prepared to sleep. In the dark he tried to arrange his limbs on the sagging couch. Rocking, the caravan sounded like a rusty cradle.

He slept. He wasn't sure whether he was asleep when he heard his mother's low voice. He must be awake, for he could feel her breath on his face. "Don't stay here." Her voice trembled. "Your girlfriend's got the right idea. Go away with her if that's what you want. Just get away from here."

His father's voice reached for her out of the dark. "That's enough. He's asleep. You come to bed."

Silence and darkness settled down for the night. But in the night, or in Michael's dream, there were noises: the stealthy departure of a car from the park; heavy footsteps trying not to disturb the caravan; the gingerly closing of his parents' door. Sleep seemed more important.

His father's voice woke him, shouting into the bedroom. "Wake up. The car's gone. It's been stolen."

Daylight blazed through Michael's eyelids. He was sure at once what had happened. His father had hidden the car, so that nobody could get away. Michael lay paralysed, waiting for his mother's cry of panic. Her silence held time immobile. He squeezed his eyelids tighter, filling his eyes with red.

"Oh," his mother said at last, dully. "Oh dear."

There was more in her voice than resignation: she sounded lethargic, indifferent. Suddenly Michael remembered what he'd read in June's book. Witches used drugs. His eyes sprang wide. He was sure that his father was drugging his mother.

V

It didn't take the police long to find the car, abandoned and burnt out, near the windmill. "Kids, probably," one of the policemen said. "We may be in touch with you again." Michael's father shook his head sadly, and they left.

"I must have dropped the car keys while we were out." Michael thought his father hardly bothered to sound convincing. Why couldn't he tell the man so, confront him? Because he wasn't sure; he might have dreamed the sounds last night—He raged at his own cowardice, staring at his mother. If only he could be certain of her support! She wandered desultorily, determinedly cleaning the caravan, as though she were ill but expecting company.

When his gagged rage found words at last it weakened immediately. "Are you all right?" he demanded of her, but then could only stammer "Do you think you'd better see a doctor?"

Neither of his parents responded. His unsureness grew, and fed his frustration. He felt lethargic, unable to act, engulfed by his father's presence. Surely June would be at the club tonight. He had to talk to someone, to hear another interpretation; perhaps she would prove that he'd imagined everything.

He washed and shaved. He was glad to retreat, even into the cramped bathroom; he and his parents had been edging uneasily around one another all day—the caravan made him think unpleasantly of a tin can full of squirming. As he shaved, the bathroom door sprang open, as it often did. His father appeared behind him in the mirror, staring at him.

Steam coated the mirror again. Beneath the steam, his father's face seemed to writhe like a plastic mask on fire. Michael reached to clear the mirror, but already his father and the man's emotions were upon him. Before Michael could turn his father was hugging him violently, his flesh quivering as though it would burst. Michael held himself stiff, refusing to be engulfed. What are you doing? Get away! In a moment his father turned clumsily and plodded out. The caravan rumbled, shaking.

Michael sighed loudly. God, he was glad that was over. He finished shaving and hurried out. Neither of his parents looked at him; his father pretended to read a book, and whistled tunelessly; his mother turned vaguely as he passed. He cycled to the club.

"Parents all right?" the barman said indifferently.

"I'm not sure."

"Good of you to come." Perhaps that was sarcasm. "There's some things for you to wash."

Michael could still feel his father's clinging embrace; he kept trying to wriggle it away. He welcomed the press of bodies at the bar, shouting "Mike!"—even though June wasn't among them. He welcomed the companionship of ordinary people. He strode expertly about, serving, as the crowd grew, as smoke gathered. He could still feel swollen flesh pressed hotly against his back. He won't do that to me again, he thought furiously. He'll never—A tankard dropped from his hand, beneath a beer-tap. "Oh my God," he said.

"What's up with you now?" the barman demanded.

When his father had embraced him, Michael had thought of nothing but escape. Now at last he realised how final his father's gesture had been. "My parents," he said. "They're, they're worse."

"Just sent you a message, did they? Off home again now, I suppose? You'd better see the manager, or I will—Will you watch that bloody beer you're spilling!"

Michael slammed the tap shut and struggled through the crowd. People grimaced sympathetically at him, or stared. It didn't matter, his job didn't matter. He must hurry back to head off whatever was going to happen. Someone bumped into him in the doorway, and hindered him when he tried to push them aside. "What's the matter with you?" he shouted. "Get out of the way!" It was June.

"I'm really sorry I didn't come last night," she said. "My parents dragged me out to dinner."

"All right. Okay. Don't worry."

"You're angry. I really am sorry, I wanted to see you—You're not going, are you?"

"Yes, I've got to. Look, my parents aren't well."

"I'll come back with you. We can talk on the way. I'll help you look after them." She caught at his shoulder as he tried to run upstairs. "Please, Mike. I'll feel bad if you just leave me. We can catch the last bus in five minutes if we run. It'll be quicker than your bike."

God! She was worse than his father! "Listen," he snarled, having clambered to street level. "It isn't ill, they aren't ill," he said, letting words tumble wildly as he tried to flee. "I've found out what they do at night. They're witches."

"Oh no!" She sounded shocked but delighted.

"My mother's terrified. My father's been drugging her." Now that he was able to say so, his urgency diminished a little; he wanted to release all he knew. "Something's going to happen tonight," he said.

"Are you going to try and stop it? Let me come too. I know about it. I showed you my book." When he looked doubtful she said "They'll have to stop when they see me."

Perhaps she could look after his mother while he confronted his father. They ran to the bus, which sat unlit in the square for minutes, then dawdled along the country roads, hoping for passengers who never appeared. Michael's frustration coiled tighter again. He explained to June what he'd discovered: "Yeah," she kept saying, excited and fascinated. Once she began giggling uncontrollably. "Wouldn't it be weird if we saw your father dancing naked?" He stared at her until she said "Sorry." Her pupils were expanding and contracting slightly, randomly.

As they ran along the Pine Dunes road the trees leaned closer, creaking and nodding. Suppose his parents hadn't left the caravan yet? What could he say? He'd be tongue-tied again by his unsureness, and June would probably make things worse. He gasped with relief when he saw that the windows were dark, but went inside to make sure. "I know where they've gone," he told June.

Moonlight and unbroken cloud spread the sky with dim milk; dark smoky breaths drifted across the glow. He heard the incessant restlessness of the sea. Bare black silhouettes crowded beside the road, thinly intricate against the sky. He hurried June towards the path.

Why should his parents have gone that way? Something told him they had—perhaps the maze he remembered, the tunnel of undergrowth: that was a secret place. The path wound deeper into the woods, glinting faintly; trees rapidly shuttered the glow of the moon. "Isn't this fantastic," June said, hurrying behind him.

The pines gave out, but other trees meshed thickly overhead. The glimpses of flat whitish sky, smouldering with darker cloud, dwindled. In the forest everything was black or blanched, and looked chill, although the night was unseasonably mild.

Webs of shadow lay on the path, tangling Michael's feet; tough grass seized him. Bushes massed around him, towering, choking the gaps between trees. The glimpses of sky were fewer and smaller. "What's that?" June said uneasily.

For a moment he thought it was the sound of someone's foot, unplugging itself from the soft ground: it sounded like a loud slow gulp of mud. But no, it wasn't that. Someone coughing? It didn't sound much like a human cough. Moreover, it sounded as though it were straining to produce a sound, a single sound; and he felt inexplicably that he ought to know what that was.

The bushes stirred, rattling. The muddy sound faded, somewhere ahead. There was no point in telling June his vague thoughts. "It'll be an animal," he said. "Probably something's caught it."

Soon they reached the tunnel. He knelt at once and began to crawl. Twigs scraped beside his ears, a clawed dry chorus. He found the experience less disturbing now, less oppressive; the tunnel seemed wider, as though someone stout had recently pushed his way through. Behind him June was breathing heavily, and her voice fluttered in the dark. "There's something following us outside the tunnel," she said tightly, nervously.

He crawled quickly to the end and stood up. "There's nothing here now. It must have been an animal."

He felt odd: calm, safe, yet slyly and elusively excited. His eyes had grown equal to the dark. The trees were stouter, and even closer; they squeezed out masses of shrub between them. Overhead, a few pale scraps of sky were caught in branches. The ground squelched underfoot, and he heard another sound ahead: similar, but not the same.

June emerged panting. "I thought I'd finished tripping. Where are we going?" she said unevenly. "I can't see."

"This way." He headed at once for a low opening in the tangled growth. As he'd somehow expected, the passage twisted several times, closing almost impenetrably, then widened. Perhaps he'd noticed that someone before him had thrust the bushes apart.

"Don't go so fast," June said in the dark, almost weeping. "Wait for me."

Her slowness annoyed him. His indefinable excitement seemed to affect his skin, which crawled with nervousness like interference on the surface of a bubble. Yet he felt strangely powerful, ready for anything. Wait until he saw his father! He stood impatiently, stamping the mushy ground, while June caught up with him. She gripped his arm. "There it is again," she gasped.

"What?" The sound? It was only his feet, squelching. But there was another sound, ahead in the tangled creaking dark. It was the gurgling of mud, perhaps of a muddy stream gargling ceaselessly into the earth. No: it was growing louder, more violent, as though the mud were straining to spew out an obstruction. The sound was repeated, again and again, becoming gradually clearer: a single syllable. All at once he knew what it was. Somewhere ahead in the close dark maze, a thick muddy voice was struggling to shout his name.

June had recognised the sound too, and was tugging at his arm. "Let's go back," she pleaded. "I don't like it. Please."

"God," he scoffed. "I thought you were going to help me." The muddy sounds blurred into a mumble, and were gone. Twigs shook in the oppressive dark, squeaking hollowly together. Suddenly, ahead of him, he heard his father's voice; then, after a long silence, his mother's. Both were oddly strained and muffled. As though this were a game of hide and seek, each had called his name.

"There," he said to June. "I haven't got time to take you back now." His excitement was mounting, his nervous skin felt light as a dream. "Don't you want to look after my mother?" he blurted.

He shouldered onwards. After a while he heard June following him timidly. A wind blundered through the forest, dragging at the bushes. Thorns struggled overhead, clawing at the air; the ground gulped his feet, sounding to his strained ears almost like words. Twice the walls of the passage tried to close, but someone had broken them apart. Ahead the passage broadened. He was approaching an open space.

He began to run. Bushes applauded like joyful bones. The thick smoky sky rushed on, fighting the moonlight. The vociferous ground was slippery; he stumbled as he ran, and almost tripped over a dark huddle. It was his parents' clothes. Some of them, as he glanced back impatiently, looked torn. He heard June fall slithering against bushes. "Don't!" she cried. But he had reached the space.

It was enclosed by trees. Ivy thickened the trunks, and had climbed to mat the tangle overhead; bushes crowded the cramped gaps between the trees. In the interstices of the tangle, dark sky smouldered.

Slowly his eyes found the meagre light; outlines gathered in the clearing, dimmer than mist. Bared wooden limbs groped into the space, creaking. The dimness sketched them. He could see now that the clearing was about thirty feet wide, and roughly circular. Dimness crawled on it, as though it were an infested pond. At the far side, a dark bulk stood between him and the trees.

He squinted painfully, but its shape persisted in eluding him. Was it very large, or was the dark lying? Across the clearing mud coughed and gurgled thickly, or something did. Dimness massed on the glistening shape. Suddenly he saw that the shape was moving lethargically, and alive.

June had hung back; now she ran forward, only to slip at the edge of the clearing. She clutched his arm to steady herself, and then she gazed beyond him, trembling. "What is it?" she cried.

"Shut up," he said savagely.

Apart from her interruption, he felt more calm than he had ever felt before. He knew he was gazing at the source of his dreams. The dreams returned peacefully to his mind and waited to be understood. For a moment he wondered whether this was like June's LSD. Something had been added to his mind, which seemed to be expanding awesomely. Memories floated free, as though they had been coded deep in him: wombs of stone and submarine depths; hovering in a medium that wasn't space, somehow linked to a stone circle on a hill; being drawn closer to the circle, towards terrified faces that stared up through the night; a pregnant woman held writhing at the centre of the circle, screaming as he hovered closer and reached for her. He felt primed with centuries of memories. Inherited memories, or shared; but whose?

He waited. All was about to be clarified. The huge bulk shifted, glistening. Its voice, uncontrollably loud and uneven, struggled muddily to speak. The trees creaked ponderously, the squashed bushes writhed, the sky fled incessantly. Suddenly, touched by an instinct he couldn't define, Michael realised how he and June must look from the far side of the clearing. He took her arm, though she struggled briefly, and they stood waiting: bride and bridegroom of the dark.

After a long muddy convulsion in the dimness, words coughed free. The voice seemed unable to speak more than a phrase at a time; then it would blur, gurgling. Sometimes his father's voice, and occasionally his mother's—high-pitched, trembling—seemed to help. Yet the effect was disturbing, for it sounded as though the muddy voice were attempting muffled imitations of his parents. He held himself calm, trusting that this too would be clarified in due course.

The Great Old Ones   still lived, the halting voice gurgled loudly. Their dreams   could reach out. When the human race was young and strayed near the Old Ones   the dreams could reach   into the womb and make   the unborn in their image. Something like his mother's voice spoke the last words, wavering fearfully. June struggled, but he gripped her arm.

Though the words were veiled and allusive, he understood instinctively what was being said. His new memories were ready to explain. When he read the notebooks again he would understand consciously. He listened and gazed, fascinated. He was in awe of the size of the speaking bulk. And what was strange about the head? Something moved there, rapid as the whirl of colours on a bubble. In the dark the face seemed to strain epileptically, perhaps to form words.

The Old Ones   could wait, the voice or voices told him. The stars would   come right. The people the Old Ones   touched before birth   did not take on their image   all at once but gradually, down   the centuries. Instead of dying,   they took on the form that the Old Ones had placed in the womb   of an ancestor. Each generation came closer to the perfect image.

The bulk glistened as though flayed; in the dimness it looked pale pink, and oddly unstable. Michael stared uneasily at the head. Swift clouds dragged darknesses over the clearing and snatched them away. The face looked so huge, and seemed to spread. Wasn't it like his father's face? But the eyes were swimming apart, the features slid uncontrollably across the head. All this was nothing but the antics of shadows. A tear in the clouds crept toward the dimmed moon. June was trying to pull away. "Keep still," he snarled, tightening his grip.

They would serve   the Old Ones, the voice shouted thickly, faltering. That was why they   had been made: to be   ready when the time came. They   shared the memories of the   Old Ones and at the change   their bodies were transformed   into the stuff of the Old Ones. They mated   with ordinary people in the human   way, and later in the way   the Old Ones had   decreed.   That way was...June screamed. The tear in the clouds had unveiled the moon. Her cry seemed harsh enough to tear her throat. He turned furiously to silence her; but she dragged herself free, eyes gaping, and fled down the path. The shadow of a cloud rushed towards the clearing. About to pursue June, he turned to see what the moon had revealed.

The shadow reached the clearing as he turned. For a moment he saw the huge head, a swollen bulb which, though blanched by moonlight, reminded him of a mass dug from within a body. The glistening lumpy forehead was almost bare, except for a few strands that groped restlessly over it—strands of hair, surely, though they looked like strings of livid flesh. On the head, seeming even smaller amid the width of flesh, he saw his mother's face. It was appallingly dwarfed, and terrified. The strands flickered over it, faster, faster. Her mouth strained wordlessly, gurgling.

Before he could see the rest of the figure, a vague gigantic squatting sack, the shadow flooded the clearing. As it did so, he thought he saw his mother's face sucked into the head, as though by a whirlpool of flesh. Did her features float up again, newly arranged? Were there other, plumper, features jostling among them? He could be sure of nothing in the dark.

June cried out. She'd stumbled; he heard her fall, and the thud of her head against something: then silence. The figure was lumbering towards him, its bulk quaking. For a moment he was sure that it intended to embrace him. But it had reached a pit, almost concealed by undergrowth. It slid into the earth, like slow jelly. The undergrowth sprang back rustling.

He stood gazing at June, who was still unconscious. He knew what he would tell her: she had had a bad LSD experience, that had been what she'd seen. LSD reminded him of something. Slowly he began to smile.

He went to the pit and peered down. Faint sluggish muddy sounds retreated deep into the earth. He knew he wouldn't see his parents for a long time. He touched his pocket, where the envelope waited. That would contain his father's explanation of their disappearance, which he could show to people, to June.

Moonlight and shadows raced nervously over the pit. As he stared at the dark mouth he felt full of awe, yet calm. Now he must wait until it was time to come back here, to go into the earth and join the others. He remembered that now; he had always known, deep in himself, that this was home. One day he and June would return. He gazed at her unconscious body, smiling. Perhaps she had been right; they might take LSD together, when it was time. It might help them to become one.

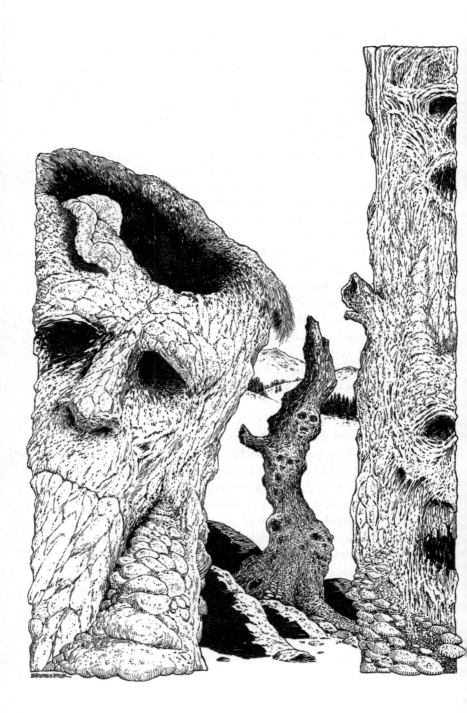

BLACKED OUT

ONCE OUT OF THE MUNICH TRAFFIC, LAMB DROVE leisurely. Painted giants, elaborate and luminous as frescoes, adorned the walls of houses, which looked as though you had only to lift their roofs to make them chime. Flowers blazed on a multitude of balconies. Between villages cows wandered, gently jangling with bells, in fields near barns. August sunlight glided over chalky lakes. Here and there he glimpsed crucifixes in wayside shrines like wooden alcoves on stalks.

He'd neglected to buy a road map. He ought to buy one before dark, at the latest. But he was enchanted with Bavaria. Occasionally, outside houses, he saw tree-stumps or even entire trunks carved with grotesque faces. Sometimes they bunched together like a knot of gnarled and incomplete old men, grimacing at him. He drove by, smiling.

While the landscape around Munich had been absolutely flat, mountains were rising now. They bristled with pines. Gazing ahead, he distinguished layer on layer of peaks, which grew paler with mist and distance. Were the furthest shapes mountains or clouds? In squinting to be certain, he passed the signpost. When he failed to make it out by craning he had to creep irritably back to it in reverse.

Yes, something was odd. The direction in which he had be heading was erased by a slash of black paint. A warning or vandalism? The pointer to the side road indicated Munich. He didn't want to backtrack if it could be avoided. Besides, there was a church ahead: he could see the tip of its spire, a pointed onion which glinted green, beyond a rise. Surely the road was safe.

As he neared the church, the priest came out to meet him. At least, that was how it looked; certainly the man appeared to be gesturing to him—though Lamb found it difficult to be sure, for the light of late afternoon which barred the road with the shadow of the spire also submerged the porch in dimness. The approach of twilight had taken Lamb unawares; it seemed at least an hour earlier than in England. British Summer Time must be the explanation—and of course the days were dwindling. Was the priest beckoning, or gesturing him away?

Before Lamb could tell, the priest was engulfed by his congregation. Movements in the dim porch developed into people, who emerged and stood outside the church: a man like a barrel for the beer that rouged his face, which drooped as though melting in the sullen heat; a thin man whose hands clambered incessantly over each other, spider-like; a young buxom blonde. Of the gazes which fastened on Lamb, and which multiplied as more of the worshippers emerged, only hers was timid. Lamb felt absurd; the priest had withdrawn into the church; the dawdling car panted fumes at the watchers. He drove on.

As it occurred to him that the congregation must come from somewhere nearby, he glimpsed the village. Its lights—or, considering the time of day, more likely reflections of sunlight on windows—gleamed through trees at the foot of the hill. Perhaps he could stay in the village, and gain experience of making himself understood.

Outside the village, horned heads stared over a gate at him. Their eyes were stagnant, but their jaws shifted, chewing. Why did the eyes look ringed by mascara? He wound down the window in order to lean out; then, faintly dismayed, he accelerated into the village. The eye-sockets were crawling with flies.

He had in fact glimpsed lights. All along the narrow clean street they hovered, pale but steady, in their globes. Perhaps a fault refused to let them be extinguished. They were dazzled not only by the daylight but by flowers which crowded the verges of lawns and swarmed on tiers of wooden balconies. Scents roamed the streets.

The village felt oddly artificial, dream-like: an exhibit constructed for tourists. Only when he had halted the car and was searching his phrasebook for aid—'Helfen Sie mir, bitte' meant 'Help me, please,' which seemed an excessively melodramatic way to ask for directions—did he realise what was odd: the street was deserted. Every window was brightly blank; flowers alone leaned out from the balconies. Nothing moved, for even the lawns were weighed down by the hot still air.

All at once the stillness was unnerving. Light clung to the village as though paralysed by the heat. The place seemed too perfect, its cleanliness oppressive. The rustling of pages was close and nerve-racking—besides being pointless: it looked as though he wouldn't need phrases. He stowed the book beneath the dashboard and drove on.

The Gasthaus sign halted him. He understood that word without referring to the book. He couldn't afford to drive past the chance of a meal and a room. Ahead there might be only ski resorts, their hotels full. With its balconies that made it resemble a chest of ajar drawers, the building seemed too attractive to pass.

But it was empty. Heat lent the emptiness a presence which swallowed the ring of the bell on the counter, like fog. The low beams troubled him; he felt caged by dark wood. The bright lights only made them more solid and heavy. He couldn't bring himself to call "Anyone here?"—even assuming he might be understood. He hurried back to the car.

Houses sailed by. The sense of unreality intensified; had he allowed his concentration to falter, he might have imagined himself to be coasting through a dream of a model village grown man-size. Still, he had almost reached the end. The road curved, to reveal a house whose windows were crowded with large unlit candles. Presumably it was a candlemaker's, though there was no sign. Beyond it, at the limit of the village, stood a small church.

What kind of church might belong to so silent a village? Though his curiosity was not altogether enjoyable, he left the car. On some of the graves which surrounded the church, candles flickered within glass, in the Bavarian tradition. He climbed the path, which was uneven and pitted as a bad road, and pushed open the door beneath the pointed arch. There he halted, taken aback.

Once, to judge by the onion spire, this had been a typical Bavarian church. What remained of the frescoes—a spotless feathered wing here, there the tatters of a face and its halo—suggested that it had been worth admiring. But only these fragments clung to the scaling walls, and most of the roof was gone. Pews leaned against one another for support; they looked merged by their crust of fallen plaster. The inner door lay within the porch, splintered into several pieces.

That door looked more recent than the building. What had broken it outwards? A stray, perhaps dormant, bomb? Momentarily Lamb suffered a twinge of vague historical guilt. Systematic desecration could not have ruined the church more thoroughly, nor have made it feel less like a church.

Late afternoon light seeped through the grimy windows. Once that light must have ignited a gilded altar. Now it groped over flakes and wounds of raw plaster. As clouds chased across the sun, the tattered discoloured patch of wall appeared to writhe stealthily, to crawl.

Where the altar had stood was a jagged hole in stone. If what Lamb could hear was plaster sifting over the edge, disturbed presumably by his entering the church, then the hole sounded deep as a pit. He didn't intend to check. The floor might well be unsafe, and the church must certainly be damp, for its chill had reached him; he suppressed a shiver. There was a stench of mould—of something growing, anyway.

He ought to be moving on, to make sure of accommodation before dark. Or should he head back a few miles, to that hotel overlooking the lake? He was still hesitating within the porch when he heard footsteps behind him.

For a moment, as he turned, the waking dream of the village toppled into nightmare. He knew all the several faces in the street; yet equally he knew he had met none of them. Then everything fitted together. He'd seen them emerging from the previous church. That was why the village had been deserted. Even the superfluous lighting of the streets seemed explained, just as you might leave lights burning while you went out of the house for a few minutes, to show you would return shortly. Of course that was nonsense, but its absurdity expressed his surge of relief. And mightn't there be someone in the Gasthaus now? As he hurried past the nervous flames to his car, he saw the thin man with the restless hands entering the candle-maker's. Perhaps those hands were calmed by making candles.

What else could the barrel-shaped man have been except the innkeeper? Yes, he could give Lamb *ein Zimmer* for the night. His spaniel jowls drooped beneath the dark beams; the lights made his face vivid as an elaborately melted candle. He seemed morosely preoccupied, and hardly interested in Lamb. Was he distracted by the heat? But as Lamb hefted his suitcase upstairs, he caught the man gazing sidelong at him. Perhaps he was too proud to welcome Lamb openly. To judge by the silence of the Gasthaus, Lamb might be the only guest.

In that case he ought to refuse the room. When he arrived, having panted up three flights of steep dark wood, he found that it was cramped beneath the eaves. At least the window in the slanting wall was low enough for him to look down on the street. He wondered where the shapely blonde might be. In a fit of resentful frustration, he took from his case the magazines he'd bought in Munich. Weren't they the next best thing? But the explicit photographs seemed clinical rather than erotic. They succeeded only in making him feel alone at the top of the house. Abruptly he strode downstairs to demand another room.

He couldn't make himself understood. The phrasebook allowed him to say "No, I don't like it"—but not to name his dislike. "Es ist zu—" Cold/hot/dark/small/noisy? He couldn't find the words for "lonely" or "misshapen" or "depressing", even assuming that he could have made himself say such things. The small dim preoccupied eyes watched him from beneath the dark beams with a spaniel's glum patience. At last Lamb desisted, feeling stupid and inept, and turned aside into the restaurant.

The waitress seemed aloof, almost loath to serve him. If only she had been the blonde! Was he expected to buy a meal to justify his beer? Too bad; he didn't intend to eat dinner too early—he would have little else to use up his evening, except a stroll afterwards. He emptied his stein quickly, for the restaurant was too bright, hostile to the vague gloomy haze of beer he craved. Hardly a corner was left alone with its shadows.

Perhaps his room was preferable, at least for a while. He could lock himself in with the magazines—though however he restrained himself, they would occupy too little time. His shadow humped like a segmented larva over the stairs before him; it looked alone amid the brightness. The upper reaches of the building sounded hollow. But as he reached the top landing, the door of his room opened. As he faltered, one foot dangling, the blonde emerged.

His emotions collided and almost overbalanced him: delight,

embarrassment, disbelief, suspicion. He pretended that his gasp had
been a prelude to a cough. What had she been doing in his room?
Her sidelong glance at him seemed less timid than slyly enticing, for
she smiled.

Whether or not that was meant to attract him, it allowed him to
stride forward. As she stood aside in the narrow passage, the strong
light rendered all of her intensely vivid: her large firm breasts, her
wide blue eyes, her skin that looked both sculpted and tanned, her
gradual shy smile. What were her eyes telling him? Before he could
judge, she was heading for the stairs. Was she swaying her round
bottom beneath the tight black uniform just for him?

Of course, she was a chambermaid. Anything beyond that was a
fantasy. He saw that as soon as he glimpsed the towel draped over
the end of his bed. But he had hardly stepped into the room when
he and his thoughts froze. His magazines, which he had left closed
on the floor, lay side by side on the bed, and open.

How dare she pry! What he read was his business! By God, if he
caught her he would—Suddenly he realised how carefully the magazines were arranged on the bed, open to the most explicit pages. At
once he realised what her smile and her gaze had meant to tell him.

By the time he'd hurried out onto the landing, the staircase was
empty, even of shadows. Nor could he hear her. He must be meant
to wait. He lay on his bed and dreamed of her—or tried to, but the
harsh light kept interrupting. Where on earth was the switch? Not
in the room, apparently. He could unscrew the light, except that the
junction of bulb and socket was bandaged with insulating tape.
Perhaps it was unsafe. No doubt the girl would know how to switch
out the light—supposing that he had any time for sleep.

He lay with her on the bed. Darkness and their warmth cradled
them. It took her footsteps in the street to start him from his dream
of her. He stumbled to the window. The sky was muddy with
clouds; the street, perhaps by contrast, looked even brighter. Yes, it
was the blonde whose footsteps he'd heard. She was talking to the
thin man with the scrambling hands.

Lamb tried to open the window stealthily, in the hope of hearing
words which he could understand. But the window rattled in its
frame, and the man looked up. His face seemed to pinch into an
expression of puritanical contempt, though at that distance Lamb
could well have been mistaken. He turned curtly to the girl, and
Lamb heard their discussion, incomprehensible save for one reas-

suring word: she called the man 'father'. All seemed well, and could hardly have been better, for as she hurried after her father the girl glanced up at Lamb and, unmistakably, smiled.

So there was to be a plot between her and Lamb. If she was going home to cook her father's dinner, then Lamb had best eat now. Yet this strategy was so rooted in the banal that it made him hesitate. Could all this really be happening? Was he making a fool of himself? At the same time, the day's adventures seemed to promise further surprises. He felt as though not knowing where he was, not even the name of the town, freed him to explore new possibilities.

Still, in the restaurant the unreality grew threatening. Beneath the multitude of lights, faces surrounded him, clinically detailed. He recognised every one, but understood not a word of their chatter. Under the circumstances, it seemed just as well that nobody sat at his table or spoke to him. But that left him alone with a mounting paranoia: how many of them knew about him and the girl? Some of them kept glancing at him as they talked; most of them seemed nervously restless, no doubt because of the heat.

Of course he must simply be imposing his own doubts on them. He ate dinner, a rich unfamiliar spiced meat. It was surely not what he had ordered, but it gave him no other cause to complain. He would have liked to savour it, but felt that he ought not to dawdle here; the girl was unlikely to come to him except in his room.

He was glad to retreat upstairs, even to the dwarf room. Above the naked bulb a blazing patch hovered on the canted ceiling, which looked prepared to descend on him. He wished he had complained that the room was too small—but he mustn't change his room now.

He lay waiting. Night gathered in the window; the brightness of the village made it look more like fog. How long had he been waiting? It was impossible to tell; his watch had stopped—it must have done so during the meal. Had the girl's father forbidden her to meet him? Surely she couldn't have discussed the plan, surely that hadn't been the reason for the man's hostile glare, the glances of the diners. Lamb's loneliness was talking nonsense. Just relax, don't nag at the dream, just let things happen. He drifted through clumps of grimacing faces; their eyes were unequal knotholes. Before he could reach the church beyond their branches, darkness swallowed him. He woke, and saw that the door of his room was open.

Had she visited him and been afraid to wake him? He stumbled to the window. The street was theatrically bright, and quite empty.

His mouth tasted sour with awakening and with disappointment. Had he been tricked, or had he tricked himself? As much to waken himself thoroughly as in any hope, he trudged onto the landing. Movement made him peer down, and the girl turned at the foot of the staircase to smile timidly at him.

At once she slipped out of sight. She must be leaving the inn. Fumbling in his pocket to make sure he had the key, Lamb slammed the door and hurried down. Dark wood thundered beneath him. Good God, he sounded like a stampede all by himself. She could hardly want to attract attention.

Had his noise scared her off? The street looked clean as bone, cleared even of shadows. It looked like a dream of perfection, in which his car outside the Gasthaus provided incongruity. Had her face at the foot of the stairs been the remnant of a dream? No, for he glimpsed her black dress vanishing beyond the curve of the street.

He strode in pursuit, not yet wondering where she meant to lead him. The heat and the lingering numbness of sleep closed him into himself, dulled his thoughts; he felt feverish. She seemed to have chosen her time well, for the street remained deserted, though here and there another window lit up. Of course she would know when the villagers would be occupied in their houses or in the Gasthaus.

The street was too short to give him time for many doubts. But the silence, the isolation of his steps and hers, seemed dauntingly unreal, as though he had been lured into miming a sexual chase. Scents wafted at him, enticing him onwards. He quickened his pace, frustrated that the curve blocked his view of her. He heard her pace increase too. She was nearly at her father's house.

Was her father away from home—or was he expecting them both? Lamb wasn't about to perform for an audience. Adventure was one thing, perversion which he didn't enjoy quite another. But as he rounded the curve he saw her clearly. Passing the house without a glance, she marched stiffly towards the church.

Apparently she meant to lead him into the fields. That had a certain primitive appeal, but was hardly alluring. He had no time to reflect, for the church had seized his attention. Was the building on fire?

Venturing forward, he saw the flames. He had the impression that they numbered thousands; their glass jars stood not only on the graves but on the paths between. The entire churchyard blazed with a multitude of candles.

The restless light made the church appear to stir on its foundations. Had someone propped a tree-trunk in the porch? The glimpse must be a trick of the light, for momentarily he thought that the object was carved with a writhing face as long and thin as the doorway. When he squinted, his eyes only grew more dazzled, unable to make out the interior of the porch.

Nor could he distinguish the girl at first. As he peered into the dark beyond the village, a stench came welling up from somewhere. Was it fertiliser, or over-ripe crops? Good Lord, how long did they leave things to rot? If the girl had gone into that dark, he was no longer so anxious to follow her.

Then he saw her. She was stealing along the outer edge of the churchyard. Only the fluttering oval of her face was visible above the dance of the railings; her clothes merged with the dark. Still, there was enough light on her path to make him feel safe.

When he trod on the path, it stirred sluggishly beneath its pelt of grass. He spent time gingerly ensuring that it was firm enough. Along the railings he heard the clash of a metal gate, and a quick rattling. The girl was out of sight now. Good Lord, what was he dawdling for? He ran past the dazzling graveyard, to the end of the railing. There was the gate, and beyond it a narrow path between hedges—but the gate was chained and padlocked.

So she was a teaser, was she? Before his anger could gather momentum it subsided, cowed. Something more was wrong than sexual trickery, though he couldn't yet tell how he knew. What was troubling him? The sharp points on the railings and on the gate, which imprisoned him in the dark? The bright street locked into itself? The desertion? By the church, something moved.

His hand clenched convulsively on a railing. Then he relaxed a little. The movement had only been a leap of darkness: a few adjacent candles, closest to the porch, had gone out. But before he had time to look away, the next flames were engulfed.

That was the only word. It was as though a shadow had fallen on them, a shadow composed of mud: he saw the flames sputter, shrink, die. Above them, at the edge of his dazzled vision, a shape tall as the doorway seemed to lean out of the porch. The stench of growth or decay flooded over Lamb, choking him. He remembered the smell of the church. A clammy chill, like the cold he had felt in the church, reached for him and set his body trembling.

When the third rank of candles was doused, he ran. Before he reached the churchyard gate, the stain of darkness had spread across half the graves. Was a shape advancing beyond the dazzle? He moaned, though air had to struggle through his constricted throat to his shaking lips, and ran.

All seemed inevitable as a nightmare. Everything was planned. He was hardly surprised to see, as he ran stumbling into the village, that every window was lit. The blaze showed him the girl in the act of retreating into her father's house.

Perhaps she had been forced to entice him. Might she shelter him now? Please, for God's sake, let her help—for behind him the entire graveyard was dark. He might not have time to reach his car, if the lights of the village failed to protect him. The stench rushed at him, the chill embraced him. The silence of the graveyard seemed altogether dreadful. He staggered towards her. 'Help me,' he cried.

She turned in the doorway. Her face was unreadable, though certainly not timid. "Helfen Sie mir," he managed to pronounce. It sounded absolutely unconvincing, and absurd. "Bitte!" he cried. "Bitte!" The sound chattered in his mouth, and would have seemed comic if its unimpressiveness had not been terrifying.

All at once Lamb saw that behind the girl stood her father. Avoiding Lamb's gaze, she reached back and grabbed—Lamb flinched away, but it wasn't a weapon, only a wide pan and a wooden spoon. At once she began to clatter them together. Still unable to look at Lamb, she kicked the door shut in his face. As though her noise had been a signal—which no doubt it was—the locked houses came alive with an uproar of utensils.

The row was deafening. It tumbled his thoughts in disarray. He couldn't plan, only run wildly as he realised that the street had dimmed behind him. The first lamps had been swallowed. The violent clamour must be meant to keep the pursuit away from the houses, in the middle of the street—Lamb and the other.

He ran, moaning desperately to himself. His chest felt raw, unable to grasp breath. His ankles gave way, pierced with pain, and tried to throw him headlong. How short the street had appeared before! The metal uproar drove him onwards, mindlessly terrified.

When he came in sight of the Gasthaus and saw that his car was gone, he cried out inarticulately. He stumbled to the Gasthaus door, though he knew it would be locked, and pounded on it, sobbing. From the edge of his eye he glimpsed darkness flooding the street. The clattering urged it towards him.

As his fist thumped the door, no longer in the hope of entry but because the whole of his arm was shivering, he saw a glow ahead, beyond the village. It was pale, and looked gnawed. He limped in that direction, for there was nowhere else to go. Then he realised that it was moonlight rising over mountains. The gnawing was silhouettes of pines.

Surely nothing could douse that light. He forced himself to run, rasping air into his lungs. But at the edge of the village he faltered. There were several hundred yards to run through darkness before he reached the crest of the road, where the glow might be waiting for him. But—he squinted from the edge of the light of the village, not daring yet to risk the dark—the crest was not deserted. A car was parked there, which must be his.

Perhaps he had a chance. He sucked air into his lungs until they throbbed—then, with a gasp of pure panic, he drove himself forward, into the dark. Behind him the village dimmed to an ember, and went out.

There was only the distant toothed glow. But almost at once the village sprang alight, and the metal clamour dwindled jaggedly into silence. At once he knew that whatever had emerged from the broken church was out here in the dark with him, barring him from the village.

In any case, the insidious chill and the advancing stench would have told him so. Why had the villagers pushed his car to the hill? In case he managed to reach the Gasthaus or in order to lure him onwards? He wished that the silence had not allowed these thoughts to form. He ran, trying to stumble faster and to deafen himself and his thoughts with his panting—for behind him in the dark he could hear a leisurely creaking which could be both the sound of limbs and, worse, a kind of laughter.

BROECKER

The Voice of the Beach

I

I MET NEAL AT THE STATION.
Of course I can describe it, I have only to go up the road and look, but there is no need. That isn't what I have to get out of me. It isn't me, it's out there, it can be described. I need all my energy for that, all my concentration, but perhaps it will help if I can remember before that, when everything looked manageable, expressible, familiar enough—when I could bear to look out of the window.

Neal was standing alone on the small platform, and now I see that I dare not go up the road after all, or out of the house. It doesn't matter, my memories are clear, they will help me hold on. Neal must have rebuffed the station-master, who was happy to chat to anyone. He was gazing at the bare tracks, sharpened by June light, as they cut their way through the forest—gazing at them as a suicide might gaze at a razor. He saw me and swept his hair back from his face, over his shoulders. Suffering had pared his face down, stretched the skin tighter and paler over the skull. I can remember exactly how he looked before

"I thought I'd missed the station," he said, though surely the station's name was visible enough, despite the flowers that scaled the board. If only he had! "I had to make so many changes. Never mind. Christ, it's good to see you. You look marvellous. I expect you can

149

thank the sea for that." His eyes had brightened, and he sounded so full of life that it was spilling out of him in a tumble of words, but his handshake felt like cold bone.

I hurried him along the road that led home and to the He was beginning to screw up his eyes at the sunlight, and I thought I should get him inside; presumably headaches were among his symptoms. At first the road is gravel, fragments of which always succeed in working their way into your shoes. Where the trees fade out as though stifled by sand, a concrete path turns aside. Sand sifts over the gravel; you can hear the gritty conflict underfoot, and the musing of the sea. Beyond the path stands this crescent of bungalows. Surely all this is still true. But I remember now that the bungalows looked unreal against the burning blue sky and the dunes like embryo hills; they looked like a dream set down in the piercing light of June.

"You must be doing well to afford this." Neal sounded listless, envious only because he felt it was expected. If only he had stayed that way! But once inside the bungalow he seemed pleased by every-thing—the view, my books on show in the living-room bookcase, my typewriter displaying a token page that bore a token phrase, the Breughel prints that used to remind me of humanity. Abruptly, with a moody eagerness that I hardly remarked at the time, he said "Shall we have a look at the beach?"

There, I've written the word. I can describe the beach, I must describe it, it is all that's in my head. I have my notebook which I took with me that day. Neal led the way along the gravel path. Beyond the concrete turn-off to the bungalows the gravel was engulfed almost at once by sand, despite the thick ranks of low bushes that had been planted to keep back the sand. We squeezed between the bushes, which were determined to close their ranks across the gravel.

Once through, we felt the breeze whose waves passed through the marram grass that spiked the dunes. Neal's hair streamed back, pale as the grass. The trudged dunes were slowing him down, eager as he was. We slithered down to the beach, and the sound of the unfurling sea leapt closer, as though we'd awakened it from dreaming. The wind fluttered trapped in my ears, leafed through my notebook as I scribbled the image of wakening and thought with an appalling inno-cence: perhaps I can use that image. Now we were walled off from the rest of the world by the dunes, faceless mounds with unkempt green wigs, mounds almost as white as the sun.

Even then I felt that the beach was somehow separate from its surroundings: introverted, I remember thinking. I put it down to the shifting haze which hovered above the sea, the haze which I could never focus, whose distance I could never quite judge. From the self-contained stage of the beach the bungalows looked absurdly intrusive, anachronisms rejected by the geomorphological time of sand and sea. Even the skeletal car and the other debris, half engulfed by the beach near the coast road, looked less alien. These are my memories, the most stable things left to me, and I must go on. I found today that I cannot go back any further.

Neal was staring, eyes narrowed against the glare, along the waste of beach that stretched in the opposite direction from the coast road and curved out of sight. "Doesn't anyone come down here? There's no pollution, is there?"

"It depends on who you believe." Often the beach seemed to give me a headache, even when there was no glare—and then there was the way the beach looked at night. "Still, I think most folk go up the coast to the resorts. That's the only reason I can think of."

We were walking. Beside us the edge of the glittering sea moved in several directions simultaneously. Moist sand, sleek as satin, displayed shells which appeared to flash patterns, faster than my mind could grasp. Pinpoint mirrors of sand gleamed, rapid as Morse. My notes say this is how it seemed.

"Don't your neighbours ever come down?"

Neal's voice made me start. I had been engrossed in the designs of shell and sand. Momentarily I was unable to judge the width of the beach: a few paces, or miles? I grasped my sense of perspective, but a headache was starting, a dull impalpable grip that encircled my cranium. Now I know what all this meant, but I want to remember how I felt before I knew.

"Very seldom," I said. "Some of them think there's quicksand." One old lady, sitting in her garden to glare at the dunes like Canute versus sand, had told me that warning notices kept sinking. I'd never encountered quicksand, but I always brought my stick to help me trudge.

"So I'll have the beach to myself."

I took that to be a hint. At least he would leave me alone if I wanted to work. "The bungalow people are mostly retired," I said. "Those who aren't in wheelchairs go driving. I imagine they've had enough of sand, even if they aren't past walking on it." Once, further up the beach, I'd encountered nudists censoring themselves with towels or straw hats as they ventured down to the sea, but Neal could find out about them for himself. I wonder now if I ever saw them at all, or simply felt that I should.

Was he listening? His head was cocked, but not towards me. He'd slowed, and was staring at the ridges and furrows of the beach, at which the sea was lapping. All at once the ridges reminded me of convolutions of the brain, and I took out my notebook as the grip on my skull tightened. The beach as a subconscious, my notes say: the horizon as the imagination—sunlight set a ship ablaze on the edge of the world, an image that impressed me as vividly yet indefinably symbolic—the debris as memories, half-buried, half-comprehensible. But then what were the bungalows, perched above the dunes like boxes carved of dazzling bone?

I glanced up. A cloud had leaned towards me. No, it had been more as though the cloud were rushing at the beach from the horizon, dauntingly fast. Had it been a cloud? It had seemed more massive than a ship. The sky was empty now, and I told myself that it had been an effect of the haze— the magnified shadow of a gull, perhaps.

My start had enlivened Neal, who began to chatter like a television wakened by a kick. "It'll be good for me to be alone here, to get used to being alone. Mary and the children found themselves another home, you see. He earns more money than I'll ever see, if that's what they want. He's the head of the house type, if that's what they want. I couldn't be that now if I tried, not with the way my nerves are now." I can still hear everything he said, and I suppose that I knew what had been wrong with him. Now they are just words.

"That's why I'm talking so much," he said, and picked up a spiral shell, I thought to quiet himself.

"That's much too small. You'll never hear anything in that."

Minutes passed before he took it away from his ear and handed it to me. "No?" he said.

I put it to my ear and wasn't sure what I was hearing. No, I didn't throw the shell away, I didn't crush it underfoot; in any case, how could I have done that to the rest of the beach? I was straining to hear, straining to make out how the sound differed from the usual whisper of a shell. Was that it seemed to have a rhythm that I couldn't define, or that it sounded shrunken by distance rather than cramped by the shell? I felt expectant, entranced—precisely the feeling I'd tried so often to communicate in my fiction, I believe. Something stooped towards me from the horizon. I jerked, and dropped the shell.

There was nothing but the dazzle of sunlight that leapt at me from the waves. The haze above the sea had darkened, staining the light, and I told myself that was what I'd seen. But when Neal picked up another shell I felt uneasy. The grip on my skull was very tight now. As I regarded the vistas of empty sea and sky and beach my expectancy grew oppressive, too imminent, no longer enjoyable. "I think I'll head back now. Maybe you should as well," I said, rummaging for an uncontrived reason, "just in case there is quicksand."

"All right. It's in all of them," he said, displaying an even smaller shell to which he'd just listened. I remember thinking that his observation was so self-evident as to be meaningless.

As I turned toward the bungalows the glitter of the sea clung to my eyes. After-images crowded among the debris. They were moving; I strained to make out their shape. What did they resemble? Symbols—hieroglyphs? Limbs writhing rapidly, as if in a ritual dance? They made the debris appear to shift, to crumble. The herd of faceless dunes seemed to edge forward; an image leaned towards me out of the sky. I closed my eyes, to calm their antics, and wondered if I should take the warnings of pollution more seriously.

We walked toward the confusion of footprints that climbed the dunes. Neal glanced about at the sparkling of sand. Never before had the beach so impressed me as a complex of patterns, and perhaps that means it was already too late. Spotlighted by the sun, it looked so artificial that I came close to doubting how it felt underfoot.

The bungalows looked unconvincing too. Still, when we'd slumped in our chairs for a while, letting the relative dimness soothe our eyes while our bodies guzzled every hint of coolness, I forgot about the beach. We shared two litres of wine and talked about my work, about his lack of any since graduating.

Later I prepared melon, salads, water ices. Neal watched, obviously embarrassed that he couldn't help. He seemed lost without Mary. One more reason not to marry, I thought, congratulating myself.

As we ate he kept staring out at the beach. A ship was caught in the amber sunset: a dream of escape. I felt the image less deeply than I'd experienced the metaphors of the beach; it was less oppressive. The band around my head had faded.

When it grew dark Neal pressed close to the pane. "What's that?" he demanded.

I switched out the light so that he could see. Beyond the dim humps of the dunes the beach was glowing, a dull pallor like moonlight stifled by fog. Do all beaches glow at night? "That's what makes people say there's pollution," I said.

"Not the light," he said impatiently. "The other things. What's moving?"

I squinted through the pane. For minutes I could see nothing but the muffled glow. At last, when my eyes were smarting, I began to see forms thin and stiff as scarecrows, jerking into various contorted poses. Gazing for so long was bound to produce something of the kind, and I took them to be after-images of the tangle, barely visible, of bushes.

"I think I'll go and see."

"I shouldn't go down there at night," I said, having realised that I'd never gone to the beach at night and that I felt a definite, though irrational, aversion to doing so.

Eventually he went to bed. Despite all his travelling, he'd needed to drink to make himself sleepy. I heard him open his bedroom window, which overlooked the beach. There is so much still to write, so much to struggle through, and what good can it do me now?

II

I had taken the bungalow, one of the few entries in my diary says, to give myself the chance to write without being distracted by city life—the cries of the telephone, the tolling of the doorbell, the omnipresent clamour—only to discover, once I'd left it behind, that city life was my theme. But I was a compulsive writer: if I failed to write for more than a few days I became depressed. Writing was the way I overcame the depression of not writing. Now writing seems to be my only way of hanging onto what remains of myself, of delaying the end.

The day after Neal arrived, I typed a few lines of a sample chapter.

It wasn't a technique I enjoyed—tearing a chapter out of the context of a novel that didn't yet exist. In any case, I was distracted by the beach, compelled to scribble notes about it, trying to define the images it suggested. I hoped these notes might build into a story. I was picking at the notes in search of their story when Neal said "Maybe I can lose myself for a bit in the countryside."

"Mm," I said curtly, not looking up.

"Didn't you say there was a deserted village?"

By the time I directed him I would have lost the thread of my thoughts. The thread had been frayed and tangled, anyway. As long as I was compelled to think about the beach I might just as well be down there. I can still write as if I don't know the end, it helps me not to think of "I'll come with you," I said.

The weather was nervous. Archipelagos of cloud floated low on the hazy sky, above the sea; great Rorschach blots rose from behind the slate hills, like dissolved stone. As we squeezed through the bushes, a shadow came hunching over the dunes to meet us. When my foot touched the beach a moist shadowy chill seized me, as though the sand disguised a lurking marsh. Then sunlight spilled over the beach, which leapt into clarity.

I strode, though Neal appeared to want to dawdle. I wasn't anxious to linger; after all, I told myself, it might rain. Glinting mosaics of grains of sand changed restlessly around me, never quite achieving a pattern. Patches of sand, flat shapeless elongated ghosts, glided over the beach and faltered, waiting for another breeze. Neal kept peering at them as though to make out their shapes.

Half a mile along the beach the dunes began to sag, to level out. The slate hills were closing in. Were they the source of the insidious chill? Perhaps I was feeling the damp; a penumbra of moisture welled up around each of my footprints. The large wet shapes seemed quite unrelated to my prints, an effect which I found unnerving. When I glanced back, it looked as though something enormous was imitating my walk.

The humidity was almost suffocating. My head felt clamped by tension. Wind blundered booming in my ears, even when I could feel no breeze. Its jerky rhythm was distracting because indefinable. Grey cloud had flooded the sky; together with the hills and the thickening haze above the sea, it caged the beach. At the edge of my eye the convolutions of the beach seemed to writhe, to struggle to form patterns. The insistent sparkling nagged at my mind.

I'd begun to wonder whether I had been blaming imagined pollution for the effects of heat and humidity—I was debating whether to turn back before I grew dizzy or nauseous—when Neal said "Is that it?"

I peered ahead, trying to squint the dazzle of waves from my eyes. A quarter of a mile away the hills ousted the dunes completely. Beneath the spiky slate a few uprights of rock protruded from the beach like standing stones. They glowed sullenly as copper through the haze; they were encrusted with sand. Surely that wasn't the village.

"Yes, that's it," Neal said, and strode forward.

I followed him, because the village must be further on. The veil of haze drew back, the vertical rocks gleamed unobscured, and I halted bewildered. The rocks weren't encrusted at all; they were slate, grey as the table of rock on which they stood above the beach. Though the slate was jagged, some of its gaps were regular: windows, doorways. Here and there walls still formed corners. How could the haze have distorted my view so spectacularly?

Neal was climbing rough steps carved out of the slate table. Without warning, as I stood confused by my misperception, I felt utterly alone. A bowl of dull haze trapped me on the bare sand. Slate, or something more massive and vague, loomed over me. The kaleidoscope of shells was about to shift; the beach was ready to squirm, to reveal its pattern, shake off its artificiality. The massive looming would reach down, and

My start felt like a convulsive awakening. The table was deserted except for the fragments of buildings. I could hear only the wind, baying as though its mouth was vast and uncontrollable. "Neal," I called. Dismayed by the smallness of my voice, I shouted "Neal."

I heard what sounded like scales of armour chafing together—slate, of course. The grey walls shone lifelessly, cavitied as skulls; gaping windows displayed an absence of faces, of rooms. Then Neal's head poked out of half a wall. "Yes, come on," he said. "It's strange."

As I climbed the steps, sand gritted underfoot like sugar. Low drifts of sand were piled against the walls; patches glinted on the small plateau. Could that sand have made the whole place look encrusted and half-buried? I told myself that it had been an effect of the heat.

Broken walls surrounded me. They glared like storm-clouds in lightning. They formed a maze whose centre was desertion. That image stirred another, too deep in my mind to be definable. The place was—not a maze, but a puzzle whose solution would clarify a pattern, a larger mystery. I realised that then; why couldn't I have fled?

I suppose I was held by the enigma of the village. I knew there were quarries in the hills above, but I'd never learned why the village had been abandoned. Perhaps its meagreness had killed it—I saw traces of less than a dozen buildings. It seemed further dwarfed by the beach; the sole visible trace of humanity, it dwindled beneath the gnawing of sand and the elements. I found it enervating, its lifelessness infectious. Should I stay with Neal, or risk leaving him there? Before I could decide, I heard him say amid a rattle of slate "This is interesting."

In what way? He was clambering about an exposed cellar, among shards of slate. Whatever the building had been, it had stood furthest from the sea. "I don't mean the cellar," Neal said. "I mean that."

Reluctantly I peered where he was pointing. In the cellar wall furthest from the beach, a rough alcove had been chipped out of the slate. It was perhaps a yard deep, but barely high enough to accommodate a huddled man. Neal was already crawling in. I heard slate crack beneath him; his feet protruded from the darkness. Of course they weren't about to jerk convulsively—but my nervousness made me back away when his muffled voice said "What's this?"

He backed out like a terrier with his prize. It was an old notebook, its pages stuck together in a moist wad. "Someone covered it up with slate," he said as though that should tempt my interest.

Before I could prevent him he was sitting at the edge of the beach and peeling the pages gingerly apart. Not that I was worried that he might be destroying a fragment of history—I simply wasn't sure that I wanted to read whatever had been hidden in the cellar. Why couldn't I have followed my instincts?

He disengaged the first page carefully, then frowned. "This begins in the middle of something. There must be another book."

Handing me the notebook, he stalked away to scrabble in the cellar. I sat on the edge of the slate table, and glanced at the page. It is before me now on my desk. The pages have crumbled since then—the yellowing paper looks more and more like sand—but the large writing is still legible, unsteady capitals in a hand that might

once have been literate before it grew senile. No punctuation sepa-
rates the words, though blotches sometimes do. Beneath the
relentless light at the deserted village the faded ink looked unreal,
scarcely present at all.

> FROM THE BEACH EVERYONE GONE NOW
> BUT ME ITS NOT SO BAD IN DAYTIME EXCEPT
> I CANT GO BUT AT NIGHT I CAN HEAR IT
> REACHING FOR (a blot of fungus had consumed a
> word here) AND THE VOICES ITS VOICE AND
> THE GLOWING AT LEAST IT HELPS ME SEE
> DOWN HERE WHEN IT COMES

I left it at that; my suddenly unsteady fingers might have torn the
page. I wish to God they had. I was on edge with the struggle
between humidity and the chill of slate and beach; I felt feverish. As
I stared at the words they touched impressions, half-memories. If I
looked up, would the beach have changed?

I heard Neal slithering on slate, turning over fragments. In my
experience, stones were best not turned over. Eventually he
returned. I was dully fascinated by the shimmering of the beach; my
fingers pinched the notebook shut.

"I can't find anything," he said. "I'll have to come back." He took
the notebook from me and began to read, muttering "What? Jesus!"
Gently he separated the next page from the wad. "This gets
stranger," he murmured. "What kind of guy was this? Imagine what
it must have been like to live inside his head."

How did he know it had been a man? I stared at the pages, to
prevent Neal from reading them aloud. At least it saved me from
having to watch the antics of the beach, which moved like slow
flames, but the introverted meandering of words made me nervous.

> IT CANT REACH DOWN HERE NOT YET BUT
> OUTSIDE IS CHANGING OUTSIDES PART OF
> THE PATTERN I READ THE PATTERN THATS
> WHY I CANT GO SAW THEM DANCING THE
> PATTERN IT WANTS ME TO DANCE ITS ALIVE
> BUT ITS ONLY THE IMAGE BEING PUT
> TOGETHER

Neal was wide-eyed, fascinated. Feverish disorientation gripped my skull; I felt too unwell to move. The heat-haze must be closing in: at the edge of my vision, everything was shifting.

> WHEN THE PATTERNS DONE IT CAN COME BACK AND GROW ITS HUNGRY TO BE EVERY-THING I KNOW HOW IT WORKS THE SAND MOVES AT NIGHT AND SUCKS YOU DOWN OR MAKES YOU GO WHERE IT WANTS TO MAKE (a blotch had eaten several words) WHEN THEY BUILT LEWIS THERE WERE OLD STONES THAT THEY MOVED MAYBE THE STONES KEPT IT SMALL NOW ITS THE BEACH AT LEAST

On the next page the letters are much larger, and wavery. Had the light begun to fail, or had the writer been retreating from the light—from the entrance to the cellar? I didn't know which alternative I disliked more.

> GOT TO WRITE HANDS SHAKY FROM CHIP-PING TUNNEL AND NO FOOD THEYRE SINGING NOW HELPING IT REACH CHANTING WITH NO MOUTHS THEY SING AND DANCE THE PATTERN FOR IT TO REACH THROUGH

Now there are very few words to the page. The letters are jagged, as though the writer's hand kept twitching violently.

> GLOW COMING ITS OUT THERE NOW ITS LOOKING IN AT ME IT CANT GET HOLD IF I KEEP WRITING THEY WANT ME TO DANCE SO ITLL GROW WANT ME TO BE

There it ends. "Ah, the influence of Joyce," I commented sourly. The remaining pages are blank except for fungus. I managed to stand up; my head felt like a balloon pumped full of gas. "I'd like to go back now. I think I've a touch of sunstroke."

A hundred yards away I glanced back at the remnants of the village—Lewis, I assumed it had been called. The stone remains

wavered as though striving to achieve a new shape; the haze made
them look coppery, fat with a crust of sand. I was desperate to get
out of the heat.

Closer to the sea I felt slightly less oppressed—but the whispering
of sand, the liquid murmur of the waves, the bumbling of the wind,
all chanted together insistently. Everywhere on the beach were
patterns, demanding to be read.

Neal clutched the notebook under his arm. "What do you make
of it?" he said eagerly.

His indifference to my health annoyed me, and hence so did the
question. "He was mad," I said. "Living here—is it any wonder?
Maybe he moved there after the place was abandoned. The beach
must glow there too. That must have finished him. You saw how he
tried to dig himself a refuge. That's all there is to it."

"Do you think so? I wonder," Neal said, and picked up a shell.

As he held the shell to his ear, his expression became so withdrawn and unreadable that I felt a pang of dismay. Was I seeing a
symptom of his nervous trouble? He stood like a fragment of the
village—as though the shell was holding him, rather than the
reverse.

Eventually he mumbled "That's it, that's what he meant.
Chanting with no mouths."

I took the shell only very reluctantly; my head was pounding. I
pressed the shell to my ear, though I was deafened by the storm of
my blood. If the shell was muttering, I couldn't bear the jaggedness
of its rhythm. I seemed less to hear it than to feel it deep in my skull.
"Nothing like it," I said, almost snarling, and thrust the shell at
him.

Now that I'd had to strain to hear it, I couldn't rid myself of the
muttering; it seemed to underlie the sounds of wind and sea. I
trudged onwards, eyes half shut. Moisture sprang up around my
feet, the glistening shapes around my prints looked larger and more
definite. I had to cling to my sense of my own size and shape.

When we neared home I couldn't see the bungalows. There
appeared to be only the beach, grown huge and blinding. At last
Neal heard a car leaving the crescent, and led me up the path of
collapsed footprints.

In the bungalow I lay willing the lights and patterns to fade from
my closed eyes. Neal's presence didn't soothe me, even though he
was only poring over the notebook. He'd brought a handful of shells

indoors. Occasionally he held one to his ear, muttering "It's still there, you know. It does sound like chanting." At least, I thought peevishly, I knew when something was a symptom of illness—but the trouble was that in my delirium I was tempted to agree with him. I felt I had almost heard what the sound was trying to be.

III

Next day Neal returned to the deserted village. He was gone for so long that even amid the clamour of my disordered senses, I grew anxious. I couldn't watch for him; whenever I tried, the white-hot beach began to judder, to quake, and set me shivering.

At last he returned, having failed to find another notebook. I hoped that would be the end of it, but his failure had simply frustrated him. His irritability chafed against mine. He managed to prepare a bedraggled salad, of which I ate little. As the tide of twilight rolled in from the horizon he sat by the window, gazing alternately at the beach and at the notebook.

Without warning he said "I'm going for a stroll. Can I borrow your stick?"

I guessed that he meant to go to the beach. Should he be trapped by darkness and sea, I was in no condition to go to his aid. "I'd rather you didn't," I said feebly.

"Don't worry, I won't lose it."

My lassitude suffocated my arguments. I lolled in my chair and through the open window heard him padding away, his footsteps muffled by sand. Soon there was only the vague slack rumble of the sea, blundering back and forth, and the faint hiss of sand in the bushes.

After half an hour I made myself stand up, though the ache in my head surged and surged, and gaze out at the whitish beach. The whole expanse appeared to flicker like hints of lightning. I strained my eyes. The beach looked crowded with debris, all of which danced to the flickering. I had to peer at every movement, but there was no sign of Neal.

I went out and stood between the bushes. The closer I approached the beach, the more crowded with obscure activity it seemed to be—but I suspected that much, if not all, of this could be blamed on my condition, for within five minutes my head felt so tight and unbalanced that I had to retreat indoors, away from the heat.

Though I'd meant to stay awake, I was dozing when Neal returned. I woke to find him gazing from the window. As I opened my eyes the beach lurched forward, shining. It didn't look crowded now, presumably because my eyes had had a rest. What could Neal see to preoccupy him so? "Enjoy your stroll?" I said sleepily.

He turned, and I felt a twinge of disquiet. His face looked stiff with doubt; his eyes were uneasy, a frown dug its ruts in his fore-head. "It doesn't glow," he said.

Assuming I knew what he was talking about, I could only wonder how badly his nerves were affecting his perceptions. If anything, the beach looked brighter. "How do you mean?"

"The beach down by the village—it doesn't glow. Not any more."

"Oh, I see."

He looked offended, almost contemptuous, though I couldn't understand why he'd expected me to be less indifferent. He with-drew into a scrutiny of the notebook. He might have been trying to solve an urgent problem.

Perhaps if I hadn't been ill I would have been able to divert Neal from his obsession, but I could hardly venture outside without growing dizzy; I could only wait in the bungalow for my state to improve. Neither Neal nor I had had sunstroke before, but he seemed to know how to treat it. "Keep drinking water. Cover your-self if you start shivering." He didn't mind my staying in—he seemed almost too eager to go out alone. Did that matter? Next day he was bound only for the library.

My state was crippling my thoughts, yet even if I'd been healthy I couldn't have imagined how he would look when he returned: excited, conspiratorial, smug. "I've got a story for you," he said at once.

Most such offers proved to be prolonged and dull. "Oh yes?" I said warily.

He sat forward as though to infect me with suspense. "That village we went to—it isn't called Lewis. It's called Strand."

Was he pausing to give me a chance to gasp or applaud? "Oh yes," I said without enthusiasm.

"Lewis was another village, further up the coast. It's deserted too."

That seemed to be his punch line. The antics of patterns within my eyelids had made me irritable. "It doesn't seem much of a story," I complained.

"Well, that's only the beginning." When his pause had forced me to open my eyes, he said "I read a book about your local unexplained mysteries."

"Why?"

"Look, if you don't want to hear—"

"Go on, go on, now you've started." Not to know might be even more nerve-racking.

"There wasn't much about Lewis," he said eventually, perhaps to give himself more time to improvise.

"Was there much at all?"

"Yes, certainly. It may not sound like much. Nobody knows why Lewis was abandoned, but then nobody knows that about Strand either." My impatience must have showed, for he added hastily "What I mean is, the people who left Strand wouldn't say why."

"Someone asked them?"

"The woman who wrote the book. She managed to track some of them down. They'd moved as far inland as they could, that was one thing she noticed. And they always had some kind of nervous disorder. Talking about Strand always made them more nervous, as though they felt that talking might make something happen, or something might hear."

"That's what the author said."

"Right."

"What was her name?"

Could he hear my suspicion? "Jesus *Christ*," he snarled, "I don't know. What does it matter?"

In fact it didn't, not to me. His story had made me feel worse. The noose had tightened round my skull, the twilit beach was swarming and vibrating. I closed my eyes. Shut up, I roared at him. Go away.

"There was one thing," he persisted. "One man said that kids kept going on the beach at night. Their parents tried all ways to stop them. Some of them questioned their kids, but it was as though the kids couldn't stop themselves. Why was that, do you think?" When I refused to answer he said irrelevantly "All this was in the 1930s."

I couldn't stand hearing children called kids. The recurring word had made me squirm: drips of slang, like water torture. And I'd never heard such a feeble punch line. His clumsiness as a storyteller enraged me; he couldn't even organise his material. I was sure he hadn't read any such book.

After a while I peered out from beneath my eyelids, hoping he'd decided that I was asleep. He was poring over the notebook again, and looked rapt. I only wished that people and reviewers would read my books as carefully. He kept rubbing his forehead, as though to enliven his brain.

I dozed. When I opened my eyes he was waiting for me. He shoved the notebook at me to demonstrate something. "Look, I'm sorry," I said without much effort to sound so. "I'm not in the mood."

He stalked into his room, emerging without the book but with my stick. "I'm going for a walk," he announced sulkily, like a spouse after a quarrel.

I dozed gratefully, for I felt more delirious; my head felt packed with grains of sand that gritted together. In fact, the whole of me was made of sand. Of course it was true that I was composed of particles, and I thought my delirium had found a metaphor for that. But the grains that floated through my inner vision were neither sand nor atoms. A member, dark and vague, was reaching for them. I struggled to awaken; I didn't want to distinguish its shape, and still less did I want to learn what it meant to do with the grains—for as the member sucked them into itself, engulfing them in a way that I refused to perceive, I saw that the grains were worlds and stars.

I woke shivering. My body felt uncontrollable and unfamiliar. I let it shake itself to rest—not that I had a choice, but I was concentrating on the problem of why I'd woken head raised, like a watchdog. What had I heard?

Perhaps only wind and sea: both seemed louder, more intense. My thoughts became entangled in their rhythm. I felt there had been another sound. The bushes threshed, sounding parched with sand. Had I heard Neal returning? I stumbled into his room. It was empty.

As I stood by his open window, straining my ears, I thought I heard his voice, blurred by the dull tumult of waves. I peered out. Beyond the low heads of the bushes, the glow of the beach shuddered towards me. I had to close my eyes, for I couldn't tell whether the restless scrawny shapes were crowding my eyeballs or the beach; it felt, somehow, like both. When I looked again, I seemed to see Neal.

Or was it Neal? The unsteady stifled glow aggravated the distortions of my vision. Was the object just a new piece of debris? I found its shape bewildering; my mind kept apprehending it as a symbol printed on the whitish expanse. The luminosity made it seem to shift, tentatively and jerkily, as though it was learning to pose. The light, or my eyes, surrounded it with dancing.

Had my sense of perspective left me? I was misjudging size, either of the beach or of the figure. Yes, it was a figure, however large it seemed. It was moving its arms like a limp puppet. And it was half-buried in the sand.

I staggered outside, shouting to Neal, and then I recoiled. The sky must be thick with a storm-cloud; it felt suffocatingly massive, solid as rock, and close enough to crush me. I forced myself towards the bushes, though my head was pounding, squeezed into a lump of pain.

Almost at once I heard plodding on the dunes. My blood half deafened me; the footsteps sounded vague and immense. I peered along the dim path. At the edge of my vision the beach flickered repetitively. Immense darkness hovered over me. Unnervingly close to me, swollen by the glow, a head rose into view. For a moment my tension seemed likely to crack my skull. Then Neal spoke. His words were incomprehensible amid the wind, but it was his voice.

As we trudged back towards the lights the threat of a storm seemed to withdraw, and I blamed it on my tension. "Of course I'm all right," he muttered irritably. "I fell and that made me shout, that's all." Once we were inside I saw the evidence of his fall; his trousers were covered with sand up to the knees.

IV

Next day he hardly spoke to me. He went down early to the beach, and stayed there. I didn't know if he was obsessed or displaying pique. Perhaps he couldn't bear to be near me; invalids can find each other unbearable.

Often I glimpsed him, wandering beyond the dunes. He walked as though in an elaborate maze and scrutinised the beach. Was he searching for the key to the notebook? Was he looking for pollution? By the time he found it, I thought sourly, it would have infected him.

I felt too enervated to intervene. As I watched, Neal appeared to vanish intermittently; if I looked away, I couldn't locate him again for minutes. The beach blazed like bone, and was never still. I couldn't blame the aberrations of my vision solely on heat and haze.

When Neal returned, late that afternoon, I asked him to phone for a doctor. He looked taken aback, but eventually said "There's a box by the station, isn't there?"

"One of the neighbours would let you phone."

"No, I'll walk down. They're probably all wondering why you've let some long-haired freak squat in your house, as it is."

He went out, rubbing his forehead gingerly. He often did that now. That, and his preoccupation with the demented notebook, were additional reasons why I wanted a doctor: I felt Neal needed examining too.

By the time he returned, it was dusk. On the horizon, embers dulled in the sea. The glow of the beach was already stirring; it seemed to have intensified during the last few days. I told myself I had grown hypersensitive.

"Dr Lewis. He's coming tomorrow." Neal hesitated, then went on "I think I'll just have a stroll on the beach. Want to come?"

"Good God no. I'm ill, can't you see?"

"I know that." His impatience was barely controlled. "A stroll might do you good. There isn't any sunlight now."

"I'll stay in until I've seen the doctor."

He looked disposed to argue, but his restlessness overcame him. As he left, his bearing seemed to curse me. Was his illness making him intolerant of mine, or did he feel that I'd rebuffed a gesture of reconciliation?

I felt too ill to watch him from the window. When I looked I could seldom distinguish him or make out which movements were his. He appeared to be walking slowly, poking at the beach with my stick. I wondered if he'd found quicksand. Again his path made me think of a maze.

I dozed, far longer than I'd intended. The doctor loomed over me. Peering into my eyes, he reached down. I began to struggle, as best I could: I'd glimpsed the depths of his eye-sockets, empty and dry as interstellar space. I didn't need his treatment, I would be fine if he left me alone, just let me go. But he had reached deep into me. As though I was a bladder that had burst, I felt myself flood into him; I felt vast emptiness absorb my substance and my self. Dimly I understood that it was nothing like emptiness—that my mind refused to perceive what it was, so alien and frightful was its teeming.

It was dawn. The muffled light teemed. The beach glowed fitfully. I gasped: someone was down on the beach, so huddled that he looked shapeless. He rose, levering himself up with my stick, and began to pace haphazardly. I knew at once that he'd spent the night on the beach.

After that I stayed awake. I couldn't imagine the state of his mind, and I was a little afraid of being asleep when he returned. But when, hours later, he came in to raid the kitchen for a piece of cheese, he seemed hardly to see me. He was muttering repetitively under his breath. His eyes looked dazzled by the beach, sunk in his obsession.

"When did the doctor say he was coming?"

"Later," he mumbled, and hurried down to the beach.

I hoped he would stay there until the doctor came. Occasionally I glimpsed him at his intricate pacing. Ripples of heat deformed him; his blurred flesh looked unstable. Whenever I glanced at the beach it leapt forward, dauntingly vivid. Cracks of light appeared in the sea. Clumps of grass seemed to rise twitching, as though the dunes were craning to watch Neal. Five minutes' vigil at the window was as much as I could bear.

The afternoon consumed time. It felt lethargic and enervating as four in the morning. There was no sign of the doctor. I kept gazing from the front door. Nothing moved on the crescent except wind-borne hints of the beach.

Eventually I tried to phone. Though I could feel the heat of the pavement through the soles of my shoes, the day seemed bearable; only threats of pain plucked at my skull. But nobody was at home. The bungalows stood smugly in the evening light. When I attempted to walk to the phone box, the noose closed on my skull at once.

In my hall I halted startled, for Neal had thrown open the living-room door as I entered the house. He looked flushed and angry. "Where were you?" he demanded.

"I'm not a hospital case yet, you know. I was trying to phone the doctor."

Unfathomably, he looked relieved. "I'll go down now and call him."

While he was away I watched the beach sink into twilight. At the moment, this seemed to be the only time of day I could endure

watching—the time at which shapes become obscure, most capable
of metamorphosis. Perhaps this made the antics of the shore acceptable, more apparently natural. Now the beach resembled clouds in
front of the moon; it drifted slowly and variously. If I gazed for long
it looked nervous with lightning. The immense bulk of the night
edged up from the horizon.

I didn't hear Neal return; I must have been fascinated by the
view. I turned to find him watching me. Again he looked relieved—
because I was still here? "He's coming soon," he said.

"Tonight, do you mean?"

"Yes, tonight. Why not?"

I didn't know many doctors who would come out at night to
treat what was, however unpleasant for me, a relatively minor illness.
Perhaps attitudes were different here in the country. Neal was
heading for the back door, for the beach. "Do you think you could
wait until he comes?" I said, groping for an excuse to detain him.
"Just in case I feel worse."

"Yes, you're right." His gaze was opaque. "I'd better stay with
you."

We waited. The dark mass closed over beach and bungalows. The
nocturnal glow fluttered at the edge of my vision. When I glanced at
the beach, the dim shapes were hectic. I seemed to be paying for my
earlier fascination, for now the walls of the room looked active with
faint patterns.

Where was the doctor? Neal seemed impatient too. The only
sounds were the repetitive ticking of his footsteps and the irregular
chant of the sea. He kept staring at me as if he wanted to speak;
occasionally his mouth twitched. He resembled a child both eager to
confess and afraid to do so. Though he made me uneasy I tried to
look encouraging, interested in whatever he might have to say. His
pacing took him closer and closer to the beach door. Yes, I nodded,
tell me, talk to me.

His eyes narrowed. Behind his eyelids he was pondering.
Abruptly he sat opposite me. A kind of smile, tweaked awry,
plucked at his lips. "I've got another story for you," he said.

"Really?" I sounded as intrigued as I could.

He picked up the notebook. "I worked it out from this."

So we'd returned to his obsession. As he twitched pages over, his
feet shifted constantly. His lips moved as though whispering the
text. I heard the vast mumbling of the sea.

"Suppose this," he said all at once. "I only said suppose, mind you. This guy was living all alone in Strand. It must have affected his mind, you said that yourself—having to watch the beach every night. But just suppose it didn't send him mad? Suppose it affected his mind so that he saw things more clearly?"

I hid my impatience. "What things?"

"The beach." His tone reminded me of something—a particular kind of simplicity I couldn't quite place. "Of course we're only supposing. But from things you've read, don't you feel there are places that are closer to another sort of reality, another plane or dimension or whatever?"

"You mean the beach at Strand was like that?" I suggested, to encourage him.

"That's right. Did you feel it too?"

His eagerness startled me. "I felt ill, that's all. I still do."

"Sure. Yes, of course. I mean, we were only supposing. But look at what he says." He seemed glad to retreat into the notebook. "It started at Lewis where the old stones were, then it moved on up the coast to Strand. Doesn't that prove that what he was talking about is unlike anything we know?"

His mouth hung open, awaiting my agreement; it looked empty, robbed of sense. I glanced away, distracted by the fluttering glow beyond him. "I don't know what you mean."

"That's because you haven't read this properly." His impatience had turned harsh. "Look here," he demanded, poking his fingers at a group of words as if they were a Bible's oracle.

WHEN THE PATTERNS READY IT CAN COME BACK.
"So what is that supposed to mean?"

"I'll tell you what I think it means—what he meant." His low voice seemed to stumble among the rhythms of the beach. "You see how he keeps mentioning patterns. Suppose this other reality was once all there was? Then ours came into being and occupied some of its space. We didn't destroy it—it can't be destroyed. Maybe it withdrew a little, to bide its time. But it left a kind of imprint of itself, a kind of coded image of itself in our reality. And yet that image is itself in embryo, growing. You see, he says it's alive but it's only the image being put together. Things become part of its image, and that's how it grows. I'm sure that's what he meant."

I felt mentally exhausted and dismayed by all this. How much in need of a doctor was he? I couldn't help sounding a little derisive.

"I don't see how you could have put all that together from that book."

"Who says I did?"

His vehemence was shocking. I had to break the tension, for the glare in his eyes looked as unnatural and nervous as the glow of the beach. I went to gaze from the front window, but there was no sign of the doctor. "Don't worry," Neal said. "He's coming."

I stood staring out at the lightless road until he said fretfully "Don't you want to hear the rest?"

He waited until I sat down. His tension was oppressive as the hovering sky. He gazed at me for what seemed minutes; the noose dug into my skull. At last he said "Does this beach feel like anywhere else to you?"

"It feels like a beach."

He shrugged that aside. "You see, he worked out that whatever came from the old stones kept moving toward the inhabited areas. That's how it added to itself. That's why it moved on from Lewis and then Strand."

"All nonsense, of course. Ravings."

"No. It isn't." There was no mistaking the fury that lurked, barely restrained, beneath his low voice. That fury seemed loose in the roaring night, in the wind and violent sea and looming sky. The beach trembled wakefully. "The next place it would move to would be here," he muttered. "It has to be."

"If you accepted the idea in the first place."

A hint of a grimace twitched his cheek; my comment might have been an annoying fly—certainly as trivial. "You can read the pattern out there if you try," he mumbled. "It takes all day. You begin to get a sense of what might be there. It's alive, though nothing like life as we recognise it."

I could only say whatever came into my head, to detain him until the doctor arrived. "Then how do you?"

He avoided the question, but only to betray the depths of his obsession. "Would an insect recognise us as a kind of life?"

Suddenly I realised that he intoned "the beach" as a priest might name his god. We must get away from the beach. Never mind the doctor now. "Look, Neal, I think we'd better—"

He interrupted me, eyes glaring spasmodically. "It's strongest at night. I think it soaks up energy during the day. Remember, he said that the quicksands only come out at night. They move, you know—they make you follow the pattern. And the sea is different at night. Things come out of it. They're like symbols and yet they're alive. I think the sea creates them. They help make the pattern live."

Appalled, I could only return to the front window and search for the lights of the doctor's car—for any lights at all. "Yes, yes," Neal said, sounding less impatient than soothing. "He's coming." But as he spoke I glimpsed, reflected in the window, his secret triumphant grin.

Eventually I managed to say to his reflection "You didn't call a doctor, did you?"

"No." A smile made his lips tremble like quicksand. "But he's coming."

My stomach had begun to churn slowly; so had my head, and the room. Now I was afraid to stand with my back to Neal, but when I turned I was more afraid to ask the question. "Who?"

For a moment I thought he disdained to answer; he turned his back on me and gazed towards the beach—but I can't write any longer as if I have doubts, as if I don't know the end. The beach was his answer, its awesome transformation was, even if I wasn't sure what I was seeing. Was the beach swollen, puffed up as if by the irregular gasping of the sea? Was it swarming with indistinct shapes, parasites that scuttled dancing over it, sank into it, floated writhing to its surface? Did it quiver along the whole of its length like luminous gelatin? I tried to believe that all this was an effect of the brooding dark—but the dark had closed down so thickly that there might have been no light in the world outside except the fitful glow.

He craned his head back over his shoulder. The gleam in his eyes looked very like the glimmering outside. A web of saliva stretched between his bared teeth. He grinned with a frightful generosity; he'd decided to answer my question more directly. His lips moved as they had when he was reading. At last I heard what I'd tried not to suspect. He was making the sound that I'd tried not to hear in the shells.

Was it meant to be an invocation, or the name I'd asked for? I knew only that the sound, so liquid and inhuman that I could almost think it was shapeless, nauseated me, so much so that I couldn't separate it from the huge loose voices of wind and sea. It seemed to fill the room. The pounding of my skull tried to imitate its rhythm, which I found impossible to grasp, unbearable. I began to sidle along the wall towards the front door.

His body turned jerkily, as if dangling from his neck. His head laughed, if a sound like struggles in mud is laughter. "You're not going to try to get away?" he cried. "It was getting hold of you before I came, he was. You haven't a chance now, not since we brought him into the house," and he picked up a shell.

As he levelled the mouth of the shell at me my dizziness flooded my skull, hurling me forward. The walls seemed to glare and shake and break out in swarms; I thought that a dark bulk loomed at the window, filling it. Neal's mouth was working, but the nauseating sound might have been roaring deep in a cavern, or a shell. It sounded distant and huge, but coming closer and growing more definite—the voice of something vast and liquid that was gradually taking shape. Perhaps that was because I was listening, but I had no choice.

All at once Neal's free hand clamped his forehead. It looked like a pincer desperate to tear something out of his skull. "It's growing," he cried, somewhere between sobbing and ecstasy. As he spoke, the liquid chant seemed to abate not at all. Before I knew what he meant to do, he'd wrenched open the back door and was gone. In a nightmarish way, his nervous elaborate movements resembled dancing.

As the door crashed open, the roar of the night rushed in. Its leap in volume sounded eager, voracious. I stood paralysed, listening, and couldn't tell how like his chant it sounded. I heard his footsteps, soft and loose, running unevenly over the dunes. Minutes later I thought I heard a faint cry, which sounded immediately engulfed.

I slumped against a chair. I felt relieved, drained, uncaring. The sounds had returned to the beach, where they ought to be; the room looked stable now. Then I grew disgusted with myself. Suppose Neal was injured, or caught in quicksand? I'd allowed his hysteria to gain a temporary hold on my sick perceptions, I told myself—was I going to use that as an excuse not to try to save him?

At last I forced myself outside. All the bungalows were dark. The beach was glimmering, but not violently. I could see nothing wrong with the sky. Only my dizziness, and the throbbing of my head, threatened to distort my perceptions.

I made myself edge between the bushes, which hissed like snakes, mouths full of sand. The tangle of footprints made me stumble frequently. Sand rattled the spikes of marram grass. At the edge of the dunes, the path felt ready to slide me down to the beach.

The beach was crowded. I had to squint at many of the vague pieces of debris. My eyes grew used to the dimness, but I could see no sign of Neal. Then I peered closer. Was that a pair of sandals, half buried? Before my giddiness could hurl me to the beach, I slithered down.

Yes, they were Neal's, and a path of bare footprints led away towards the crowd of debris. I poked gingerly at the sandals, and wished I had my stick to test for quicksand—but the sand in which they were partially engulfed was quite solid. Why had he tried to bury them?

I followed his prints, my eyes still adjusting. I refused to imitate his path, for it looped back on itself in intricate patterns which made me dizzy and wouldn't fade from my mind. His paces were irregular, a cripple's dance. He must be a puppet of his nerves, I thought. I was a little afraid to confront him, but I felt a duty to try.

His twistings led me among the debris. Low obscure shapes surrounded me: a jagged stump bristling with metal tendrils that groped in the air as I came near; half a car so rusty and misshapen that it looked like a child's fuzzy sketch; the hood of a pram within which glimmered a bald lump of sand. I was glad to emerge from that maze, for the dim objects seemed to shift; I'd even thought the bald lump was opening a crumbling mouth.

But on the open beach there were other distractions. The ripples and patterns of sand were clearer, and appeared to vibrate restlessly. I kept glancing toward the sea, not because its chant was troubling me—though, with its insistent loose rhythm, it was—but because I had a persistent impression that the waves were slowing, sluggish as treacle.

I stumbled, and had to turn back to see what had tripped me. The glow of the beach showed me Neal's shirt, the little of it that was left unburied. There was no mistaking it; I recognised its pattern. The glow made the nylon seem luminous, lit from within.

His prints danced back among the debris. Even then, God help me, I wondered if he was playing a sick joke—if he was waiting somewhere to leap out, to scare me into admitting I'd been impressed. I trudged angrily into the midst of the debris, and wished at once that I hadn't. All the objects were luminous, without shadows.

There was no question now: the glow of the beach was increasing. It made Neal's tracks look larger: their outlines shifted as I squinted at them. I stumbled hastily toward the deserted stretch of beach, and brushed against the half-engulfed car.

That was the moment at which the nightmare became real. I might have told myself that rust had eaten away the car until it was thin as a shell, but I was past deluding myself. All at once I knew that nothing on this beach was as it seemed, for as my hand collided with the car roof, which should have been painfully solid, I felt the roof crumble—and the entire structure flopped on the sand, from which it was at once indistinguishable.

I fled towards the open beach. But there was no relief, for the entire beach was glowing luridly, like mud struggling to suffocate a moon. Among the debris I glimpsed the rest of Neal's clothes, half absorbed by the beach. As I staggered into the open, I saw his tracks ahead—saw how they appeared to grow, to alter until they became unrecognisable, and then to peter out at a large dark shapeless patch on the sand.

I glared about, terrified. I couldn't see the bungalows. After minutes I succeeded in glimpsing the path, the mess of footprints cluttering the dune. I began to pace toward it, very slowly and quietly, so as not to be noticed by the beach and the looming sky.

But the dunes were receding. I think I began to scream then, scream almost in a whisper, for the faster I hurried, the further the dunes withdrew. The nightmare had overtaken perspective. Now I was running wildly, though I felt I was standing still. I'd run only a few steps when I had to recoil from sand that seized my feet so eagerly I almost heard it smack its lips. Minutes ago there had been no quicksand, for I could see my earlier prints embedded in that patch. I stood trapped, shivering uncontrollably, as the glow intensified and the lightless sky seemed to descend—and I felt the beach change.

Simultaneously I experienced something which, in a sense, was worse: I felt myself change. My dizziness whirled out of me. I felt light-headed but stable. At last I realised that I had never had sunstroke. Perhaps it had been my inner conflict—being forced to stay yet at the same time not daring to venture onto the beach, because of what my subconscious knew would happen.

And now it was happening. The beach had won. Perhaps Neal had given it the strength. Though I dared not look, I knew that the sea had stopped. Stranded objects, elaborate symbols composed of something like flesh, writhed on its paralysed margin. The clamour

which surrounded me, chanting and gurgling, was not that of the
sea: it was far too articulate, however repetitive. It was underfoot
too—the voice of the beach, a whisper pronounced by so many
sources that it was deafening.

I felt ridges of sand squirm beneath me. They were firm enough
to bear my weight, but they felt nothing like sand. They were
forcing me to shift my balance. In a moment I would have to dance,
to imitate the jerking shapes that had ceased to pretend they were
only debris, to join in the ritual of the objects that swarmed up from
the congealed sea. Everything glistened in the quivering glow. I
thought my flesh had begun to glow too.

Then, with a lurch of vertigo worse than any I'd experienced, I
found myself momentarily detached from the nightmare. I seemed
to be observing myself, a figure tiny and trivial as an insect, making
a timid hysterical attempt to join in the dance of the teeming beach.
The moment was brief, yet felt like eternity. Then I was back in my
clumsy flesh, struggling to prance on the beach.

At once I was cold with terror. I shook like a victim of electricity,
for I knew what viewpoint I'd shared. It was still watching me, indifferent as outer space—and it filled the sky. If I looked up I would see
its eyes, or eye, if it had anything that I would recognise as such. My
neck shivered as I held my head down. But I would have to look up
in a moment, for I could feel the face, or whatever was up there,
leaning closer—reaching down for me.

If I hadn't broken through my suffocating panic I would have
been crushed to nothing. But my teeth tore my lip, and allowed me
to scream. Released, I ran desperately, heedless of quicksand. The
dunes crept back from me, the squirming beach glowed, the light
flickered in the rhythm of the chanting. I was spared being
engulfed—but when at last I reached the dunes, or was allowed to
reach them, the dark massive presence still hovered overhead.

I clambered scrabbling up the path. My sobbing gasps filled my
mouth with sand. My wild flight was from nothing that I'd seen. I
was fleeing the knowledge, deep-rooted and undeniable, that what I
perceived blotting out the sky was nothing but an acceptable
metaphor. Appalling though the presence was, it was only my
mind's version of what was there—a way of letting me glimpse it
without going mad at once.

V

I have not seen Neal since—at least, not in a form that anyone else would recognise.

Next day, after a night during which I drank all the liquor I could find to douse my appalled thoughts and insights, I discovered that I couldn't leave. I pretended to myself that I was going to the beach to search for Neal. But the movements began at once; the patterns stirred. As I gazed, dully entranced, I felt something grow less dormant in my head, as though my skull had turned into a shell.

Perhaps I stood engrossed by the beach for hours. Movement distracted me: the skimming of a windblown patch of sand. As I glanced at it I saw that it resembled a giant mask, its features ragged and crumbling. Though its eyes and mouth couldn't keep their shape, it kept trying to resemble Neal's face. As it slithered whispering toward me I fled toward the path, moaning.

That night he came into the bungalow. I hadn't dared go to bed; I dozed in a chair, and frequently woke trembling. Was I awake when I saw his huge face squirming and transforming as it crawled out of the wall? Certainly I could hear his words, though his voice was the inhuman chorus I'd experienced on the beach. Worse, when I opened my eyes to glimpse what might have been only a shadow, not a large unstable form fading back into the substance of the wall, for a few seconds I could still hear that voice.

Each night, once the face had sunk back into the wall as into quicksand, the voice remained longer—and each night, struggling to break loose from the prison of my chair, I understood more of its revelations. I tried to believe all this was my imagination, and so, in a sense, it was. The glimpses of Neal were nothing more than acceptable metaphors for what Neal had become, and what I was becoming. My mind refused to perceive the truth more directly, yet I was possessed by a temptation, vertiginous and sickening, to learn what that truth might be.

For a while I struggled. I couldn't leave, but perhaps I could write. When I found that however bitterly I fought I could think of nothing but the beach, I wrote this. I hoped that writing about it might release me, but of course the more one thinks of the beach, the stronger its hold becomes.

Now I spend most of my time on the beach. It has taken me months to write this. Sometimes I see people staring at me from the bungalows. Do they wonder what I'm doing? They will find out when their time comes—everyone will. Neal must have satisfied it for a while; for the moment it is slower. But that means little. Its time is not like ours.

Each day the pattern is clearer. My pacing helps. Once you have glimpsed the pattern you must go back to read it, over and over. I can feel it growing in my mind. The sense of expectancy is overwhelming. Of course that sense was never mine. It was the hunger of the beach.

My time is near. The large moist prints that surround mine are more pronounced—the prints of what I am becoming. Its substance is everywhere, stealthy and insidious. Today, as I looked at the bungalows, I saw them change; they grew like fossils of themselves. They looked like dreams of the beach, and that is what they will become.

The voice is always with me now. Sometimes the congealing haze seems to mouth at me. At twilight the dunes edge forward to guard the beach. When the beach is dimmest I see other figures pacing out the pattern. Only those whom the beach has touched would see them; their outlines are unstable—some look more like coral than flesh. The quicksands make us trace the pattern, and he stoops from the depths beyond the sky to watch. The sea feeds me.

Often now I have what may be a dream. I glimpse what Neal has become, and how that is merely a fragment of the imprint which it will use to return to our world. Each time I come closer to recalling the insight when I wake. As my mind changes, it tries to prepare me for the end. Soon I shall be what Neal is. I tremble uncontrollably, I feel deathly sick, my mind struggles desperately not to know. Yet in a way I am resigned. After all, even if I managed to flee the beach, I could never escape the growth. I have understood enough to know that it would absorb me in time, when it becomes the world.

THE HORROR UNDER WARRENDOWN

YOU ASK ME AT LEAST TO HINT WHY I REFUSE EVER TO open a children's book. Once I made my living from such material. While the imitations of reality hawked by my colleagues in the trade grew grubbier, and the fantasies more shameful, I carried innocence from shop to shop, or so I was proud to think. Now the sight of a children's classic in a bookshop window sends me fleeing. The more apparently innocent the book, the more unspeakable the truth it may conceal, and there are books the mere thought of which revives memories I had prayed were buried for ever.

It was when I worked from Birmingham, and Warrendown was only a name on a signpost on a road to Brichester—a road I avoided, not least because it contained no bookshops. Nor did I care for the route it followed a few miles beyond the Warrendown sign through Clotton, a small settlement which appeared to be largely abandoned, its few occupied houses huddling together beside each side of a river, beside which stood a concrete monument whose carvings were blurred by moss and weather. I had never been fond of the country-side, regarding it at best as a way of getting from town to town, and now the stagnant almost reptilian smell and chilly haze which surrounded Clotton seemed to attach itself to my car. This unwelcome presence helped to render the Cotswold landscape yet more forbidding to me, the farmland and green fields a disguise for the ancient stone of the hills, and I resolved to drive south of Brichester on the motorway in future and double back, even though this added half an hour to my journey. Had it not been for Graham Crawley I would never again have gone near the Warrendown road.

In those days I drank to be sociable, not to attempt to forget or to sleep. Once or twice a month I met colleagues in the trade, some of whom I fancied would have preferred to represent a children's publisher too, for a Balti and as many lagers as we could stay seated for. Saturdays would find me in my local pub, the Sutton Arms in Kings Heath. Ending my week among people who didn't need to be persuaded of the excellence of my latest batch of titles was enough to set me up for the next week. But it was in the Sutton Arms that Crawley made himself, I suppose, something like a friend.

I don't recall the early stages of the process, in his case or with any of the folk I used to know. I grew used to looking for him in the small bare taproom, where the stools and tables and low ceiling were the colour of ash mixed with ale. He would raise his broad round stubbled face from his tankard, twitching his nose and upper lip in greeting, and as I joined him he would duck as though he expected me either to pat him on the head or hit him when he'd emitted his inevitable quip. "What was she up to in the woods with seven little men, eh?" he would mutter, or "There's only one kind of horn you'd blow up that I know of. No wonder he was going after sheep", or some other reference to the kind of book in which I travelled. There was a constant undercurrent of ingratiating nervousness in his voice, an apology for whatever he said as he said it, which was one reason I was never at my ease with him. While we talked about our week, mine on the road and his behind the counter of a local greengrocer's, I was bracing myself for his latest sexual bulletin. I never knew that so many women could see in him, and hardly any of them lasted for more than an encounter. My curiosity about the kind of girl who could find him attractive may have left me open to doing him the favour he asked of me.

At first he only asked which route I took to Brichester, and then which one I would follow if the motorway was closed, by which point I'd had enough of the way he skulked around a subject as if he was ready to dart into hiding at the first hint of trouble. "Are you after a lift?" I demanded.

He ducked his head so that his long hair hid even more of his ears and peered up at me. "Well, a lift, you know, I suppose, really, yes."

"Where to?"

"You won't know it, cos it's not much of a place. Only it's not far, not much out of your way, I mean, if you happened to be going that way anyway sometime."

When at last he released the name of Warrendown like a question he didn't expect to be answered, his irritating tentativeness provoked me to retort "I'll be in that square of the map next week."

"Next week, that's next week, you mean." His face twitched so hard it exposed his teeth. "I wasn't thinking quite that soon . . . "

"I'll forgive you if you've given up on the idea."

"Given up—no, you're right. I'm going, cos I should go," he said, fiercely for him.

Nevertheless I arrived at his flat the next day not really expecting to collect him. When I rang his bell, however, he poked his nose under the drawn curtains and said he would be down in five minutes; which, to my continuing surprise, he was, nibbling the last of his presumably raw breakfast and dressed in the only suit I'd ever seen him wear. He sat clutching a small case which smelled of vegetables while I concentrated on driving through the rush hour and into the tangle of motorways, and so we were irrevocably on our way before I observed that he was gripping his luggage with all the determination I'd heard in his voice in the pub. "Are you expecting some kind of trouble?" I said.

"Trouble." He added a grunt which bared his teeth and which seemed to be saying I'd understood so much that no further questions were necessary, and I nearly lost my temper. "Care to tell me what kind?" I suggested.

"What would you expect?"

"Not a woman."

"See, you knew. Be tricks. The trouble's what I got her into, as if you hadn't guessed. Cos she got me going so fast I hadn't time to wear anything. Can't beat a hairy woman."

This was a great deal more intimate than I welcomed. "When did you last see her?" I said as curtly as I could.

"Last year. She was having it then. Should have gone down after, but I, you know. You know me."

He was hugging his baggage so hard he appeared to be squeezing out the senseless vegetable smell. "Afraid of her family?" I said with very little sympathy.

He pressed his chin against his chest, but I managed to distinguish what he muttered. "Afraid of the whole bloody place."

That was clearly worth pursuing, and an excuse for me to stay on my usual route, except that ahead I saw all three lanes of traffic halted as far as the horizon, and police cars racing along the hard shoulder towards the problem. I left the motorway at the exit which immediately presented itself.

Framilode, Saul, Fretherne, Whitminster . . . Old names announced themselves on signposts, and then a narrow devious road enclosed the car with hedges, blotting out the motorway at once. Beneath a sky clogged with dark clouds the gloomy foliage appeared to smoulder; the humped backs of the hills glowed a lurid green. When I opened my window to let out the vegetable smell, it admitted a breeze, unexpectedly chill for September, which felt like my passenger's nervousness rendered palpable. He was crouching over his luggage and blinking at the high spiky hedges as if they were a trap into which I'd led him. "Can I ask what your plans are?" I said to break the silence, which was growing as relentless as the ancient landscape.

"See her. Find out what she's got, what she wants me to." His voice didn't so much trail off as come to a complete stop. I wasn't sure I wanted to know where his thoughts had found themselves. "What took you there to begin with?" was as much as I cared to ask.

"Beat ricks."

This time I grasped it, despite his pronouncing it as though unconvinced it was a name. "She's the young lady in question."

"Met her in the Cabbage Patch, you know, the caff. She'd just finished university but she stayed over at my place." I was afraid this might be the preamble to further intimate details, but he continued with increasing reluctance "Kept writing to me after she went home, wanting me to go down there, cos she said I'd feel at home."

"And did you?"

He raised his head as though sniffing the air and froze in the position. The sign for Warrendown, drooping a little on its post, had swung into view along the hedge. His half-admitted feelings had affected me so much that my foot on the accelerator wavered. "If you'd prefer not to do this . . . "

Only his mouth moved, barely opening. "No choice."

No reply could have angered me more. He'd no more will than one of his own vegetables, I thought, and sent the car screeching into the Warrendown road. As we left behind the sign which appeared to be trying to point into the earth, I had an impression of movement beyond the hedge on both sides of the road, several figures which had been standing absolutely still leaping to follow the car. I told myself I was mistaking at least their speed, and when ragged gaps in the hedge afforded me a view of oppressively green fields weighed down by the stagnant sky, nobody was to be seen, not that anyone could have kept pace with the car. I hadn't time to ponder any of this, because from the way Crawley was inching his face forward I could tell that the sight a mile ahead among the riotous fields surrounded by hunched dark hills must indeed be Warrendown.

At that distance I saw it was one of the elements of the country-side I most disliked, an insignificant huddle of buildings miles from anywhere, but I'd never experienced such immediate revulsion. The clump of thatched roofs put me in mind of dunes surmounted by dry grass, evidence less of human habitation than of the mindless actions of nature. As the sloping road led me down towards them, I saw that the thatch overhung the cottages, like hair dangling over idiot brows. Where the road descended to the level of the village, it showed me that the outermost cottages were so squat they appeared to have collapsed or to be sinking into the earth of the unpaved road. Thatch obscured their squinting windows, and I gave in to an irrational hope that the village might prove to be abandoned. Then the door of the foremost cottage sank inwards, and as I braked, a head poked out of the doorway to watch our arrival.

It was a female head. So much I distinguished before it was snatched back. I glanced at Crawley in case he had recognised it, but he was wrinkling his face at some aspect of the village which had disconcerted him. As the car coasted into Warrendown, the woman reappeared, having draped a scarf over her head to cover even more of her than her dress did. I thought she was holding a baby, then decided it must be some kind of pet, because as she emerged into the road with an odd abrupt lurch the small object sprang from her arms into the dimness within the cottage. She knotted the scarf and thrust her plump yet flattish face out of it to stare swollen-eyed at my passenger. I was willing to turn the vehicle around and race for the main road, but he was lowering his window, and so I slowed the car. I saw their heads lean towards each other as though the under-side of the sky was pressing them down and forcing them together. Their movements seemed obscurely reminiscent, but I'd failed to identify of what when she spoke. "You're back."

Though her low voice wasn't in itself threatening, I sensed he was disconcerted that someone he clearly couldn't put a name to had recognised him. All he said, however, was "You know Beatrix."

"Us all know one another."

She hadn't once glanced at me, but I was unable to look away from her. A few coarse hairs sprouted from her reddish face; I had the unpleasant notion that her cheeks were raw from being shaved. "Do you know where she is?" Crawley said.

"Her'll be with the young ones."

His head sank as his face turned up further. "How many?"

"All that's awake. Can't you hear them? I should reckon even he could."

As that apparently meant me I dutifully strained my ears, although I wasn't anxious to heighten another sense: our entry into Warrendown seemed to have intensified the vegetable stench. After a few moments I made out a series of high regular sounds—childish voices chanting some formula—and experienced almost as much relief as my passenger audibly did. "She's at the school," he said.

"That's her. Back where her was always meant for." The woman glanced over her shoulder into the cottage, and part of a disconcertingly large ear twitched out of her headscarf. "Feeding time," she said, and began unbuttoning the front of her dress as she stepped back through the doorway, beyond which I seemed to glimpse something hopping about a bare earth floor. "See you down there later," she told Crawley, and shut the door.

I threw the car into gear and drove as fast through the village as I reasonably could. Faces peered through the thick fringes over the low windows of the stunted cottages, and I told myself it was the dimness within that made those faces seem so fat and so blurred in their outlines, and the nervousness with which Crawley had infected me that caused their eyes to appear so large. At the centre of Warrendown the cottages, some of which I took to be shops without signs, crowded towards the road as if forced forward by the mounds behind them, mounds as broad as the cottages but lower, covered with thatch or grass. Past the centre the buildings were more sunken; more than one had collapsed, while others were so overgrown that only glimpses through the half-obscured unglazed windows of movements, ill-defined and sluggish, suggested that they were inhabited. I felt as though the rotten vegetable sweetness in the air was somehow dragging them all down as it was threatening to do to me, and had to restrain my foot from tramping on the accelerator. Now the car was almost out of Warrendown, which was scarcely half a mile long, and the high voices had fallen silent before I was able to distinguish what they had been chanting—a hymn, my instincts told me, even though the language had seemed wholly unfamiliar. I was wondering whether I'd passed the school, and preparing to tell Crawley I hadn't time to retrace the route, when Crawley mumbled "This is it."

"If you say so." I now saw that the last fifty or so yards of the left-hand side of Warrendown were occupied by one long mound fattened by a pelt of thatch and grass and moss. I stopped the car but poised my foot on the accelerator. "What do you want to do?"

His blank eyes turned to me. Perhaps it was the strain on them which made them appear to be almost starting out of his head. "Why do you have to ask?"

I'd had enough. I reached across him to let him out, and the door of the school wobbled open as though I'd given it a cue. Beyond it stood a young woman of whom I could distinguish little except a long-sleeved ankle-length brown dress, my attention having been caught by the spectacle behind her—at least half a dozen small bodies in a restless heap on the bare floor of the dark corridor. As some of them raised their heads lethargically to blink big-eyed at me before subsiding again, Crawley clambered out of the vehicle, blocking my view. "Thanks for, you know," he muttered. "You'll be coming back this way, will you?"

"Does that mean you'll be ready to leave?"

"I'll know better when you come."

"I'll be back before dark and you'd better be out here on the road," I told him, and sped off.

I kept him in view in the mirror until the hedges hid Warrendown. The mirror shook with the unevenness of the road, but I saw him wave his free hand after me, stretching his torso towards the car as though he was about to drop to all fours and give chase. Behind him a figure leapt out of the doorway, and as he swung round she caught him. I could distinguish no more about her than I already had, except that the outline of her large face looked furry, no doubt framed by hair. She and Crawley embraced—all her limbs clasped him, at any rate—and as I looked away from this intimacy I noticed that the building of which the school was an extension had once possessed a tower, the overgrown stones of which were scattered beyond the edge of the village. It was none of my business whether they took care of their church, nor why anyone who'd attended university should have allowed herself to be reduced to teaching in a village school, nor what hold the place seemed to have over Crawley as well. They deserved each other, I told myself, and not only because they looked so similar. Once they were out of sight I lowered the windows and drove fast to rid the car of the stagnant mindless smell of Warrendown.

Before long the track brought me to an unmarked junction with the main road. I wound the windows tight and sped through the remains of Clotton, which felt drowned by the murky sky and the insidious chill of the dark river, and didn't slow until I saw Brichester ahead, raising its hospital and graveyard above its multiplying streets. In those streets I felt more at ease; nothing untoward had ever befallen me in a city such as Brichester, and nothing seemed likely to do so, especially in a bookshop. I parked my car in a multistorey at the edge of Lower Brichester and walked through the crowds to the first of my appointments.

My Christmas titles went down well—in the last shop of the day, perhaps too well. Not only did the new manager, previously second in command, order more copies than any of her competitors, but in a prematurely festive mood insisted on my helping her celebrate her promotion. One drink led to several, not least because I must have been trying to douse the nervousness with which Crawley and Warrendown had left me. Too late I realised my need for plenty of coffee and something to eat, and by the time I felt fit to drive the afternoon was well over.

Twilight had gathered like soot in cobwebs as wide as the sky. From the car park I saw lights fleeing upwards all over Brichester, vanishing home. The hospital was a glimmering misshapen skull beside which lay acres of bones. Even the fluorescent glare of the car park appeared unnatural, and I sat in my car wondering how much worse the places I had to drive back through would seem. I'd told Crawley I would collect him before dark, but wasn't it already dark? Might he not have decided I wasn't coming for him, and have made his own arrangements? This was almost enough to persuade me I needn't return to Warrendown, but a stirring of guilt at my cowardice shamed me into heading for that morning's route.

The glow of the city sank out of view. A few headlights came to meet me, and then there were only my beams probing the dim road that writhed between the hills, which rose as though in the dark they no longer needed to pretend to slumber. The bends of the road swung back and forth, unable to avoid my meagre light, and once a pair of horned heads stared over a gate, rolling their eyes as they chewed and chewed, rolling them mindlessly as they would when they went to be slaughtered. I remembered how Crawley's eyes had protruded as he prepared to quit my car.

Well outside Clotton I was seized by the chill of the river. Though my windows were shut tight, as I reached the first abandoned house I heard the water, splashing more loudly than could be accounted for unless some large object was obstructing it. I drove so fast across the narrow bridge and between the eyeless buildings that by the time I was able to overcome my inexplicable panic I was miles up the road, past the unmarked lane to Warrendown.

I told myself that I mustn't use this as an excuse to break my word, and when I reached the Warrendown signpost, which looked as though the weight of the growing blackness was helping the earth drag it down, I steered the car off the main road. Even with my headlight beams full on, I had to drive at a speed which made me feel the vehicle was burrowing into the thick dark, which by now could just as well have been the night it was anticipating. The contortions of the road suggested it was doing its utmost never to reach Warrendown. The thorns of the hedges tore at the air, and a gap in the tortured mass of vegetation let me see the cottages crouching furtively, heads down, in the midst of the smudged fields. Despite the darkness, not a light was to be seen.

It could have been a power failure—I assumed those might be common in so isolated and insignificant a village—but why was nobody in Warrendown using candles or flashlights? Perhaps they were, invisibly at that distance, I reassured myself. The hedges intervened without allowing me a second look. The road sloped down, giving me the unwelcome notion that Warrendown had snared it, and the hedges ended as though they had been chewed off. As my headlights found the outermost cottages, their long-haired skulls seemed to rear out of the earth. Apart from that, there was no movement all the way along the road to the half-ruined church.

The insidious vegetable stench had already begun to seep into the car. It cost me an effort to drive slowly enough through the village to look for the reason I was here. The thatched fringes were full of shadows which shifted as I passed as though each cottage was turning its idiot head towards me. Though every window was empty and dark, I felt observed, increasingly so as the car followed its wobbling beams along the deserted lane, until I found it hard to breathe. I seemed to hear a faint irregular thumping—surely my own unsteady pulse, not a drumming under the earth. I came abreast of the church and the school, and thought the thumping quickened and then ceased. Now I was out of Warrendown, but the knowledge that I would be returning to the main road whichever direction I chose persuaded me to make a last search. I turned the car, almost backing it into one of the overgrown blocks of the fallen tower, and sounded my horn twice.

The second blare followed the first into the silent dark. Nothing moved, not a single strand of thatch on the cottages within the congealed splash of light cast by my headlamps, but I was suddenly nervous of what response I might have invited. I eased the car away from the ruins of the tower and began to drive once more through Warrendown, my foot trembling on the accelerator as I made myself restrain my speed. I was past the school when a dim shape lurched into my mirror and in pursuit of the car.

Only my feeling relatively secure inside the vehicle allowed me to brake long enough to see the face. The figure flared red as though it was being skinned from head to foot, and in the moment before its hands jerked up to paw its eyes I saw it was Crawley. Had his eyes always been so sensitive to sudden light? I released the brake pedal and fumbled the gears into neutral, and saw him let his hands fall but otherwise not move. It took some determination on my part to lower the window in order to call to him. "Come on if you're coming."

I barely heard his answer; his voice was indistinct—clogged. "I can't."

I would have reversed alongside him, except there wasn't room to pass him if he stayed put in the middle of the road. I flung myself out of the car in a rage and slammed the door furiously, a sound that seemed to provoke a renewed outbreak of muffled drumming, which I might have remarked had I not been intent on trying to wave away the suffocating vegetable smell. "Why not?" I demanded, staying by the car.

"Come and see."

I wasn't anxious to see more of Warrendown, or indeed of him. In the backwash of the car's lights his face appeared swollen with more stubble than an ordinary day could produce, and his eyes seemed dismayingly enlarged, soaking up the dimness. "See what?" I said. "Is it your young lady?"

"My what?"

I couldn't judge whether his tone was of hysterical amusement or panic or both. "Beatrix," I said, more loudly than I liked to in the abnormal silence and darkness. "Is it your child?"

"There isn't one."

"I'm sorry," I murmured, uncertain whether I should be. "You mean Beatrix . . . "

I was loath to put into words what I assumed she must have done, but he shook his blurred head and took an uncertain step towards me. I had the impression, which disturbed me so much I was distracted from the word he'd inched closer to mutter, that he couldn't quite remember how to walk. "What are you saying?" I shouted before my voice flinched from the silence. "What's absurd? Never mind. Tell me when you're in the car."

He'd halted, hands dangling in front of his chest. His protruding teeth glinted, and I saw that he was chewing—seemed to glimpse a greenishness about his mouth and fattened cheeks. "Can't do that," he mumbled.

Did he mean neither of us would be able to return to the car? "Why not?" I cried.

"Come and see."

At that moment no prospect appealed to me less—but before I could refuse he turned his back and leapt into the dark. Two strides, or at least two convulsive movements, carried him to the doorless entrance to the church. The next moment he vanished into the lightless interior, and I heard a rapid padding over whatever served for a floor; then, so far as the throbbing of my ears allowed me to distinguish, there was silence.

I ran to the church doorway, which was as far as the faintest glow from my headlights reached. "Crawley," I called with an urgency meant to warn him I had no intention of lingering, but the only response from the dark was a feeble echo of my call, followed by a surge of the omnipresent vegetable stench. I called once more and then, enraged almost beyond the ability to think, I dashed to my car. If I had still been rational—if the influence of Warrendown had not already fastened on my mind—I would surely have left my acquaintance to his chosen fate and driven for my life. Instead I fetched my flashlight from under the dashboard and, having switched off the headlamps and locked the car, returned to the rotting church.

As the flashlight beam wavered through the doorway I saw that the place was worse than abandoned. The dozen or so pews on either side of the aisle, each pew broad enough to accommodate a large family, were only bloated green with moss and weeds; but the altar before them had been levered up, leaning its back against the rear wall of the church and exposing the underside of its stone. I swung the beam through the desecrated interior, and glimpsed crude drawings on the mottled greenish walls as shadows of pews pranced across them. There was no trace of Crawley, and nowhere for him to hide unless he was crouching behind the altar. I stalked along the aisle to look, and almost fell headlong into a blackness that was more than dark. Just in time the flashlight beam plunged into the tunnel which had been dug where the altar ought to have stood.

The passage sloped quite gently into the earth, further than my light could reach. It was as wide as a burly man, but not as tall as I. Now I realised what my mind had been reluctant to accept as I'd heard Crawley disappear into the church—that his footfalls had seemed to recede to a greater distance than the building could contain. I let the beam stray across the pews in a last desperate search for him, and was unable to avoid glimpsing the images scrawled on the walls, an impious dance of clownish figures with ears and feet so disproportionately large they must surely be false. Then Crawley spoke from the tunnel beyond the curve which my light barely touched. "Come down. Come and see."

A wave of the stench like a huge vegetable breath rose from the tunnel and enveloped me. I staggered and almost dropped the flashlight—and then I lowered myself into the earth and stumbled in a crouch towards the summons. The somnolence audible in Crawley's voice had overtaken me too, and there seemed no reason why I should not obey, nor anything untoward about my behaviour or my surroundings. Even the vegetable stench was to my taste, because I had inhaled so much of it since venturing back to Warrendown. Indeed, I was beginning to want nothing more than to be led to its source.

I stooped as far as the bend in the tunnel, just in time to see Crawley's heels vanishing around a curve perhaps fifty yards ahead. I saw now, as I had resisted hearing, that his feet were unshod— bare, at any rate, although the glimpse I had of them seemed hairier than any man's feet should be. He was muttering to me or to himself, and phrases drifted back: ". . . the revelations of the leaf . . . the food twice consumed . . . the paws in the dark . . . the womb that eats . . . " I thought only my unsteady light was making the scraped passage gulp narrower, but before I gained the second bend I had to drop to all fours. Far ahead down the increasingly steep tunnel the drumming I'd heard earlier had recommenced, and I imagined that the models for the figures depicted on the church walls were making the sound, drumming their malformed feet as they danced in some vast subterranean cavern. That prospect gave me cause to falter, but another vegetable exhalation from below coaxed me onwards, to the further bend around which Crawley's heels had withdrawn. I was crawling now, content as a worm in the earth, the flashlight in my outstretched hands making the tunnel swallow in anticipation of me each time my knees bumped forward. The drumming of feet on earth filled my ears, and I saw Crawley's furred soles disappear a last time at the limit of the flashlight beam, not around a curve but into an underground darkness too large for my light to begin to define. His muttering had ceased as though silenced by whatever had met him, but I heard at last the answer he had given me when I'd enquired after the child: not "absurd" at all. He'd told me that the child had been *absorbed*. Even this was no longer enough to break through the influence of whatever awaited me at the end of the tunnel, and I crawled rapidly forward to the subterranean mouth.

The flashlight beam sprawled out ahead of me, doing its best to illuminate a vast space beneath a ceiling too high even to glimpse. At first the dimness, together with shock or the torpor which had overcome my brain, allowed me to avoid seeing too much: only a horde of unclothed figures hopping and leaping and twisting in the air around an idol which towered from the moist earth, an idol not unlike a greenish Easter Island statue overgrown almost to featurelessness, its apex lost in the darkness overhead. Then I saw that one of the worshipping horde was Crawley, and began to make out faces less able to pass for human than his, their great eyes bulging in the dimness, their bestial teeth gleaming in misshapen mouths. The graffiti on the church walls had not exaggerated their shapes, I saw, nor were they in costume. The earth around the idol swarmed with their young, a scuttling mass of countless bodies which nothing human could have acknowledged as offspring. I gazed numbly down on the ancient rite, which no sunlight could have tolerated—and then the idol moved.

It unfurled part of itself towards me, a glimmering green appendage which might have been a gigantic wing emerging from a cocoon, and as it reached for me it whispered seductively with no mouth. Even this failed to appal me in my stupor; but when Crawley pranced towards me, a blasphemous priest offering me the unholy sacrament which would bind me to the buried secrets of Warrendown, some last vestige of wholesomeness and sanity within me revolted, and I backed gibbering along the tunnel, leaving the flashlight to blind anything which might follow.

All the way to the tunnel entrance I was terrified of being seized from behind. Every inhabitant of Warrendown must have been at the bestial rite, however, because I had encountered no hindrance except for the passage itself when I scrambled out beneath the altar and reeled through the lightless church to my car. The lowered heads of the cottages twitched their scalps at me as I sped recklessly out of Warrendown, the hedges beside the road clawed the air as though they were determined to close their thorns about me, but somehow in my stupor I managed to arrive at the main road, from where instincts which must have been wholly automatic enabled me to drive to the motorway, and so home, where I collapsed into bed.

I slept for a night and a day, such was my torpor. Even night-mares failed to waken me, and when eventually I struggled out of bed I half-believed that the horror under Warrendown had been one of them. I avoided Crawley and the pub, however, and so it was more than a week later I learned that he had disappeared—that his landlord had entered his room and found no bed in there, only a mound of overgrown earth hollowed out to accommodate a body—at which point my mind came close to giving way beneath an onslaught of more truth than any human mind should be required to suffer.

Is that why nobody will hear me out? How can they not under-stand that there may be other places like Warrendown, where monstrous gods older than humanity still hold sway? For a time I thought some children's books might be trying to hint at these secrets, until I came to wonder whether instead they are traps laid to lure children to such places, and I could no longer bear to do my job. Now I watch and wait, and stay close to lights that will blind the great eyes of the inhabitants of Warrendown, and avoid anywhere that sells vegetables, which I can smell at a hundred yards. Suppose there are others like Crawley, the hybrid spawn of some unspeakable congress, at large in our streets? Suppose they are feeding the unsuspecting mass of humanity some part of the horror I saw at the last under Warrendown?

What sane words can describe it? Partly virescent, partly glaucous . . . pullulating . . . internodally stunted . . . otiose . . . angiospermous . . . multifoliate . . . Nothing can convey the dreadfulness of that final revelation, when I saw how it had overcome the last traces of humanity in its worshippers, who in some lost generation must have descended from imitating the denizens of the underworld to mating with them. For as the living idol unfurled a sluggish portion of itself towards me, Crawley tore off that living member of his brainless god, sinking his teeth into it to gnaw a mouthful before he proffered it, glistening and writhing with hideous life, to me.

The Other Names

THEY WERE PAST THE TOP OF BRICHESTER AND NEARLY AT
the twisted house when Arnold started. "What's the sign say,
Sylly? What's it say?"

"It says BEWARE OF KILLER DOG," Bruce suggested, raising
his fists as he did whenever he spoke.

"No, it says TRESPASSERS. WILL. BE. CASTARATED,"
Denzil said, pointing the fattest finger of his right hand at each
bunch of marks on the signboard.

"Shut up, you. And you and all. I'll tell you what it says," Arnold
said, and rubbed his scalp as if to conjure hair out of the grey shaved
skin. "It says SYLLY'S TURN NOW WE'VE ALL BEEN IN OR
HE'S A WIMP."

"Don't call me that," Sylvester told him. "It doesn't, either."

"Go on then." Arnold shoved his blotchy face and broken eleven-
year-old nose at him. "You say what it says."

A wind blustered down from the dark Cotswold hills and tried to
find its way under Sylvester's leather jacket. While he didn't shiver,
everything around the abandoned house did: the tall scrawny trees
like charred bones hanging from the black sky, the knee-high grass
and shrivelled weeds that sprawled over the cracked mossy path
beyond the fallen gate, the segments of rotted fence leaning away
from one another on top of the crumbling wall. Even the board
shook as though impatient, but the marks on it conveyed no more

to him. "It says JUST AN OLD HOUSE WITH NOTHING IN," he muttered.

If that was true, it hadn't been. He remembered the items the others had brought back to show they'd gone all the way in. Bruce had run out carrying a mask that couldn't have been meant to be worn, since it had only one eye-hole and far too big a grinning face—he'd run so fast that he'd dropped it to smash on the path. Denzil had found a bowl that seemed to have been used to grow fungus in, but when he'd felt underneath it he'd thought it was somebody's skull cut in half down the middle and had thrown it over the fence. And Arnold had returned with a screw-topped jar so grimy it had been impossible to tell whether its contents were a little hand or a spider with not enough legs, particularly once he'd tipped it out and they had all trampled on it when it had appeared to try to crawl away. Perhaps Arnold was recalling this as he said into Sylvester's face "If there's nothing in it, why aren't you going?"

"Give us the light and I will."

Arnold handed him the club of a flashlight so readily that Sylvester demanded "Have you messed with it?"

"You'll find out," Arnold said in a tone that left him no other choice.

Sylvester poked the beam of Bruce's stolen flashlight through the gateway with dried-up rasping weeds for gates. The light found the mouldering front of the house, but that was as far as it reached. Six windows showed him darkness which appeared to go back further than it should. The way the pairs of windows shrank as they went higher was not the only reason why he saw the house tilting backwards, tipping the unhinged front door into the dark. As he and the others had swaggered along the lane with no other houses in it he'd seen how the rear of the building was at least a foot lower than the front, and twisted to the left as though it was trying to drag the rest of the house with it. Now that the wind was holding its breath he saw that all the grass and weeds leaned towards the house, suggesting that it was stronger than sunlight. He fancied that the path was sloping downwards underfoot, though his eyes told him otherwise. He slashed at weeds with the flashlight and wished he could feel like an explorer in the jungle as the dark beyond the windows lurched at him.

It was only a house that was falling down, and it wasn't going to fall on him. The owner who'd died in it while it was starting to collapse had just been a crazy old man who used to shout and sing at night in a language nobody could understand. No wonder the people who lived nearest had told stories about him when he'd kept wakening them at all hours—how on the night he died they'd heard a voice joining in with his, and then the old man trying to shout it down, maybe because it had been much bigger than his and had seemed not to need to breathe, until his voice had come apart as if the other one had been tearing him open. Could his mouth really have been wider than the hands with which he'd tried to shut it? Only the police who had found him would know. Sylvester was a very few steps from the house now, yet the flashlight was making no appreciable difference to the dark beyond the fallen door. "Don't come out till you've got something," Arnold called along the path, so that Sylvester couldn't hesitate for being watched, even though the doorstep seemed to tilt slyly inwards as he trod on it and aimed the flashlight beam into the house.

At first the light slid over the darkness, which only gradually admitted to containing walls and bare floorboards and, when he raised the beam, the lofty ceiling of a hall. Every surface was as black as the sky between the stars. Although doors were open in both walls, the darkness of the openings was virtually indistinguishable from the walls themselves. "There's nothing left down there," Bruce advised from the safety of the pavement. "You'll have to go up."

Sylvester showed him a vicious finger and stepped over the skewed door, and felt himself being tilted down into the house. Perhaps it was the way the light seemed unable to keep hold of the surfaces of the interior—crept over them even when he gripped the flashlight with both hands—that made him feel in danger of sliding all the way down the hall, past a fallen chandelier like a translucent stranded deep-sea creature, to the point where the house was most warped. A spasm of panic sent him onto the stairs which the darkness to his left had abruptly produced. At least their angles caught more of the light than the hall did. He'd go as far as the first window from which he would be visible, and then the others would have to admit he'd ventured further than they had.

The creak of each stair echoed into the distance, enlarging the darkness and sounding as though the house was continuing to warp. He had to believe that the black underside of the roof was coming closer only because he was climbing towards it, not lowering itself, but he was beginning to feel as though he was being trapped under a stone with whatever might live there unseen. He was wishing he'd hidden some object in a pocket before leaving home so that he could say he'd found it in the house when all at once there were no more stairs between him and the middle floor.

At least he was able to see outside the house. Beyond a doorway to his left the hole of a window showed him the highest streetlamps of Mercy Hill leading down into Brichester. He took a step towards the room, and was unable to halt. Whatever had taken place in the house had warped this corridor even more steeply than the ground floor, and he seemed to have no option other than to stagger into the room, flailing the air with his fists and the cone of light, unless he wanted to be carried helplessly deeper into the house.

The room was almost bare. A bedstead off which a mattress lolled had been dragged away from the window, leaving deep scratches in the floorboards. The mattress had been torn open, and its dangling innards were unpleasantly suggestive of withered dusty entrails. Protruding from beneath the heap of them as though it had been concealed within the mattress was a book whose covers were as black as the inside of the house. His sense of how useless a book would be to him was so overwhelming that he almost forgot he could take it to show. He ran across the room, pursued by footsteps that must be his and, grabbing the book by a corner, snatched it out of the clinging mass. The cover fell open, and he saw the first page.

Except the book, which was bound like a real one but had lines ruled on its pages, didn't just fall open. It twisted in his hand, and he had an impression of its warping exactly as the house had, a notion which overwhelmed him so powerfully he thought he felt his mind change shape. Before he could grasp the impression it vanished, and the book was straightened out. It was just a book, yet he couldn't take his eyes off it, and nothing else mattered. He could read the page.

Charles Horus, his book so long as he shall live. Copied under the protection of Nyarlathotep, Stalker in the Shadows. Written from memory of the Necronomicon, *British Museum, 1985—1995...*

Each shakily handwritten word in the midst of the shrinking island of light seemed to be forming itself especially for him. He squatted to turn the page, then considered perching on the edge of the bedstead, at which point his awareness of his surroundings returned to him. That didn't cow him, not when he suddenly had so much more of a mind. He ran to the window and saw the three boys throwing chunks of the wall at streetlamps, having lost interest in watching for him. He'd show them a prize that was worth all of theirs, one they wouldn't believe until he proved it. Hugging the book with both arms, he bore it from the room.

The tilted corridor didn't bother him. He only had to walk uphill to the stairs, and he did. The stairs themselves were worse—as he clattered down them he had a sense of climbing towards the secretive darkness beneath the roof, and grabbing the banister was like trying to hold onto a dead eel—but by telling himself he was on his way out he managed to keep going. His heels struck the canted floor of the hall at last. Three upward strides took him past the torn-off door and onto the path, whose roughness prevented him from sliding back. He was almost at the gateway before the others saw him.

Denzil pointed so wildly that Sylvester thought there was something at his back until he realised the subject of the gesture was himself. "Look at him," Denzil scoffed, and when he'd finished laughing at that "Look what he's got."

Bruce told the joke a different way. "Sylly's got a book."

"Let's see it," Arnold demanded as if the sight of it wasn't convincing enough.

Sylvester thrust the flashlight into his hand before opening the middle of the book. "It's only wrote in," Bruce complained.

Denzil gave the pages twice as much of a look while he dragged his finger along the air in front of them. "Isn't even a diary," he decided as soon as he could.

"Give us a look, I said." Arnold shoved the flashlight under his arm and slammed his hands on top of Sylvester's on the edges of the book. When Sylvester refused to let go, Arnold wrested the book towards the light of a surviving streetlamp. "Thought so," he said. "It's just mad stuff. Let's tear it up."

"Don't." Sylvester backed away, taking the book with him, and could have imagined he felt it helping him, nudging its edges into his grip like a creature settling into its lair. "I found it. I want to keep it. It's mine."

"Reckon he's going to try and make out he can read."

"Bet his dad'll give him a kicking if he does," Bruce exulted.

"Couldn't even read that sign," said Denzil.

Sylvester closed the book and clutched it to himself, and looked at the signboard above the fence. "Well, I can," he said as the letters

instantly fitted themselves to his mind. "It says BUILDING PLOT
FOR SALE."

"He's guessing," said Arnold, then glared at the others. "Or somebody told him."

"I never," Bruce said, shaking his fists at the idea.

"Wasn't me," protested Denzil.

Sylvester wished he hadn't revealed his new ability until he'd seen
what he could do by hiding it. "Wasn't any of you," he said, "but
I'm not saying who."

"See, I told you someone did," said Arnold, and considered
punching him in the face, but contented himself with leading a fresh
bout of derision. "Let's do something down the hill," he said at last
and strutted off, pausing only to shatter the undamaged lamp.

Sylvester looked back from the slope. The twisted house was
sinking out of view beyond the crest of the hill, as if it was collapsing
for want of a support he'd taken away with him. He had little time
to reflect on this, because once they'd marched down the steeply
terraced street he was too busy trying to outdo the others in causing
a row outside the hospital, playing the railings with a bit of
someone's fence and yelling the worst words he knew. He couldn't
let on that he knew the sign said PLEASE BE QUIET NEAR
HOSPITAL. Soon a guard with a truncheon that whooped through
the air chased the boys down past the graveyard, and Sylvester
glimpsed a few of the inscriptions on the stones. He would have
liked to read more until he grasped how the reduction of lives to
hyphenated dates affected him. Shortly, however, he and his
companions were in central Brichester, and there was much to read.

The pedestrianised streets were plates of neon, and the night
crowds were out—children sharing bottles they'd persuaded
someone to buy or to sell them, young couples pretending they
could afford everything they wanted, people buying commodities
in doorways, gangs in search of a pub and a fight—but all
Sylvester could see were signs. LATEST FASHIONS. 20 KING
SIZE. INSTANT PRIZES. SHOPLIFTERS WILL BE
PROSECUTED. BEER OF THE MONTH. ALL DAMAGE
MUST BE PAID FOR. EVERYTHING HALF PRICE OR LESS.
24 HOUR SECURITY. ADULT BOOKS...In particular his
understanding that the sign he'd always thought said SHOP in
nearly every window was SALE came as a revelation, yet the more he
deciphered, the more he seemed to sense the yearning of the book in

his embrace to be read. When his companions began looking for burglar alarms to set off or, better still, that were already triggered so that the boys could break in, he said "I have to go now."

"He's going home to read," shouted Denzil, jabbing the book with his favourite finger.

"Going to show his book to his dad," Bruce crowed between his fists.

"Hide it from him, more like," Arnold said, and lowered his head in case it was required for butting.

Sylvester hurried to the bus station full of sleeping people being woken up by guards. A bus not much larger than his father's van was about to leave for Lower Brichester. It smelled at the very least of booze and tobacco, but he hardly noticed once he turned to the book. Perhaps it was the lurch of the bus as it raced to overtake one from a different company which made the book open itself.

Daoloth is truth. Before the eyes and minds of men shrank from all about them and within themselves was Daoloth. Daoloth knows all names and is all names, and all names are Its name. All things within the universe, and all which are beyond and so are part thereof, must yield their true names to the power of Daoloth. He who utters the name of Daoloth shall hear Its voice in all things and so learn their names. As those names are called in Its name, so must those called shed the cloak which men have draped about them and reveal their veritable aspect in Daoloth...

Though Sylvester couldn't have paraphrased any of this, he felt it settling into the depths of himself. He seemed hardly to have started reading when he grew aware that he was about to be carried past his stop. Ordinarily he would have seen how far he could travel beyond his fare before he was thrown off, but now he wanted to give himself up to the miracle of reading. He depressed the bell until the infuriated driver stopped the bus and came for him, at which point Sylvester dodged around him to haul on the lever that released the doors and sprint into the nearest back alley which led home.

His father's van, which he saw at last said BENNY BENTLEY BUILDER, was parked mostly on the pavement in front of the house, and casting its shadow across the sliver of a garden as though to cover up some of the work his father had done—the yellow paint outlines too large for the windows, the plastic gutter sagging from the roof, the cracked pebbledash. The bespectacled old woman who always complained about any children in sight was dragging her wheezing tartan-lagged dog out of the house opposite. "Don't you be looking at me, Sylvester Bentley," she said at once, "or I'll set him on you."

Sylvester turned away without speaking, which gave her a reason to start an extended complaint, and let himself into the house. He was hoping to sneak upstairs now that the front door didn't stick, since his father had been at too much of it with a plane. Besides, in the front room he could hear a video making the kinds of noises his parents sometimes emitted when they thought he was asleep. He was halfway up the stairs, and just had time to sit on the book, when his father came out glowering and stuffing his shirt into his jeans. 'Where've you been? How long have you been hanging round there?'

"He's not been pinching," Sylvester's mother called or groaned.

"You heard your ma. Have you?'

"I've just been with Arn and them."

"I hope you didn't let them take advantage of you," his invisible mother said.

"You want to get yourself some decent mates." Having dealt with that, his father withdrew. "Don't come in here," he said, and slammed the door.

Sylvester might have listened outside if he hadn't been eager to return to his book. He ran up the stairs, above which the highest of a trio of plaster ducks had begun an inadvertent nose-dive, and into his room, where he set the book down on the bed while he leafed through his computer manual. Although he could read it at last, it told him nothing he hadn't been shown at school. He threw it on top of the bookcase stuffed with computer games and sat down with the book from the twisted house.

It skewed itself open at the page he'd read. He went through the sentences again and felt them slither between his thoughts. Perhaps he wouldn't understand them until he had obeyed them. He carried the book to the window and stared along the concertinaed terrace, and had an inkling of how long the book had occupied him when he saw the old woman already dragging her dog homeward from its lavatorial quest. "Miss Whittle," he whispered, and added what the book seemed to want him to say. 'Day oh loth.'

The dog insisted on halting at the streetlamp closest to home, and the old woman saw Sylvester. He almost flinched back as she raised her face into the white glare of the lamp, but she couldn't know what he'd done when he didn't know himself. Despite the promise of the book, he didn't quite hear a voice, unless that included the one in his head. It was more as though he glimpsed, or had a memory of glimpsing, shapes that were hidden by Miss Whittle and her dog—that were hiding either behind or within them or, somehow, both. However nearly indefinable it was, the glimpse suggested words to him, words that would help him see it. "Old Bones That Crawl," he said like answering at school. "Day oh loth says."

The dog lowered its leg, and the old woman's spectacles aimed the glare at Sylvester's window as if her eyes had grown white and blind before she and the dog waddled up their path. It seemed to him that a bit of the world had twisted in the instant he'd ceased to speak. He wasn't sure that he wanted to see the outcome, but he watched while Miss Whittle appeared to have some trouble with wielding her key in her door. As the dog yanked her into the unlit house the door swung closed, so that Sylvester couldn't be certain whether he saw her fall or be pulled to all fours, and her spectacles fly off. Perhaps it was only the darkness that made her seem to shrink. He observed how the house remained dark, and listened until he began to nod, which put him in danger of dropping the book. He slid it under his quilt for safety while he prepared to join it in bed.

Sleep was unwilling to come near him. Whenever he drifted towards it he was pulled up short by a fear of talking in it, not that he was aware of ever having done so. The possibility that he might change things without knowing, or of dreaming he had only to find it was true, unnerved him. When at last he slept he dreamed of going to the window to shout "Old Bones That Crawl." He watched Miss Whittle's door falter open, and a crouched shape begin to grope into the light before he managed to awaken. He had to venture to the window to confirm her door was shut and her house dark, at which point he realised that he hadn't heard the wheezy yapping of the dog since they'd vanished into her house.

In bed again, he was awakened by his mother's morning screech. "What do you think you're up to, Sylvester?" He thought she'd found him out until she added 'Never mind trying to be late for school.' While he was in the bathroom she shouted upstairs three times that his breakfast was going cold, though he knew it wouldn't be on the table yet, and when he stumbled downstairs she kept telling him not to eat so fast or he would make himself ill. His father confined himself to saying to do as she said. No wonder Sylvester was glad to leave the house, though not for school. Nevertheless he headed for it, to confirm what he already knew.

The narrow streets lined with failed trees were full of second-hand cars and people to go with them, and puddles doubling both. All the activity around him was infinitely less meaningful than the words of the book in his bed. Opposite the school he hid in the bus shelter, or rather under it, since its glass sides had been smashed. He saw some of his classmates being led into the schoolyard by their parents, and expelling the noises they were supposed to try not to make in class: Kevin sounding like a seal, Jimmy like a mega-phone forgetting how to talk. Their special teacher was representing order in the yard, and greeted them in his tone of telling a joke at which nobody was expected to laugh. "And how are we this inclement day?" Mr Westle said, and Sylvester saw the joke was on the teacher—felt as though the words he had read in his book were sharing this secret with him. By including himself with the people he addressed Mr Westle meant to appear sympathetic, but in truth there wasn't much to choose between their minds and his, which was smaller than his head. Before Sylvester could be noticed he turned away from the school and all its Mr Westles for ever. He wanted to be where he could read as much as he liked without having to explain his ability.

The central library was one of the largest buildings in Brichester, and so heavy with books it needed six pillars to hold up its front. Once he'd climbed the wide steps and passed beyond the giant doors, he felt as he imagined you were supposed to feel in church. Everybody kept their voices down, yet the murmurs rose to have their own mysterious conversations under the dome where the sun was starting to appear. He walked beneath the echoes of his foot-steps to the History section and pulled an armful of thick volumes off a shelf to set down gently on a table. At last he was going to learn what books had to offer.

Those he'd selected were histories of the world, and they didn't detain him for long. He had a go at the Religion shelves, then went to Science, his reading of which only affected him the same way. The more he read, the more he knew that the secret which the book from the twisted house had lodged in his brain rendered every other book untrue. Books were lies the world told about itself, he saw, and went to the window in case the spectacle beyond it might seem more real.

Groups of people were crossing the pedestrianised street from every direction. Their only function appeared to be to form meaningless patterns, just as the rain drying on the pavement had to. He watched until a librarian tapped him on the shoulder. "Shouldn't you be at school, son? If you don't want to read, you're distracting folk who are, and we'll have to ask you to make yourself scarce."

"I'm not doing anything," Sylvester said to her fat reflection infested by the herd.

"Then go and do your nothing somewhere else like a good boy before I have to call security."

She was trying to patronise him into insignificance, but he knew whom to call to demonstrate his power. "Daoloth says," he muttered, and trailed off before words for her had time to suggest themselves; he wasn't certain that he wanted all the readers to see what would happen then, especially if he got the blame. He shouldered his way through her heavy perfume, which he couldn't help thinking was meant to disguise her true nature that he had almost revealed, and let the clamour of his footsteps crowd him out. He was trying to escape the words he'd muttered, but they came with him.

They paced him as he wandered home. They lurked behind everyone he met and everything he passed, so that all this seemed to be trying to hold on to its appearance for fear that by completing his sentence he would change it into its true self. "Faces that slide over the earth ... cells that store the night ... hands that swarm ... eyes worming in the earth ... leaves that suck the dead ... windows of the buried ... rotting brains ... " He had no idea where all this came from; he was afraid that simply thinking it might cause it to emerge from the concealment of itself. Once he was home he could read his book, which perhaps would calm his thoughts down. But as he returned to his street he couldn't avoid realising that he'd spent the day so far in staying clear of seeing what he might have done to the old woman.

He shut the front door and fled to his room. His father was out damaging somebody's property with a view to mending it, and his mother had gone to call Bingo for the afternoon, leaving a premonitory smell of her stew which never tasted as good as that promise. He could do what he wanted, but he discovered that wasn't reading the book while he didn't know how the old woman had lived up to his words. He stood at his window and gazed at her silent darkening house.

The sight focused his sense of a presence hidden by the world, and he no longer felt urged to finish his sentence; in her case, after all, he already had. He was prompting himself to call her when people began to appear in the street, mothers wheeling babies home or rather couples that looked like that and then, as the streetlamps produced their flutter, older children walking. Sylvester had become preoccupied with the gathering of darkness in the old woman's house when he saw his mother at the end of the street. He retreated and sat on the bed, clutching his book, but all too soon she and his father summoned him down for dinner. He hadn't taken a mouthful from the plate that had been laden to await him when the questions began with his father pointing a fork at him. "Good day at school?"

"Fair."

That was usually sufficient, and Sylvester tried to say it in his habitual manner, but his father persisted in staring at him. Sylvester would have been grateful to his mother for interrupting except for her question. "Have you seen Miss Whittle today?"

"Who," Sylvester blurted, "me?"

"Why, what's up with her?" his father said.

Sylvester fed himself a mouthful of stew while he braced himself for the reply. "That's what I want to know," his mother said, however. "She wasn't in her seat at the Bingo where she always is."

"Maybe the kids have scared her off the streets at last."

"So long as it wasn't you, Sylvester."

"It wouldn't be him, would it? He's not capable of anything."

That sounded as patronising as the librarian had, and Sylvester was keeping his mouth full so as to be unable to disprove the statement when his mother said "When we've finished I'll go over and see how she is."

Sylvester almost emptied the tasteless mouthful outwards before he could swallow. "No," he spluttered. "I mean, she's gone away to stay. I heard."

"What did you hear?"

"Heard her saying to some friend of hers about going away for a week. When I was going to school. And," he gabbled once the necessity occurred to him, "taking her dog."

His mother gazed at him for so long he thought his haste had betrayed him. "Peculiar nobody at the Bingo said," she eventually revealed herself to have been thinking. "What's the matter, don't you like my stew any more? It's the same stew you've always had."

That aggravated his sudden fear of how the food might taste if he even thought of words for it. "I'm a bit sick," he wailed.

"Maybe he'd better go up and lie down," his father said.

"He can have it tomorrow if you don't finish it."

Sylvester didn't know which of them that was intended to threaten, but managed to stifle the idea of food as he hurried to his room—to his window. The house in the midst of the terrace opposite was unlit, and seemed to be holding itself still in anticipation of his voice. He eased the wobbly sash up and poked his head out to survey the deserted street, and drew a breath which tasted of the chilly night, and spoke. "Daoloth says you have to come out now, Old Bones That Crawl."

In the white glare of the streetlamp the door of the house resembled the entrance to a tomb—a marble entrance which he realised he was dreading to see opened from within. When it appeared to shift, he thought that was because his eyes were nervous. Then the glare slid off the door as it faltered ajar, revealing darkness and a dim shape that was hunched within it. Just as he guessed that the door was moving awkwardly because its opener was, the tenant of the house sidled into the pitiless light, and Sylvester saw its difficulty in managing so many limbs. It raised its face, or more accurately the front of its head, towards him, and he ground his elbows against the windowsill as if the pain could anchor him in the world whose reality he used to take for granted. Then the misshapen figure robbed of flesh crouched even lower, veiling its head with the material that sprouted from it, and scuttled into the concealment of the garden wall. The hedge between the wall and the house quivered, and Sylvester understood that the thing had writhed through.

He wanted to see where it went and what it did. It couldn't touch him or come closer than he liked if he told it Daoloth said not to; in any case, it seemed anxious to conceal itself from view. He leaned on the sash to lower it and rubbed his bruised elbows; then, pausing only to hide the book in his bed and grab a jacket, he tiptoed quickly downstairs. He might as well not have bothered with stealth, since as he reached the hall his mother turned from pegging her rubber gloves above the gargling kitchen sink. 'Where do you think you're going?'

"Out."

"I can see that all by myself. I thought you were meant to be ill."

"I'm better," Sylvester said, and felt it—no longer needing to eat, filled up and energised by the words from the book.

"Your mother still wants to know where you're going," his father said, draping a dish-towel next to the gloves.

"To see—" Sylvester was suddenly afraid that if he didn't escape at once he would give in to the temptation to release himself by using his secret on his parents, not least because their banality felt like a weight they were loading onto his head. "To see Arn and them," he blurted.

"Just you make sure you're back by ten. By half past nine." As Sylvester sprinted for freedom, having agreed to both of her stipulations, he heard her say rather defensively "Fresh air ought to do him good if anything will."

Sylvester dashed across the whitened glaring road and slammed the door of Miss Whittle's house before anyone could wonder why it was open. His haste was such that only then did he think to peer at the hedge, beneath which he made out a dim twisted shape. By straining his eyes he was able to distinguish that it was a tangle of roots and branches which looked not unlike the object he was searching for. He raised his eyes to the rest of the blocks of stained marble foliage dividing the cramped gardens, and saw the furthest hedge shudder as though with loathing of whatever had just crawled through it. "I see you," he cried and ran to the corner.

Fewer houses were occupied in the cross street, which was even narrower than his. Some of the windows had been walled up, and quite a number of the cars parked on the pavement between the destroyed streetlamps looked abandoned. All the same, the street wasn't as deserted as Sylvester would have wished. He was watching hedges twitch and creak one after the other along the left side of the road when the three boys emerged jostling and yelling from Bruce's house on the right. They saw Sylvester, but not the surreptitious activity that had passed beyond them. "Look who it isn't," Denzil shouted.

"It isn't Sylly," Bruce agreed, and looked to Arnold to top his wit, which Arnold did: "It's Building Plot For Sale."

"Read us something if you're not Sylly," Bruce yelled, raising his fists while he scowled around him in search of an appropriate task for Sylvester.

"Read us that," said Denzil, jabbing a finger at the plaque on the wall at the alley entrance halfway down the street.

"You heard, let's see you read it," Arnold said and rubbed his scalp as if to increase its baldness.

Sylvester was tired of skulking inside himself and besides, he needed to distract them from the movements that had nearly reached the alley. "It says DOMESTIC ACCESS ONLY AND NO CYCLING OR TIPPING."

"Does not," Denzil scoffed, then jerked his finger along the first line of the plaque across the street, and frowned hard. "Doesn't, does it?"

"If it does someone told him," Bruce said, readying his fists for the culprit.

"This time you just tell us who did," Arnold warned Sylvester, and led the advance towards him.

Sylvester glimpsed movement in the nearer of the gardens bordering the alley—a shape that clambered rapidly over the low wall between the garden and its neighbour and huddled in the shadows, awaiting its chance. "Nobody," he said. "I read it myself."

By the time the others had done jeering at him they were around him, so that he could smell their sweat and their breaths. Arnold took hold of his left upper arm and began to roll the flesh and muscles of it in his grip. "Thinks we're stupid."

"Stupid like him," said Denzil, and poked him in the chest.

"Must be stupid to think that," Bruce said, and was in the process of selecting which area of him to punch first when there was a clatter in the alley, and a dustbin fell out, spilling its meagre contents. "Hey," Bruce threatened, spinning round so fast that he almost punched Arnold.

"Cat," said Denzil, though his finger seemed less sure of it.

"Dog," Arnold said without looking, and intensified his treatment of Sylvester's arm.

Sylvester kept his gaze on the passage leading to the dark between the back yards. "Wasn't either."

"Who says?" Arnold demanded, and when that produced no response, pinched Sylvester's muscle. "What was it then, eh, Sylly?"

"Ow. Something you'd be scared of."

"Me, right." Arnold let go in order to rub his scalp, kindling the glower in his eyes. "Like you were scared to go in the house up the hill. You'll be dead before you see me scared."

"Go on then, go and look."

"Right, so you can get away." Arnold grabbed his arm again, but only while he said "You two hold him and I'll look. And tell him he'd better be scared of me when I come back."

"You'd better be scared," said Bruce, having seized Sylvester's bruised arm, and dug his knuckles into it. Denzil contented himself with digging Sylvester in various ribs. The boy succeeded in ignoring the discomfort, which after all would soon be over. He watched as Arnold stalked into the passage and stared both ways into the dark at the end. "Can't see a thing," Arnold declared.

It would try to hide from him unless it was called, Sylvester realised. "Daoloth says go to him, Old Bones That Crawl."

Denzil pointed violently at him. "What'd he say?"

"Sounded like he was telling something something," Bruce said, and shoved his face at Sylvester. Before he could enact the proffered butt, Arnold disappeared into the alley. "Hang on, there's . . . "

Sylvester couldn't quite contain a grin. Denzil stared at it, then at the entrance to the alley. "What's he done?" he muttered, and raised his voice. "Arn, wait. He—"

Arnold's response, or at least the noise he uttered, cut him off. It sounded as though Arnold was trying to scream while being sick. Deeply satisfying though Sylvester found it, he couldn't have it attracting attention. "Daoloth says you're not Arn now," he murmured. "Daoloth says you're Scalp For A Face."

He felt the world twist a little more, and his mind too. Arnold's noise ceased instantly as if a gag had been applied to its source. Denzil was at the mouth of the passage, having shouted to Arnold that he was coming. He wavered there and glanced back furiously at the other boys, and fished in the air for them with his finger as he dared another step. It was time, thought Sylvester, to continue what he'd started. "Daoloth says stop being Denzil, Worms For Bones."

He didn't see the result—he was busy dodging a punch Bruce threw at him—but Bruce did. His face clenched like a fist, then opened to release a howl as Bruce fled along the street, waving his splayed fingers to ward off everything around him. Sylvester let him almost reach the crossroads before addressing him. "Daoloth says goodbye to Bruce and hello to Living Inside Out."

He had to look away at once, and to turn his back as he heard the new thing flounder through the shadows of the walls to join its companions. The sounds they made in the alley, blundering and slithering and slopping about, were enough for now, in fact rather too much before long. "Daoloth says go to the house on the hill where the book was," he called. "Daoloth says not to let anyone see you and when you get there go under the floor."

He was able to bear the ungainly confusion of their retreat. Quite soon with distance they sounded more like insects than anything else remotely familiar, and then they were gone. He'd done enough for one night. Tomorrow he would go to the twisted house and call them out and have some fun. As he turned homewards, it occurred to him that he mightn't live there for much longer. Perhaps soon he would know, and call himself by, his name.

THE CORRESPONDENCE OF
CAMERON THADDEUS NASH

Annotated by Ramsey Campbell

I N 1968 AUGUST DERLETH WAS SENT A NUMBER OF LETTERS that had apparently been received by H. P. Lovecraft. The anonymous parcel bore no return address. Although the letters had been typed on a vintage machine and on paper that appeared to be decades old, Derleth was undecided whether they were authentic. For instance, he was unsure that someone living in a small English village in the 1920s would have had access to issues of *Weird Tales*, and he could find no obvious references to Nash in any of Lovecraft's surviving correspondence. Derleth considered printing some or all of Nash's letters in the *Arkham Collector* but decided against using them in the Winter 1969 issue devoted to Lovecraft. Later he asked me to think about writing an essay on Lovecraft for a new Lovecraftian volume that might offer the letters a home, but the project was shelved. Intrigued by his references to the Nash letters, I persuaded him to send me copies, including the other documents. It isn't clear what happened to the originals. When I visited Arkham House in 1975, James Turner knew nothing about them, and he was subsequently unable to trace them. He did mention that in *HPL: Dreamer on the Nightside*, Frank Belknap Long referred to an English writer who "thought it was amusing to call people names", by whom Lovecraft had supposedly been troubled for several years.

Since Long was unable to be more specific, Turner deleted the reference. I reproduce all the letters here, followed by the final documents. Nash's signature is florid and extends across the page. It grows larger but less legible as the correspondence progresses.

> 7, Grey Mare Lane,
> Long Bredy,
> West Dorset,
> Great Britain.
> April 29th, 1925.

My dear Mr. Lovecraft,

Forgive a simple English villager for troubling such a celebrated figure as yourself. I trust that the proprietors of your chosen publication will not think it too <u>weird</u> that a mere reader should seek to communicate with his idol. As I pen these words I wonder if they might not more properly have been addressed to the <u>eerie</u> letter-column of that magazine. My fear is that the editor would find them unworthy of ink, however, and so I take the greater risk of directing them to you. I pray that he will not find me so presumptuous that he forwards them no farther than the bin beside his desk.

May I come swiftly to my poor excuse for this intrusion into your inestimably precious time? I have sampled six issues of the <u>Unique Magazine</u>, and I am sure you must be aware that it has but a single claim to uniqueness—the contributions of your good self. I scarcely know whether to marvel or to be moved that you should allow them to appear amongst the motley fancies which infest the pages of the journal. Do you intend to educate the other contributors by your example? Are you not concerned that the ignorant reader may be repelled by this commonplace herd, thereby failing to discover the visions which you offer? The company in which you find yourself reads like the scribbling of hacks who have never dared to dream. I wish that the magazine would at least emblazon your name on the cover of every number which contains your prose. I promise you that on the occasion when I mistakenly bought an issue which had neglected to feature your work, I rent it into shreds so small that not a single vapid sentence could survive.

I am conscious how far any words of mine will fall short of conveying my admiration of your work. May I simply isolate those elements which remain liveliest in my mind? Your parable of Dagon seems to tell a truth at which the compilers of the Bible scarcely dared to hint, but I am most intrigued by the dreams which the narrator is afraid to remember in daylight. The quarry of your hideous hound declares that his fate is no dream, yet to this English reader it suggests one, brought on by the banal Baskerville investigations of Sherlock Holmes. Your narrator de la Poer dreams whilst awake, but are these reveries shaped by awful reality or the reverse? As for the descendant of the African union, perhaps he never dreams of his own nature because he has a <u>germ</u> <u>in</u> him—the same germ which infects the minds of all those who believe we are as soulless as the ape. But it is your <u>hypnotic</u> tale of Hypnos which exerts the firmest hold on my imagination. May I press you to reveal its source? Does it perhaps hint at your own experience?[1]

As to myself, I am sure you will not want to be fatigued by information about me. I am but a player at the human game. However long I sojourn in this village, none of its natives will tempt me to grow <u>breedy</u>. While my body works behind a counter, my spirit is abroad in the infinity of imagination. At least the nearby countryside offers solitude, and it harbours relics of the past, which are keys to dreams. Please accept my undying gratitude, Mr. Lovecraft, for helping to enliven mine. If you should find a few moments to acknowledge this halting missive, you will confer existence on a dream of your most loyal admirer.

I have the honour to remain, Mr. Lovecraft,

Your respectful and obedient servant,

Cameron Thaddeus Nash.

7, Grey Mare Lane,
Long Bredy,
West Dorset,
Great Britain.
August 12th, 1925.

My esteemed Mr. Lovecraft,

I am sorry that you find New York inhospitable and that you have been inconvenienced by burglary. May I counsel you to reflect that such disadvantages are negligible so long as one's fancies remain

---

[1] Nash refers here to Lovecraft's tales "Dagon", "The Hound", "The Rats in the Walls", "Arthur Jermyn" and "Hypnos", all recently published in *Weird Tales*

unfettered? Your corporeal experiences count for naught unless they prevent you from dreaming and from communicating your dreams. Let me assure you that they have reached across the ocean to inspire a fellow voyager.

I was sure that your stories which I have read gave voice to your dreams, and I rejoice to understand that other tales of yours do so. But why must these pieces languish in amateur publications? While the mob would doubtless greet them with brutish incomprehension, surely you should disseminate your visions as widely as possible, to give other dreamers the opportunity to chance upon them. I hope some of our kind made themselves a Yuletide present of your tale about the festival in the town which you had never visited except in dreams. I fear that any reader with a brain must have been seasonally inebriated to enjoy the other contents of that number of the magazine. How can it still neglect to advertize your presence on the cover? I remain appalled that the issue which contained your tale of Hypnos chose to publicize Houdini's contribution instead. How misguided was the editor to provide a home for those ridiculous Egyptian ramblings? Houdini even dares to claim that the tale is the report of a dream, but we genuine dreamers see through his charlatanry. I believe he has never dreamed in his life, having been too bent on performing tricks with his mere flesh.[2]

May I presume to pose a question? I wonder if Hypnos represents only as terrible an aspect of dream as you believe the reader could bear to confront, unless this evasion is born of your own wariness. For myself, I am convinced that at the farthest reach of dream we may encounter the source, whose nature no deity ever imagined by man could begin to encompass. Perhaps some Greek sage glimpsed this truth and invented Hypnos as a mask to spare the minds of the multitude. But, Mr. Lovecraft, our minds stand above the mass, and it is our duty to ourselves never to be daunted from dreaming.

I wish you could have shared my midsummer night's experience, when I spent a midnight hour with the Grey Mare and her colts. They are fragments of an ancient settlement, and I seemed to dream that I found the buried entrance to a grave. It led into a labyrinth illuminated only by my consciousness. As I ventured deeper I became aware that I was descending into an unrecorded past. I

---

[2] In this paragraph Nash refers to "The Festival" and "Imprisioned with the Pharaohs".

understood that the labyrinth was the very brain of an ancient mage, the substance of which had fertilized the earth, where his memories emerged in the form of aberrant subterranean growths. One day I may fashion this vision into a tale.

I have done so, and I take the great liberty of enclosing it. Should you ever be able to spare the time to glance over it, I would find any comments that you cared to offer beyond price. Perhaps you might suggest a title more fitting than <u>The</u> <u>Brain</u> <u>beneath</u> <u>the</u> <u>Earth</u>?

I bid you adieu from a land which you have dreamed of visiting.

Yours in inexpressible admiration,
Cameron Thaddeus Nash.

18, Old Sarum Road,
Salisbury,
Wiltshire,
Great Britain.
October 30th, 1925.

Dear H. P. Lovecraft,

Thank you for your kind praise of my little tale, and thank you for taking the trouble to think of a title. Now it sounds more like a story of your own. Please also be assured of my gratitude for the time you spent in offering suggestions for changes to the piece. I am sure you will understand if I prefer it to remain as I dreamed it. I am happy that in any case you feel it might be worthy of submission to the "unique magazine", and I hereby authorise you to do so. I am certain that <u>Beneath</u> <u>the</u> <u>Stones</u> can only benefit from your patronage.

I must apologize for my mistake over the "Houdini" tale. Had it appeared as <u>Under</u> <u>the</u> <u>Pyramids</u> by none other than the great Howard Phillips Lovecraft, I promise you that it would have excited a different response from this reader. I should have guessed its authorship, since it proves to be the narration of a dream. May I assume that Houdini supplied some of the material? I believe this robs the tale of the authenticity of your other work. Only genuine dreamers can collaborate on a dream.

I was amused to learn that you had to devote your wedding night to typing the story afresh. Perhaps your loss of the original tran-scription was a lucky chance which you should continue to embrace.

I trust you will permit a fellow dreamer to observe that your courtship and marriage appear to have distracted you from your true purpose in the world. I fervently hope that you have not grown unable to dream freely now that you are no longer alone. May your wife be preventing you from visiting sites which are fertile with dreams, or from employing relics to bring dreams to your bed? You will have noticed that I have moved onwards from my previous abode, having exhausted the site of which I wrote to you. I believe my new situation will provide me with a portal to dreams no living man has begun to experience.

In the meantime I have read your brace of tales which recently saw publication. The musician Zann and his street are dreams, are they not? Only in dreams may streets remain unmapped. Is the abyss which the music summons not a glimpse or a hint of the source of the ultimate dream? And Carter's graveyard reverie conjures up the stuff of dream[3]. It rightly stays unnameable, for the essence of dreams neither can nor should be named. You mentioned that these tales were composed before your courtship. May I take the liberty of suggesting that they remind you what you are in peril of abandoning? The dreamer ought to be a solitary man, free to follow all the promptings of his mind.

At least while you are unable to write, you are still communicating visions—my own. Now that you have become my American representative I shall be pleased if you will call me Thad. It is the name I would ask a friend to use, and it sounds quite American, does it not? Let me take this opportunity to send you three more tales for your promotion. I am satisfied with them and with their titles. May I ask you not to show them to any of your circle or to mention me? I prefer not to be heard of until I am published. I hope that the magazine will deign to exhibit both of our names on the cover. Let the spiritless scribblers be confined within, if they must continue to infest its sheets.

Yours in anticipation of print,

Thad Nash.

---

[3] Nash is referring to "The Music of Erich Zann" and "The Unnamable".

18, Old Sarum Road,
Salisbury,
Wiltshire,
Great Britain.
February 14th, 1926.

Dear Howard Phillips Lovecraft,

I am grateful to you for your attempt to place my work. You had previously mentioned that Farthingsworth Wrong[4] tends to be unreceptive to the truly <u>unique</u>. I am certain that you must have done everything in your power to persuade him to your opinion of my tales. Are there other markets where you will do your best to sell them, or is it more advisable to wait for his tastes to mature? You will appreciate that I am relying on your experience in these matters.

I do not recall your mentioning that you had written new fiction last summer. I am relieved to learn that your marital subjugation has not permanently crippled your ability to dream. May I assume that these stories did not hinder your marketing of my work? I believe that our writing has little in common other than the title you provided, but I wonder if the editor's judgement may have been adversely affected by your sending him too many pieces all at once. Perhaps in future it would be wise to submit my work separately from your own, and with a reasonable interval between them.

I am heartened by the information that you plan to write a history of supernatural literature. I am sure that your appreciation of the form will produce a guide which should be on the shelves of every dreamer. I look forward eagerly to reading it. If I can advise or in any way aid you, please do not hesitate to ask.

You will be anxious to hear about the progress of my own work. Please reassure yourself that your failure to place my stories has not cast me down. Rather has it goaded me to venture deeper into dream, whence I shall return bearing prizes no less wonderful than dreadful. I shall tell ancient truths which no reader will be able to deny and no editor dare to suppress. I am certain that the nearby sites contain unsuspected relics, although soon I may have no more need of them. However it is used, a relic is but the germ of a dream, just as your dreams are the germs of your fiction. I wonder to what

---

[4] Farnsworth Wright, editor of *Weird Tales*.

extent your dreams have become fixed on your native Providence? Perhaps your desire to return there is draining your imagination of the energy to rise higher and voyage farther. I hope you will ultimately find as congenial an environment as I have myself.

I await news of your efforts.

Yours for the supremacy of dream,
Cameron Thad Nash.

                                              1, Toad Place,
                                                  Berkeley,
                                          Gloucestershire,
                                            Great Britain.
                                          May 23rd, 1926.

Dear HPL,

I write to alert you that, like yours, my body has found a new lodging. It became necessary for me to decamp to an unfamiliar town. I had been surprised one night in the process of obtaining a relic. The donor of the item could have made no further use of it, but I fear that the mob and its <u>uninformed</u>, <u>uniformed</u> representatives of <u>unformed</u> <u>uniformity</u> have little understanding of the dreamer's needs. The resultant pursuit was unwelcome, and a source of distraction to me. For several nights I was annoyed by dreams of this mere chase, and they led to my seeking a home elsewhere.

Well, I am done with graves and brains and the infusion of them. I am safe inside my skull, where the mob cannot spy, nor even dreamers like yourself. I have learned to rise above the use of material aids to dream. I require but a single talisman—the night and the infinite darkness of which it is the brink. Let the puny scientists strive to design machines to fly to other worlds! This dreamer has preceded them, employing no device save his own mind. The darkness swarms with dreams, which have been formed by the consciousnesses of creatures alien beyond the wildest fancies of man. Each dream which I add to my essence leads me deeper into uncharted space. A lesser spirit would shrivel with dread of the ultimate destination. In my tales I can only hint at the stages of my quest, for fear that even such a reader as yourself may quail before the face of revelation.

I see you are content to have reverted to your native Providence. I hope that your contentment will provide a base from which you may venture into the infinite. I have read your recent contributions to Farthingsworth's rag. Will you forgive my opining that your story of the dreamer by the ancestral tomb seems a trifle earthbound? I had higher expectations of the other tale, but was disappointed when the narrator's dreams urged him to climb the tower not to vistas of infinity but to a view of the dull earth. No wonder he found nothing worthy of description in the mirror.[5] I wonder if, while immolated in your marriage, you became so desperate to dream that you were unable to direct the process. I counsel you to follow my example. The dreamer must tolerate no distractions, neither family nor those that call themselves friends. None of these is worth the loss of a solitary dream.

At your urging I recently viewed the moving picture of <u>The Phantom of the Opera</u>. You mentioned that you fell asleep several times during the picture, and I have to inform you that you must have been describing your own dream of the conclusion rather than the finale which appears on the screen. I assure you that no "nameless legion of <u>things</u>" welcomes the Phantom to his watery grave. I am glad that they at least remained nameless in your mind. No dream ought to be named, for words are less than dreams.

I look forward to reading your short novel about the island raised by the marine earthquake, although would an unknown island bear such a name as "L'yeh" or indeed any name?[6] And I am anxious to read your survey of supernatural literature when it, too, is completed. In the meantime, here are three new tales of mine for your perusal and advancement. Please do make all speed to advise me as soon as there is news.

Yours in the fellowship of dreams and letters,
CTN.

P.S. Could you make sure to address all correspondence to me under these initials?

---

[5] "The Tomb" and "The Outsider".
[6] Lovecraft's original name for the island in "The Call of Cthulhu".

1, Toad Place,
Berkeley,
Gloucestershire,
Great Britain.
April 17th, 1927.

Dear HPL,

I trust that you have not been alarmed by my prolonged silence. I thought it wise not to attract the attention of the mob for a judicious period. I also felt obliged to give you the opportunity to place some of your fiction and to compose new tales before I favoured you with the first sight of my latest work. I think now you have been amply represented in Farthingsworth's magazine, and I am encouraged to learn that you have recently been productive. I believe it is time that you should have reports of my nocturnal voyaging, and I shall include all those which I judge to be acceptable to my audience. Some, I fear, might overwhelm the mind of any other dreamer.

I hope those which I send you will go some way towards reviving your own capacity to dream. May I assume that the anecdote about the old sea captain and his bottles was a sketch for a longer story and saw publication by mistake? I suppose it was trivial enough for Farthingsworth's mind to encompass. I note that the narrator of your tale about the Irish bog is uncertain whether he is dreaming or awake, but his dream scarcely seems worth recording. Your tale of the nameless New Yorker is no dream at all, since the narrator's night is sleepless, and the only fancy you allow him is your own, which you have already achieved—to return to New England. As for the detective in Red Hook, he needs specialists to convince him that he dreamed those subterranean horrors, but I am afraid the medical view failed to persuade this reader.[7]

I am glad to hear that you wrote your story of the upraised island. May I trust that it has greater scope than the tales I have discussed above? Perhaps this may also be the case with your most recent piece, though I confess that the notion of a mere colour falls short of rousing my imagination. No colour can be sufficiently alien to paint the far reaches of dream, which lie beyond and simultaneously at the core of the awful gulf which is creation. Of the two novels you have recently completed, does the celebration of your return to

---

[7] "The Terrible Old Man", "The Moon-Bog", "He" and "The Horror at Red Hook".

Providence risk being too provincial? I hope that the account of your dream-quest is the opposite, and I am touched that you should have hidden my name within the text for the informed reader to discover. But I am most pleased by the news that you have delivered your essay on supernatural literature to the publisher. Could you tell me which living writers you have discussed?[8]

Let me leave you to do justice to the enclosed pieces. Perhaps in due time I may risk sending those I have withheld, when you have sufficiently progressed as a dreamer. Have you yet to loose your mind in the outer darkness? Every dream which I encounter there is a step towards another, more ancient or more alien. I have shared the dreams of creatures whose bodies the mob would never recognise as flesh. Some have many bodies, and some have none at all. Some are shaped in ways at which their dreams can only hint, and which make me grateful for my blindness in the utter dark. I believe these dreams are stages in my advance towards the ultimate dream, which I sense awaiting me at the limit of unimaginable space.

Yours in the embrace of the dark,
CTN.

1, Toad Place,
Berkeley,
Gloucestershire,
Great Britain.
June 23rd, 1927.

Dear HPL,

Of course you are correct in saying that my new pieces have progressed. I hope that you will be able to communicate your enthusiasm to Farthingsworth and to any other editors whom you approach on my behalf.

Thank you for the list of living writers whose work you have praised in your essay. May I take it that you have withheld one name from me? Perhaps you intended me to be surprised upon reading it in the essay, unless you wished to spare my modesty. Let me reassure you that its presence would be no surprise and would cause me no embarrassment. If by any chance you decided that my work should not be discussed in the essay because of its basis in actual experience,

---

[8] "The Call of Cthulhu", "The Colour out of Space", *The Case of Charles Dexter Ward*, *The Dream-Quest of Unknown Kadath* and *Supernatural Horror in Literature*.

pray do remind yourself that the material is cast in fictional form. In the case of such an omission, I trust that the error will be rectified before the essay sees publication.

Yours in urgency,
CTN.

1, Toad Place,
Berkeley,
Gloucestershire,
Great Britain.
August 25th, 1927.

Dear HPL,

I was glad to receive your apology for neglecting to include me in your essay. On reflection, I have concluded that your failure to do so was advantageous. As you say, my work is of a different order. It would not benefit from being discussed alongside the fanciful yarns of the likes of Machen and Blackwood. It is truth masquerading as fiction, and I believe you will agree that it deserves at least an essay to itself. I hope its qualities will aid you in placing your appreciation in a more prestigious journal, and one which is more widely read. To these ends I sent you yesterday the work which I had previously kept back. I trust that your mind will prove equal to the truths conveyed therein. While you assimilate their implications, I shall consider how far they are suitable for revelation to the world.

Yours in the darkest verities,
CTN.

1, Toad Place,
Berkeley,
Gloucestershire,
Great Britain.
November 1st, 1927.

Dear HPL,

I am assured by the postmistress that the parcel of my work has had ample time to reach you. I hope that the contents have not rendered you so speechless that you are unable to pen a response.

Pray do not attempt to comment on the pieces until you feel capable of encompassing their essence. However, I should be grateful if you would confirm that they have safely arrived.

Yours,
CTN.

1, Toad Place,
Berkeley,
Gloucestershire,
Great Britain.
January 1st, 1928.

Lovecraft,

Am I meant to fancy that the parcel of my work faded into nothingness like a dream? You forget that my dreams do not fade. They are more than common reveries, for they have grasped the stuff of creation. The accounts which I set down may be lost to me, but their truths are buried in my brain. I shall follow wherever they may lead, even unto the unspeakable truth which is the core of all existence.

I was amused by your lengthy description of your Halloween dream of ancient Romans. I fear that, like so many of your narrators, you are shackled to the past, and unable to release your spirit into the universe. I read your <u>amazing</u> story of the alien colour, but I failed to be <u>amazed</u> except by its unlikeness[9]. How can there be a colour besides those I have seen? The idea is nothing but a feeble dream, and your use of my name in the tale is no compliment to me. When I read the sentence "The Dutchman's breeches became a thing of sinister menace", I wonder if the story is a joke which you sought to play on your ignorant audience.

Nevertheless, it has some worth, for it convinces me that you are by no means the ideal agent for my work. I ignored your presumption in suggesting changes to my reports as if they were mere fiction, but I am troubled by the possibility that you may regard your work as in any way superior to mine. Is it conceivable that you altered the pieces which you submitted on my behalf? I suspect you of hindering them for fear that your fiction might be unfavourably

---

[9] "The Colour out of Space" was published in *Amazing Stories*.

compared to them, and in order that it might reach the editors ahead of them. I am sure that you excluded my work from your essay out of jealousy. I wonder if you may have resented my achievement ever since I gave you my honest appraisal of your Houdini hotchpotch. For these reasons and others which need not concern you, I hereby withdraw my work from your representation. Please return all of it immediately on receipt of this letter.

Sincerely,

Cameron Thaddeus Nash.

1, Toad Place,
Berkeley,
Gloucestershire,
Great Britain.
March 3rd, 1928.

Loathecraft,

Where is my work? I have still not had it back.

C. T. Nash.

1, Toad Place,
Berkeley,
Gloucestershire,
Great Britain.
May 1st, 1928.

Lovecramped,

So a second parcel has vanished into the void! How capricious the colonial post must be, or so you would have me believe. I am not to think that you are fearful of my seeing any alterations that you made to my work. Nor should I suspect you of destroying evidence that you have stolen elements of my work in a vain attempt to improve your own. You say that I should have kept copies, but you may rest assured that the essence is not lost. It remains embedded in my brain, where I feel it stirring like an eager foetus as it reaches for the farthest dream.

I wonder if its undeveloped relative may have made its lair in your brain as you read my work. Perhaps it is consuming your dreams instead of helping send them forth, since your mind falls so short of the cosmos. Your limits are painfully clear from your tale of the regurgitated island. Could you imagine nothing more alien than a giant with the head of an octopus? You might at least have painted it your non-existent colour. Giants were old when the Greeks were young, and your dreams are just as stale. No doubt your acolytes— Augur Dulldeath and Clerk Ashen Sniff and Dullard Wantdie and Stank Kidnap Pong and the rest of your motley entourage[10] —will counterfeit some admiration of the tale.

I assume they have been deluded into valuing your patronage, and are so afraid of losing it that they dare offer you no criticism. I would demonstrate to you how your tale should have been written if it included any matter worthy of my attention. In any case, all my energy is necessary to dealing with my dreams. I doubt that I shall write them down in future. I am unaware of anyone who deserves to learn of them. Let mankind experience them for itself when it has sufficiently evolved to do so.

C. T. Nash.

1, Toad Place,
Berkeley,
Gloucestershire,
Great Britain.
December 25th, 1929.

Lugcraft,

Did you dream that you would never hear from me again? Had you, perhaps, even forgotten my existence, since reading my work has evidently taught you nothing as a writer? You are but a shell in which a few dreams writhed and then withered when exposed to daylight. I had the misfortune to leaf through your claptrap about Dunwich[11]. I suppose you must have chosen to write about the submarine village before you remembered that you had already written about a submarine island[12]. You would have done better to leave both of them sunken. Can you dream of nothing except tentacles? It seems to me that your writing is a decidedly <u>fishy</u> business. Has my mislaid work yet to put in a mysterious reappearance?

---

[10] August Derleth, Clark Ashton Smith, Donald Wandrei and Frank Belknap Long.
[11] "The Dunwich Horror".   [12] Dunwich is a submerged town off the Suffolk coast.

I was reminded of you upon recently encountering Mr. Visiak's novel <u>Medusa</u>.[13] He, too, writes of a tentacled colossus which inhabits an uncharted rock. His prose is infinitely subtler and more skilled than your own, and evokes the dream which must have been its seed. Have you read the book? Perhaps it is one reason why you appear to have written so little of late. He has achieved all that you strain to achieve and more, with none of your symptoms of labour. He is rightly published by a reputable London house, whereas your efforts are removed from view within a month. Pulp thou art, and pulp thou shalt remain.

Are you struggling to shape some kind of myth out of the mumbo-jumbo in your recent effusions? It does not begin to hint at any kind of truth. You can never hope to touch upon that until you approach the ultimate, the source, the solitary presence, the very secret of all being. What is the universe but the greatest dream, which dreamed itself into existence? At its core, which is also its farthest boundary, is the lair of its creator. That awful entity is the essence of all dreams, and so it can be glimpsed only through them. The visionary dreams of the inhabitants of the universe are frag- ments of its nature, and it is jealous of bestowing them. Could you convey any of this in your spiritless fiction? I am certain you could not. Even I flinched from the merest distant glance upon the pres- ence which hovers in the deepest dark, mouthing vast secrets while it plucks many-legged at the fabric of the universe. Perhaps I shall capture its essence in a final literary offering, <u>The Eater of Dreams</u>. Should it see print, your attempts and those of all your acolytes will fade into deserved oblivion.

C. T. Nash.

> 1, Toad Place,
> Berkeley,
> Gloucestershire,
> Great Britain.
> November 1st, 1931.

Lumpcraft,

Have you still failed to lay your hands on my misplaced work? It is evident that you have learned nothing from its example. When I

---

[13] *Medusa: A Story of Mystery, and Ecstasy, & Strange Horror* (Gollancz, 1929).

saw the title of your latest washout I wondered if the whisperer might have been your feeble version of the truth to which I previously alluded, but it is even weaker than I would have expected of you[14]. The conclusion of the tale was obvious to me before I read the first page. You have always donned the mask of fiction to aid you in your pitiful attempts to scare your few admirers, but now it should be plain to the dullest of them that there is nothing behind the mask.

Your day is done, Lumpcraft, such as it ever was. I was amused to see that you have rendered Farthingsworth's rag even less <u>unique</u> by reprinting your tired tales of the hound and the rats. Are you now so bereft of imagination that you must resort to reanimating these soulless cadavers? Perhaps you have realised that, enervated though they are, they have more life than your latest efforts.

Which of those has lured in your new lickspittle, Rabbity Cowherd[15]? I presume he is avid for the world to notice that he refers in his own scribblings to your mumbo-jumbo. Is this intended to delude the reader into mistaking your puerile fancies for truth, or is it simply a game which you and your courtiers play? If you had been granted even the briefest glimpse of the denizen of the ultimate darkness, you would not dare to misuse your dreams in this fashion. You would recognise that you are but the least of its countless dreams. If you had discerned the merest hint of its nature, you would know that by attempting to perceive it, you had attracted its attention. How shall I describe the experience in words that the likes of you may understand? It feels as though some embryonic organ has become embedded in my brain. Sometimes I feel it stir, and then I know that I am observed by a consciousness so vast and so indifferent to me that it shrivels my being to less than an atom. Perhaps these moments are immeasurably brief, and yet they last for an eternity, both of which are constant states of the denizen of the infinite. In such a moment I become aware that time is as much of an illusion as space and all the materials which compose the universe. Nothing is real except the dreams of the source that clutches with its countless limbs at its creation. What would you write if you grasped even a fraction of its nature, Lumpcraft? I believe that you would never write again. What a boon that would

---

[14] "The Whisperer in Darkness".
[15] Robert E. Howard.

be! For myself, I have done writing to you. You are no more to me than I am to the boundless dreamer.

C. T. Nash.

1, Toad Place,
Berkeley,
Gloucestershire,
Great Britain.
September 3rd, 1933.

Pulpcraft,

Well, you have outdone yourself. Who else could have written your tale about the witch's house[16]? Who else would have wanted to do so? Who, having committed the offence, would have put his name to it? I am beginning to think that you may indeed not have received my later work. Certainly its example is nowhere to be seen, although the same may equally be said of my work which you admitted to receiving. This latest farrago is an insult to the very name of dream, and I suspect that even your fawning friends will search in vain for elements to praise. Since they all write fiction, no doubt they will produce some to comfort you. Are you so timid or so dishonest that you cannot admit your failings as a writer even to yourself? Were I you, Pulpcraft, I should give up the struggle before I perpetrated worse embarrassments. I writhe in disgust at your humdrum pulpy prose, and so does the mouth in my brain.

It is indeed the semblance of a mouth. Just as the glimpses of the presence with which I tantalized you were no more than similes, so this may be the merest hint of the reality. All the same, I often feel its moist lips shift within my cranium, and sometimes I have felt a tongue explore the folds of my brain, probing among them. Increasingly I seem to sense its whispered secrets seeping into the substance of my cerebrum. At times I have to overcome a compulsion to voice them as I deal with the mob beyond the counter. Does this raise your hope that I may reveal some of them to you? You will have no further opportunity to steal the fruits of my dreaming. You lack the courage to venture where my spirit travels, and so you are unworthy of the reward. Let your prudent <u>providence</u> provide you with the prize you earn.

C. T. Nash.

[16] "The Dreams in the Witch House".

1, Toad Place,
Berkeley,
Gloucestershire,
Great Britain.
October 24th, 1935.

Cravecraft,

Behold, you have enticed a new follower to yourself! Bobby Blob writes like a very young man[17]. Was Dulldeath not one, too? Doubtless you find their kind easiest to influence. Do you now require your lackeys to imitate your awkward prose besides including your mumbo-jumbo in their fiction? Perhaps you should be wary of accepting young Blob's tale of the shambler as a tribute[18]. The narrator appears to need very little excuse to do away with the writer from Providence. I am reminded that Stank Pong also exterminated such a writer.[19] He had an even better reason, since his image of the hand which plays with brains comes closer to the cosmic truth than all your slime and tentacles and gibberish.

You should heed the message of your minions. You are redundant, Cravecraft, and a burden on your scanty audience. Do you not see that your friends feel obliged to praise you? I believe your lack of inspiration has finally overwhelmed you, since your pen appears to have dribbled its last. You are reduced to disinterring the decayed carcasses of tales which should have been left in their unmarked graves. The fiddler Zann begs for pennies once more, and the white ape joins in with a jig. Why, you have given the tale of the ape a new name in the hope of misleading the reader that its publication is unique[20]! I doubt that even Farthingsworth's dull audience will be deluded. No mask can disguise material which is so uninspiringly familiar, and all the perfumes in the world cannot swamp the stench of rot.

You will be interested to learn that one of the conduits through which I was dreamed into the world has ceased to function. He leaves a sizeable amount of money and his fellow channel, my mother. Both are useful in relieving me of the need to remain in prosaic employment. As well as dealing with domestic matters, my

---

[17] Robert Bloch.   [18] "The Shambler from the Stars".
[19] "The Space-Eaters" by Frank Belknap Long.
[20] The tale originally published as "The White Ape" was reprinted as "Arthur Jermyn".

mother will act as my envoy to the mundane world. I am glad to be free of the distractions of customers and fellow butchers, for their incomprehension was becoming an annoyance. The secrets that are mouthed within my brain must be pronounced aloud, but only the enlightened should hear them. Do not dream for an instant that you are numbered among that fellowship.

C. T. Nash.

1, Toad Place,
Berkeley,
Gloucestershire,
Great Britain.
June 19th, 1936.

Strivecraft,

Never imagine that you can pass off my discoveries as your own. Wherever you are published, I shall find you. Do you now seek to astound? You appear to have astounded your new readers solely by your unwelcomeness[21]. They are as unimpressed by all your slime and tentacles as any audience should be. What possessed you to inflict your outmoded fancies on a readership versed in science? Since you claimed Farthingsworth as your most sympathetic editor, have you perhaps thrown yourself upon an agent? He must be poor, both financially and intellectually, to accept your work. At least, if I am not mistaken, he has revised it to improve your prose. No doubt your craven sycophants will chorus that your enfeebled work goes from strength to strength.

The true visionary neither requires supporters nor expects them. My mother's only functions are to keep the house in order and to deal with the mob on my behalf. Her interpretations of my pronouncements are none of my concern, and I shall not allow them to annoy me. It is only to retain her usefulness that I exert myself to keep my secrets from her, instead sharing them with the lonely hills when the night permits. There I can release the truths which the lips constantly shape in my brain. Sometimes things consumed by ancientness gather about me to listen to my utterances, and sometimes I am witnessed by creatures that will inhabit the earth when the mob is no more.

[21] On its appearance in *Astounding Stories,* "*At the Mountains of Madness*" attracted hostile comment in the letter-column.

As to you, Strivecraft, will you persist in scribbling when you have less than nothing to communicate? Perhaps you should be shown what a true seer looks like. The next time I dispatch my mother to the shops I may have her bring me a camera. While your mind would shrivel at the merest glimpse of the source of all dreams, perhaps you can bear to look upon its human face, although I do not think you will survive the comparison. I think you will never again want to face yourself in a mirror.

C. T. Nash.

> 1, Toad Place,
> Berkeley,
> Gloucestershire,
> Great Britain.
> October 12th, 1936.

Limpcraft,

I see that Rabbity Coward has ceased to play the brave barbarian. His dreams must have been as frail as your own. Or might he have intended to set you an example by ridding the world of himself? How long will you persist in loitering where you are unwanted? The readers of the scientific fiction magazine have made your unwelcomeness plainer still. What delusion drives you to seek publication where you must know you will be loathed? Even Farthingsworth is not so desperate that he feels compelled to disseminate your latest flops. Limpcraft, you are but a dismal caricature of the man I once sought to be. As well as burdening literature, your inert presence weighs me down and binds me to the earth. My brain aches at the thought that you continue to infest the world, just as my jaws ache with declaration.

I have the camera, but I do not think any technician could look upon the photograph which would be developed. Whenever my mother is at home I keep to my room. I have trained her to leave my meals outside the door, since it would be inconvenient to have her flee. The curtains shut out the attentions of the mob. I have no need of mirrors, because I know that I am transformed by dreaming. Perhaps I am growing to resemble the source, or perhaps its awareness has begun to consume me. Perhaps I am how it mouths its way into the world. By now the lips that gape within me feel as vast as space. Your puny skull could never contain even the notion of them.

C. T. Nash.

1, Toad Place,
Berkeley,
Gloucestershire,
Great Britain.
January 18th, 1937.

Lovecrass,

So you are dreaming of me, are you? Or you are so bereft of dreams that you have to write tales about me. I am a <u>haunter</u> of the <u>dark</u>, am I, and a shell which owes its vitality to the presence of a woman[22.] It is time that you were confronted with the truth. I shall convey a revelation from which even your mind will be unable to hide. I vow that you will no longer be able to ignore your ignorance.

I shall enclose my photograph. There is, of course, no need for my to delegate my mother to obtain a print, since you can have the film developed yourself. Have you the courage to gaze upon the face of dream, or has all your dreaming been a sham? Perhaps you will never sleep again while you remain in the world, but whenever you dream, there shall I be. Do not imagine that your death will allow you to escape me. Death is the dream from which you can never awaken, because it returns you to the source. No less than life, death will be the mirror of your insignificance.

C. T. Nash.

This was apparently Nash's final letter. Two items are appended to the correspondence. One is a page torn from a book. It bears no running title, and I have been unable to locate the book, which seems to have been either a collection of supposedly true stories about Gloucestershire or a more general anthology of strange tales, including several about that area. Presumably whoever tore out the sheet found the following paragraph on page 232 relevant:

Residents of Berkeley still recall the night of the great scream. Sometime before dawn on the 15th of March 1937, many

---

[22] Nash is referring to "The Haunter of the Dark" and "The Thing on the Doorstep", published in the most recent issues of *Weird Tales*.

people were awakened by a sound which at first they were unable to identify. Some thought it was an injured animal, while others took it for a new kind of siren. Those who recognised it as a human voice did so only because it was pronouncing words or attempting to pronounce them. Although there seems to have been general agreement that it was near the river, at some distance from the town, those who remember hearing it describe it as having been almost unbearably loud and shrill. The local police appear to have been busy elsewhere, and the townsfolk were loath to investigate. Over the course of the morning the sound is said to have increased in pitch and volume. A relative of one of the listeners recalled being told by her mother that the noise sounded "as if someone was screaming a hole in himself". By late morning the sound is supposed to have grown somehow more diffuse, as though the source had become enlarged beyond control, and shortly before noon it ceased altogether. Subsequently the river and the area beside it were searched, but no trace of a victim was found.

The second item is a photograph. It looks faded with age, a process exacerbated by copying. The original image is so dim as to be blurred, and is identifiable only as the head and shoulders of a man in an inadequately illuminated room. His eyes are excessively wide and fixed. I am unable to determine what kind of flaw in the image obscures the lower part of his face. Because of the lack of definition of the photograph, the fault makes him look as if his jaw has been wrenched far too wide. It is even possible to imagine that the gaping hole, which is at least as large as half his face, leads into altogether too much darkness. Sometimes I see that face in my dreams.

The Last Revelation of Gla'aki

THE MOST FAMOUS VICTORIAN RARITY MAY BE A STAMP— the Penny Black—but it is several times more common than the rarest Victorian book. It is possible that no copy of *The Revelations of Glaaki* still exists anywhere in the world.

The only printed edition was published in nine volumes in 1865, by the Matterhorn Press of Highgate in London. A spurious "Liverpool edition" is unrelated to it, and consists of text fabricated by modern gamesters for use in role-playing games. The Matterhorn set was published for subscribers, supposedly numbering fewer than two hundred, most of whom are thought to have belonged to cults or occult fellowships. It appears to have been the only work published by Matterhorn Press. The founder of the publishers may have been connected with the Ghost Club of Cambridge University, revived in London in 1862.

The nine volumes are described as "edited, organised, and corrected by Percy Smallbeam." The name is almost certainly a pseudonym. The text is reputedly founded on the contents of eleven volumes composed over an indeterminate period by members of an obscure cult founded at Starfall Water near Brichester in Gloucestershire. While the original text is said to have been understandably haphazard, it is uncertain how much the Matterhorn edition was rewritten rather than simply reorganised. For instance, the occult writer John Strong claimed that Smallbeam dropped the apostrophe from the name Gla'aki to make for ease of reading.

The original content was apparently provided by an unidentified defector from the Gla'aki cult, though some sources maintain that the man responsible had been charged with propagating the material. He appears to have approached the Ghost Club for help with publication but was turned down by religious members of the society. Among its founders was E. W. Benson, later Archbishop of Canterbury and father of several writers of supernatural tales, including E. F. and A. C. Benson. In his *Life* of his father, A. C. comments that he "was more interested in psychical phenoemna (sic) than he cared to admit, but would have no truck with the dissemination of occult secrets. A dupe who approached him for aid in the publication of a grimoire or the like was swiftly shown the door." Some have cited this as a reference to the cultist from Brichester.

The Matterhorn edition attracted no significant comment at the time. It would not be noticed by the public until the 1920s, when the campaign against Aleister Crowley ("the wickedest man in the world") by *John Bull* and the *Sunday Express* was at its height. A set of the books had been observed in Crowley's library, and Crowley described it as "an inspiration, the source of many secret truths." *John Bull* proceeded to attack it as "the most evil book ever published" while the *Express* exhorted its readers to burn every copy they could find. While the attacks were very largely if not entirely speculative, showing no acquaintance with the content of the books, the journalists were able to condemn the titles of two volumes, *On the Purposes of Night* (which was reviled as betraying the furtiveness of anyone associated with the books) and in particular *Of the Uses of the Dead*.

Most of the edition may have been destroyed as a result of the campaign. Subscribers who were still alive no doubt felt vulnerable and could have been easily influenced, and few if any descendants of the original owners would have cared to be associated with the books. Since then no copies have come to light, and in an unrelated incident the set held by Brichester University was among the volumes destroyed by a student at the turn of the last century. The most evil book, or a lost contribution to the literature of occultism? Like the contents of the Library of Alexandria, it may have passed into legend.

Leonard Fairman
Archivist, Brichester University
(guest columnist, *Rarae Aves*:
Bookhunter Monthly, May 2012)

As the coast road brought him in sight of Gulshaw, Fairman thought this was how a writer must feel: you never knew where anything you wrote might lead you. The fat grey bricks of the small town looked as though the September sky had settled to the earth and grown solid. Beyond a wide church with tall thin arched windows and a squat tower, a line of stocky hotels overlooked a half-mile curve of beach. Behind them houses crowded uphill towards a wood, both ends of which reached down almost to the shore. At the near end of the promenade a town sign stood on stilts over an arrangement of large shells embedded in the pavement. **WELCOME TO GULSHAW—SO MUCH MORE THAN SEA!** There certainly was, Fairman thought, for him.

Just now the town seemed to be slumbering. A few families lay on towels on the beach as if they were hoping to bring out the sun. Old folk in wheelchairs drifted along the promenade while parents pushed children in buggies at the pace of the somnolent waves. At the ends of several pedestrian crossings Belisha beacons exchanged somnolent blinks. A Crazy Golf course was in use, though the players weren't much livelier than the statue that appeared to be shading its eyes to watch them as it gazed stonily out to sea. Beyond the hotels Fairman saw amusement arcades jittering with multi-coloured lights, souvenir shops wearing bunches of hats, a fish standing as tall as a man to hold a menu in its fins. Close to the far end of the woods a string of cars crawled up the incline of a roller coaster, and a big wheel turned sluggishly for a few seconds before reverting to stillness.

Fairman slowed down as he passed the Church of the First Word. Though he hadn't been speeding, he felt as if he had, and in any case he needed to find his hotel. There was the Staymore, the Toprooms, the Seaside Dreams, the Kumbak . . . Eventually he located the Wyleave, a hefty structure with three storeys and a stained-glass awning, near the middle of the row. Across the road graffiti were attempting to bring a Victorian shelter up to date. Fairman drove around the Wyleave to the car park, where half a dozen vehicles took up almost half the space, and trundled his overnight bag into the hotel.

He suspected that the wallpaper along the corridor leading to Reception had been there before he was born. It was embossed with a pattern of fish leaping out of equally stylised waves, an image no doubt meant to evoke the seaside. The pattern flocked into the lobby, where a woman with silvery curls and a long heavy suntanned face sat behind a massive counter of dark wood. For an instant she looked drowsy, and then she stood up from her desk, her pearl necklace emitting a tiny chatter as it shifted on her embroidered white blouse. "Mr Fairman?" she said, and with a widening smile "I'm Mrs Berry. Call me Janine. Welcome to the Wyleave."

She held out a hand that proved to be soft and moist and possibly frail, so that Fairman refrained from taking too much of a grip. "I've given you a view," she said. "Can you put your details down for us?"

He was surprised by how much the registration form required: not just his name and address and the registration number of his car but date of birth, occupation, even next of kin and where to phone them—his father's name and the number of the retirement home. "Such a lot for just one night," Janine Berry said. "Won't you give us more of a chance?"

"I'd be happy to, but my holiday's arranged."

"So what's brought you to us?"

"Books."

"Of course," she said as though it had been less a question than a joke.

"We librarians do have other interests too, you know."

"I expect so," she said, though with a blink that looked a little puzzled, and slapped the nipple of a bell on the counter. "Tom, can you show Mr Fairman up to six."

The porter was a pudgy youth whose tan put Fairman in mind of batter on a fish, quite possibly a staple of Tom's diet. As he carried Fairman's luggage up a staircase enclosed by the omnipresent wallpaper Fairman tried asking "Been away for some sun?"

"Not likely," Tom said without turning to him.

Did Fairman sense resentment? Perhaps the tan was artificial. Tom was silent until he unlocked a room on the first floor. "We've got you here."

As soon as the door opened Fairman could see all the way to the watery horizon. Heavy purple velvet curtains scragged by bands of the same material framed the extensive window. A mauve plush chair sat by a dressing-table surmounted by a wide oval mirror, which was flanked by massive wardrobes of the same dark wood as the reception counter. The double bedspread and the plump head-board kept up the empurpled look. At least the wallpaper was pale blue, and decorated with stylised waves but no fish. While Fairman could live with all this, he was taken aback by the absence of a bath-room. Perhaps the porter saw him frown at the sink in the corner, because he pointed along the corridor at a pair of doors marked WC and BATH. "You'll not be sharing long," he said.

Once Tom had dumped the case at the foot of the bed Fairman pressed a pound coin into his hand. The clammy palm yielded so much that he thought he'd been too forceful, but the porter didn't react. "Call us if you need us," he muttered before retreating into the corridor.

Fairman sat on the bed, which emitted a creak and a scent of lavender. As he took out his mobile he heard the sea, a sound like a great protracted sleepy breath. The breath was held while a phone rang somewhere in Gulshaw, and then a mellifluous male voice said "Home of the Gulshaw Players. How can we help you?"

"Could I speak to Mr Lunt?"

"I'm your man and no other, and I believe I may be speaking to Mr Fairman."

"That's so," Fairman said, wondering if he had more of an accent than he imagined. "I'm in town. When might it be convenient for me to come by?"

"No better time than now. Toddle over whenever you're ready. Anyone will tell you where we are."

Fairman rather hoped the fellow wouldn't prove to be even more effusive in the flesh. He let himself out of the room and dawdled on the stairs to search for a pocket that might accommodate the brass baton attached to the key. "Don't go lugging that about with you," Mrs Berry protested. "We're always here. If you need us, wake us up."

"Could you direct me to the Shaw Theatre?"

"Our only one. Along the front and turn up by the Goodnight. You're on your mission, then." As Fairman granted that, she said "You'll have a look round too, won't you? There's so much more to see."

Was that a joke about the town slogan or a slip of her tongue? Fairman forgot about it before he reached his car. He couldn't recall

having passed a Goodnight, and he found it at the far end of the row
of hotels, on the corner of a street that separated them from the
amusement arcades. The theatre was halfway up the street, which it
divided into lanes that passed on either side. As Fairman parked
below it, a couple leading their children by the hand plodded uphill
towards him. The boy and the equally sleepy-eyed girl watched him
feed coins into a machine that performed a routine of clicks and
whirs before producing a coquettish ticket. The children even
seemed to find him worth watching while he stuck the ticket inside
the windscreen, and he wasn't unhappy to leave them behind as he
made for the Shaw.

A dormant neon sign identified the squat grey building, but not
by its original name. The lingering outlines of letters betrayed that it
had once been called the Gulshaw. On either side of the glass doors
a poster advertised **THE GULSHAW PLAYERS** IN **FOR
YOU TO SEA**, which Fairman thought made no sense. As he
tried to open the nearest door a young woman crossed the foyer to
admit him, miming more speed than she achieved. "Mr Fairman?"
she said with a smile that multiplied creases on her plump tanned
face. "Mr Lunt is ready for you. You're to go straight through."

Beyond the ticket counter a corridor was decorated with posters
older than Fairman. He'd squinted at just a couple—the grudging
light and the befogged glass within the frames blurred the outlines of
the faces—when the door at the end of the corridor swung inwards.
"Mr Fairman," the manager boomed. "Frank Lunt. Welcome to the
Shaw."

He was a small man capped with glossy black hair. He wore a
lounge suit and a white shirt stretched so tight over his prominent
stomach that dark hairs peeked between more than one pair of
buttons. His bow tie was as black as his neat moustache, which
appeared to be sharing its gloss with his round face. His handshake
was somewhat prolonged for Fairman's taste, since it was damp and
pliable. "Step in," he urged. "Will you have a drink to celebrate?"

"I'd better not when I'm driving. Being here is enough of a celebration for me."

"Not for you alone, sir." Lunt lowered himself into a venerable
leather chair behind his broad squat desk while Fairman sat on a
pudgy stool. "It's good to meet someone who knows all about our
book," Lunt said.

"I wouldn't say quite all. Only what you read." When the

manager looked politely unconvinced Fairman added "Do you mind if I ask how you came by the book?"

"Father gave it me."

That was brusque enough to be a warning, especially since it didn't sound like the man's style. Perhaps Fairman had touched on a family secret, in which case he shouldn't pry. "I don't doubt he was right to trust you," he said.

"I'll say as much for you."

Fairman supposed he should feel vindicated, but he said "Would you like to see some identification?"

"No need." Lunt might even have been offended. "Nobody's doubting who you are."

"Well then, may I see what you've been looking after?"

"My privilege." Lunt stood up as if he were stretching after a rest, but gestured Fairman to stay seated. "It's here for you," he said.

Fairman had expected to be taken somewhere else. The safe to which Lunt turned behind his desk seemed hardly large enough to hold nine books, though Fairman had learned from a nineteenth-century auction catalogue that the volumes were small quartos. Having typed on the keypad, the manager pressed a final key so hard that his thumb appeared to swell and flatten, and then he stood back as the door swung ajar.

The safe was full of papers and, as far as Fairman could make out, nothing else. He had to restrain himself from craning for a better view as Lunt hauled the door wide and reached in. For a few moments that felt longer than a breath Fairman had the odd impression that the man was extending his arm quite a distance. He let out the breath as Lunt produced a small black volume from the safe. "All yours now, Mr Fairman," he said.

Fairman must look as if he were bowing in obeisance as he rose in a crouch to take the book that Lunt passed him with both hands. It was bound in soft black leather, with a colophon embossed on the front cover. At first Fairman took the image for a spider clutching a ball of its eggs, and then he saw that it showed the world held aloft by a claw with many digits, unless those were meant for the limbs of some creature lurking on the far side of the globe. He was cataloguing the volume in his mind—it was indeed a small quarto, measuring about seven inches by a little over three—but despite his attempt to stay professional, his pulse was quickening. The spine was devoid of any title, and as he turned the cover towards him again the colophon appeared to rise out of its own blackness. "Thank you, Mr Lunt," he said. "You can't know how much this means to me."

"Just so it's in the right hands, Mr Fairman. That's all we need."

As Fairman opened the book a musty odour reminiscent of stagnant water rose to greet him. In a breath it dissipated, giving way to the familiar aroma of old paper, though the pages had hardly yellowed. He seemed to taste both smells on the long breath he took as he read the title page.

Of the World as Lair
Tome III of the Revelations of Glaaki
edited, organised, and corrected by Percy Smallbeam

His hands grew a little clammy, and the covers felt as if they had, while he turned to the first page.

How many secrets hath the world! Some are hid by water, and so Glaaki may be known to few men but in the dreams He sends . . .

It occurred to Fairman that scarcely anyone alive might have read these words. He could imagine himself reading to the end without looking up, but he mustn't presume on Lunt's hospitality. He regained some professionalism by noting that while the subscribers weren't named or numbered, this volume belonged to the sixty-first set. He shut the book and saw Lunt closing the safe. "May I have the rest now?" he said.

"A rest," Lunt said and gazed at him.

"All the rest." Fairman added a laugh to take responsibility for the mistake. "The others," he said. "The other books."

"There's what I told you I had, Mr Fairman."

For a moment Fairman was as bewildered as the fellow seemed to be, and then he was able to laugh afresh. "I don't mean different ones. Forgive me, I'm talking about the rest of this set."

"We know that."

"You mean," Fairman said more sharply than he was able to control, "this is all?"

"I hope you don't think you'd have been brought here if it wasn't worthwhile."

"Please don't think I'm ungrateful," Fairman resigned himself to saying. "It's a more than welcome acquisition. I'll see that you're named as the donor."

"No need to single me out, Mr Fairman."

"Whatever you're comfortable with, Mr Lunt." When this brought no response Fairman said "I suppose we'll never know what happened to the rest, then."

"You will."

Fairman had to take a breath before he asked "How shall I?"

"Go to Dr Stoddart. He's got something for you just like me."

"You don't mean the rest."

As Lunt gave him a slow grin Fairman felt as if he'd been made the butt of a ponderous joke. Perhaps it was a local brand of humour if not simply Lunt's, and Fairman couldn't really call it malicious. A number of questions came to mind, but he only said "Would you know his number?"

"It'll be the surgery, but he's shut for the night."

"I'd like to try calling to be sure."

"It's your time." Lunt intoned the number and said "Tell him you're at Frank's."

A receptionist answered, though only on a tape that hissed like waves. Once she'd recited the surgery hours she provided an emergency number. Fairman didn't feel justified in using this, especially when it mightn't connect him with the person he was after. "Dr Stoddart, I'm Leonard Fairman of the Brichester University archive," he said. "Mr Lunt has just presented me with his valuable addition and says you'll be able to complete it. Let me leave my number and I'd appreciate your giving me a call."

He looked up just too late to interpret Lunt's vanishing expression. He would have felt presumptuous to call him Frank after so brief an acquaintance. "Thank you once again for your generous bequest," he said and stood up.

"We've another present for you," Lunt said and handed him a slip of paper that had been lying on the desk.

It was a ticket for the Gulshaw Players on Thursday night. "That's very kind of you, Mr Lunt," Fairman said, "but I don't imagine I'll be here by then."

"You mustn't run away from us, Leonard. There's so much more to see."

Fairman didn't know which peeved him more—the lurch into

familiarity or the mangling of the slogan. He thanked Lunt once more as the manager held the door open for him. In the foyer the young woman did, and gave Fairman's prize a look not far short of reverential. Presumably Lunt had told his staff about the book. Outside the theatre Fairman might have fancied that everyone trudging uphill towards him was aware of it. Of course he was simply mindful of how vulnerable it was out here in the open, and he hurried to unlock the car.

He'd brought nine stout cartons filled with excelsior. As he made space in one for the book and covered it up, quite a few passers-by stared at him. At least one man slowed down to watch, humming some old melody under his breath. Was Fairman betraying how valuable the book was? He made haste to stow the carton in the boot and lock the car before driving back to the hotel.

Janine Berry glanced over the reception counter at the solitary item in his hands. "I hope you don't think Gulshaw's let you down, Mr Fairman."

"Don't worry." He'd told her he was here for more than one book, of course. "I've more to look forward to before I go home," he said.

In his room he opened the safe that was hidden in the left-hand wardrobe. While there was nowhere near enough space for nine cartons, of course he wouldn't need it; he would be driving back to Brichester as soon as he took charge of the rest of the books. He laid the carton in the safe and typed his birthday—5475—on the keypad. Once he'd made certain the safe was secure he went out for dinner.

He didn't want much. He was eager to spend time with the book. He walked along the promenade, overtaking the occasional stroller. The sun had gone down, though he couldn't judge exactly where, given the grey haze that merged the horizon with the sea. Beyond the hotels he was met by the clamour of the amusement arcades: the electronic jingles of fruit machines, the repetitive ditties of toddlers' rides, the robot voices of video games. Between two of the arcades a giant fish stood on its tail in a pool of mossy light from the green tube in the window of Fishing For You. As Fairman let himself into the fish and chip shop the proprietor, an unexpectedly scrawny woman in a white uniform not unlike a nurse's, said "The word's out, then."

"Sorry, I'm not with you."

She gave that a look he could have thought was skeptical. "The word about the best fish dinners," she said. "You've come a distance."

Presumably Fairman's accent had betrayed him again. "Everybody's favourite," she said as she perched a battered fish on top of a heap of chips on a sheet of greaseproof paper. "See if you aren't back for more."

He didn't bother saying that he wouldn't be in Gulshaw long enough. She wrapped the package in a page of the *Gulshaw Gannet* and wiped her glistening hands on a towel before she gave Fairman his change. He took the hot package across the road to a bench overlooking the beach. Could people really still be swimming in the sea? He had to squint into the gathering dusk to be sure that the restless shapes were large jellyfish. As he unwrapped his dinner a wind fluttered the newspaper; in the dimness it looked as if the fish was struggling to demonstrate some kind of life. The batter was crisp, and though he might have called the fish a little rubbery, it tasted as he remembered cod tasting in his childhood. He ate most of it and nearly all the chips, and stuffed the remains into a concrete bin that appeared not to have been emptied for some time. He was turning back towards the Wyleave when an old phone began to trill.

Although he wouldn't have been surprised to see a vintage phone box on the promenade, the sound was in his pocket. He was hoping Dr Stoddart had returned his call, but the phone display showed him Sandra's name. "Sorry," he said. "I ought to have called you by now."

"You're there, I take it."

He heard affection underlying that, but he didn't know if anybody else would have. "I have been for a little while," he said. "It feels longer, somehow."

"That's a bit imprecise for you, Leonard."

"I'm sure it's because I'm away from you." He imagined her making the face she kept for compliments—almost too deprecatory to betray appreciation—but when he heard no response he said "It reminds me of the kind of holiday I never had as a child."

"I didn't realise you preferred that kind."

"I don't. I'm looking forward to ours. Art galleries and churches are fine as far as I'm concerned."

"So have you acquired your prize?"

"I've made a start."

"You either have it or you haven't, Leonard."

"I thought the chap who emailed me had all nine volumes. You saw yourself what he said." When she gave him a silence to interpret, Fairman told her "It turns out he just had one."

"So you'll be on your way after breakfast, I suppose."

"Not quite so soon. I'm waiting to hear from the fellow who has the rest of the set."

"Why on earth would they split it up?"

"To tell you the truth, I didn't enquire. I don't think the chap I saw was anxious to discuss its history. We can't expect everyone to care about books as much as we do, can we? I'm just happy it still exists."

"Don't let them take advantage of you, Leonard."

"How is anybody going to do that? It's not as though I'm being asked for payment. We ought to appreciate how generous that is."

"Unless they're glad to see the last of it. Perhaps the man who gave you the book didn't want too much of that kind of thing in his house, and that's why he had only one volume."

"It wasn't in his house, it was in his office safe."

"There you are, then."

She could be imprecise when it suited her, Fairman thought as he retorted "It doesn't matter what he thinks of it, does it? It's our job as archivists to preserve books like those."

"That doesn't mean we have to promote what they represent."

"Nobody's promoting anything. I've hardly even started reading it."

"Do you really need to, Leonard?"

"I wouldn't be much of a librarian if I didn't know my stock."

"In that case I'd better leave you to get on with your job."

"I'll give you a call when I'm about to start back if you like." When she let him assume her response he said "Have a good night."

"I expect I shall." As he began to think the call was over she said "I hope you do as well."

He'd learned to find fondness in her voice, since she hadn't much time for nicknames or other expressions of intimacy. The conversation had brought him to the shelter opposite the Wyleave. In the open cabin four benches formed a cross. On the bench that faced the sea the names MELANIE and SETH were united by a heart so inexpertly rendered that it looked malformed. Another seat bore misshapen figures merged by the enthusiasm of the cartoonist, while the bench facing the hotel was covered with initials bunched closely enough to resemble words, especially since they could have been scrawled in a single hand. Fairman found himself attempting to pronounce the gibberish in his head, if only to prove the graffiti weren't words, as he crossed the promenade to the hotel.

Mrs Berry was rising from behind her desk when he stepped into the lobby. He might have thought she'd been waiting up for him. His key gave a hollow rattle as she retrieved it from its pigeonhole. "Ready for bed, Mr Fairman?"

"I've some reading to do first."

"Of course," she said as though he'd reconfirmed her notion of the typical librarian. He was heading for the stairs when she murmured "Dream well."

"I don't really go in for it."

"We all do, Leonard." She touched her forehead, and the patch of brow as well as her fingertip grew momentarily pale. "If you don't," she said, "you'll never know what's in there."

That was the kind of observation Sandra had least patience for, he thought as he climbed the stairs. She hadn't even let him finish telling her what he knew about Starfall Water, although it wasn't a great deal. He'd found none of it worth mentioning in the essay that had ended up online.

Had a cult ever really made its home beside the unfrequented lake? In the 1960s the notion had been revived after Thomas Cartwright, a minor artist specialising in fantastic and occult themes, moved into one of the lakeside houses and died as the result of some kind of attack. A police investigation had proved inconclusive, and a family who were supposed to have abandoned the house before Cartwright took it over had never been tracked down. If the houses had at some stage been served by a private graveyard, no identifiable trace was found, though some tales suggested that the stone tombs had been pulverised beyond recognition. *We Pass from View*, an occult book by local author Roland Franklyn, even claimed that they'd been destroyed by the police.

Fairman had thought this unsuitable for mentioning in *Book Hunter Monthly*, and Sandra hadn't wanted to hear any more. She would have liked his other anecdotes even less—schoolboy stupidity, he imagined she would call them. They dated from his days at Brichester High, a quarter of a century after the Cartwright business. The lake had become a place you dared your friends to visit after dark, and he'd assumed his fellow pupils had borrowed the idea from films, though the originator of the challenge had lived on the edge of Brichester nearest the lake. Those who ventured there brought back increasingly extreme stories: the lake had begun to throb like an enormous heart, or a procession of figures as stiff as bones had been glimpsed among the trees on the far side of the water, or a globular growth on a stalk in the middle of the lake had turned so as to keep a party of teenagers in sight, and they'd realised it was an eye. How could any of this have been visible at night? At the time Fairman hadn't been surprised that the adventurers had ended up with nightmares, but once the headmaster learned of the visits to the lake he'd forbidden them. Apparently his fierceness was daunting enough, since the lake reverted to the status of a rumour. Since then, so far as Fairman knew, it had been visited mostly by the kind of people who tried to plumb the depths of Loch Ness, and they'd found just as little evidence of anything unnatural.

He didn't think he would ever tell Sandra that he'd visited Starfall Water. He'd hoped to bring his essay more to life, but perhaps he also meant to prove that he wasn't quite the bookish introverted fellow his schoolmates had thought him. He could see no reason to go at night, and even on a February afternoon the place had seemed unnecessarily dark, no doubt because of the trees that stooped close to the unpaved track from the main road as well as surrounding the lake. They overshadowed the row of three-storey houses that huddled alongside a cobblestone pavement at the edge of the water. All six roofs had caved in, and some of the floors were so rotten that they'd collapsed under the weight of debris. Great leaves of blackened wallpaper drooped off the walls of a house in the middle of the terrace, and Fairman had wondered if this was the one most recently occupied, nearly half a century ago. None of the windows contained even a fragment of glass, and he suspected his old schoolmates might have been at least partly responsible. The buildings seemed to gape at the expanse of water like masks lined up to demonstrate they had no identity of their own. He'd found the thought oddly disturbing as he went to the edge of the lake.

The murky water stretched perhaps half a mile to the trees where some of his schoolfellows had claimed to see a procession that shouldn't have been walking. He doubted you could see that even with a flashlight, given how close together the trees grew. The depths of the lake were even harder to distinguish. It was fringed by large ferns, but he'd made out just a few inches of the stalks beneath the surface, which was so nearly opaque that he might have imagined the mud was being stirred up by some activity in the lake. In fact the water had been absolutely stagnant, and he'd peered harder into it as though he was compelled to find some reason to have visited Starfall Water. He'd had the odd impression that around it all the trees were craning to imitate him, enclosing the lake with an iris of darkness that was capable of shrinking the sky overhead. That must have been an effect of his concentration, along with the idea that his scrutiny could waken some presence in the depths; in fact, a sluggish ripple had begun to spread from the middle of the lake, followed by another and another. They'd advanced so slowly that their lethargy had seemed to take hold of him; he could have fancied that the waves of his brain had been reduced to the pace of the hypnotic ripples. The thought had jerked him back to consciousness, not least of the unnaturally premature dark. As the ripples grew audible he'd turned his back and retreated to his car. He'd heard water splashing the edge of the pavement by the time he'd succeeded in starting the engine. Of course the ripples must have been caused by a wind, since all the trees around the lake had bent towards the water.

Besides these impressions, he'd seemed to take something else home. Like Sandra, for whom it was a reason to be proud of her rationality and control, he didn't dream or at least never remembered having done so, but for some nights after visiting Starfall Water he'd been troubled by wakeful thoughts. Whenever he drifted close to sleep he'd found himself thinking of the investigators who had tried to search the lake. The notion of sounding it had brought to mind a disconcertingly vivid image of a vast shape burrowing deeper into the bed of the lake, raising a cloud of mud so thick that it blotted out the denizen. No doubt this betrayed how preoccupied he was with the impossibly rare book, but he'd been assailed by the vision several times a night, until he'd begun almost to dread attempting to sleep. If dreaming was like that, it wasn't for him.

By the time he'd completed his essay the vision had left him, which surely proved they were related. He didn't mention it to Sandra, and he supposed he should be grateful that they'd been living apart. Perhaps this might change soon, along with her view of his find here in Gulshaw. Surely no librarian could be unaffected by the sight of one of the rarest books in the world.

He locked the door of his room and hurried to the safe. When he typed his birthday digits he was assailed by a panicky notion that the safe wouldn't open, as though the book might be too precious to release. But the black door edged open, and he reached into the dimness to cradle the box in his hands, laying it on the bed to lift the book out of its papery nest. The leather covers felt unexpectedly chill, as he thought a reptile's hide might feel. He sat on the solitary chair and opened the book as carefully as he might have handled an infant. "How many secrets hath the world . . . "

Was he exhausted after the long drive from Brichester to the northern coastal town? Perhaps not only tiredness was affecting his concentration. Whatever the incantatory prose might be meant to achieve, he wouldn't call it lucid. To what extent had Percy Smallbeam rewritten the material? Certainly the style read like a single author's. Fairman felt as though he wasn't so much interpreting the text as waiting for it to take shape in his brain, an experience that seemed unnecessarily similar to dreaming, and he turned the stiff pages in search of some reference his mind could fasten on. What was Glaaki meant to be, for instance? Perhaps that was made clear in an earlier volume, but around the middle of this one he found a reference to Brichester.

The theory appeared to be that certain areas of the world were foci of alien or occult forces—the book made no distinction. Whether this was a result of magical practices performed there over many centuries, or whether the sites had initially attracted the practices, was left unclear. Massachusetts around the town of Arkham was such a place, and other American locations included the Sesqua Valley and the Derry area of Maine. In Britain the Yorkshire moors near Marske were mentioned, along with Caerleon and Liverpool, where the chronic overcrowding of the slums at the time the book was published "allowed the ancient denizens to flourish unremarked save by those who had carnal recourse to them." As for Brichester, the book suggested that the surrounding Severn Valley area was a node of occult activity and the lair of creatures far older than humanity. Supposedly some of the latter had survived beneath the village of Clotton, a name no longer on the map, "where they ape the voice of the blind waters that pour into the abyss beneath the earth." Other legends spoke of Temphill, where an attempt to render an ancient site Christian had merely given sustenance to the forgotten things that were drawn to a subterranean vault, and

Goatswood, in Roman times a place of worship of an inhuman entity the Romans called the Magna Mater. In the forest that gave Goodmanswood its name you might encounter a man composed of insects that would swarm into your brain. And here at last was a reference to Gla'aki, although spelled in Percy Smallbeam's way. "So steeped in arcane power was the valley that it acted as a beacon to which Glaaki guided His stone cocoon across the gulfs of space."

Fairman hadn't realised that the area around his home town had given rise to so many myths. Perhaps they were simply delusions of the cult that had written the original text, or Percy Smallbeam might have elaborated on them; who was to know? Nevertheless Fairman had an odd elusive sense that he'd already been aware of some of them. It felt as he imagined trying to recall a dream would feel, and he was gazing into his own bemused eyes in the mirror when his phone rang. He might almost have been jerking awake as he saw the number was unidentified. "Hello?"

"Leonard Fairman? I believe you want me."

"I might if I knew who you were."

"It's Dennis Stoddart, Leonard. You left me a message."

"Dr Stoddart." Fairman couldn't quite bring himself to match the familiarity, and hoped this conveyed that he didn't welcome it either. "Thanks for calling back. Mr Lunt said—"

"I'll bet he said a lot and at least half of it worth hearing. That's our Frank and it's how we all like him." The doctor cut a chortle short and said "But if he told you where to find your sacred item, that's the truth."

While Farman might have demurred about the sacredness, especially if Sandra had been there, he said "When could I—"

"As soon as you like in the morning. Sleep sound," the doctor said—it could almost have been medical advice—and rang off.

No doubt Mrs Berry would be able to direct Fairman to the surgery. The front cover of the book he'd placed on the dressing-table had begun to twitch upwards as though it and its reflection were beckoning to him. He no longer felt sufficiently awake to concentrate, and returned the book to its carton, which he locked in the safe. Slinging a towel over his arm, he ventured into the corridor.

He might have preferred the hotel to be somewhat less quiet. He'd been inhibited in public toilets ever since his childhood. He flushed the shared toilet before using it and hoped that his uncontrollably intermittent pouring would be drowned out by or at least

indistinguishable from the filling of the cistern. He waited for that
to finish so that he could pull the chain, the handle of which wore a
mauve sheath that matched the shaggy cover of the lid and the
curtains at the dinky window. At last he was free to dodge next door
to the bathroom.

Apparently the previous user had left the light on beyond the
frosted glass that was additionally obscured by condensation.
Fairman pushed the door open and recoiled so hastily that he lost
his grasp on the handle. "Sorry," he gasped.

"My fault." It was a woman's voice, though until she spoke he
wasn't sure it would be. "Forgot to bolt," she said. "Just getting in
shape for the night."

"You carry on. Don't hurry for me. I can do without the bathroom."

He still couldn't see her except as a blurred shape under the steam
on the mirror. The bathroom had an oddly stagnant smell; perhaps
she had lingered too long in the bath. Fairman was retreating when
the door shut, though the imprecisely outlined figure in the mirror
hadn't seemed to move. No doubt she'd used her foot to close the
door, though it must have been quite a stretch. Presumably the door
was still unbolted, a thought that hastened him back to his room.
He washed his face and brushed his teeth at the sink, above which a
small mirror showed him his back above the dressing-table. He
could do with keeping himself in better shape; perhaps he ought to
use a gym, as Sandra did.

Outside the window the streetlamps blanched the promenade
and blackened the graffiti in the shelter. The pale glare illuminated
just a narrow strip of the beach, so that he couldn't be sure whether
there were jellyfish in the receding sea. He unlatched the sash and
pushed it up, which didn't help him to distinguish the indistinct
restless shapes from the movements of the waves. As he leaned over
the sill a wind brought him the smell of the sea—at least, the smell
of Gulshaw beach. It hadn't previously occurred to him that the
place didn't smell as the seaside should; he was reminded of the
stagnant smell he'd noticed in the bathroom. Although he believed
it was healthier to sleep with the bedroom window open, he dragged
the sash all the way down.

The stagnant odour seemed to linger in the dark. It held him back
from sleep, and so did thoughts of the book. The reference to a
stone cocoon kept catching at his mind, and he found himself visu-
alising an enormous stone oval suspended in outer space, an object

that resembled a monstrous egg or an island torn loose from its world to wander among the stars. As it plummeted towards a familiar planet he had a sense that it was being held together from within and reinforced against the friction that would have consumed a lesser meteor. What kind of entity could exert so much control over matter? The vision troubled him like the one he'd experienced after visiting Starfall Water, and made him feel as he had while reading the book—that he was reaching for memories he hadn't known were his. He was glad the image of the cocoon went no further, and eventually it let him sleep.

Daylight wakened him, and so did an idea. While it might be too much to hope that each volume was indexed, he ought to check. He opened the safe and the carton, and leafed to the end of the book. "Good God," he said with very little sense of what he was expressing.

There was no index. The text was followed by the flyleaves, which were covered with handwriting. However nearly illiterate the sprawling script looked, it might be senile or written under some influence. Fairman didn't think it could be Lunt's, though it must be relatively recent, having been written with a ballpoint. *Do not trust all which is herein*, it said. *Some visions were imperfectly set down, and some came damaged at the source. Some were spoiled by the minds employed to convey them, while others were misinterpreted by the editor. Not the bible nor the Quran is so worthy of restoration.*

By the time Fairman had read this he no longer thought the book had been defaced. If anything the comments seemed to make the copy rarer still, but how could anyone establish what the original text had been? The set would be available for experts to decipher if they could, and Fairman was content to be its guardian. He closed the book more carefully than ever and returned it to its nest in the safe before he emerged from the room.

A smell of breakfast greeted him in the corridor, and he heard voices murmuring downstairs. He flushed the toilet and then used it while the fattened lid nestled against his lower back. The stagnant smell had departed from the bathroom, and the shower he took didn't revive it, though condensation turned the mirror into a block of fog. Once he was dressed he reassured himself that the safe was locked and went down to the breakfast room.

Two teenage girls in grey track suits were on their way out while their parents told another family "See you next year." The seated party were the only breakfasters just now. They were a stocky lot, consisting of a dumpy son and daughter who resembled their parents so much that Fairman was reminded of those wooden dolls that unscrewed to produce miniatures of themselves. As he sat by the window, beyond which a whitish haze was curtaining the sea off from the beach, the mother twisted her top half around on the chair to face him. "First time?"

"Forgive me, I'm not sure what you mean."

Her husband squirmed around to stare at him. "We've not seen you before," he said in a Lancashire accent at least the equal of his wife's, "she's saying."

"Just here for the night," Fairman said.

The man gave a grunt that might have been doubling as some kind of laugh. "There's not many do that in Gulshaw."

Fairman was wondering if this deserved an answer when Mrs Berry bustled into the room, though not at much speed. "Good morning," she cried. "Any dreams?"

As the boy and girl opened their mouths in unison Fairman said "Nothing I'd call one."

"What would you call it, then?"

The question seemed all the more unwelcome for coming from the stocky man. "Just night thoughts," Fairman resented having to explain.

Apparently it was the mother's turn to speak. "It can bring them, right enough."

"We'll leave them there for now, shall we?" Janine Berry said. "Are you having our big breakfast, Leonard?"

"That'd set anyone up for the day," the stocky man declared.

"Thank you, Mrs Berry," Fairman said. "I'll indulge myself this once."

The parents turned their back to him as Mrs Berry left the room, but the children continued to gaze at him as if he were some kind of specimen until they were told to eat up. As soon as they'd both wiped their glistening mouths the family took leave of Fairman. "Make the most of your stay," the man advised him, and his wife added "So much more to see."

Was everybody in on that joke, supposing it could be called one, or was nobody capable of reading the slogan? The family plodded away before Fairman could find a response. He watched people tramp down to the beach, vanishing into the haze that the sunlight had turned more opaque, until Mrs Berry brought his plateful. "There's a Gulshaw breakfast for you," she said.

It certainly seemed regional. The yolks of the pair of fried eggs were unusually large and pale, and oddly irregular. Both sausages were almost the colour of the slices of white pudding, and all these were tinged patchily purple, like the mushrooms and the bacon. Fairman mightn't have been ready to sample his breakfast if Mrs Berry hadn't lingered to watch. In fact it tasted as it should, so that he was able to reward her with an enthusiastic smile, and then he thought to say "I need to see your Dr Stoddart."

"Already?" Mrs Berry said and rubbed her mouth as if to erase the word—rubbed so hard that the skin around her lips looked bruised. "Oh, you mean—"

"He has something for me."

"Of course. I'm going to say it's a book."

"I hadn't realised I was so predictable."

"Nobody's laughing at you, Mr Fairman. You mustn't think you're anything but welcome."

She seemed close to offended. As she turned away he said "I was going to ask if you have a directory I could find him in."

"I can tell you where he is, of course. Eat up," she said not unlike a mother, "and I'll show you where you have to go."

Fairman was surprised to find how hungry the mouthfuls he'd taken had made him for more. People stared towards him as they lagged along the promenade, possibly looking for vacancy signs. He'd just laid down his knife and fork when Mrs Berry returned. "Here's what you need," she said.

It was a map of Gulshaw with the slogan from the town sign along the upper margin. On the back were advertisements for local attractions: the Shaw, the Bywood Zoo, the Promenade Ballroom, the Woody Ramble forest trail, the Ridem amusement park. "That's his surgery," Mrs Berry said, flattening a fingertip close to the sketch of the woods. "Past all the fun and up Bywood Road."

"I should think he might be keeping what he has for me at home."

"That's where he lives as well, Leonard," Mrs Berry said with an indulgent smile. "He's always there. We have to go to him. Dennis will do all he can for you, never fret."

"I'd better see him before I overstay my welcome with you."

"Don't you bother giving that a thought," Mrs Berry said.

Bywood Road was at the opposite end of the promenade from the church. As he drove past the Ridem rides Fairman saw how the haze that fringed the sea was helping the woods to enclose the town. At the ballroom he turned uphill past a number of large houses with their backs to the trees. The doctor's house displayed a nameplate on a gatepost, where the name was followed by so many unpronounceable clumps of letters that Fairman was reminded of the graffiti in the shelter. He parked on the street and let himself in through the grey stone porch.

In the wide hall beyond the massive door that gleamed white as marble, a receptionist sat behind a desk outside a closed room opposite an open one. She wore a voluminous flowered dress that covered nearly all of her without disguising how disproportionately small her head and hands were. Cropped spiky silver hair framed her face, which might have been more delicate until it had grown padded. "Mr Fairman," she said in a familiar voice rather younger than she looked—of course, he'd heard it on the answering machine. "You're here already, then."

He was bemused by being recognised, and spoke more sharply than he meant to. "The doctor said I should come as soon as I liked."

"He'd have meant before surgery. He's got his patients now."

Fairman felt as if he had to struggle past the professionally bland expression that hadn't changed since he'd come in. "What am I supposed to do? I haven't much time left."

"I'm sure you have more than some of us, Mr Fairman." Before he could clear up her mistake, if indeed she had made one, the receptionist said "You can wait with the others by all means."

"Couldn't you ask the doctor if that's what he wants?"

She was giving this her fixed expression when a man lurched out of the doctor's office behind her. His patchily empurpled face and the disconcerting flexibility of his gait suggested that his trouble might have to do with drink. As the man fumbled to open the front door Fairman said to the receptionist "Can't you ask him now?"

While her expression didn't waver, she pressed the key on a vintage intercom, an action that pulled back her cuff and sent a quiver up her pale inflated arm. Fairman heard a rasping buzz, and then a muffled voice said on both sides of the door "I'm afraid Mr Fairman will have to follow my patients, Doris."

"Doctor says—"

"I understood what he said," Fairman informed her, the nearest he could come to expressing his dissatisfaction, and tramped across the hall into the waiting-room.

All the people seated on straight chairs against the walls stared at him as a harsh metallic rattle appeared to announce him. The buzzer above the lintel was summoning the next patient, a young woman whose baby squirmed so vigorously in her arms that its one-piece suit had almost abandoned its shape. The infant favoured Fairman with a sleepy blink that he would have been foolish to mistake for recognition, and he was working on a responsive smile when the mother carried her exuberant burden out of the room.

A solitary table strewn with copies of the *Gulshaw Gannet* squatted in the middle of the dun carpet. Fairman took one to a chair, but the content was so trivial—graffiti on the seafront shelters made the front page under the headline **RESIDENTS CONDEMN VANDALISM**—that the paper might have been designed to reassure visitors that nothing very untoward ever happened in Gulshaw. He'd read all sixteen pages and forgotten virtually every one by the time the buzzer called the next invalid, a pasty-faced man who flattened his hand against the wall at each step he took. That left nine patients, and Fairman found some of them difficult to ignore—a woman with grey swellings reminiscent of fungi on her legs, a man whose chin seemed to merge with his spongy throat whenever he was overcome by an apparently uncontrollable nod, a woman whose every protracted breath sounded like a renewed task. If everyone was seated in order she would be the last to see the doctor, and Fairman didn't think he could endure her sounds for however long that would entail—perhaps an hour. He dropped the newspaper on the table and made for the hall. "I'm nearly at your zoo, aren't I?" he said. "I think I'll kill my time there if you don't mind."

There was no reason why the receptionist should, and her unassailable expression might have been telling him so. "Would you mind letting me know when the doctor's free?" he said. "I'll give you my number."

"We have it, Mr Fairman."

As he stepped out of the porch he saw the zoo at the top of the hill. He thought he wouldn't care to live so close to it, but perhaps the neighbours took it as part of living in a holiday resort. Or perhaps they were determined to ignore it, since all the windows he passed were curtained, as if there had been a death or the houses were occupied by night workers catching up on their sleep.

The signboard for the zoo had broken out in lumps of moss, one of which transformed the name into Byword. Beyond a small gate in the wire fence a man sat in a wooden booth that was piebald with lichen. His long pointed chin rested on his gloved hands, and he wore a floppy hat so nearly shapeless that he might almost not have known how to fit it to his cranium. As he saw Fairman he lifted his head, which seemed to elongate while his eyes took their time over widening, and the hat sagged backwards to reveal the slogan **GULSHAW BY GUM**. Fairman was reaching in his pocket for the fee posted on the booth when the man waved at him so vigorously that his fingers appeared to writhe—just the glove, of course. "Sorry?" Fairman said.

"Keep it." The fellow poked a greyish tongue between his lips as if rediscovering his mouth and muttered "It's on the town."

Perhaps this was a concession they made at the end of the season. Before long Fairman thought he wouldn't have been too happy if he'd paid. The exhibits weren't identified by signs, so that he couldn't tell what he was supposed to look for in the cages and concrete pits beside the winding mossy paths. Did the pits contain bears or big cats? None of those were visible, and the trees along the paths blocked off so much of the hazy sunlight that he could see nothing except darkness inside the bunkers in the pits. If the cages were for apes or monkeys, why weren't the enclosures roofed? Fairman could imagine their occupants leaping from the trees into the forest to make their escape. Even the windowless aquarium and reptile house didn't offer much; once his eyes adjusted to the dimness he had to conclude that most of the glass cases were presently disused, unless their tenants were lurking behind the rocks inside. Several panes bore large greyish fingerprints or more probably some other kind of marks, since they lacked whorls and appeared to be on the other side of the glass. He couldn't help recoiling when a boneless hand stretched out its pallid fingers to him from behind a submerged rock, but of course it was a squid or octopus, even if he couldn't see any suckers on the tentacles that darted back as though imitating his retreat. He shivered with the stony chill of the building and made for the open air.

It was less open than before. The haze had crept closer, dousing the grey sun. No wonder the animals had taken refuge wherever they could. He'd pretty well abandoned looking for them, and had begun to think of returning to the surgery, when he glimpsed movement in a cage. An ape was hiding behind a tree, gripping it with a large grey hand disconcertingly reminiscent of the object that had seemed to gesture at him from the tank in the aquarium. As he peered at it the fingers wormed away around the trunk. He watched for it to reappear until he grew cold with the dank stagnant air, and then he headed for the exit. He'd taken just a few steps when he seemed to hear a murmur behind him. "So much more to see," it said.

Nobody else was on the path. Were those fingertips or fungi on the glistening tree trunk in the cage? He needn't care, and he was making rather faster for the gate when a voice called out somewhere ahead. "Mr Fairman."

"Yes?"

"Leonard Fairman."

"Yes," Fairman yelled and put on speed until he saw the pay booth. The man in the misshapen hat was craning his top half over the counter and around the side of the booth at an angle that looked decidedly painful. "There you are," the man said. "Doctor's ready for you now."

Fairman could only assume the receptionist thought it was cheaper to phone the zoo than call him on his mobile. "Thank you," he said as the man's upper body shrank with a sinuous motion into the booth. "I'm afraid I didn't see very much."

"They're shy, some of them. You mightn't want to be seen in that kind of a shape." When Fairman frowned at this the man said "They're getting on or they're not well."

Fairman hadn't time to question this. He hurried past the dormant houses and let himself into the doctor's. When he thanked the receptionist for the call her expression didn't change, and he could have thought it was hiding bemusement if not convicting him of sarcasm, though he didn't see why it should do either. She bent her dwarfed head towards the intercom. "Doctor—"

"That's all right, Doris. Send in our visitor."

The moistness of the brass doorknob reminded Fairman of the atmosphere at the zoo. Beyond the door, chairs and a sketchy bed with a screen beside it faced a desk across a large white room. The man behind the desk rose from gazing at a computer monitor to extend a hand to Fairman. His bald head was rendered more egg-like by jowls, and his shoulders were so broad that Fairman had a grotesque sense that they'd slumped outwards. Presumably he'd acquired his tan abroad or in a studio. "Glad to meet you in the flesh, Leonard," he said. "What did you make of our zoo?"

His handshake was resolutely firm but clammier than Fairman cared for. "I couldn't see much," Fairman said and at once felt unreasonable; the doctor had nothing to do with the menagerie, after all. "Don't tell me," he said, "there's so much more to see."

The doctor raised his almost hairless brows, and his heavy eyelids crept back from his pale protruding eyes. "So much more than sea."

"I know that's how it's meant to go."

"We'll let it lie for now." Dr Stoddart wrinkled his wide nose, an action that twitched his thick lips. "What would you like me to prescribe?"

No doubt this was a sort of joke. "Just the books," Fairman said. "They're why I'm here."

"Nobody's forgetting that, Leonard. You don't know how much you're appreciated."

Embarrassment made Fairman change the subject. "Can you tell me anything about them?"

"They've been waiting for someone just like you."

Fairman had meant where the books had come from, but it needn't matter. "May I take possession, then?"

"All yours," the doctor said, reaching for the left-hand drawer. The desk quivered as the drawer emerged with a prolonged cavernous creak, and he lifted out a book that was the twin of the one Fairman had. The black cover was embossed with the image of a hand contorted in an occult gesture, the second and fourth fingers curving inwards while the others arched bonelessly backwards and the thumb jutted up from the palm. Fairman opened the book to find it was the first volume, *On Conjuration*. "The tongues of men reduce the world to words . . . " He shut the book before he could be tempted to linger over reading and looked up at the doctor, who was resting his hand on the open drawer. "Forgive my haste," Fairman said, "but may I trouble you for the others?"

The doctor shut the drawer and gave him an oddly distant look. "That's my contribution, Leonard."

Fairman tried not to feel let down; he had two considerable rarities for the archive, after all. "You mean there are just the two volumes."

"Just that one. That's all I ever had."

Fairman didn't bother to clear up the misunderstanding. He held the book in both hands as he rose to his feet. "Was it in your family?"

As Dr Stoddart made to open the door he said "Father gave it me."

He had his back to Fairman, who could almost have imagined that the doctor had borrowed someone else's words. Perhaps they betrayed how local he was, much as Fairman's accent seemed to place him. "Do you know your way around our town yet?" Dr Stoddart said.

"I don't mean to be rude, but why should I need to do that?"

"Because now you'll want to see Don Rothermere."

Fairman waited until the doctor turned to face him, having opened the door. "To what end?"

"For the same reason you've seen me."

"Another volume of the book?" Less enthusiastically and with some unease Fairman said "Just one?"

"That's how it's going to be, Leonard."

"But why has it to be? Why do I need to go through all this?"

His outburst was unprofessional, and he regretted it as Dr Stoddart and the receptionist gazed distantly at him. "It isn't for you, Leonard," the receptionist said.

Fairman might have expected her to be rebuked for being too familiar. He supposed she must think she was defending her employer. "So who's this Mr Rothermere?" he said. "Where shall I find him?"

"It's Suit Your Book on Station Road," the doctor said. "If you ask anyone—"

"I've got a map. I assume he's a bookseller."

"Our only one," Dr Stoddart said, and the receptionist added "Your kind of person, Leonard."

Fairman hoped so. Most booksellers would surely have completed the set of books by now and sold it for a considerable profit. Once the first volume was safely boxed in the car boot he consulted the map and drove uphill. Below the menagerie he turned right along Tree View, a name that made him feel as if he were following some kind of diagram. Beyond a sloping junction the twin terraces of small houses, which looked as if they'd been squeezed fat and grey, met Station Road. Cast-iron awnings set with coloured glass overhung the shops, and halfway along the road a railway station was composed of the omnipresent stone. Families were dragging luggage across the forecourt with a ponderous thunder of wheels while they did their best to hasten for a train. Suit Your Book was almost opposite the station, next to a doorway bristling with nets on canes and hung with plastic buckets. Fairman parked in a side street, where Vacancy signs dwindled downhill to the hazy promenade, and tramped up to the bookshop.

The window display wasn't encouraging. All the books—hardcovers of various sizes and a scattering of paperbacks—had plainly spent years in the sun, leaving them almost as pale as the haze above the sea. As Fairman stepped into the shop a bell sprang its clapper above his head, and a man hastened over to him. "Leonard Fairman?" he said, if it was even a question. "Don Rothermere. Kindred spirits, eh?"

Presumably the doctor had phoned ahead. The bookseller was a lanky man who moved as loosely as his grey suit hung on him. His face looked as if the dewlaps at his throat had drawn it narrower, and it was topped by an outburst of hair that might almost have leached colour from his skin so as to stay reddish. Prodigious glasses magnified his blinking eyes, and his pale lips kept twitching at a smile. "I'd hope we are," Fairman said.

Rothermere thrust out a long hand to hold Fairman's in a clammy grasp while he jerked his head to indicate the contents of the shelves—new or at least unread volumes along the side walls and in the middle of the floor, second-hand books at the back. "We don't read many books in Gulshaw," he said.

"Not the best place for you, then."

"I've got all I want to read." Apparently grasping that Fairman hadn't meant this, the bookseller said "And it isn't much of a trot to the post office."

Fairman wondered how much postal business Rothermere could do, given the state of his stock. "Have you been reading much here?" the bookseller said.

"Just the new acquisition."

"Of course." Rothermere's eyes widened, filling the lenses. "How's it affecting you?" he said.

"I wouldn't say it is."

"We mustn't deny it, Leonard."

Fairman was uneasily aware of being in the presence of some kind of believer. It hardly seemed possible for the eyes behind the lenses to have opened further, but he had the unpleasant fancy that they weren't far from touching the glass. "Have you read yours?" he felt compelled to ask.

"How couldn't I? It changes everything."

Fairman was loath to enquire into this. "Could I have it, then?"

"It's yours," the bookseller said and made for the back of the shop.

His office was between the shelves of second-hand books. Most of these were jacketless, a state Fairman used to describe as in their shirt-sleeves until Sandra made her unamusement plain. The office was unlit, but he was able to distinguish a large heavy desk surrounded by piles of books. Without switching on the light Rothermere retrieved a volume from the desk. "Yours," he said again.

Fairman stayed in an aisle of shelves to bring the man out of the gloom. With the book held in both hands Rothermere looked rather too much like the celebrant of a ritual. As he came forward Fairman could easily have imagined that some of the darkness had clung to the book. The colophon represented a hand that bore a lantern from which black rays were streaming. "Which one is this?" Fairman said.

"*On the Purposes of Night*," Rothermere said with reverence.

Fairman had asked so as not to linger over examining the book, but he couldn't help adding "Did you never want to find out what you could get for it?"

"I got everything it needs, Leonard."

"I meant," Fairman said more sharply, "had you no interest in discovering what it could fetch?"

"We did." Before Fairman could think of any answer he might risk, the bookseller said "If you're asking whether I'd have sold it to the highest bidder, that wouldn't have entered my mind."

"Would you care to say why?"

"The book says it for us."

When Rothermere stretched out his hands as though yearning to reclaim the book, Fairman said "Never mind, I'll look into it later."

"I can tell you what it says." The bookseller's gaze seemed to turn inwards if not somewhere else entirely. "Let none read who will not understand," he said like a priest intoning a sermon. "Let the great secrets be kept close lest they grow blurred by the unshaped minds of the uninitiated."

"That's what Percy Smallbeam said, do you think?"

"One solitary mind speaks through the book." It wasn't clear if the bookseller was still quoting, nor when he said "The world will know the book once it has done its work."

"What work would that be?" Fairman demanded.

"You'll come to know it, Leonard. Will you promise one thing?"

"That will have to depend."

"Never put any of it online, will you? You heard what it said."

"I've no intention of scanning it," Fairman told him and was so anxious to be gone that he almost forgot to ask "Can you tell me whom I need to see next?"

"Heidi Dunscombe. She represents our town."

"Represents in what way?"

"I thought you'd know more about us by now. She's our tourist officer."

"And where can I find her? No, don't tell me." Fairman saw Rothermere take this for an admission of knowledge, and felt bound to add "I have to get back."

Rothermere's earnestness seemed to befog his glasses. "You aren't leaving us, Leonard."

"Back to the hotel. They can direct me. Thank you for keeping this safe." Having reached the door, Fairman couldn't resist adding "You haven't told me there's so much more to see."

"There's no need." The lenses looked not merely blurred now but smeared. "You're beginning to," the bookseller said.

Fairman let that go. As he stepped out of the bookshop, triggering the bell again, he glanced back. The bookseller had withdrawn into his office and was fitting the spectacles to his face, no doubt having wiped the lenses. Fairman barely glimpsed the naked eyes, but they appeared to glimmer at him out of too much of the face, so that he could have imagined that the lenses were plain glass. He had an unwelcome impression of a creature watching him from the depths of its lair. Then Rothermere emerged from the gloom, blinking through his glasses at the light, and Fairman reassured himself that the illusion had been brought on by too little sleep. It wasn't why he hastened to his car.

He was tramping up the passage to the lobby of the Wyleave when Mrs Berry called "Don't put yourself out, Mr Fairman. No rush at all."

She was waiting at the counter. "We've given you another day," she said. "We knew you couldn't leave us so soon."

"I don't mean to be any longer than that."

"We'll have to see, won't we?" Mrs Berry said and gave the cartons he was cradling a slow nod. "More for our collection?"

This was a different kind of familiarity, one that he found patronising too, but he only said "Can you tell me where to find your tourist office?"

"Up in the square," Mrs Berry said and spread out a map on the counter. He supposed she had recently painted her nails, since the one she was using to point glistened like the surface of a lake. "Heidi will see to you," she said. "She'll give you what you need."

Fairman wished that were the case rather than just a single book. He hurried upstairs in time to see a chambermaid leaving his room. She wheeled a trolley next door as he let himself into the room, to find she'd been so eager to finish her work that she'd left the wardrobe open an inch—the wardrobe that contained the safe. The sight made him feel worse than careless, unworthy of the trust that had been placed in him, however irrational his reaction was. He planted the cartons on the bed and threw the wardrobe door wide.

The safe was locked, but as he typed the combination he saw marks on the black metal beside the keypad—the prints of a pair of moist hands. He could only think the chambermaid had left them, although they were larger than he'd seen her hands to be, as if they'd been pressed so fervently against the door that they'd spread to nearly twice their size. Presumably their clamminess had magnified the prints, which faded and vanished as he peered at them. He thought of confronting the girl or informing Mrs Berry, but what could he possibly say? Surely all that mattered was for the book to be there in the safe.

It was, and he unpacked it to make sure. The three cartons darkened the inside of the safe so much that he could almost have imagined there was space for nine of them. He wouldn't need it—he would be going home tomorrow. When he shut the safe he thought he heard a stealthy movement, as if the books were settling into their nests. He typed the code and was on his way out of the room until he remembered there was a call he ought to make. However important his search was, he shouldn't let it occupy quite so much of his mind.

The distant phone took some time to respond, which was how the head librarian treated any question. "Nathan Brighouse," he said at last.

"Nathan, it's Leonard Fairman. I thought I should report in."

"So glad you have, Leonard. All secured?"

"Up to a point, certainly."

"That'll be a negative, will it? Where's the hindrance?"

"I've acquired several volumes but the set has turned out to be somewhat scattered."

"Yes, Sandra Byers was telling me as much. Odd business, I must say. You haven't made the opportunity to assemble the set, then."

"I'm sure I will have by tomorrow."

"I'd be glad if that were the case. I'm sure the archives can survive without you for another day, but much longer and it may have to be put down as annual leave. You know how strict I'm forced to be in these straitened times."

"I assure you I'm doing all I can," Fairman told him, by no means as resentfully as he felt entitled to, and hurried downstairs to leave the key at Reception, where Mrs Berry was waiting. "Keep up the good work," she called after him.

As he drove onto the promenade Fairman saw that the haze had receded across the sea, giving the impression that the horizon had been drawn closer to the town. Before he came abreast of the theatre he turned uphill to the town hall, a massive grey edifice as plump as the statues of dignitaries that stood guard on either side. Perhaps the town didn't have much of a budget for the upkeep of monuments, since the stone faces were fattened by masks of lichen. He parked on the forecourt in front of an annexe, where the automatic doors of the tourist office deferred to him with a faint glassy squeal.

The walls were decorated with vintage posters, all of which showed the seafront very much as it still was. **IMMERSE YOUR-SELF IN GULSHAW** and **BREATHE IN GULSHAW** were two of the slogans that caught Fairman's eye, but the one that provoked a wry laugh said **SO MUCH MORE TO SEE**. So the townsfolk hadn't been mistaken after all, and perhaps he should take more notice of them. He was making for the counter at the far side of the room when a woman called "With you right now, Mr Fairman."

She was beyond a door at the end of the counter, applying makeup or retouching it so vigorously that she might have been trying to squeeze her cheeks smaller. They looked as carelessly expansive as the rest of her, most of which was contained by a loose blouse and a capacious overall. Unruly auburn curls framed nearly all of her round face, which stayed sleepily jovial as she waddled to the counter, sticking out a hand. "Heidi Dunscombe," she said, "as if you didn't know."

Her grasp felt slippery, no doubt with makeup. "What have you made of our town so far, Leonard?" she said.

"I should think that's your job."

It had taken her so little time to turn familiar that his reply was sharper than he liked, but she only said "What's that?"

"Making the most of your town."

"We'd love to have your thoughts."

Did she think he was being too unfriendly? Though her face stayed so genial that she might almost have been lost in a dream, Fairman said "Forgive me. I've been having rather an odd day."

"There's the night to come as well."

He might have expected such a comment from the bookseller, not from her. "May I have the book you're holding for me?"

"Of course."

Fairman thought for a moment that she was repeating herself, except that someone else he'd met had used the phrase. She waddled to a wall safe behind a desk in the office and then swung around languidly to ask "What do you think was odd?"

For a disconcerting moment Fairman had a sense of being watched from an unexpected distance, not just across her room. "Someone I met," he said.

"You'll get used to us, Leonard," Heidi Dunscombe said and turned ponderously away to spin the wheel on the safe. "What was odd about him?"

"He seemed to believe in the book he had. I don't imagine you do."

The safe lumbered open, gaping with darkness, a lump of which Heidi Dunscombe brought forth. She hugged it to her breast while she shut the metal door and twirled the wheel. As she advanced to the counter she said "It's belief that makes us what we are, Leonard."

Despite her equable expression, he assumed this was a rebuke. When she handed him the book, her breasts seemed to swell as if she were taking an enormous breath. The cover of the volume was imprinted with unfamiliar constellations, presumably somehow illustrating the title, *Of the Secrets behind the Stars*. "Thank you," Fairman said and hesitated. "May I ask how you came by it?"

"The same as everybody. From our father."

The wording unsettled Fairman, and so did the remoteness of her gaze. "Can you tell me whom I should see now?" he said.

"Of course." Her pause might almost have implied that he should know as well. "Rhoda Bickerstaff," she said. "She looks after our old folk."

"Not all of them, surely."

"Just the worst ones, Leonard." Her face suggested she had taken his bemused comment as a joke. "We like to think our town's a healthy place," she said.

She added a heavy nod, not just for emphasis. When Fairman looked where she was indicating he saw a brace of joggers down on the promenade. He assumed she had them in mind rather than the people plodding uphill, though even the joggers didn't seem especially energetic. "You'll find Rhoda at the Leafy Shade," Heidi Dunscombe said.

"Would you happen to have the number? I ought to let her know I'm coming."

"If you think so," Heidi Dunscombe said and told him the number.

As he keyed it he was conscious of her watching him across the dormant book on the counter. Her gaze seemed as remote as the bell that began to ring in his ear—to ring at considerable length. He was preparing to leave a message on a machine when at last a woman's voice said "Leafy Shade."

She sounded at the very least harassed. "Could I speak to Rhoda Bickerstaff?" Fairman said.

"Who is it?"

"Don't you know?" Fairman almost retorted, having come close to thinking everybody knew about him in advance. "I'm from the Brichester University archive," he said. "Is that Ms Bickerstaff?"

"What do you want, Mr Fairman?"

So she did know who he was, in which case she didn't need to ask this question either. "I believe you have a book for me," Fairman said.

"I can't talk about it right now."

Her voice was growing more agitated, while her breath seemed in danger of falling short of her words. "No need to," Fairman said. "Just tell me when I can collect it. I'd appreciate the soonest you can manage."

"I told you, not now."

Although he didn't think she had, arguing would waste time. "Forgive me if I've caught you in the middle of a crisis, but when is it likely to be convenient?"

"I don't know. Not today."

"It really won't take long at all." When this failed to earn a response Fairman said "Couldn't you leave it with someone for me to pick up and then I wouldn't need to trouble you?"

"Who?" This came out not unlike a gasp, but she found enough breath to add "I can't. You'll have to wait for me."

He supposed whatever problems were preoccupying her could involve her staff as well. "Then could you just tell me whom else I can see while I'm waiting?"

"I can't. You'll have to wait. You've got enough to occupy your mind."

"You mean you—" Fairman said, only to find he was talking to waves of static.

Heidi Dunscombe hadn't even glanced away from him. "Isn't she ready?"

"Apparently not," Fairman said and couldn't restrain his frustration. "She won't give me a time and she won't say who else there is to see. Can you?"

"She's next, Leonard."

"Yes, but I can get the other volumes in the meantime. Who has them, do you know?"

"I can't tell you."

He was angered not just by her words but by the jovial expression that seemed independent of her distant gaze. "Can't or won't?" he blurted.

"You'll understand us better soon, Leonard."

He was almost furious enough to give this the answer it deserved. The glass doors had squealed shut by the time he muttered "I hope I never need to." Perhaps his muted outburst was the reason people stared at him as he marched to his car. While he drove along the promenade he looked out for signs of the healthiness Heidi Dunscombe had wanted him to notice, but he couldn't see much. A man sitting rather less than upright in a wheelchair was waving one floppy hand beside a wheel as though to urge it to turn faster. Several people were walking dogs whose faces seemed almost to scrape the pavement, and at least one owner's could compete for pendulousness. There were joggers, but none of them appeared to be capable of overtaking the walkers or the chair. Their energy seemed to flag even further as they came abreast of his hotel.

The thump of the club attached to his key greeted him as he made for the reception counter. "Another one for the vault?" Janine Berry said, pressing her brow pallid with a fingertip.

"You could put it that way if you like," Fairman said despite thinking that somebody other than her might have—Frank Lunt, for instance, or the bookseller. All the way to his room the key rattled against the carton as though eager to unlock the secrets within. The wardrobe and the safe inside it were shut tight, and no marks were visible on the metal door. It didn't matter that the safe had space for just one more carton; he was determined to be back at the archive tomorrow with the entire set of books. He removed the four volumes from their cartons and lined them up on the dressing-table, where they seemed to bring too much darkness into the room—because the mirror doubled them, of course. Presumably this was what people called daydreaming, and he ought to be examining the books, but not until he'd made a call.

By the time Sandra answered he'd begun to wonder if she had switched her mobile off. "Are you only just starting out?" she said.

"Hasn't Nathan kept you informed? I hear you've been discussing me."

"It was library business, Leonard. You surely don't object to that."

"Not in the slightest. Keep him posted by all means. He already knows I won't be back today, though."

"You mean you told him but not me."

"I'm telling you now, Sandra." Fairman wasn't going to be made to feel unreasonable. "And he might have passed the information on to you," he said.

No doubt her pause was a form of rebuke. "So what's keeping you where you are?"

"What else except the books?" He'd turned towards the window, but seemed to feel their massed blackness behind him, making him impatient to read. "I still have to lay my hands on some of them," he said. "I will tomorrow."

"I don't understand. How many are you leaving until then?"

"About half. Well, just more than half." With mounting irritation Fairman said "I told you they're being held by a number of people. The one I have to see next isn't available today."

"I'm not grasping this at all. Why can't you deal with the others while you're waiting?"

"Because apparently it isn't done like that. Don't bother asking me why." This left him feeling so inadequate that he blurted "If you talk to Nathan you might like to know he's suggesting I'll have to take my time here as leave."

"But you haven't any left this year, Leonard. Our holiday is all you have."

"You don't need to tell me that." In a bid to make up for his abruptness Fairman said "You might try to use your wiles to change his mind."

"I really don't believe we have that kind of relationship."

"Then maybe you should work on having one for both our sakes." When she gave him another silence to construe Fairman said "I'll call you tomorrow as soon as I'm done here."

"Meanwhile you'll be enjoying the sort of holiday you wish you'd had, will you?"

"No," Fairman said, not seeing why he should feel accused. "I'll be doing my job."

He gazed through the window as he ended the call. Several old folk had their backs against the graffiti in the shelter on the promenade, hiding the unreadable clumps of letters. Dozens of people were sitting or lying on the beach, and there were even swimmers in the sea despite the greyish haze that enclosed it. The haze made the more distant ones hard to distinguish, but the most unstable of the shapes among the waves had to be jellyfish. In any case he ought to be attending to the books.

It made sense to start with the first volume, but he found himself lingering over the colophon. He wasn't far from imagining that the inhumanly distorted hand could conjure up some idea in his mind, and perhaps this had been the book designer's aim, since the volume was *On Conjuration*. "The tongues of men reduce the world to words . . . " Was that supposed to mean that gestures achieved something else? In that case, what was the point of this book entirely composed of words? Surely he oughtn't to expect it to make too much sense. Ah, here was some kind of enlightenment further down the page. "Let no man utter the secret words who has not first prepared his mind and spirit in the occult ways, for otherwise the words shall batten on him and shape him to their liking . . . "

"No chance of that," Fairman said and was glad that Sandra

couldn't hear him talking to himself. He stared at his reflection as though holding it responsible, and it stared at him across the inverted volume in its hands. He glimpsed it ducking its head to read "The beliefs to which the mass of men cling are the foes of revelation" and imagined it reading not just the words but all the letters in reverse. "The prating of the prophets chatters down the centuries without beginning to encompass the truths which shape the world. Still less can the gewgaws of religion challenge forces older than the universe we know. In his enfeebled Christian travesty of Al-Hazred, John Dee speaks of a glowing cross which appeared above the sabbats to confound the summoned powers. Say rather that the sabbats were no more than puerile parodies of ancient rituals, so mired in the tradition of the celebrated Jew that the biblical bauble could be misapprehended as a talisman . . . "

Fairman took a few moments to consider the Dee allusion. It referred to the alchemist's unpublished English paraphrase of the *Necronomicon*, which survived only in the form of fragments held by the British Museum, together with a fifteenth-century Latin translation, and Fairman couldn't have said why it left him feeling oddly vulnerable. His reflection gave him a conspiratorial nod as he bent his head once more to the book.

"And what shall be said of the star-signs which some claim as protection against entities no less immemorial than creation? How blurred the ancient truths become in the minds of the uninitiated! What are these signs but imperfect renderings of a stage in the formation of the universe? None but the ignorant seek to invest them with power, and only the most imbecilic of the old survivals may mistake them for a hostile charm, to be cowed by them for a short while. Let the star-signs never be confused with the secret gesture of the Children of the Moon, whose true nature is disguised in many a fairy-tale. Whereas to the rudimentary minds of lesser entities the star-sign may appear to threaten a return to primal chaos, and on occasion may temporarily interfere with the ethereal sendings of the dormant masters of our world, the gesture of the Children recalls that paradisiacal state of fluidity which the Bible bids to deny with its fabricated tales about the father of the Jew. Even these betray their imperfectly veiled secrets to the initiate, for the serpent in the garden is but a symbol of fluidity, an occult promise that the upstart race and its beliefs cannot wholly trammel the potential of the world . . . "

Was the image on the cover meant to illustrate the gesture? Fairman had the irrational thought that it was just a human approximation; perhaps that was the kind of thing the book was meant to put into your mind. He held up his left hand and could only laugh at his pathetic attempt to describe the sign. His reflection did no better, but at least its fingers didn't twinge. It watched him until they bowed their heads over the book.

The more he read, the less he seemed to grasp, and yet he felt close to understanding, as if the incantatory prose were leading him in that direction. Of course this wasn't the original text, it was whatever Percy Smallbeam had made of it. How much did that matter? Why should it matter to Fairman at all? He could almost have imagined that he was dreaming the material, letting it take shape in his head. He had no sense of how long it took him to read to the end, where he found he was eager to continue, in case the next volume helped him understand. He shut the book and saw that darkness had gathered behind him.

Night was at the window. It had fallen more than an hour ago, according to his watch. He couldn't recall switching on the standard lamp beside him, though why should a librarian feel troubled by having been engrossed in a book? He should at least eat, and he returned the books to the safe without boxing them up. Once he'd pressed his hands against the metal door to reassure himself that it was locked, he let himself out of the room.

Janine Berry was waiting at the counter by the time he came in sight. "Will you be having our dinner?" she said.

"Would you excuse me if I just nip out for something quick so I can get back to work?"

"The work you're doing here, you mean."

"Examining what I've acquired." In case this was unclear Fairman added "Yes."

"Then we've nothing to excuse." As she took hold of the bludgeon attached to his room key her fingernails glistened, and he thought the skin around them did; she must have been painting them again. "There won't be much difference," she said. "It's all our own produce."

The glare of the streetlamps blanched the promenade and blackened the cars parked outside the hotels but left the buildings as grey as the fog that had crept back across the sea. For the moment the seafront was deserted, though Fairman heard a metallic rattle that might have belonged to a restless car on the roller coaster or a shutter at a shop window, if it wasn't the sound of the bars of a cage. He made his way past Fishing For You to another such establishment among the noisily wakeful arcades. "Trying us tonight?" said the blubbery man at the counter of Fish It Up, dabbing the infirm pallid ridges of his brow with a paper napkin. "It's the only thing to have while you're here."

"Seaside food, you mean? I expect you're right. Fish and chips for me."

He was relieved not to see the man touch the food, instead using a spade like a child's seaside toy to scoop chips out of the fryer and employing tongs to crown them with a fish. At first he'd thought the man was wearing plastic gloves, since his rudimentary nails were virtually indistinguishable from the stubby fingers. He was careful not to touch the man's hand when he paid—he still remembered vividly how the coin with which he'd tipped the porter had seemed to sink into the moist palm—and took the package from the sweating metal counter.

When he crossed the promenade to a bench he was surprised to see how many people were still on the beach, but he supposed he wasn't behaving entirely unlike them. Most were seated, which made them look as if they were protruding from the pebbly sand, and a few were lying down. He saw none of them move even slightly while he ate his dinner; in the pasty light he could have taken them for dummies that had strayed out of a waxworks. The meal was very much like last night's, with the same odd texture to the fish, but he felt as if he wasn't quite able to grasp the familiar taste. Perhaps he was too anxious to be back at the books, though he was also distracted by the sight of a supine figure on the beach lurching upright at the waist as though roused from a dream. The man's face was covered by a floppy hat, which had slipped so far down the head that Fairman could easily have imagined it had taken the face with it; there certainly appeared to be an unreasonable amount of greyish brow beneath the glistening hairless cranium. He finished his dinner as quickly as digestion would allow, while the figure stayed half upright with the hat dangling from the unseen face, and then he made some haste to the hotel.

As he reached it a chorus bade him good evening from the shelter opposite. The voices were feeble enough to add up to a single one, and they belonged to several old folk—surely not the same ones he'd seen earlier—who sat facing the Wyleave. For an absurd moment he wondered if they were about to address him by name. "Good night," he called and felt as if the chilly fog had lurched across the seafront after him.

The thump of the metal club on the counter reminded him of a gavel. "Here for good now?" Mrs Berry said.

"In for the night, if that's what you mean."

"That's good." As Fairman took the key she said "You know who to ring if you need anything at all."

Perhaps he was making too much of this, but he blurted "Isn't Mr Berry with you?"

"We don't leave Gulshaw, Mr Fairman. I think you saw him at the zoo."

Fairman was so embarrassed by his own question that he could only protest "I didn't see very much."

"The season's over for this year." As if she were reassuring a disappointed child Mrs Berry said "We promise you won't miss them."

"I appreciated your husband's help," Fairman said to leave his peevishness behind. "Please do thank him for me."

He wasn't expecting this to be met with a stare so distant he couldn't identify an expression. "Dream well, then," she said as he moved away. "Try and lose yourself."

He wondered if the state of the man in the booth at the zoo was her excuse for seeking solace elsewhere. In any case she mustn't look to Fairman. Once he'd checked the safe he hurried to the bathroom. He couldn't hear a sound in the hotel, and the silence seemed so expectant that it made him even more conscious of the noise he tried to muffle by flushing the toilet. As soon as he was able he retreated like a culprit to his room.

He left the first book in the darkness of the safe and lined up the others in front of the mirror before opening the second volume, *On the Purposes of Night*. "What is daylight but the ally of brutish creation, the progenitor of mindless growth? Let the night be celebrated as friend to the true possessors of the world. Let its powers be roused that it may reveal the nocturnal truth which lies even within men . . . "

Did this refer to dreams? It would take more than a book to rouse any within him, although while reading he did feel as if the night was growing not just darker but more substantial—the fog, of course. The book wasn't capable of persuading him that the night was pregnant with secrets, let alone teeming with creatures best left unseen, but he was quite glad to reach the final page. He'd finished the third volume last night—however little of it he recalled, he felt as though its burden had lodged somewhere in his head—and so he turned to *Of the Secrets of the Stars*, the fourth book. "Cry out the names of the ancient constellations . . . "

The night was always beyond the sky, however bright the sun strove to appear. The infinite darkness was older than time, and the stars were simply playthings that its avatar had shaped and scattered in patterns to which the universe was in the process of reverting. Fairman understood this much; at least, he saw the meaning of the words, although the further he progressed the more he felt that the book was a kind of reverie, incomprehensible to a waking mind. By the time he reached the end he was little better than asleep, and the reflections of the trinity of volumes in the mirror made him feel as if the books were dreaming of companionship. He laid the books to rest in the safe and stumbled to the window.

The old folk in the shelter raised their heads as he dragged up the sash. The beach was still peopled as well. Most of the occupants were supine, but Fairman saw a woman stand up and waddle away from the edge of the sea, leaving a rubbery cushion on which she'd been seated. The roundish object glistened and stirred feebly, having been caught by a wave. As Fairman shut the window and turned away, unenlivened by the stagnant smell he'd let into the room, he saw a man carrying a large plastic bucket down a ramp to the beach.

Fairman went to bed expecting to be kept awake by thoughts of the books, but the vision that was waiting for him to lie down in the dark came from somewhere earlier. Once more he was beset by the image of the stone cocoon, but this time he imagined the end of its wanderings. He saw it blaze like an enormous coal as it plummeted into the depths of a forest, blasting a crater many times its size and setting fire to the surrounding trees. He had to watch as it cooled and split open, a spectacle too reminiscent of the hatching of an egg. Through the fissure he glimpsed a whitish spongy lump that must be some species of face, since eyes reared up from it to peer in all directions from the crack in the meteor—two eyes and then another. He managed to avoid imagining its size until the meteor tumbled apart in huge fragments to let its contents crawl forth. The ovoid body was as vast as a cathedral, a similarity that was brought to mind by the spines protruding all over the ponderous bulk. As it used the spines to scrabble deep into the earth Fairman could almost have been watching a cathedral bury itself, and he had an uneasy sense that the idea was how his mind coped with the vision, which surely derived from one of the books he'd read. He was relieved not to see more of the face as it sank into the earth; the other sight was bad enough—the eyes withdrawing like a snail's out of the glare of the forest fire. Then there was only the expanse of disturbed earth surrounded by great flames, but it was imbued with a dreadful sense of waiting. At last the notion of settling into the earth merged with the prospect of subsiding into sleep, and that was all he knew.

A thumping sound roused him. It seemed to gain definition, growing less large and loose, as he struggled awake. Somebody was at the door. "What is it?" Fairman demanded, trying to control his slack voice. "What's wrong?"

"It's only Janine, Mr Fairman. Just wondered if you wanted to miss breakfast."

Fairman fumbled at the bedside table for his watch. From the greyish light that seeped into the room he would have taken it to be not much later than dawn, and he had to blink his eyes clear before he could believe it was almost eleven o'clock. "Good God, I've slept in," he called. "I meant to be up hours ago."

"Don't you worry even the tiniest bit. It's ready when you are."

Did he have time for breakfast? As his panic faded he saw that he would almost certainly need to stay overnight to complete the set of books. It might very well have been necessary even if he'd wakened when he should have. The thought left him feeling almost lethargically calm, no doubt because he hadn't quite woken up.

Nobody was in the bathroom or the toilet, and the corridor was deserted, though he seemed to recall having heard quite a few people come upstairs last night while he was intent on the books. Of course they would have been up and about today long before him, unless he'd imagined hearing them, and could he really have seen anybody lying or otherwise occupied on the beach last night? The breakfast room was empty, and just one couple was checking out at the desk. "See you next year," the man told Fairman, and the equally rotund wife joined in.

Fairman mumbled ambiguously and made for his breakfast table by the window. A thick curtain of fog was trailing its hem in the sea about half a mile from the promenade, and he couldn't locate the sun. Just now the sea looked no wider than a lake. As he saw that the fog had sent the old folk away from the shelter, Mrs Berry arrived with a plateful very similar to yesterday's. "Here's your favourite," she said.

He thanked her before saying "I'm afraid I'll need the room tonight as well."

"No need at all to be afraid."

She closed her mouth and then rounded her lips, suggesting that she'd realised she had more to say. If she meant to bring up dreams again, Fairman wasn't anxious to discuss them. "Would you excuse me?" he said and took out his phone. "I should make some calls."

"You do what you have to, Leonard."

The bell shrilled in his ear and continued shrilling. At last a reluctant voice said "Yes, Mr Fairman."

"Good morning, Ms Bickerstaff. Have things improved for you today?"

"Some have and some haven't. It's always like that for us here."

"Well, I'm glad to hear some have. When should I pay you a visit?"

"I still can't say."

"I thought you said the situation—"

"Nothing's changed there."

"I'm sorry to hear it. I'm obviously sorry, but I really do need—"

"Don't attempt to bully me, Mr Fairman. Some of our residents have tried that on, but it doesn't work."

"I give you my word I don't mean to, Ms Bickerstaff, but I would ask you to appreciate that I've come quite a long way on the understanding that these books will be made available to me."

"That isn't what Frank said, is it? He just wrote to you about his one."

"It's what I've been led to believe by everybody else." Fairman felt as if the argument had grown as slow as trying to run in a dream. "The sooner I take charge of the book," he said, "the sooner it'll be one less responsibility for you."

"I don't shirk any of my responsibilities, Mr Fairman."

"I'm sure I didn't say otherwise. I'm simply trying—"

"I haven't got time for this. As you say, I have responsibilities," Rhoda Bickerstaff said and immediately rang off.

As Fairman listened to the hiss of static, which he could have mistaken for the long breaths of the sea, Janine Berry came into the room. "Have you gone past your appetite?" she said like a reproving mother, and when he frowned at her "Don't keep it to yourself. We don't do that in Gulshaw."

"I'm finding someone isn't as forthcoming as everybody else has been."

"That won't do at all. We mustn't have anyone giving you trouble."

"It's Rhoda Bickerstaff. She's in charge of your Leafy Shade Home."

"I know that." With a look so distant it made her face resemble a mask, Mrs Berry said "Don't let her use that as an excuse. You go up there and don't take no for an answer."

"She does have plenty to deal with as it is, I suppose."

"Then like you said, she'll have less when you take what's yours." Before Fairman could object to having been overheard, Mrs Berry turned maternal again. "Just you eat up," she said, "and then I'll show you where to go."

Fairman gazed out at the fog while he ate, and had the fanciful notion that he was tasting it. A watery hint seemed to underlie every mouthful, though the textures were firm enough. The taste grew more indefinite as he fetched his coat and took the town map to the reception counter. "You go straight there now," Mrs Berry urged, but called him back as he headed for the car park. "You'll be thinking we don't trust you," she said and twisted the key off the ring on the metal club, so vigorously that her fingernails became indistinguishable from the flesh around them. "Now you can come and go like all of us."

Fairman pocketed the key on his way to the car. He was glad to leave the promenade where the stagnant greyish light appeared to seep into every face, not that the pavements were anything like crowded. He drove up a lane between the Kumbak and the Seesea, across the shopping streets to Edgewood Row, where several large houses had apparently lost their boundaries to form the Leafy Shade. While the single garden wall they shared beside the pavement had been cared for, the wall that backed onto the hazy colonnades of the woods was in some disrepair; more than one gap was wide enough for residents to wander through. As Fairman parked on the road, he saw that one of the vehicles in the grounds was a police car.

Presumably the crisis was at least as serious as Rhoda Bickerstaff had made it sound. He couldn't justify adding to her problems, however frustrated he might feel; surely even Nathan Brighouse wouldn't expect it of him. He was restarting the engine when a woman hurried out of the central building of the Leafy Shade complex. "Mr Fairman," she shouted. "Leonard Fairman."

Her gangling run emphasised how tall she was. Her head was disproportionately large, though with a small mouth and miniature chin. She wore a padded coat over a billowing black dress that exposed ankles thicker than he would have thought to see and black shoes too big for the elegance they aimed for. As Fairman left the car she unlocked the tall iron gate. "Mrs Bickerstaff," he said. "I'm sorry, I didn't realise—"

"No call for an apology. I'm not Rhoda Bickerstaff."

"Even so, I'm sorry if I'm adding to your difficulties."

"You're doing nothing of the kind." This sounded closer to an accusation than a reassurance, and her tone didn't change as she said "I'm Eunice Spriggs."

Her gaze went with the tone, but in a moment it relented— receded, at any rate. "I'm the mayoress," she said.

Did a wig come with the title? The hairline above the chubby brows that overshadowed her sizeable eyes seemed unusually regular, while the black hair that hung straight down beside her cheeks looked as inert as the grey light through the ceiling of fog. As she offered Fairman her disconcertingly small hand she said "Thank you for everything you're doing for us."

"I'm just doing what's expected of me."

"I wish some others of us would. Please accept my apologies on behalf of the town for the hindrance." Before he could tell her they weren't necessary the mayoress said "Do come and take over."

Fairman refrained from wiping his hand until she turned along the gravel drive. "Are you visiting someone?"

"Regrettably I had to," she said and stalked loosely although purposefully towards the central building. "Rhoda Bickerstaff."

Beyond a wide hall a pair of broad staircases not unlike pincers framed the entrance to a room full of old folk in armchairs. French windows let in the murky daylight, which seemed to tint all the ageing flesh. One old man was opening his mouth wide and circular to expose his greyish gums, and several of his companions joined in, as though they were competing to produce the roundest mouth. An old woman was dangling her arms on either side of her chair to touch the carpet, and Fairman might have thought her hands were too long for the arms. Outside the windows a number of apparently unsupervised residents were shuffling and wobbling about the grounds; several had gathered to stare through a gap in the wall into the ill-defined depths of the woods. Fairman didn't want to distract anyone from keeping an eye on the residents, but Eunice Spriggs was gesturing him towards a room to the left of the stairs. She didn't bother knocking on the door.

A dumpy woman stuffed into a suit not much greyer than her face and hair sat behind a desk on the far side of the office. If she wasn't grimacing, a good deal was wrong with the left side of her face. Her lips were drawn towards it, and that eye was half shut, while the cheek harboured a purplish tinge. She was flanked at a distance by a policeman and a woman in the identical uniform. Fairman could almost have taken them for twins, not least because their rounded faces bore the same blank determined look. "Here he is at last," Eunice Spriggs said. "I believe someone owes you something, Leonard."

She gazed at the woman behind the desk, and then the police did. Since none of this broke the silence, Fairman felt he should. "Thank you for making time for me, Mrs Bickerstaff."

The woman sat forward and folded her arms with a thump on the desk. The sound seemed to echo, but the repetitions grew louder as they continued to reverberate. Fairman felt as if the floor were growing unstable, even when he realised that she was drumming a heel beneath the desk. "Rhoda," the mayoress said.

Rhoda Bickerstaff dug her fingers into her upper arms as she raised her head. "I've got to say I'm sorry, Mr Fairman."

"I'm sure I understand." When her eyes denied it Fairman said "Why should you?"

"For not scurrying to let you have your book like everybody else."

"I don't think anybody's quite done that."

"Then you don't know much about our town."

Fairman almost retorted that he knew there was so much more to see; it was like hearing a chorus in his head of all the voices that had told him. This time the mayoress brought a silence to an end. "Safe, Rhoda," she said. "Safe."

Though it could have been a reassurance, Fairman thought it was an order. Rhoda Bickerstaff's eyes remained defiant while the drumming of her heel seemed to dissipate through the floorboards, and her gaze seemed to retreat without leaving him. She lurched to her feet so abruptly that her suit bunched up around her midriff, and Fairman could have thought her flesh had. The floor shook again as she paced to the safe behind the desk. She spun the combination wheel and hauled the door wide, leaving the interior in darkness, so that Fairman couldn't see the book until she clutched it to her breast. As she swung around her face twisted further to the left, and she seemed to find it hard to work her mouth. "I hope you're ready, Leonard," she said indistinctly. "There's your next step."

He had to extend both hands—he might almost have been reaching to take charge of an infant—before she relinquished the volume. As he took it she let out a breath that sounded capable of leaving her entire self hollow, and he saw the mayoress relax. It was the sixth volume, *Of Things Seen by the Moon*, with a colophon depicting a full moon where a lunar sea resembled the pupil of an eye. "Thank you," Fairman said, which seemed inadequate. "I hope your crisis will be resolved soon."

Rhoda Bickerstaff's face twisted leftward so convulsively that it seemed to drag the hairline of her greying curls askew. "Don't you really know what's going on here, Leonard?"

"The book was the only crisis," Eunice Spriggs told him. "Rhoda got a bit too used to looking after it, that's all."

"Is all this necessary?" Fairman said and stared at the police. "You mustn't think I'm being unprofessional, but when it comes right down to it, it's just a book."

"You're the last one I'd hope to hear saying that, Leonard."

He was disconcerted not just because it was Rhoda Bickerstaff who told him so but by a sense that at least one other person in the room might have. "I assure you I'll take care of it," he said, not without resentment. "Who's next on my list?"

"Eric Headon. He's our local historian."

This time it was the mayoress who spoke, but Fairman kept his eyes on Rhoda Bickerstaff. "You couldn't have told me that yesterday."

"That's not how things are done here, Leonard," Eunice Spriggs said.

"Why not?" Fairman demanded and turned on her. "How much do you know about all this?"

"All I need to," she said with an odd faraway look. "You will when it's time."

He oughtn't to be loitering, not least since the police had brought blank looks to bear on him. "Can someone give me Mr Headon's number?"

He had no idea who might respond until Rhoda Bickerstaff scrawled the information on the back of a Leafy Shade card that bore the slogan REST IS BEST. He was hurrying along the drive, and acutely relieved to have left the episode behind, when he glimpsed movement out of the corner of his eye. Had one of the residents fallen out of bed? Beyond a ground-floor window to his left a quilt was sprawling towards the floor. The pale shapeless object floundered out of sight beneath the low sill before he could distinguish it more clearly, but he couldn't have seen arms and legs protruding from it; nobody's limbs could be so unequal, in length as well as thickness. All the same, the bed was empty, and an occupant might have been entangled in the quilt. As Fairman thought of alerting someone, a uniformed nurse came into the room. His face grew blank as he saw what was there, and Fairman headed for his car.

He boxed up his prize and locked the boot, and then he hesitated. However uncomfortable the intervention of the mayoress and the police had made him, they'd helped him secure the book. Suppose the historian was as unforthcoming as Rhoda Bickerstaff had tried to be? Fairman might appreciate some official help, and so he phoned from outside the Leafy Shade. A somnolent hiss gave way to the simulation of a bell before a man mumbled "Yes."

There were fewer consonants to it than there might have been—perhaps none. "Mr Headon," Fairman said.

"Miss a fair un."

Was Headon drunk? He seemed to find it hard to shape his words. "That's who I am," Fairman nevertheless said.

"Goo to he fum you. Reach me alas."

"Good to speak to you. I'm sorry that I couldn't reach you sooner. Is it convenient to see you now?"

"Seem eel layer. Attach oh."

"I'm sorry, I didn't quite catch that."

"Lair. Lair." With a distinctly peevish effort Headon succeeded in pronouncing "Later. You'll be at the show."

"I may be, but couldn't you possibly—"

"I have Tourette's." As Fairman wondered how much this might explain, Headon added a resentful translation. "Have to rest before the show."

"You're involved in it, you mean."

"I'm image all wry." Headon's words were growing worse than blurred again. "Arrest him," he muttered, "when you caw."

"Forgive me, I didn't catch that either."

"I said," Headon complained, "I was resting when you called."

"I'm sorry, I didn't realise." Fairman had a distinct impression that Headon thought he should have. "I don't suppose," he said, "before I go you could tell me who else—"

"Seethe am altar night. See you deny," Headon said so indistinctly that his voice seemed to merge with the static as he rang off.

Had he really believed Fairman was asking who else would be onstage tonight? At least Fairman had done all he reasonably could, and he had a book to examine. As he drove downhill he saw that the haze had advanced to the near edge of the sea and blocked off both ends of the promenade, which the grey light helped to resemble an old faded image of itself. Near the Wyleave the people on the seafront reminded him of the posters in the tourist office, since they appeared to be moving hardly at all.

Not to be met by Mrs Berry felt like a form of acceptance, though not one he needed to welcome. He unpacked the carton once he'd checked the contents of the safe. From the window he saw that despite the fog on the beach, people were sitting at the water's edge. They were so blurred that he couldn't be sure how scantily dressed they might be. Were those the same old folk as yesterday in the shelter? It was impossible to tell, given the scarves they'd wrapped around the lower sections of their faces, presumably to keep out the fog. Fairman ought to be making a call, and he took out his phone. "Leonard," Brighouse said. "Surprise me."

"I'm past the halfway mark."

"You mean you've nearly as far to go? What's the obstacle this time?"

"Some of the people with the books have been keeping me waiting."

"Perhaps you shouldn't let them. Do you think they're sufficiently aware of the importance of our acquisition?"

"I don't believe that's the problem. I'm sure they know how much the books mean."

"And what about the other people? Have you contacted them all?"

"I can't do that." Fairman braced himself for the reaction as he said "I have to collect the volumes in a certain order."

"Why on earth are you bothering to do that?"

"Because that's what everyone wants me to do."

"And you're letting yourself be dictated to in that fashion? It sounds to me as if somebody is amusing themselves at your expense."

Fairman felt defensive not just on his own behalf. "I honestly don't think that's the situation."

"Well, perhaps you know best." Brighouse's tone fell short of supporting the notion. "Is there any point in asking when you'll have completed the task?"

"I don't think I can say just now," Fairman said and heard himself echoing some of the townsfolk.

"I'd remind you what I mentioned yesterday about leave."

"If that's all the university thinks these books are worth—" For a breath Fairman was on the edge of threatening to resign. "They're the most significant acquisition we'll ever make," he said.

"No need to proselytise, Leonard. I'm just as aware of their rarity as you."

Fairman felt as if he'd meant more than this but couldn't put it into words. Either this or Brighouse's attitude infuriated him so much that he blurted "Would you mind not telling Sandra I'm further delayed?"

"I can't imagine why you'd think I would."

"You've been discussing me, haven't you? I'd prefer to let her know myself."

After quite a pause Brighouse said "I'd like to see you here as soon as practicable. There are issues that may need to be clarified."

Had Fairman jeopardised his position after all? "I'll be back as soon as the books let me," he said, and once he was rid of Brighouse the situation at the university seemed too remote to trouble him. Surely his acquisitions would protect him against dismissal, and he sat down with *Of Things Seen by the Moon*. "How many fools dismiss the moon as borrowing its illumination from the sun! In truth its light reveals more to the mage's eye than the sunlight of midsummer . . ."

The book went on to peer behind lunar myths. The transformation of the werewolf was "but the brutish display of the changes which are wrought on every aspect of the world by the illumination the night brings." Some old tales of the fairies named them as the

Children of the Moon because their shapes mutated with its phases. At the time Percy Smallbeam compiled the edition, some women were apparently still afraid to conceive or give birth on nights of the full moon in case they produced a mooncalf, "a thing whose shape betrays how life was formed in the infancy of the universe." Other sections of the book suggested that "the mage shall learn to see as the moon does", but if the pages that followed were meant to instruct, Fairman seemed incapable of grasping so much as a word. The prose grew meditative and mystical, presenting the dark side of the moon as a symbol of concealment; surely the notion that it "swarms with monstrous and inhuman life, as does the underside of any stone" was metaphorical, despite the unappealing detail in which it was discussed at length. Then the book proposed that "what is closest is most hidden", but Fairman felt as if the paragraphs that followed were taking refuge in his mind without entering his consciousness. Whenever he glanced up he was met by his own gaze, so remote that it must be betraying the incomprehension that lay like a weight in his brain as he finally closed the book. He didn't need to understand; his mission was simply to keep the books safe. Wasn't there something else he ought to do? He let out a sigh like one of the waves at his back as he realised who he'd neglected to call.

She sounded wearily resigned. "I won't ask, Leonard."

"Nathan hasn't spoken to you, then."

"Not about you, no." When Fairman only gazed into the depths of his own eyes Sandra added "What would he have said?"

"I'm still where you've gathered I am, and he's talking about leave again."

"You don't seem very anxious about it."

"I'm anxious to be with you, if that's what you mean." With an inspiration that hardly felt like his Fairman said "Of course if you wanted I could be soon enough."

"How are you proposing to achieve that?"

"You've the weekend off, haven't you? If I haven't finished here by tomorrow you could join me."

"I'm sure you'd be surprised if I did."

"Pleasantly so, yes."

"It sounds to me as if you're having a pleasant enough time by yourself. You certainly don't seem to be in a hurry to leave."

"We can't hurry these books."

Fairman saw a hand besides his own come to rest on the black volume. No, it was his hand in the mirror, where he looked as if he were about to swear an oath or use the book in some other solemn ritual. "Then I won't try to hurry you any more," Sandra said with nothing like enthusiasm.

He could speak to her again tomorrow. Perhaps sleep would bring some kind of change. Once they'd said their goodbyes he saw that he had nearly an hour to spare, though he wouldn't have guessed that from the muffled light outside the window. He had the irrational notion that it might be hard to judge when the moon replaced the sun behind the fog. He had time to walk to the Shaw and for a quick dinner as well. He returned the book to the safe and took an empty carton with him.

Joggers were trotting doggedly along the promenade. They looked as if they were struggling to forge their way through the befogged twilight, and Fairman could have imagined that he felt the medium weighing him down. Certainly the joggers needed exercise; some were so obese that every step sent a flabby wobble upwards through the whole of them, even quivering their faces. Each of them raised a hand to greet Fairman, and more than one used theirs to mop their foreheads with such vigour that he could have thought the flesh was quaking like tripe. He was surprised that any of them could find breath to hum snatches of an old tune, whatever it might be.

The Shaw appeared not to be open. The lobby was as dim as any of the glass cases he'd seen at the zoo. As he crossed the junction with the promenade he had to dodge a pushchair wheeled by a young but pudgy mother. The plastic cover that protected the chair from the elements blurred the occupant's wide flat face so much that it looked featureless apart from the eyes, which the plastic distorted until the left one seemed twice the size of the other. Fairman could have thought the toddler was naked as well; presumably the plastic and the clogged twilight were lending its skin and its one-piece suit the same greyish pallor. He'd seen people complimenting parents on their offspring when they met them in the street, but he couldn't think of anything appropriate to say. In any case the woman's distant stare didn't strike him as inviting a remark.

The machines in the arcades were jingling and prattling, while video games carried on shouting in unnatural voices meant to pass for human. Fairman could have fancied that the show was being put on just for him, to persuade him that Gulshaw was lively even so late in the season. The plastic eyes of a horse outside an arcade glistened with moisture, and as its innards burst into electronic song he might have been reminded of the kind of life that swarmed in corpses or on the hidden side of the moon, according to the *Revelations*. Was that still the sun behind the fog? He was growing unduly fanciful—he didn't need to think that the murk was capable of hiding a vast presence—though as he tramped past the arcades their mindless clamour crowded all thoughts out of his head.

The proprietor of Fishing For You was in her hospital uniform, or at least the outfit that made her resemble a nurse. "Decided in our favour?" she said.

"I've had no better since I've come to town."

"You won't, either." Presumably this was a boast, even if her eyes held back from admitting to it. "The usual?" she said.

He supposed this meant everybody's preference, since she could hardly know his. "That's fine with me."

As he sat at a picnic table on the tiled floor she said "Eating in? You've not got used, then."

"To this weather? I don't think I'd want to be."

"Don't be too quick to think."

No doubt that kind of advice went with her blunt accent. He'd found no more to say by the time she brought him fish and chips in a squeaky polystyrene container. As she planted it in front of him, leaving moist marks on the table, the lid shuddered upwards as if some of the contents were making an ineffectual bid to escape. Fairman was disconcerted to observe that her thinness ended well above the waist, suggesting that much of her flesh had sunk to be held up by her extensive hips. Once she returned to the far side of the counter he fed himself a mouthful with the plastic fork. The increasingly familiar taste made him ask "Is this actually cod?"

"It says fish, doesn't it?" Having poked a long finger at the menu on the wall, she said "It's our kind."

"Don't think I'm complaining, but what kind is that?"

"The kind we have here. The kind that brings everyone back."

Fairman gave up and reverted to eating while the proprietor hummed under her breath. It sounded like a folk song, especially once she added a few words about someone coming home from the sea. When he heard shuffling he glanced up to see that the woman was performing a kind of dance on the spot. He found it disconcerting, not least because her eyes were shut, revealing how flat the lids were, hardly distinguishable from the skin around them. He left quite an amount of his dinner and was easing himself off the bench when her eyes sprang open, bulging at him. "We'll be seeing you," she said.

Fairman nearly asked who else she thought she was speaking for. The streetlamps had come on, appearing to draw the fog inland. He felt as if it was shutting him in with the arcades, where the shrill piping of the fruit machines and the challenging roars of the games had begun to put him in mind of a zoo. As he turned uphill towards the theatre the lights were switched on in the lobby, and Frank Lunt emerged onto the marble steps to wait for him. "Here's our audience," the manager announced.

"Not all of it, I hope."

"Enough for us." Lunt's black moustache and clipped hair glistened as if they shared the moistness of his unavoidable handshake. "So long as we don't disappoint," he said.

"To be truthful, I'm mostly here for Eric Headon."

At once Fairman felt tactless and ungrateful for the complimentary admission, but Lunt's face remained enthusiastic. "They're all the stuff stars are made of," he said, releasing Fairman's hand at last. "You'll see."

He made for the auditorium with a wallowing gait that reminded Fairman of a sailor just home from the sea. Beyond the double doors a wide aisle divided at least thirty rows of seats, every one of them unoccupied. "Have I got the time wrong?" Fairman blurted.

"Nothing's wrong that shouldn't be." Lunt bowed towards the curtained stage like a priest making obeisance to an altar. "Sit wherever you like," he said. "The closer the better. You won't be on your own long."

Despite if not because of having slept so late, Fairman felt less than entirely awake. He would prefer not to be singled out from the stage, and so he chose an aisle seat halfway down the auditorium, which he hoped was close enough to placate Lunt without being too conspicuous. "Now we'll let you see some of our gifts," the manager said. "We aren't just a sleepy town."

"I've never said you were," Fairman protested, but Lunt was already making for the foyer. The doors shut with a muffled plushy thud, and then Fairman heard a noise somewhere ahead of him. It sounded oddly reminiscent of the murmur of an audience before a show, but it was beyond the curtains. Or was it more like a chant—

some formula to inspire the performers? He was straining to identify any words—he could have thought they were too unfamiliar to grasp—when the lights went out, flooding the auditorium with blackness dense as earth.

Fairman sucked in a breath that felt like inhaling the dark. As his eyes began to ache with his bid to see even a hint of light, he heard a sluggish movement ahead of him. Something of considerable size was being dragged across the floor, and the idea that it was advancing towards him robbed him of breath. It had split in two, dividing like some primitive form of life, and the halves were crawling to either side of him. They hadn't halted when lights blazed up to reveal that he'd been hearing the curtains, between which Frank Lunt stepped forward, holding out his hands as though to present the struggle of the buttons of his dress suit to restrain his midriff. "Welcome to the last show of the season," he said. "I give you the Gulshaw Players. A century and half another one of artfulness."

Fairman assumed this meant the skills had been passed down the generations, though the observation wasn't addressed just to him. As the curtains stumbled to a standstill, light from the foyer had spilled into the auditorium, and he heard people taking their seats at the back. The movements subsided as Lunt wallowed backwards and a performer sprang onstage to either side of him.

They were acrobats in white leotards, and they brought a merry march with them. Presumably the band was recorded, because a technical problem was warping it out of tune, if so slightly that Fairman couldn't quite grasp where the music had gone wrong. Another pair of acrobats joined their fellows as Lunt swayed into the wings. No doubt all the pale faces were meant to resemble pierrots, though their costumes failed to sustain the notion. Despite the tightness of the leotards, Fairman couldn't identify their gender, and the identical caps of cropped black hair didn't help. The acrobats leapt and tumbled and stacked themselves on top of one another while their small brightly smiling faces remained as changeless as four masks from the same mould. He was unsettled by their sinuousness, which along with their pallor reminded him rather too much of the squirming of grubs, and he had to fend off the idea that whenever they stood on one another's shoulders, their toes grasped like fingers, extending to sink into the flesh. His need for sleep must be forcing fancies that resembled dreams into his waking mind. Now the topmost of the tower of acrobats was bending backwards in an arc, and one by one the others did until the performer who'd stood highest was able to flatten his cranium against the stage. Each of them regained their feet with a somersault, and as Fairman applauded he heard moist puffy handclaps break out behind him. "So much more to see," the acrobats chorused as they ran in pairs into the wings, and he thought they were echoed from the back of the auditorium.

As soon as the stage was deserted a newcomer lurched into view. Was he meant to be drunk? Having floundered to the centre of the stage, he tried to tell a joke about falling into water that he'd thought was solid ground, but by the time he reached the punch line, which involved telling his wife where he'd been, he was so effortfully incoherent that Fairman couldn't understand a word. The comedian's struggles with articulation seemed to drag his lanky body more lopsided, and his helpless gestures grew increasingly extravagant until they unbalanced him, throwing him on his face. Apparently this was the joke, and Fairman felt a duty to laugh, which prompted everyone behind him to join in. He was disconcerted to see the comedian leap to his feet and go through the entire routine again, not by any means just once. Each time his language ended up less speakable, until Fairman was reminded of the graffiti in the shelter opposite the Wyleave. At the end of every repetition the man fell flatter on his face, and took to pointing at the pallid slab it appeared to have become. Fairman had to laugh in order not to be dismayed, especially by the finale, where the comic wiped his hand across his face to demonstrate how level the surface was. "So much more to see," the mouth in it declared as he made way for a juggler.

At first she seemed conventional enough, if almost painfully thin. The indefinably dissonant band had fallen silent during the comedian's act, but now it was back. Surely only the juggler's swiftness made her arms appear to stretch to unequal lengths to catch the airborne objects—balls, skittles, knives—unless the illusion was another symptom of sleeplessness. At times Fairman imagined that her hands had grown unduly long as well, perhaps an effect of the light, which was dimmer than he would have expected stage illumination to be. She ended with the Gulshaw slogan, and her place was taken by a pair of contortionists so unnervingly supple that Fairman wondered why they needed to contort their faces too. He wished their mouths and nostrils and especially their eyes wouldn't gape so wide; less than half would be more than enough. He was glad that the contortionists were eventually ousted by a mind-reader with a black cloth covering the top half of his face, though less happy to be chosen as a subject by the man's assistant, who extended her forefinger quite some distance towards Fairman. He was putting together something very large, the blindfolded man told him. Fairman supposed that was true—the set of books, not to mention their importance—as true as the suggestions that he couldn't tell when he was dreaming and that his head contained more thoughts than he knew. He wondered why the performer needed to be blindfolded to come up with all this, until the assistant who had led him onstage untied the cloth to reveal that above the man's mouth was a single nostril twitching in a featureless expanse of pallid flesh.

Fairman was acutely relieved to see the man ushered into the wings once he'd uttered the familiar slogan. He'd scarcely vacated the stage before it was occupied by a troupe of singers, the foremost of whom swelled his chest like an amphibian to perform a solo. Was it a folk song or an unfamiliar hymn? Fairman had heard it before, but now he realised he hadn't quite caught the words; the refrain was "Thou great inspiration, come in from the sea," the first word of which seemed to turn the singer's mouth more nearly circular with every repetition. The woman behind the counter at Fishing For You might also have been practicing the dance with which the troupe supported the soloist. Fairman took it for a folk dance, a spiky jig interspersed with tortuously fluid movements and describing patterns on the stage too intricate for him to follow. The melody seemed related to the tune the band had played, and as hypnotic as the dance was proving to be—so mesmeric that when the performance ended, having grown slower on the way to stillness, he wakened himself by starting to clap. How long had he been asleep? Longer than he'd realised, to judge by the faces of the performers who crowded onstage to bow to him; they might almost have been honouring him, though surely that would have to be ironic. At least his having dozed must explain some of the spectacle he'd imagined he was seeing, even if he wasn't sure how much. As the players made their various ways offstage, the blindfolded man resting his fingertips on his assistant's arm, Fairman heard the audience depart, isolating uneven imprecise footsteps close behind him—Frank Lunt's footsteps. "What did you make of us?" the manager said.

"Most impressed." Fairman might have liked to leave it there but added "I hope everyone will forgive me. I've been up late with the books and I did nod off a little."

"So long as you dreamed of us."

Fairman wasn't about to admit it. He could have asked why the manager was counting himself in—it seemed to be a local trait—but said only "I wasn't expecting so much home-grown talent."

"Some of it is. Some came and stayed." Lunt motioned to him, crooking or rather curving a forefinger. "You'll be wanting Eric," he said.

Fairman could have thought they were alone in the building. Certainly the audience had gone, unless they were keeping quieter than made any sense. He couldn't help wondering somewhat uneasily which of the players he was about to meet. Lunt preceded him into the office and beckoned him again with that uncommonly flexible finger. "Eric, this is Leonard."

The man who rose with ponderous suppleness from a chair in front of the desk was the solo singer. Up close his expansive whitish face looked as though it needed all its chins to prevent it from collapsing out of somnolence. As he swallowed, his throat swelled so much that Fairman could have thought he was about to burst into song. "Leonard," he said. "Allow me to thank you personally for the part you're playing."

His handshake was as moist as any Fairman had been offered—perhaps that had something to do with the Gulshaw air—and oddly imprecise. At least his voice was more defined than it had sounded on the phone. "You were the stars, not me," Fairman told him. "And I apologise if I wasn't as attentive as I should have been."

"We entirely understand." Headon gazed at him with some kind of appreciation and said "Shall we walk? It's close."

Lunt shut the glass doors after them and stepped back into the sudden darkness of the theatre. Headon turned uphill past the Shaw and then along another deserted street, this one running parallel to the promenade. It included a number of clothes shops: Tall Boy, Lots of Woman, Stout Fellow, Skinny Girl, Fat Lad. Fairman reflected ruefully that he might have to patronise some outfitters like the last one if he ate many more Gulshaw dinners. The shops gave way to terraces of houses, all of them unlit despite the relatively early hour. "People seem to like their sleep round here," he said.

"We all need it, Leonard."

Fairman hadn't meant to seem to be referring to their earlier conversation. Now that Headon's voice was more distinct it was apparent that he wasn't local. "How long have you lived here?" Fairman said.

"Long enough."

"You aren't a native, I mean."

"I am now."

If Sandra had been there she would certainly have queried that use of language, but Fairman only said "What kept you here?"

"The same as you." Before Fairman could address this Headon said "I'm retired."

"I understand you were a historian."

"I still am." With some pique Headon added "It's all in here."

He was poking his forehead to demonstrate. In the inert greyish light, which resembled a luminous distillation of the fog beyond the promenade, Fairman could have imagined that the fingertip had sunk into the ridged flesh. He looked away before saying "You ought to write a book."

"Soon we'll have no more use for those."

Sometimes Fairman was afraid this would indeed be an effect of the internet, but not so long as he worked in the archive. "Better not let Don Rothermere hear you saying that," he said.

"He knows. Everybody has to."

Fairman stopped short of demanding to be left out, instead saying "So what can you tell me about Gulshaw?"

"It's shaped by its history."

"We all are, I should think."

"That's the truest word so far," Headon declared and turned his head to him.

It felt like being watched from an unreasonable distance, and Fairman was grateful to be distracted by noises ahead. Around one uphill corner of a junction he heard a series of soft irregular thuds reminiscent of the impacts of the dancers' feet onstage. When he reached the crossing he saw children at hopscotch in a floodlit schoolyard. Apparently in this version of the game they had to hop simultaneously about various sections of the yard. "Is that peculiar to this part of the world?" he said.

"A lot of things are."

Fairman was on the edge of demanding why the man's responses were so absurdly guarded, and then he wondered if they were. Might

Headon be crediting him with too much local knowledge? The schoolyard railings and the shadows of the players confused his vision, so that he could have thought the children were hopping higher than they should and adopting grotesque postures too. The patterns of the game seemed increasingly reminiscent of the Gulshaw Players' dance, and weren't the children chanting a rhyme under their breaths? As he strained to make out the jagged whisper, which reminded him less of the song than of the comedian's unknown lingo, Headon said "Don't put them off, will you? Not far to go now."

In fact his house was just across the junction. Like its neighbours, it was so tall and thin that every front window appeared to have been squeezed narrow. A haphazardly paved path wandered between rockeries, unless they were overgrown heaps of rubble, to the front door. When Headon switched on the hall light, it seemed reluctant to respond. Presumably it was designed to conserve energy, but the glow reminded Fairman of old paper and left the reaches of the house in darkness. The hall and the stairs that climbed from it stretched further than he could see, and the grudging light from a room on the left didn't help. In the room faded armchairs faced a black iron fireplace, and dozens of images of Gulshaw hung on the drab brownish walls—presumably old photographs, unless they owed their sepia tinge to the illumination. "It doesn't change much, does it?" he commented as Headon ushered him into the room.

"It does where it counts. You'll be seeing." Headon stayed in the doorway and murmured "Shall I fetch it to you?"

Fairman found the conversation a good deal too ambiguous. "The book, you mean."

"And everything it brings."

More sharply Fairman said "What are you saying that is?"

"Knowledge, Leonard. What we're all waiting for," Headon said and turned away, though not with his whole body at once. Fairman heard him pad into the depths of the house, presumably switching on at least one more light. The large soft footfalls receded into silence, and then a muffled noise might have denoted the opening of a door. Fairman had grown far too used to the moist stagnant Gulshaw smell, but it seemed more apparent in this house, and he felt oppressed by the dimness that resembled an emanation of old paper. He wasn't sure if the smell was intensifying as slow footsteps advanced towards the room, sounding furtive and yet heavier than he would have expected or invited. Apparently all of this signified the care Headon was taking with the book, which rested on his outstretched hands as he paced into the room like a priest approaching an altar. He watched Fairman lay it in its excelsior nest, having ascertained that it was the seventh volume, *Of the Symbols the Universe Shows*. Headon's throat bulged with swallow after nervous swallow, which made Fairman blurt "You aren't a believer, are you?"

"We're of the same mind, Leonard."

"Speak for yourself," Fairman almost retorted. He wasn't sure what daunted him—surely not the distant gaze that seemed bent on including him. "Well," he said awkwardly, "I'd best be off to keep it safe."

"Nobody would dream of taking any of them away from you." Headon paused to let this gain more weight before he said "And you're going to see the little ones."

"The little ones," Fairman said and felt as though he'd been overtaken by a local tendency to repeat other people's words.

"Our youngsters. The ones at the nursery."

"Why should I need to see them?"

"I expect they'd like to see you." As more of an explanation Headon added "Phyllida Barnes runs the Sprightly Sprouts, and she's got the next book."

"I'd better find out when she can accommodate me."

"I wouldn't trouble yourself, Leonard. Just go over in the morning. Nobody's going to give you any more problems."

Could Headon really undertake this on behalf of the rest of the town? Certainly he didn't seem to be giving voice just to himself. As Fairman emerged into the hall he avoided glancing into the dark that felt unpleasantly like a lair, but sensed it massing at his back all the way to the front door, an impression far too reminiscent of being spied upon. Outside the house he thanked Headon and peered along the deserted street. "Don't worry," Headon told him. "Nobody can be safer than you are."

The children were still hopping or dancing about the schoolyard. The surrounding silence magnified their footfalls, which sounded oddly loose, insufficiently defined. Fairman didn't look towards the yard as he turned downhill to the promenade, beyond which the fog hung like a vast curtain the colour of a dusty cobweb. He was put in mind of a stage with the streetlamps for footlights, and couldn't help recalling the restless anticipatory sounds he'd heard behind the curtains at the Shaw. Of course any presence behind the fog could only be the moon.

The arcades were dark and silent now. The lunar glare of the streetlamps seemed to lend more substance to the fog, which blotted out a good deal of the beach. The visible stretch was deserted apart from a scattering of plastic cushions. Could people have left them to keep their places on the beach? He remembered seeing a woman leave one near the hotel—and then, with a not especially mirthful laugh at his mistake, he saw that the objects were jellyfish.

They didn't belong to any species he recognised. Perhaps it was rare enough to be represented in the Bywood aquarium, if such creatures ever were. They glistened in the pallid light as if they'd just crawled up from the veiled sea. Obviously they were being moistened by the fog, which appeared to trail over them as Fairman advanced along the promenade. It revealed dozens of them, every one as broad as his midriff. They put him in mind of exposed flattened greyish brains, which wasn't their only unappealing aspect; each of them had stretched out gelatinous tendrils as if to help them crawl, tendrils that resembled spines gone translucent and flabby. Quite a few of the tendrils seemed to have ambitions to gain more of a shape, swelling to form excrescences reminiscent of embryonic hands. When Fairman started to fancy that he could distinguish small splayed fingers, in some cases fewer than a hand should have and in others an unpleasant profusion, he did his best to fix his attention on the promenade as he tramped faster towards the hotel.

At last all the inert misshapen lumps were behind him. He refused to imagine that he'd seen tiny greyish nails on any of the finger-like protrusions, still less that he'd glimpsed one gelatinous slab beginning to extrude features that suggested a rudimentary face. He needed sleep, that was all, once he'd spent time with the book. Just now he could hardly control his thoughts, which was why he needed to fend off the notion that all the creatures washed up on the beach were only playing dead. The prolonged slithering noise somewhere behind and below him must be a wave on the beach, but it made him look over his shoulder. As the fog surged towards him, hiding the stretch where he'd seen all the jellyfish, he was sure he glimpsed an utterly deserted beach.

He was about to hurry onwards when he heard the movement

again. It sounded close enough for its source to be hidden at the base
of the sea wall. Fairman gripped the chilly railing and made to crane
over, and then he dodged across the promenade instead. As he
hastened past the hotels, all of which were lit only by the streetlamps, he kept glancing behind him. Were lumpy greyish shapes
crouching almost flat on some of the ramps that led up from the
beach? While he couldn't be sure about that, he was glad to see
people seated in the shelter opposite the Wyleave, though the scarves
around their faces made them unidentifiable. "Sea wall," their
muffled voices called—no, surely they were telling him to sleep well,
not even to see that way. As they raised their left hands to wave to
him if not to dab at their glistening foreheads, he let himself into the
hotel.

Apart from the lobby and the upstairs corridor, it was dark. The
silence felt as expectant as a held breath, and prompted him to make
even more noise with the plumbing than usual. He was shutting
himself in his room when he thought he heard a restless movement,
too large and undefined to be anything except a wave, not an indication that all the neighbouring rooms were occupied. Just the same,
he couldn't help reminding himself of Headon's reassurance as he
sat down with the latest book.

"We are all but symbols of the vagaries of the becoming of the
universe. May a symbol read a symbol?" Presumably the book was
setting out to convey how that was possible, but Fairman found the
text at least as obscure as the colophon, a circle that appeared to be
blank until his fingertips traced a series of irregularities that might
form a secret diagram or motif. "The old dances conjure the ancient
patterns and celebrate the imminence of revelation . . . " This was
among the more intelligible sentences, and even then he felt he
hadn't entirely grasped the point. "Most potent are the words of
becoming, which shape the voice and the mouth when spoken, and
mould the brain which seeks to comprehend them. No wholly
human lips may pronounce the language of creation, and the brain
must yield its customary form to rediscover the making of the
universe . . . " Beyond this the book might as well have been
composed of the language it regarded as unfathomable by the ordinary reader. When Fairman shut the book at last he felt as though it
had been a dream he was already forgetting, its details sinking out of
reach in the depths of his mind.

He might have liked to think the view from the window was a

dream. The denizens of the shelter had entirely covered their faces with scarves, and their hands lay so slackly on their knees that there might have been no fingers inside the whitish gloves. The clumps of hair perched on their heads accentuated their resemblance to waxworks. People were still sitting on the beach in the restless fog, which blurred their outlines so much that he couldn't even tell which way they were facing. Perhaps all the pallid heads were bald, but he had the odd notion that every figure had its back to the sea. The view was enough to send him to bed.

His night thoughts were waiting for him. He saw the monstrous shape as vast and spiky as a cathedral burrowing into the earth, and then all sense of time deserted him. As the passing of ages reshaped the landscape a lake was formed, and perhaps it remained unvisited for at least as long before the inhabitant was roused from its monstrous torpor by wanderers whose dreams had been touched by its reverie. It found a crude way to bind the intruders, injecting them with a trace of its essence through its spines. Fairman had heard rumours of this relatively modern legend, which he'd assumed to be a variant on tales of alien abduction, but now it felt as if the volumes of the *Revelations* were carrying on a dialogue in his head, composing annotations there. At some point the entity was injured and retreated to its sanctuary beneath the lake. Over the ages it had withered to little more than a seed of itself, but now it rediscovered its primal substance, extending its spines through the land. Or was this yet another symbol—a veiled account of how it was reaching for the world? It was just a dream, Fairman reassured himself, or rather it would have been one if he were asleep. At some point he was, since daylight wakened him.

Not just the greyish light did, nor even the suspicion that he could have been mumbling in his sleep. He'd had an idea during the night, and his gaze drifted towards the safe. Had he been less thorough than he ought to be? He lined up the books on the dressing-table before he opened the first volume at the rear flyleaf. The breath he released felt like starting awake once again, and he saw his eyes widen in the mirror. The book and all the others had been annotated on the flyleaf.

The addition that he'd previously seen wasn't in the same handwriting as the others, although they looked similar. They were even more loosely scrawled than the first example had been. Perhaps the writers had been drunk or half asleep, which might explain the vagueness of the annotations too. "The mage need not speak the words nor shape them in his mind, for reading them has made of him a conduit for their power." This had been added to *On Conjuration*, while *On the Purposes of Night* now ended by exhorting "Embrace the night, that the old dreams may walk by day" and *Of the Secrets of the Stars* had acquired an extra scrap of wisdom. "Gaze not upon the stars but into the gulf beyond, where you may glimpse the eternal watchers whose sport is the shrivelling of worlds . . . "

Fairman was distracted by a knocking—more a series of loose flat thumps—at the door. "Mr Fairman?" Janine Berry called. "Leonard?"

His lips were unexpectedly difficult to wield, and he saw his mouth try out shapes beyond the books. "One moment," he said indistinctly.

"Don't go hurrying yourself. We know you're busy. Only wanted to make sure you know breakfast's whenever you're ready."

He couldn't have guessed the time from the clogged daylight, but his watch showed it was nearly ten o'clock. "I shouldn't be long," he called, and his lips mimed the words in the mirror.

He hadn't heard the landlady depart when he turned to the next book. The *Revelations* told how Gla'aki roamed the universe, the annotation said. "His great mind guided the vessel, but even He could not revive the denizens of the dead city which formed its carapace. The city and its secrets far older than humanity were destroyed as the vessel fell to our earth." The scrawl at the end of the following volume seemed to continue the theme. "The disciples of Gla'aki have described the dead city which lies in the depths of Starfall Water, yet none of His evangelists have understood the greater wonder. What is the apparition of the vanished city but a token of His power to shape His domain through His dreams?"

"What indeed," Fairman muttered. He turned his back on his twin once they'd both shut their books, and carried a trinity of volumes to the safe. Had he learned anything at all from the annotations? They felt to him as if the books had been talking to themselves. He locked the other volumes in the safe and headed for the bathroom.

Someone had been in it recently. The mirror was befogged, and a trickle of water was snaking into the plughole of the bath. Fairman made the plumbing muffle his noises next door and ambled downstairs once he was dressed. He'd hardly taken his place by the window, outside which the fog hovered wakefully above the beach, when Mrs Berry appeared with a trayful of breakfast. As she transferred the plate and the other items to his table she said "We saw you at the theatre last night."

Fairman was distracted by the sight of the occupants of the shelter opposite the hotel. Could they really have been there all night? Their faces were still hidden, suggesting that they could be asleep if not worse. When he saw one of them stir, flexing his floppy gloved fingers on his knees, Fairman said "What did you think of the show?"

"What you did, that's all that matters."

"Surely not all." His response seemed to drive her gaze further back in her eyes, and Fairman said "You have to be impressed by how much they can do."

"You've not seen the half yet."

He had no idea what to say to this. The empty tables all around him prompted him to murmur "I'm sorry to be putting you to trouble."

"You aren't at all, Leonard. None of us."

"Eating after everybody else, I mean."

"You're not. You're our only one."

"Haven't your other guests eaten? Someone was in the bathroom before me."

For an instant Mrs Berry hesitated. "What makes you say that?"

"It was steamed up."

"I expect the fog got in." Before he could argue she said "Look at me keeping you from your meal. That isn't what I'm for."

She stumped away softly but rapidly, returning as Fairman downed the last pliant mouthful. He was gazing at a bunch of sluggish joggers who might almost have been imitating animals from the zoo, some with their fists raised in front of them like paws while others dangled their arms from a simian crouch. "We all need to keep ourselves in shape," Mrs Berry said.

Rather than admit this Fairman said "Could you tell me where I'll find Phyllida Barnes?"

"You'll be seeing our littlest ones, of course. She has them up on Haven Way."

"Not quite the smallest, surely? They'll be at your hospital."

"We've none of those in Gulshaw."

"The nearest one, I mean. The nearest maternity."

"We like to keep it here. Us Gulshaw women don't need all that paraphernalia."

"Some people must, surely."

"If what we drop can't get on without that kind of help, it isn't meant."

Fairman wasn't anxious to learn how much she might be drawing on her own experience, and made haste to fetch his coat instead, together with a carton for the next book. The old folk in the shelter had partly uncovered their faces; the scarves had sagged below their eyes, at any rate. "Good day," they called, two syllables so muffled that he could easily have thought they formed a less commonplace word.

The light was more stifled than ever. The icy disk of the sun gleamed for a moment before vanishing into the wall of fog above the sea as if it had been engulfed by gelatin. No jellyfish were visible beyond the promenade, though at first he had the grotesque fancy that some of the people standing about on the beach were ankle-deep in them. Of course the people were wearing plastic beach shoes, which made their feet look translucent and discoloured and swollen.

A side street led uphill past Gulshaw Face & Body, apparently both a beautician's and a gym. Perhaps this was where the local folk acquired their tan, though Fairman hadn't seen much of that lately; even the ones he'd previously encountered—Janine Berry's, Frank Lunt's—had begun to fade as if there was no further need for such a sham. Though the slope wasn't especially steep, he felt sluggish by the time he reached the top. Not far around the corner was Sprightly Sprouts, a long grey single-storey building that might originally have been some sort of hall. The exterior was painted with large animals so cartoonish that they hardly seemed to belong to any species Fairman recognised. As he closed the gate of the yard, which was provided with miniature climbing equipment and infantile rides, he heard a woman cry "Here's our visitor. Let's see you all shape up."

He felt abashed and resentful of being used as some kind of threat. As he made for the merrily yellow doors, they were flung open by a buxom woman. Her voluminous dun gown hung straight to her feet from her considerable bosom, which quivered visibly inside the material when she took a step towards him. He might have thought her chubby face quaked too, twitching the tips of her fierce smile and almost closing her small eyes, not to mention jerking her greyish nostrils wider. Though her russet hair was parted well to the left, it framed her face with identical waves. "Phyllida Barnes," she said not much less vigorously than she'd addressed the children. "Good to meet you at last, Mr Fairman."

Once he'd accepted the clammy Gulshaw handshake, she made a tremulous bustling movement with her entire body to urge him over the threshold. "No ceremony, Mr Fairman. They're all waiting for you."

He could hear the children beyond the lobby, where dozens of miniature jackets and overcoats hung in an alcove. As he shut the doors behind him the hubbub seemed to swell up, growing shriller. Perhaps his face betrayed some nervousness, because Phyllida Barnes blinked at him. "Don't you care for children?"

"I've had very little to do with them."

"Maybe you should see to that," she said and appeared to realise to some extent that she was being presumptuous. "We know how much you're doing already, but still."

Without waiting for an answer she opened a door opposite the cloakroom. The babble of children subsided, isolating a few wordless sounds, as Fairman ventured into the room. Most of the toddlers were behind dwarfish desks, though a few children, not necessarily the smallest, lay on plastic mats on the wooden floor. Every child was gazing at Fairman, who had an unsettling sense that he was the focus of attention of a single mind. "We like to start them young," Phyllida Barnes declared. "You're never too young to learn, or too old either."

He supposed she was referring to the classroom ambiance. Quite a few of the toddlers were unduly plump while others were equally unhealthily thin. He was restraining any comment when Phyllida Barnes said "Diane?"

Diane was just as stout but more sluggish, and wore a gown like hers. Fairman was disconcerted to observe how similar her hair was to her colleague's, virtually a mirror image with the parting on the right. "Show Mr Fairman your pictures, everyone," she urged.

Perhaps they had recently been to the zoo or gone walking in the woods. He could just deduce that the paintings were meant to represent something like a hedgehog. Even the prostrate infants held up spiky daubs on large sheets of paper. "What do you think of that, Mr Fairman?" Phyllida Barnes cried.

"Very nice." In case this sounded insufficiently enthusiastic he said "All of them."

"There you are, children. See who thinks you're developing." Nevertheless she seemed disappointed by his reaction. "What else would you care to see?" she said.

"If you don't mind, what I came for." When she and Diane added their stares to the children's, Fairman said "The book."

"I'll bring it to you. You'll occupy him while I get it, won't you?"

Fairman couldn't tell whether she was speaking to her colleague or the children. As Phyllida Barnes left the room Diane said "What would you like to show Mr Fairman now? What shall we do for him?"

After a general murmur that might have included some words a boy or else a girl piped "Walk."

"That's right, you're good at that," Diane said so instantly that he wondered if she found them daunting. "Show Mr Fairman how well you can."

The children at the desks stood up at once with a flapping of dun overalls, and he was disconcerted by how tall some of them proved to be. Did they have difficulty in walking? Was that why the woman had made an issue of it? Or perhaps they were demonstrating as they came towards him how complicatedly they could walk. The children on the mats had raised their heads, and now they began to squirm, rustling the plastic. "Yes, go on," Diane told them. "You crawl."

They set about it as the other children shuffled and hopped and sidled to him. All of them wore slippers not unlike the beach shoes he'd seen earlier, and the room resounded with slithering. All their eyes were on him, widening with eagerness if not bulging with some effort, especially those of the infants around his feet. The children only just stopped short of touching him, instead taking elaborate steps backwards. It put him in mind of some sort of dance—even the crawlers on the floor were finding different ways to wriggle—and he heard a whisper of a song or chant that sounded nearly familiar. "Keep that up and you'll be on the stage," he said.

This didn't seem to be what they wanted to hear, since they continued to encircle him while murmuring the chant their soft loose footfalls almost drowned. Quite a few of their eyes had grown so protuberant that he was put in mind of gouts of liquid. He glanced at Diane, but she was standing well back and watching him as distantly as all the children seemed to be. He was about to appeal to her or even call a halt himself—the intricate movements were confusing him so much that he could hardly distinguish the shapes of some of the players—when they all grew still in unison, even the ones on the floor. Phyllida Barnes had come into the room. "Here's his book," she said.

Did she really need to give the pronoun so much weight? He was still more thrown by the children's response. All their mouths grew round as they stretched out their hands to the book—even the crawlers did—and almost deafened him with a cry that might have greeted a present somebody had just unwrapped on their behalf. "It isn't for you," he couldn't help blurting. "There'll be other books."

A shudder took him unawares. He felt as if he'd been assailed by a denial so concerted that its force was close to physical. As the sensation faded Phyllida Barnes gave him a blink that he could have taken for reproach. "Mr Fairman has to put it with the others," she said. "That's where it's going to live."

"Back to your places now," Diane said.

The outstretched hands sank, and the toddlers shuffled to their desks while the prone children slithered to their mats. Fairman couldn't have said whether every child resumed the same position they'd been in when he'd entered the room. He made for the door, but as he held out his hands for the book Phyllida Barnes murmured "Do you want to say something?"

She didn't let go of the volume when he took hold of it. In her grasp the cover felt clammy, even yielding. "Thank you for taking care of it," he said—presumably he was meant to set the children an example. "I'm grateful to everyone who has."

Phyllida Barnes gazed at him so distantly that he couldn't read her feelings. "I expect you'll say more when it's time," she said and relinquished the book.

She was still in the doorway, and there wasn't room to squeeze past her. As he wondered none too happily if more was expected of him, Diane said "What do we say to Mr Fairman?"

He heard an indrawn breath behind him. It was so enormous that he had to remind himself he was hearing a roomful of children. After a pause they spoke almost in chorus, some of them distinctly enough that he couldn't mistake the words. "So much more to see."

"That's right," Phyllida Barnes said. "We don't know how much."

Fairman had no idea what this was supposed to mean or whether it was addressed to him. When she stepped back, twitching her eyes even smaller and quivering her straightened lips towards some kind of smile, he dodged around her. As he lingered to package the book he said "Do you know where I'm going next?"

"Of course we do. You want Bernard Seddon at Stillwater."

"What sort of place might that be?"

"Where we all go in our time." She appeared to think this was plain, and only eventually said "The funeral parlour."

"I imagine you'll be directing me."

"Maybe you should call him first if you don't mind. We know you're not meant to be put to any more trouble, but just in case he's occupied with someone. We've had a few go lately."

Fairman supposed he should be grateful to the mayoress for making arrangements on his behalf. Phyllida Barnes recited the number for him to type on his phone. Before a bell started to ring he heard the murmur of a song or chant in the room he'd just left. A woman's voice interrupted the bell. "Stillwater. How may we be of assistance?"

"Could I speak to Bernard Seddon?"

"Is this Mr Fairman? Bernard's engaged with the departed at the present."

"When could I see him, do you know?"

"As I say, he's at the church. He'll be to and fro with the deceased till this afternoon. He asked me to tell you he'll be here for you by three."

"Three it is. If by any chance he's delayed, here's my number."

"He'll be waiting, Mr Fairman. We know better than to let you down."

Perhaps the hushed respect that had crept into her voice came with the job. As Fairman pocketed the mobile, Phyllida Barnes said "You could have asked him to put them off for you."

"I don't think I should when they can't speak for themselves."

He was trying to lighten the inexplicably oppressive mood, but he thought he'd failed even before she said "We all have a voice, Leonard."

If this was a rebuke it was beyond him. He was emerging into the yard, where the climbing frames and tiny rides were so bedewed with fog that they looked as if they'd been dredged out of water, when Phyllida Barnes murmured "It's yours now."

"It's the university's," Fairman said, but her distant look left him more confused than ever.

His route to the promenade took him past Gulshaw Face & Body, where several bald customers were exercising in the gym. They had plenty of reason, given their lumpy shapes. Some were throwing themselves backwards and forwards on bicycles to nowhere, stretching their arms and then their legs in some form of therapy unfamiliar to him. Others were running or striding on conveyor belts, and Fairman could have thought they were elongating their legs rather too vigorously at each pace. He might even have imagined that the indistinct chant that drifted down from Sprightly Sprouts was accompanying if not driving the exercises. Through another window he glimpsed a woman lying supine on a bed for some kind of facial treatment. A hulking overalled masseuse had laid a towel over the customer's face, of course, however much it looked as though she was kneading the pallid surface in order to squeeze features up from it. Fairman didn't linger over the sight but hurried downhill.

The sea had crept out of the fog. Quite a few people were ankle-deep in the water—he could have thought they hadn't moved since he'd passed that way earlier—while others clustered closer to the promenade. The greyish light looked as if it were being strained through gelatin, and lent all the flesh on display a tint unpleasantly reminiscent of jellyfish. A faint song seeped through the fog, and Fairman was near to imagining that it originated somewhere out to sea until he deduced that it came from the church beyond the murk. The congregation must be singing at one of Bernard Seddon's funerals, but could the mourners be dancing as well? Perhaps this was the activity that made the song too intermittent for Fairman to be sure how familiar it was.

As he crossed the road to the Wyleave, the denizens of the shelter raised their left hands, and one man called out. Surely he hadn't used Fairman's name, but Fairman demanded "What did you say?"

"We're saying no need to rush there, lad."

Fairman couldn't tell who had spoken first or now, and it might have been a third participant who said through his scarf "We'll all be there soon."

"The whole lot of us," another said.

Fairman had an unwelcome impression of being not just watched but addressed by a solitary senile consciousness. Presumably they had the funeral in mind. "You're right, no hurry," he said but made swiftly for the hotel.

There was nobody at Reception, and the building was quiet as fog, yet it felt no more deserted than the view from his room. As soon as he looked out of the window, the oldsters in the shelter saluted him. Waves were crawling forward on the beach as if determined to drag the fog closer to the promenade. He wasn't going to imagine that all the figures in the restless murk were facing him. He left the window and took his latest acquisition out of its papery nest. "Nearly whole," he said.

It was the fifth volume, *Of Humanity as Chrysalis*. At first glance he took the colophon for an anatomical diagram, showing a muscular skeleton next to a body parted down the middle. The stance of the bones suggested that they might have burst forth of their own volition, however, and the bony grin seemed more conscious than it ought to be. Were there eyes in the sockets? They reminded him of the distant gaze he seemed to have encountered too often in Gulshaw, and he turned to the end of the book. The flyleaf was blank.

It made the book feel oddly unfinished. He was so eager to read the text that he grudged the call he had to make. "Leonard," Nathan Brighouse said. "I hardly like to ask."

"I think I'd better plan on being done by tomorrow."

"That's Saturday." Brighouse might have been saying so in case Fairman had lost all sense of time. "Please ensure you're here on Monday," he said, "and we'll see what needs to be talked over."

"I'll do my best, of course."

"I'd expect no less." Brighouse let him interpret this for a few moments and added "I wouldn't like to think it needs assessment at this stage of your career, Leonard."

"Then don't," Fairman said, but only after ringing off. He was more aware of the book on which he and his twin were resting their hands than of still holding the phone. He should let Sandra know the situation, and as soon as she answered he said "It's me."

"I see it is, Leonard." As he grasped that she was referring to the display of his number she said "You aren't on your way, are you?"

"Who told you I'm not?"

"Nobody had to. It's in your voice."

"As it happens you're right." In a bid not to feel at the mercy of his circumstances Fairman said "I'm on my way to putting it together."

"How much do you still have to collect?"

"Just a couple of volumes. Nathan said I might as well stay the weekend."

"I shouldn't think you'll need any company when you have your books."

"I do have some reading ahead of me." Just in time he saw how she might have wanted him to interpret her remark. "You'd be most welcome if you cared to make the journey," he said hastily, "and I'm sure I wouldn't be alone in saying so."

"You can speak for the town, can you, Leonard?"

"I believe they pay someone to do that. But I think I've a pretty good sense of the place by now, yes."

"It's still the kind of place you dreamed of as a child, is it?"

"It's a lot more than whatever that was. There's so much more to see." If that was a joke, he should have known it was beyond her. "Not least the people," he said.

"What are you saying about them?"

"I started off thinking some of them were a little odd, but maybe they're no more so than I am. I'm sure you'd find them welcoming, all the ones you'll meet."

"I wonder if that's because their town is out of season."

"I'm sure they're genuine enough. They speak their mind round here. I was lectured this morning by one of them."

"Good heavens." Sandra sounded amused or ready to be. "What about, Leonard?"

"A lady told me I ought to care more about children."

"Well." Apparently this wasn't a source of amusement. "Maybe you should," Sandra said.

"I didn't know you felt that way."

"Maybe it isn't all you don't know about me."

"Then if you came here for the weekend I might have a chance to find out."

"I wasn't doing much tomorrow." She paused, perhaps to let him wonder about her decision or to attempt to persuade her, and then she said "All right, I'll take the first train in the morning."

"I'll meet you at the station. I'll make sure I'm free," Fairman said but thought it best to add "If the book should hold me up I'll let you know." That made him even keener to resume reading, and his distant gaze out of the mirror seemed to double his impatience. "Looking forward to it," he said and freed his hand to open the book.

"What need of flesh has the sorcerer? Nightly his essence springs forth and capers for glee . . . " He was surprised how unsatisfactory he found this and the pages that followed. Even if the content was meant only for the initiated, it felt unnecessarily withheld from him. "More curious still is the transformation which overtakes the child of sorcery, a change often too impatient to wait upon the death of the flesh . . . " This seemed yet more remote from his experience—as remote as the gaze that was waiting to meet his whenever he glanced up. Perhaps the whole book was symbolic, in which case he lacked the knowledge to interpret it; could that be in the volume he had yet to obtain? He was surprised how frustrated he felt by having read them out of order. "Some of the transformed owe their change to pronouncing the words of power, which shapes the body of the speaker to produce them." Might reading aloud help him under-stand? It seemed only to make him feel overheard inside the hotel and, if he let himself dream anything so absurd, outside too. "Most potent is the transformation which overtakes those who dwell within a territory which an Ancient One has made His own. As He occupies their minds, so the very landscape may revert to the age of primal shaping . . . " Fairman read to the end and shut the book at last, and as he and his counterpart each rested a hand on the cover he was put in mind of a priest who'd delivered a sermon without having grasped a word.

It was almost ten to three. He added the book to the blackness in the safe and saw the moist print of his fingers vanish from the metal door. As he padded downstairs his footsteps sounded like a muffled heartbeat he'd brought to life. Mrs Berry was behind the counter, but she appeared to be asleep. Her head was tilted back so far that he couldn't immediately distinguish her face. Surely it was only the perspective that made her eyes appear to have sunk inwards, rendering the lids concave enough to fit a thumb in, but there was also the illusion that her features had sunk into the flesh. He was attempting to steal away when she sat up, rubbing a hand over her face so violently that she might have been embarrassed to have been caught sleeping at her post. He could have fancied that he glimpsed her face quivering with emotion or with her treatment. She gazed hard at him before she said "Was there something you wanted to ask me, Leonard?"

For a moment he wondered what she might have been dreaming, and then he didn't want to know. "Just a passing thought," he said.

"All the same."

That could scarcely be an answer to the question he hadn't voiced, and so he said "Actually, it seems I'm to be joined for the weekend. I hope that won't cause any problems."

"Your lady couldn't be more welcome," Janine Berry said with a look he could have taken as coquettish. "We'll see to it she is."

He felt as if his thoughts were too obvious, hardly his own any more. "Thank you for all your hospitality," he said.

He wanted to be in time for his appointment, but he also didn't mind avoiding the tenants of the shelter on the promenade. He drove along the street behind the Wyleave towards the church and came to Stillwater Funerals at a junction above the promenade. As he caught sight of it he realised that he hadn't asked for directions. He must have noticed the place or the name on the map at some point, though he didn't remember. In any case he no longer seemed to need the map.

The funeral parlour was a single-storey building not unlike an elongated vault with windows, and as grey as the light doled out by the fog above the sea. It was overlooked by the backs of hotels, and as Fairman left the car on the forecourt he saw people seated at several hotel windows. All of them were gazing in his direction, but he couldn't distinguish what was in their eyes, even when they each raised a hand to greet or acknowledge him. While they could hardly have been waiting for him, he would rather not imagine that they spent their days watching the funeral parlour.

Beyond a glass door with a black border, a venerable desk faced an expanse of carpet that yielded underfoot like moss. Two obese black leather couches rested against the walls, where the dark wallpaper seemed to hint at a pattern like stars almost too distant to see. A table scattered with dog-eared brochures bearing the slogan **A Better Place** squatted in front of each couch. The reception area was deserted, but a hymn hung like mist in the air. At least, Fairman took it for a hymn, so muted that he couldn't grasp the melody. As he strained to identify it and perhaps put words to it he heard soft heavy footfalls approaching down a corridor, and a man in a suit as grey as discretion plodded into the room. "Mr Fairman," he said, rather loudly for the setting. "Bernard Seddon."

His oval face tapered to not much of a chin, and his shoulders sloped so precipitously that his jacket seemed in danger of slipping off. Perhaps that was why he finished buttoning it before he gave

Fairman an unctuous handshake, which came with a deferential nod that offered a view of the pallid central parting of his almost monkish tonsure. "Beg pardon for the wait," he said. "The girl's gone for a lie down. Big day tomorrow."

"I should be the one apologising. I wasn't quite on time." As the undertaker's large eyes widened while his small mouth worked on an expression, Fairman said "What kind of congratulations are in order?"

"For the girl?" Seddon's eyes grew wider still, elevating his hairless brows, and seemed to betray some kind of uneasy amusement. "She doesn't need any," he said. "If anyone does it's you, Leonard."

"I'm only doing my job."

"That's us, not you. You don't want a look at mine, do you? See how we all finish up in Gulshaw."

"I really don't think that's necessary, thank you."

Did Fairman sense disappointment before Seddon recaptured his humour? "I don't get many complaints from my customers," the undertaker said. "Even the ones that aren't from here."

"I shouldn't think you would."

Fairman saw his bid to join in the joke fall flat; certainly Seddon's gaze retreated deep into his eyes. "Shall I bring it you?" the undertaker said.

"The book." Since the undertaker seemed to think this didn't call for a reply, Fairman said "By all means."

"I won't be two shakes."

Perhaps this was more of his notion of wit, since he was gone considerably longer. Once the soft footsteps faded along the corridor Fairman reverted to trying to identify the music that seemed to permeate the room. Was there a whisper of voices as well as the murmur of the organ? He didn't know how long he had been left alone when he thought he heard his name. Or might the words have been "Let us see him"? In any case they took him into the corridor.

There were three doors in either wall. Just the furthest on the right and the nearest left-hand door were open. From somewhere came a sound like long slow effortful breaths—the noise of some kind of suction. Fairman couldn't help feeling relieved when a glance through the first doorway showed him no more than a viewing room, where two rows of straight chairs faced an open coffin. Or was it meant for viewing? The underside of the lid reflected the contents; he could make out details of a dark suit, including a breast pocket, but surely other parts of the image were distorted, since the collar and the ends of the sleeves sported greyish masses with nothing he would call a shape. The figure must be part of some kind of display too macabre for Fairman's taste or, he would have hoped, anybody else's. He needn't wonder what the swollen greyish wads resembled, and he was resisting an urge to look in the coffin when a figure with a blurred face and hands lurched into the corridor.

They had to be blurred because they were at the edge of his vision. When he looked he saw Seddon with a book in his hands. "Want to see after all?" the undertaker said. "We can show you what happens if you like."

"No. No thank you." Fairman turned away from the room, only to sense the contents of the coffin behind him. "I just wondered if you were having difficulty finding the book," he said as he retreated down the corridor.

"Saying goodbye, that was all." Seddon plodded softly after him into the reception area and passed him the book. "I didn't need to, did I?" he said as though he'd seen another joke. "There's no good-byes round here."

Fairman refrained from interpreting this. As the marks of moist fingertips faded from the cover of the book without exhibiting their prints he saw that the colophon depicted a coffin framed by a pair of open hands that might have been offering it to the reader. The volume was the ninth, *Of the Uses of the Dead*. Without taking time to think he blurted "You're the man to know."

"What are you making me, Leonard?"

"The chap who'd know about their uses." Fairman was thrown by how eager if not anxious the question had sounded. "That's supposing you think they have any," he said.

"We all have here. You most of all."

"Well, thank you," Fairman said, rather hoping Seddon thought he had the book in mind. "So who's my last custodian?"

"The father. Father Sinclough."

At once Fairman wondered how much was about to grow clearer. "The father," he said. "Did he give you this book?"

"All of us."

Fairman hadn't really needed to be told. "Why?" he said.

Seddon's face quivered as if the question had hurt him. "Seems like he thought he could trust us."

"You've proved him right, but why did he give them out at all?"

"Maybe he'll say. It wasn't up to us to ask."

Fairman suspected that the undertaker was being less than honest, but there was no need to interrogate him. "I'll call now if you have the number."

"It's here," Seddon said, poking his forehead.

Fairman glanced aside as he reached for his mobile. He'd thought Seddon's forefinger was significantly longer and thinner than the glimpse had made it seem. As he typed the digits Seddon intoned he had an odd sense of already knowing them. Of course he'd already encountered the Gulshaw prefix several times. The electronic trilling of a bell invaded the hushed music of the parlour, and eventually a man's uneven voice said "Sinclough."

He sounded short of breath if not of words. "Father Sinclough," Fairman said. "This is—"

"Mr Fairman. It couldn't be anyone other."

"And how about your people with the books?" Something like resentment of being taken for granted so much provoked Fairman to demand "Couldn't they have been either?"

"It should all be clear to you tomorrow, Mr Fairman."

"Why do I have to wait till then?"

"Preparing, Mr Fairman." The priest had begun to sound as if he grudged the breaths he was expending. "I've still got to," he said.

Fairman assumed he was thinking of the Sunday sermon. "You're telling me I can't have the book today."

"I'm sure you'll have enough to digest tonight as it is." Weightily enough to be quoting a sacred text, Father Sinclough said "All shall be ready for you in the morning."

"Where do I find you? What time?"

"My house is in Forest Avenue. Shall we say nine?"

At least Fairman would have the book well before he had to meet Sandra. As he agreed the time he heard the priest take a stuttering breath. "Don't drive, will you?" Father Sinclough said. "There may not be room to park."

"I expect the walk will do me good."

In a moment Fairman thought that a walk in the fog was scarcely likely to improve his health. As the faint music seeped into his ear he realised he was alone on the mobile. He shoved it in his pocket and was opening his mouth when the undertaker said "Don't thank me, Leonard. It's us should be thanking you for bringing it all together."

Did he think the addition to the archive would earn the town some tribute? At least one of the townsfolk preferred not to be named for the donation. "Let's say we all did," Fairman said and saw a response flicker in Seddon's eyes—appreciation, surely, but too distant to own up to its nature.

As he made for the car he felt as if the gelatinous light was gathering on his skin. By the time he'd shut the carton in the boot his skin was crawling clammily enough for fever. Along the route to the hotel all the windows looked as though the surrounding stone had expanded like fungus to coat the panes grey—condensation, of course. Nobody had rubbed them clear, but there wasn't much to see in the deserted glistening streets. He could have thought the entire town had succumbed to slumber, though he didn't blame anyone for staying indoors in this weather.

He was crossing the lobby when Janine Berry came out of the office behind the counter, massaging her cheeks as if to revive their lost tan. "Just fixing my face," she said, though for a moment her vigour had made it look alarmingly lopsided. "Will you do us the honour tonight, Leonard?"

He wasn't sure if he wanted to learn "Which one would that be?"

"Will you dine with us? No charge. Our privilege."

While he didn't relish the prospect of another walk in the fog, Fairman said "With whom?"

"Just our hotel. You're on your own till tomorrow."

"That's very kind. When would you like me?"

"Whenever suits you," Mrs Berry said and gave the carton in his hands a deferential nod. "Before you lose yourself or after if you prefer."

"These aren't the kind of books you lose yourself in." When she looked unconvinced he said "Before might be best."

"Can you give us twenty minutes? If it's less I'll let you know."

He could have thought she was eager for him to begin reading. Though it seemed early for dinner, he didn't like to protest when it was complimentary. Upstairs he transferred the book to the safe, where the mass of blackness reminded him of a lightless void. The tenants of the shelter might have been waiting for him to appear at the window so that they could salute him in unison. He couldn't tell how crowded the beach was in the fog, where every figure appeared to glisten whenever they grew visible. The sight made his mind feel incapable of grasping what was there, and he lay down on the bed until the phone rang beside it—rattled, at any rate. "We're ready for you," Janine Berry said.

She wasn't alone in the dining-room. She was flanked by Tom the porter, whose tan had grown patchy enough for a disease, and the chambermaid. All three bowed to Fairman while keeping their united gaze on him, so that he had to suppress a nervous laugh. Since Tom still wore the suit he'd worn while conducting Fairman to his room, it was perhaps not entirely surprising that the girl was dressed in her chambermaid's uniform. "Here you are by the window," Mrs Berry said as if he mightn't notice the only table that was set. "Wine, Dora," she said. "You'll have red, won't you, Mr Fairman?"

While that was his preference, he would rather not have had it taken for granted; somebody had even pulled the cork in advance. Once he'd tasted it and pronounced it fine despite an underlying ferrous tang, Mrs Berry said "Soup, Tom."

This was a greyish broth that resembled stagnant water with gelatinous fragments floating in it. "Is this seafood?" Fairman said in an attempt to prepare for a mouthful.

"Our very own," Mrs Berry said with some pride. "Brought up from the sea."

When he risked a spoonful Fairman found that it did indeed taste marine, in fact very reminiscent of meals he'd previously eaten in Gulshaw. He might have found it easier to finish if the staff of the Wyleave hadn't watched each mouthful, Dora shuffling forward to replenish his glass whenever he took a sip while Tom was equally dutiful in wielding a jug of water. When at last Fairman laid his spoon to rest in the bowl, Janine Berry said "Ready for our special?"

Fairman said he was but felt somewhat less so once Tom brought it in. The roundish steak was the same grey as the soup, and slithered towards the edge of the plate as the porter playing waiter stumbled on the threshold of the room. "Steady, son," Mrs Berry said.

Tom paid this so little attention that he might have thought she wasn't addressing him. He tilted the plate on its way to the table, and when the action threatened to dislodge the vegetables—potatoes not much more whitish than the beans and carrots—he grabbed Fairman's fork and used it to hook the dangling dewlap onto the plate. "Gently, Tom," Mrs Berry blurted.

"Could I ask what the meat is?" Fairman said, if only to delay the encounter.

"Gulshaw's best," Mrs Berry said. "Our own produce."

He supposed it would be impolite to enquire further. The knife sliced it readily enough once he'd dragged the meat across the plate with the fork. The rubbery texture suggested seafood, and it did taste rather like fish, though he wasn't able to identify the underlying flavour. He could have thought that not just his hostess and her staff but the occupants of the shelter across the road were watching him. The more conscious he became of being observed, the vaster the attention seemed, and he did his best to make short work of the fillet and the vegetables to which it lent its taste. As he laid the utensils together on the glistening plate Mrs Berry said "Pudding?"

"I'll turn into it if I eat any more." Since this failed to amuse his audience, whose gazes grew distant in unison, Fairman added "Thank you enormously, but I honestly don't think I could find room."

"You've done us proud," Mrs Berry said. "You go and finish what you're here for."

Had he drunk too much? Though he'd left wine in the bottle, having gestured Tom away, Fairman's legs felt a little rubbery on the stairs. In the upper corridor he had to support himself for a moment against the wall, leaving a moist handprint on the fishy wallpaper. His skin kept turning clammy, and when he dabbed his forehead with a hand, both of them felt infirm. Perhaps the fog had given him a touch of fever, in which case he might benefit from a bath.

As he stepped into the corridor with a towel over his arm he thought he heard activity in the bathroom. Nobody was visible through the frosted pane, but he was easing the door open when the fluid restless sound was repeated. Surely it was only water trickling into the drain. The bath glistened with moisture, and he saw movement in the plughole. A greyish substance was withdrawing out of sight, and he could have imagined that as it vanished it blinked at him. That was enough to send him back to his room, where he confined himself to splashing water on his face.

He couldn't hear Janine Berry or her staff. He wasn't far from fancying that they were still where he'd left them, standing side by side to watch him plod away replete. The idea seemed to magnify the stillness, which felt as if it were focused on him. He dragged the

curtains together without glancing through the window and released
the book from the safe. "All life is the instrument of the mage, and
remains in his power after the process men call death . . . "

The volume seemed to promise formulas to revive the dead, to
conjure forth their wakeful thoughts, to inhabit their bodies so as to
use them as disposable vessels in some form of arcane exploration,
even to prevent the newly dead from departing as long as they were
useful to the sorcerer. None of these were promises Fairman was
anxious to see kept, but he couldn't resist reading on; that was why
he was here, after all, though perhaps he was glad not to be able to
interpret much of what he read. "The mage shall be known by the
summoning of the remains . . . " Which was the summoned, and
which the summoner? If there were occult formulas they must be
lying low in the midst of the text, and he found himself trying not to
hear his own voice, though the peripheral sight of a mouth shaping
every word didn't help. He released a breath as long and slow as any
of those he'd kept hearing—the waves outside his room—when the
blank flyleaves brought the volume to an end.

Once it was locked away he ventured into the corridor, where the
stillness made him feel more observed than ever. Perhaps he ought
to blame the eyes of all the fish that were embossed in the wallpaper.
He didn't simply flush the toilet as an aid to using it but sang to
cover up his activity: "Thou great inspiration, so much more than
sea . . . " Back in his room he couldn't resist going to the window.
The tenants of the shelter raised their sluggish floppy hands, but
their faces were so much in shadow that he could have thought the
featureless grey expanses below their eyes weren't scarves. In spite of
the hour and the fog, more people than he could count were on the
beach. Some were sitting with their backs to him, but surely it was
fog, not the sea, that kept drifting over their outstretched legs. Far
too many of the motionless figures, both the seated ones and those
on their feet that rubbery shoes had enlarged, were facing the hotel.
All their eyes were so wide that they made the other features seem to
have dwindled if not shrunk into the flesh.

He couldn't be sure of that—couldn't even tell whether any of
the people on the beach had been among those he'd encountered in
Gulshaw. He felt as if he were dreaming the sights beyond the
window; perhaps he would prefer to be. When he retreated to bed
and switched off the light he was afraid that worse fancies were
waiting in the stagnant dark—more visions of the denizen of Starfall

Water. He found he was nervous of sleeping, and he didn't think he had by the time Janine Berry's voice roused him.

She was singing or more accurately crooning. At first he thought she was in the lobby beneath his room, and then he realised she was outside the hotel. He floundered out of bed and sprawled towards the window. The watchers in the shelter saluted him before growing as motionless as almost everybody on the beach. He caught Janine Berry in the act of rising to her feet at the edge of the waves. As she stooped to cradle a flabby greyish almost shapeless object in her hands her left breast emerged from her blouse, to such a disconcerting extent that it might have been reaching for the prize she lifted to it. The sea fell silent between waves, so that Fairman was just able to make out her words. "You'll shape up," she said. "You'll last. You won't be like your brother."

So this was what dreams were like, Fairman thought as he found himself back in bed. Another showed him a horde of dancers emerging from the ballroom along the promenade to take their bewilderingly elaborate dance onto the beach. While they chanted a celebratory version of a familiar tune they kicked up their legs, which were bare and unnervingly long. Beyond them, through a momentary break in the fog, he glimpsed gelatinous lumps sidling crabwise towards the woods or crawling with a caterpillar motion. His bedtime reading must have given rise to the sight of the dead slithering out of their coffins through any crack they could find and worming through the earth to cluster at the edge of the sea, extending their arms and their hands that were at least as elongated towards the fog. He might have expected this to waken him—certainly he would have hoped for that to happen—but a nagging impression did. He felt as if he'd been talking in his sleep, and to an audience.

Although he seemed to be flaccid with exhaustion, another thought sent him squirming out of bed to wobble over to the safe. Outside the window the fog was engulfing the dawn. He fumbled to switch on the light once he'd transferred his two most recent acquisitions to the dressing-table. He opened *Of Humanity as Chrysalis* at the rear endpaper and then, with resignation that felt dreamlike, *Of the Uses of the Dead*. The pages were no longer blank.

The writing was less recognisable than ever. It looked as though an intruder had been struggling to guide Fairman's hand. The words seemed wholly unfamiliar, having left no discernible trace in his brain. "While Cthulhu makes Himself known to men through their dreams, Gla'aki fastens on their minds so as to make their dreams His own and shape them to His will . . ." This had been added to the volume on humanity, and Fairman couldn't tell whether it referred to the shaping of dreams or of minds, if not both. Beneath it the sentences were increasingly skewed across the page. "The Ancient Ones are not restricted to Their lairs, since a simple thought of Them may summon Them to seep through the very substance of the world. As Gla'aki came to know the minds of men, so He ceased to need to bind them physically to Him . . ." In the other volume the handwriting was even less controlled, wandering awry and almost off the flyleaf. "Where the power of Gla'aki has been concentrated He uses all life for His dreams. In these places shall be seen the eldest ways, where whatever lived was uncertain of its form and consumed its like in a bid for vigour . . ."

This read like an imitation of Percy Smallbeam's prose, Fairman tried to think; all the annotations did. Certainly he found them just as incomprehensible. He wondered if he'd spoken them aloud while scrawling them, and in what voice. As he resisted an urge to try reading them out, the bedside phone emitted its unmelodious clatter. "You're up, aren't you, Leonard?" Janine Berry told him. "Are you breakfasting before you go out?"

Fairman was assailed by an excessively familiar taste that rose from somewhere in him. "I think I'm still fed from last night."

"You know best. You fast if you think you should." Before Fairman could find a response she said "We'll have plenty of the special for your lady friend as well. I made it for you myself."

She sounded oddly wistful. Some undefined thought made Fairman's limbs grow rubbery as he stood up, fumbling the receiver onto its stand. He really didn't need to stay in Gulshaw once he'd completed the set of books; he could pick up Sandra at the station and drive straight back to Brichester—it was too late for him to phone and tell her not to come. As he hauled the curtains wide he braced himself to be greeted by the tenants of the shelter, but then his body sagged. The promenade was deserted and so was the beach, as far as he could see for the stagnant fog that made the sea resemble an artificial lake.

Had the weather proved too much for everyone at last? Even the shelter opposite the hotel was empty, and the graffiti glistened as if they had only just been painted; the incomprehensible words appeared to writhe with moisture or with eagerness to be grasped until Fairman looked away. The sense of an unseen audience seemed to have left the hotel. Perhaps he needn't put Sandra off after all, he thought with vague relief. While he wasn't entirely alone—Mrs Berry at least was presumably still in the building—he felt sufficiently at home that he didn't use the plumbing to cover up his noises. Once he'd showered in the already damp bath he dressed and made his way uphill from the car park.

The fog had been waiting for him. The moisture seemed not simply to cling to him but to permeate his glistening skin, which felt feverishly unstable. He climbed the street as fast as he could, though that made him even clammier. The fog might have been ushering him to his destination, leaving its murky mark on every window as it fluttered sluggishly backwards just a few paces ahead of him. All the houses looked as dormant as the empty cars resting half their wheels on the pavements. Did Gulshaw shut down on Saturdays out of season? He could have thought the town was not so much resting from its summer labours as reverting to its ordinary state.

Forest Avenue was indeed beside the woods. Some of the houses on the inland side were so close to them that Fairman couldn't tell where their gardens ended and the woods began. There were no buildings on the opposite side, just a line of trees bordering the cracked uneven road. The priest's house was separated from its neighbours by walls that had partly collapsed, weakened by vines that stretched out of the forest to overgrow most of the garden and clutch at the house. Even the porch between two tall thin grimy windows was adorned with dripping tendrils and beaded leaves. Fairman felt the stone step crumble underfoot as he stepped into the porch to thumb the rusty bellpush.

He had to press so hard that his thumb swelled up around his nail. He was close to trying again by the time he heard footsteps shuffling towards the door, which wavered open to reveal a man whose age had bent him almost a head shorter than Fairman. His floppy slippers must be why his feet had sounded unduly lacking in shape. His black robe emphasised the livid tints of his skin, and his wrinkled face put Fairman in mind of a balloon that had started to deflate; even his bald whitish scalp seemed in danger of subsiding. His large eyes were virtually colourless, and gleamed up at his visitor while his thin faded lips groped for a smile. "Mr Fairman," he said. "Thank you for gracing my house."

His handshake was the loosest yet. His lank fingers writhed in Fairman's grasp as if they were trying to give him a sign, unless they were betraying how age had made them uncontrollable. "Will you sit with me for a little while?" he said.

The hall and the stairs that divided it not quite in half grew darker still as Father Sinclough shut the door. The carpets and the wallpaper weren't much less sombre than his robe, and the additional darkness felt like a weight that had settled into the house. The priest shuffled effortfully into the nearest left-hand room and grabbed the arms of a chair before lowering himself. "Please be at home," he said with the last of a breath.

He hadn't switched the light on. Fairman couldn't even make out the nails of the fingers gripping the chair. The stifled glow through the grubby windows made all the furniture look steeped in fog, though surely it was dust that had risen from the chair when the priest sank into it. A radio that might have been as old as its owner squatted on a chipped marble mantelpiece above a dark hearth strewn with dead leaves that must have fallen from the vines that enshrouded the chimney on the roof. The gloom of the walls was relieved only by a dull glint of glass in frames, all of which had been divested of whatever pictures they'd contained. As Fairman headed for the armchair closest to the window he saw a blurred version of himself slither from glass to glass like an inhabitant of an aquarium.

Having sat down, he edged gingerly forward. The chair felt soft and bloated, and he could have thought it was moist as well, perhaps from its proximity to the fog that loomed at the window. He might have moved if it hadn't given him the best view of the room. Father Sinclough seemed content to be almost somnolently quiet, but Fairman was anxious to be done with any interview. "So," he said, "I understand you're the gentleman responsible."

"I tried to be," the priest said like a sigh. "Mea culpa, I was wrong."

"In what way?"

"I thought the books were best kept apart." With another breath the priest said "You'll appreciate I've learned my error."

"You don't mean the people you gave them to." When Father Sinclough shook his head—in the dimness the pale scalp seemed to wobble—Fairman said "Why those people in particular?"

"I never questioned it." The priest held out his hands as if they were cradling a burden. "We're all one here," he said.

Fairman wanted to protest that he wasn't, whatever the priest's words were supposed to mean. Instead he demanded "And why me?"

"It becomes you, my son." Father Sinclough clasped his hands together; in the gloom they looked near to merging into a single pallid mass. "When Donald Rothermere read your essay we knew you'd take all the care that was called for," he declared. "Do you know what Eunice Spriggs said?"

His eyes were wide enough to be expecting a yes, but Fairman was disconcerted to learn that the mayoress had been involved at such an early stage. "Please say."

"She said she was sure you'd live up to your name."

All this had taken quite a few breaths out of the priest, but Fairman was provoked to try another question. "Forgive my asking, but is Sinclough really yours?"

The priest shook his head slowly, and Fairman told himself its outline hadn't shifted in the process. "It was the first change I made," Father Sinclough said.

Fairman didn't feel the need to interrogate him further, even to learn how it might be spelled. "Anyway, could I trouble you for the book?"

The priest laid his hands on the arms of the chair. "We've led you quite a dance, haven't we."

"Never mind, it's over now."

"Not entirely, Mr Fairman." Father Sinclough took a breath and said "Not here."

Fairman found he had to take a breath himself. "I'm sorry?" he said but didn't feel. "You're telling me the book is . . . "

"It's at the church."

"Because it's safer there, would that be?"

"It would be safe anywhere in Gulshaw, Leonard."

However much Fairman was failing to understand, it surely didn't matter. "Well then, shall we go?" he said and stood up.

The priest sagged if not sank back into the chair. It looked as though the stagnant gloom had donned a pallid face and hands. "It's waiting for you," he said.

"Perhaps you could tell me where to find it."

"Where else but the pulpit, my son."

"Thank you for your time," Fairman said, which seemed sarcastically inadequate. "Thank you for everything you've done," he tried saying, but the priest's face had grown even less distinguishable. Surely only the dimness was engulfing its features. Just the same, Fairman wasn't slow in letting himself out of the house.

The street was still deserted. "Not a soul," he heard himself murmur before his voice sank without a trace into the fog. There weren't even many cars on Forest Avenue; he could have driven after all. The lethargic fog receded ahead of him as if it was about to unveil the world, and he felt it leave a residue on his skin. The windows of the houses were hardly distinguishable from the grey walls that framed them, and yet he felt watched—enormously so. The street wasn't entirely silent apart from his footsteps; moisture kept dripping from the trees, spattering the wet road and occasionally drumming on car roofs. The shrouded woods put him in mind of a jungle, as if they and the line of trees opposite were reverting to the primitive. He was resisting an urge to sing if not to talk to himself—to add some sound to his muffled footfalls and the intermittent plop of condensation haphazardly accompanied by hollow metallic thumps—when he heard a noise behind him.

It was high up in the trees. It might have been a bird, although he was belatedly aware that he'd seen none in Gulshaw, not so much as a seagull. When the foliage rustled again he glanced back. The branches of more than one tree were shaking against the unseen sky, as if some creature had leapt from one to the other. Fairman couldn't help thinking of the zoo, which—together with the Leafy Shade and Sprightly Sprouts—was somewhere in the murk beyond the priest's house. Another treetop quivered, and at the same time one shook on the opposite side of the road. Whatever was on the move up there sounded larger than a bird, but it was indistinguishable from the clumps of greyish branches. Fairman turned away, and as his suddenly unstable legs threatened to let him down he grabbed the nearest tree. His fingers recoiled, and he tramped faster towards the church. Surely the trunk hadn't squirmed like a wet scaly limb in his grasp, but he didn't touch any more trees. Even when the floppy sounds in the treetops multiplied he refrained from looking back.

The trees gave out as the road brought him to the Church of the First Word. He could have fancied that the grey stone walls puffed up at his approach, just as the fog seemed to swell with a vast breath as it withdrew across the empty promenade and the deserted beach. He lingered between the mossy gateposts to examine the signboard, having noticed that the definite article had been inserted in smaller letters between the two lines of the name. Patches of lichen obscured parts of the sign, but he thought the last two words had been altered, though he couldn't be sure whether they had originally been Saint Mark.

The same grey lichen had run riot on the gravestones surrounding the church. Some of them were so distorted that Fairman could have imagined the fog had infected them with its amorphousness. A stone urn seemed to be sprouting tendrils like a giant seed if not a tentacled denizen of the sea, and the pale mass dangling from an angel's bowed head was less devoid of features than Fairman liked, as if it was on the way to forming a new face. As he hurried down the path from the rusty gate he saw that quite a number of the mounds that extended from the memorials had crumbled seawards. That needn't remind him of anything, and he tramped to grab the encrusted ring on the door within the grey stone arch.

The door lumbered inwards on its massive hinges, scraping the uneven flagstones, and the stagnant Gulshaw smell came to meet him as though the church had let out a moist breath. The interior was so dim that he left the door open. All the arched windows in the side walls and flanking the altar were at least partly overgrown by a greyish fungoid substance, but Fairman couldn't judge whether this or the fog was responsible for leeching all the colour from the stained glass, where the outlines of the figures were so malformed that it was impossible to tell who or what they were meant to be. As he made his way along the aisle between the pews, all of which were empty even of books, he saw that the form on the cross that overlooked the altar seemed bloated, its ill-defined grey shape drooping forward as though poised to plump on the floor. Whatever Father Sinclough had said, the church was surely no longer in use, at least not in any conventional sense. Had the priest espoused a new faith? That needn't concern Fairman so long as he retrieved the book.

The pulpit stood to the left of the altar. As Fairman climbed the creaky steps, the banisters seemed to turn moist in his grasp. A book was resting on the lectern, and he could have thought it quivered a little with eagerness—his own. The embossed colophon showed a night sky in which unfamiliar constellations hinted at the features of an inhuman face. A stagnant smell that Fairman recognised rose from the pages as he opened it to confirm that it was the eighth volume, *Of the Dreaming of Creation*. He felt his eyes bulge with the strain of reading in the dimness. "All creation is a dream of itself. The universe dreamed itself into being and continues to do so . . . "

In that case, he thought, the book must be a dream as well. Perhaps he was on the edge of understanding why his time in Gulshaw had grown to resemble one—and then another thought overtook him. At last he grasped something Father Sinclough had said. Although he no longer had the street map, he could visualise the layout of the town, and he had indeed been led a dance. The route he'd followed to collect the books had described the first steps of the dance he'd watched at the Shaw.

At once he felt as if more than the insight had taken hold of his mind. He heard a huge prolonged dribbling breath behind him. It was surely just a wave that had sprawled onto the beach and lingered over retreating, but it felt like a symbol or an omen. So was the book, unless it was more than that. As he read on he could have taken it for a dream he was having, even if not on his own behalf, and was about to waken from. "Who hath shared the dreams the old stones dream, or those of the earth or the sea? Who hath beheld the sleeping visions of the mountains, or been a party to the reveries of the moon? The Ancient Ones partake of the dreams of the farthest stars, where universe and void consume each other for eternity. Let the mage prepare himself before venturing to invite them into his mind . . . " This and much more seemed to sink past Fairman's comprehension to root itself in his brain. The unchanging dimness gave him no sense of how long he had been at the lectern when he became aware of activity in the churchyard. A crowd was advancing on the church.

Father Sinclough led the procession, and the mayoress supported him on her arm. Though their progress seemed so furtive that Fairman hadn't noticed them until they were past the gate, their faces suggested that they meant to be respectful. They were followed by everyone who had taken care of the books, even Rhoda Bickerstaff, who looked not quite resigned nor yet just nervously expectant. Behind them came people Fairman had encountered in the town—Janine Berry and her staff, the proprietors of Fishing For You and Fish It Up, the Gulshaw players apart from Eric Headon— and then people he thought he had passed in the street or seen on the beach. It occurred to him that while he was reading at the lectern he'd heard a good deal of traffic on the promenade but hadn't realised its significance. By the time Eunice Spriggs and Father

Sinclough crossed the threshold, much of the crowd was still outside the gate.

The priest shuffled to the front pew with the mayoress, where they sat and gazed up at Fairman. As they entered the church he'd thought Eunice was doffing her hat as a mark of respect, but did women do that? Now he saw that the object she'd stuffed into her handbag hadn't been headgear in that sense. Everyone in the crowd uncovered their bald heads as they stepped into the church, the women included. Nobody was wearing beach shoes, despite their appearance and the way their rubbery feet slithered over the stone floor. Too many eyes to count were gazing up at Fairman now; it felt like being observed by a single consciousness, and not only from within the church. He ought to have suspected something of the kind, given all the phrases they had in common. He was watching the church fill up—all the pews were occupied, and newcomers were crowding three deep along the walls—when the priest raised an unstable hand. "Read, my son," he murmured. "Read to us."

To some extent Fairman was glad to return to the book. He'd caught sight of a group of familiar figures in a pew at the back of the church. As they tugged their scarves down, he could have thought they were dragging their faces lopsided or otherwise awry. The townsfolk who couldn't find space inside the church were massing around it, although not at his back, where the waves had grown slower and louder. Some of the spectators had managed to clamber up to the side windows, though he didn't know what they were able to see; the faces flattened against the panes were so blurred that he could have taken them for lumps of the fungus that clung to the stained glass. He did his best to ignore all these sights and concentrate on the book, beginning where he'd left off. Perhaps it conveyed more to the listeners than he was aware of understanding himself, because there was rapt silence except for his voice and the sluggish progression of waves behind him on the beach. At last he came to the end of the printed text and turned to the flyleaf.

"The grimoire is a tool for the unmaking of the world. What are these volumes save a nexus of ancient power? Happy the land which is bounded by them, for it shall be irradiated and transformed. Happy the denizens of that land, for they shall renew the oldest ways of shaping, when all that lived partook of a single creation. More powerful still is the mage through whom the old words find their voice, and happiest is he whose lips Gla'aki uses to address the world. Wherever He is heard He shall manifest Himself to His worshippers . . . "

Fairman was no longer reading aloud, since the page was blank. He felt as though he was hearing someone else preach—as if the book had found a voice that wasn't his. He had to speak up, because the ponderous slithering of the waves had grown louder. He was about to continue, though he'd no idea what he would say, when he glimpsed a concerted movement in the church.

Everyone in the congregation had bowed their heads. Until he looked at them he was able to take this as a gesture of respect, and then he clutched the pulpit so hard that it seemed to sweat in his grasp. Although every head was lowered so far that he could see the back of every neck, all the faces were still turned up towards him, as if their raptness had dislodged them. They were no longer intent on him, however. All the wide dislocated eyes were gazing past him.

As the protracted cumbersome sound that he'd kept hearing was repeated at his back, he could no longer avoid realising that it wasn't the noise of waves, because it had left the beach. He felt himself tremble, and the pulpit shivered; he thought the entire church did. Perhaps the tremor that spread through the floor and rose up the walls to the gloomy timbers under the roof betrayed how massive the presence was, so weighty that it shook the earth, or perhaps the vibration was a sign of its power. Then the church grew as still as the multitude of unblinking eyes, and Fairman had to turn and look behind him.

He was being watched from beyond the altar. An eye was peering through each of the windows that framed it—an eye as large as Fairman's head. They looked as if they were using the church for a mask. He found himself struggling to feel equal to the sight; perhaps he could survive it, since the eyes were no less blurred than the vast pallid face out of which they were craning. Then a third eye swelled like a moist fleshy balloon through the wall above the crucifix and stooped towards him on a flexible greyish trunk the thickness of a tree. It was followed by the face, which absorbed the cross as it seeped through the stones around it—a whitish spongy moon-shaped face twice Fairman's height, featureless except for the stems of the eyes and a circular thick-lipped mouth. It was followed by a sample of the body, an oval mass bristling with restless spines as long as Fairman's arm, as the face leaned over the altar towards him.

He couldn't move. His hands might have been fastened to the pulpit, and his legs felt as if they would give way if he tried to flee. He did his desperate best to tell himself that he could bear the scrutiny if he closed his eyes, but worse was to come. A breath that smelled like the essence and the source of the stagnant Gulshaw odour overwhelmed him as the face descended to bestow a kiss that engulfed his head.

It made his skull feel malleable, close to gelatinous. As the sensations expanded through the whole of him he felt his flesh squirm like a grub. He even thought his brain shifted wakefully inside his cranium, an insect in a chrysalis. As long as the cold spongy lips lingered on him he seemed to forget how to breathe. At last they withdrew, and he heard a vast body shuffle backwards out of the church.

Was it dread or some other factor that made it hard for him to open his eyes? When he succeeded in raising the rubbery lids he saw that the windows beside the altar were empty, the wall bare except for the figure lolling off the cross. As he turned to the congregation he felt as if something apart from himself was looking out through his eyes; he might even have thought there was movement within them. The sensation wasn't quite enough to distract him from the spectacle before him—the sight of everybody in the church raising their heads to let the faces resume their positions on the skulls like jellyfish sliding down rocks. In a few moments he was almost able to think he couldn't have seen that, since the congregation was so innocently intent on him, as though waiting for a sign. He had no idea how to respond, but perhaps the sight of him was enough, because Father Sinclough was rising to his feet, helped by his companion. The priest shuffled forward and stooped lower still, bowing not to the altar but to Fairman.

Eunice Spriggs followed his example before supporting him along the aisle. His fellow keepers of the books stepped forward to bow, and the other occupants of the front rows did. By the time the entire congregation had done so and left the church Fairman had no sense of how long he'd spent in the pulpit, resting his loose hands beside the book. Even the crowd in the churchyard had bowed in his direction or otherwise inclined their shapes towards him. He'd glimpsed the most uncontrollably misshapen at the back of the crowd before they flopped away towards the woods, he guessed, or wherever else they hid.

When he emerged from the church with the book in his hands he found Father Sinclough waiting outside the porch. He wondered if the priest was clinging to a remnant of his old vocation until Father Sinclough said "We were guided in our choice, my son. I was never the man for the task."

Fairman moved his unwieldy tongue around his mouth until they felt more familiar. "What task?"

"When your books were entrusted to me I wasn't sure how to proceed. I confess it, I was afraid to keep them with me, to take all that upon myself. Until you spoke today I didn't realise why I was guided to distribute them." He seemed to be apologising for some presumption as he said "I'm sure I haven't got your calling. You're the one who can restore the word."

"Edit the books, do you mean?" Fairman felt as if he was trying to recapture his old self too. "You'll want to keep us in Gulshaw, then."

"Not at all." The priest shook his head so vigorously that his scalp wobbled, and the bald woman beside him did all that too. "We'll still have the benefit," Father Sinclough said. "You go forth and seed the world."

The last cars were departing uphill or along the seafront. The newborn sea glittered beneath a piercing sun all the way to the horizon. While the fog had dissipated as if Gulshaw no longer needed to be veiled, Fairman seemed to feel it on if not within him. Had it impregnated everything it touched? When he made his way along the promenade, clutching the book in both hands like a talisman, he thought he saw the hotels and the buildings beyond them swell up almost imperceptibly as a greyness merged with them. Perhaps it was just the angle of the sun, although this didn't quite explain how they glistened while his flesh prickled in a feverish response.

In his room at the Wyleave he opened the safe, even though it seemed unnecessary to protect the book. He sensed how the darkness welcomed the newcomer. He shut the door and gazed at the marks his fingers left, moist blotches without whorls. He plodded downstairs to find Janine Berry behind the counter, adjusting the hair on her head. "Would you like us to move you to the honeymoon suite?" she said with nervous coyness.

"I think that might be most appropriate."

"You'll be in there when you've fetched your lady."

"It's appreciated," Fairman said and was accosted by a thought. "Whoever moves me will need the combination of the safe."

"You don't think anybody still needs to be told that, Leonard."

He might have produced some kind of a laugh at his thoughtlessness if his mobile hadn't clanked with an incoming message. "Well," he said, having read it, "Gulshaw does it again. Think of someone and they come."

"You go and get her. Everything will be ready when you're back."

Sandra's message said that she was fifteen minutes from Gulshaw. Coming to collect you, he responded on his way to the car. As he drove uphill he saw that all the shops were open, and the streets were peopled too. It occurred to him that the Gulshaw Players weren't the only townsfolk to put on a performance. He didn't need to tell any of the inhabitants that the town had a new visitor.

He parked on the station forecourt and was on the platform in time to meet the solitary figure who left the train. She looked unexpectedly vulnerable—too slight and slim by local standards—while the profusion of red hair that framed her small delicate determined face seemed unfamiliar after his days in Gulshaw. He felt himself swell with a new emotion as he strode forward, stretching out his arms, not far enough to daunt her. "Sandra," he said. "Welcome to our town. There's so much more to see."

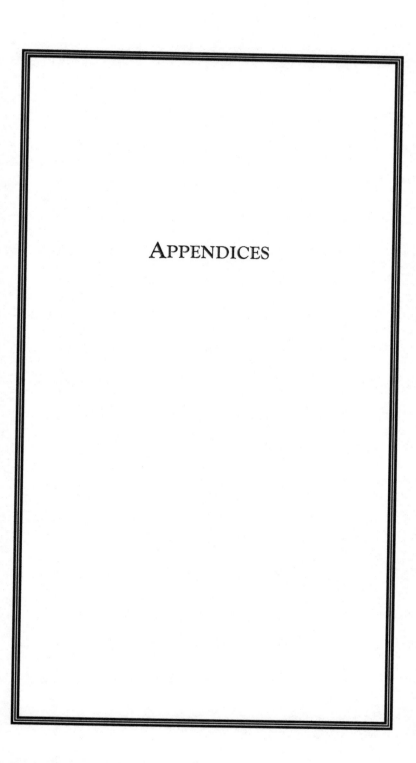

APPENDICES

APPENDICES

THE SUCCESSOR

(First draft of "Cold Print")

THE NIGHT WHIRLED WITH SNOW, BUT DEREK SHERIDAN scanned newspaper paragraphs in the warmth and protection of a bus. His eye caught a headline: *Brutal Murder in Ruined Church*—and went on to ascertain that a corpse had been discovered early that morning in a church hidden among the city centre's[1] brick alleys, that the corpse's face had been frightfully mutilated, that the mutilations had been oval and resembled, etc; but at that point his attention lost its hold. He folded the newspaper—the *Mercy Hill Chronicle*—and slipped a paperback from his inside pocket.

An expensive paperback, he thought, but worth it. The pale-blue cover showed the colophon of Sweden's Ultimate Press and the title *The Experiments of Youth*; and its price of 30/- stemmed from the fact that it was banned in Britain. For no conceivable reason, Sheridan mentally added as the bus ploughed on through the night, and began to read.

Several pages later he glanced out of the window, through which the light streamed and caught up the snowflakes. The bus was turning into Mason Street; he got up and negotiated the stairs,

---

[1] "center's" in manuscript.

jumped off the platform, skidded on the pavement. To the left, up a side street of libraries and offices, several cars had already converged on Harrison Chambers and been parked. He hastily protected the book with his newspaper, hurried along the street and beneath the arched doorway into the red-carpeted hall.

Among the framed paintings signs directed the newcomer through Harrison Chambers, but Sheridan was familiar with these halls. He clattered up the wide stone staircase on the left, across a precariously-polished landing, up a more modern flight and into a hall; where, through the first door on the left, a polite murmur, a tentative whir of projection machinery and the blare of recorded classical music located Brichester's one film society. He hung his coat in an introductory hallway and entered the cinema.

A young lady exchanged his ticket for a programme[2], and he passed on to a plush seat. The ashtray before him was opposed by a *No Smoking* mural. He checked his watch, determined to read, and withdrawing the book, opened it where finger-blackened pages touched pure white.

Something intruded on his consciousness; there was someone watching. He looked up sharply into bloodshot eyes across the aisle. He knew the man by sight; indeed, every member of the society must know him. His origins were obscure, perhaps because his irrepressible conversation clung to one subject: commercial American films of the 1930s, worthless movies which the society preferred to ignore. The man's shabby, dishevelled appearance and anxious pleas for agreement made it difficult for anybody next to whom he sat—and he insisted on seating himself amiably by anyone convenient—to make their real opinions known. And now he had turned from conversation to regard Sheridan.

Or perhaps it was Sheridan's book which had drawn his gaze. Yes, that was it—his eyes moved to the pale-blue cover, back to Sheridan. The latter filtered emotion from his own expression, waiting for some reaction from beyond the aisle: disgust, interest, enquiry—at present he could not decide. And at that point colour[3] withdrew from the watcher's face, it blurred, darkness drew across the cinema, the projector commenced to click.

The film was obscurely symbolic, and analysis preoccupied Sheridan as he brushed past his recent watcher on the way out. He

2 "program" in manuscript.
3 "color" in manuscript.

leaned into the snow which swept toward him, looked back as a car began to rev somewhere in the rear. The other man was standing under a lamppost, staring blindly through the aggressive white.

The society exhibited each Friday, excluding the summer months when the room's lack of ventilation would have been insupportable. Next Friday found Sheridan at the cinema earlier than he had intended; the Brichester buses were unpredictable. There were few members yet in their seats; he quickly read the typewritten page which preceded each film, returned to *The Pleasures of Adam and Ryan—Experiments of Youth*'s replacement. He was quite engrossed by the time someone padded down the aisle and waited for him to draw back his knees.

He looked up, saw the thin worried face above him. He expressed his resentment with a long outward breath, concentrated on the book as he stood up. The other slid past and eased himself down beside Sheridan, who angrily reread a sentence three times. There came a preparatory cough beside him. Here goes American rubbish, he thought, but his expectations were confounded by the question: "Do you like that sort of book?"

The question was toneless; Sheridan could not deduce from it its prompting emotion. "Yes," he replied with a touch of defiance. "Why?"

"Oh, I don't mean to sound impertinent," came a hasty answer. "I was just wondering where you got it."

"Got it while I was in Stockholm," said Sheridan automatically, trying to understand the anxiety which fluctuated in his questioner's eyes.

"That's where you got that other one? I mean, you don't know anywhere in Brichester that sells them?" The other leaned closer, and a slight odour[4] of must floated across. "You see, I know a place you can get some. I'll take you if you like."

"Oh, do you?" Sheridan withdrew slightly. That expression—the man was anxious to please, seemed terrified of loneliness; was he seeking companionship?—because if so, Sheridan did not relish the idea of his friendship.

"Yes, I'll take you if you want—better go soon before all the ones you want are gone. Do you want me to take you? Can you go tomorrow night?"

---

[4] "odor" in manuscript.

Sheridan held back. But after all, a local source of Ultimate Press books was something to know about; he could stay aloof from his guide, the same way he never talked to his barber. "Yes, I'm free tomorrow night," he plunged as darkness softened the outlines of plush.

And the following evening he leaned back under a shop's awning while the snow edged toward him. Couples strolled and peered in the glowing windows, ran hand in hand for a bus; figures passed back and forth on the pavements as he squinted at them; a muttering old woman scrabbled in a wastebin and passing teenagers stared at her. Through all this the man he awaited eventually arrived, hunched up against the transient snowflakes, his hands in the pocket of a dirty overcoat.

"We'll have to be quick," the other sniffed. "It's a long way."

Now he tells me, thought Sheridan, and followed his guide as he pressed into the adamant snow. The luminous windows began to fade behind them, the pavements lost their level security. Less[5] cars hissed past. Now, only ten minutes away from a main Brichester street he passed along every day, Sheridan was lost amid a web of twisting back streets and alleys behind buildings, black pubs warm against the weather, cars slanting against the kerb, here and there a wooden door leading nowhere or a set of windows ominously boarded up. From the way the man he followed darted into side turnings, Sheridan felt he was meant to become disoriented.

One side of the street gaped without warning; a patch of waste ground where lone walls and twisted metal surfaces drank the snow. They slithered over loose bricks and pits to the other side, then up another street. It was deserted; on the corner flakes sifted through a lack of plate-glass window into a desolate shop, its walls flapping posters. Over the city a dog barked at the pearly sky. A plane throbbed overhead, serving only to sharpen the cold and silence.

"How much further?" Sheridan did not call after his leader; he was determined to deter conversation. He drew his collar closed again and battled on.

And when they had hurried back and forth along roads deeper into the area, finally down a narrow alley black with water, blocked with dustbins, they emerged opposite their destination. Shops had

---

[5] Yes, I know – "fewer" – and I wince while transcribing the error.

possessed the landscape again; on street level a drably curtained café offered tea with chips, and below it rough stone steps searched out an unpainted door. Black railings protected a sunken window. Books pressing against the pane inside announced the shop's identity; snow and grime prevented further vision.

"That's it," the man remarked, his voice flat against the unlit shops. "We can go down."

Sheridan slipped on the black steps, one hand gritting on the rusty railings, the other touching for an unpleasant moment the must-exuding overcoat of the man below. The door creaked open on a long room blocked by books. There were no shelves; sets of Victorian encyclopaedias climbed the walls, children's annuals barricaded them in, travel books and biographies framed pillars between which one had to ease. Dust whirled at the opening of the door, defined by the rays which filtered through the window,[6] and irritated Derek Sheridan's nostrils.

"There they are," and a dirty hand pointed one cracked and bitten nail. "Don't knock anything over."

All that could be seen in the direction indicated was a rickety table, atop it several copies of *The Clique* ageing beside a clogged typewriter, but Sheridan followed the other. And when the journals were fanned across the tabletop, doubling back covers, a sedate little set of Ultimate Press volumes was revealed. Sheridan leaned forward, his eyes widening in pleasure. The murky atmosphere stained the pale covers, but he could decipher spinal titles: *Two Boys and a Whip*, *A Libertine's Journal*, *The Descent of William Harrison*—already he was feeling for his wallet. He turned to declare his appreciation, but his companion's bloodshot eyes were fixed on that end of the room furthest from the door; Sheridan strained his gaze in that direction. The left side of the wall contained a second door, its upper half relieved by a dusty pane of frosted glass. It denoted a room, he assumed; but the room beyond was dark.

This did, however, convey to him that the bookshop lacked an essential. "Is the shopkeeper about?" he asked, drawing the other's gaze from that noncommittal door. But was there not an alternative possibility? "I suppose you're not the shopkeeper?" he continued.

"No, I'm not," and the gaze returned—albeit rather unwill-

---

[6] comma omitted in manuscript.

ingly—to the frosted glass. "But he won't be here tonight. You can pay me, and I'll give him the money."

Sheridan hesitated; but, after all, the important thing was for him to get these books. "Very well, here you are," he said, and slid notes from the wallet.

The other pushed the books across the dirt of the table. Sheridan grimaced, picked them up and dusted them as best he could, while the notes were inexpertly folded and stuffed into a fraying pocket. Then the ragged man timidly made for the street entrance.

"Don't you intend to wrap them up? No, on second thoughts I'll do it myself." Sheridan pulled brown paper from a roller, letting a good deal of discoloured[7] wrapping coil on the floor before he discovered a satisfactory stretch. Having parcelled the novels, discarded a moist roll of adhesive tape and finally retained the package with string, he too made his way to the exit. The bookseller's assistant—one assumed that was his occupation—was staring again at the door to what must be the owner's office; but no shadow or sound betrayed an occupant.

Snow drove down the street. Sheridan, intent on holding the books, slowly realised that he was being led in a direction different from his approach; this time he almost called out—but he refused to acknowledge his dependence. After all, they must be heading in the direction he required; and eventually they came forth from a maze of tall menacing office buildings onto a wide main street where streetlamps released snowflakes and buses zoomed by. Sheridan's stop lay some yards away; but though he had tried to be alert, he had no idea how they has arrived here. He stood until the man, snorting nasal mucus back, turned away—presumably homeward. "Good night," Sheridan called, and struck out in the other direction.

The week resolved itself into routine. He stared across the roofs and glimpsed the Severn glint; might he not visit the bookshop again? "I think I may go to that bookshop again," he informed the drab figure he had deliberately sat behind, the next Friday. The member beside him threw an enquiring glance. "I'll take you whenever you want," said the man in front.

Thus increased Sheridan's familiarity with the bookshop—the

---

[7] "discolored" in the manuscript.

shop itself, not its location; for his guide seemed to have a perverse talent for seeking out new routes. He led Sheridan under arches so prolonged they became tunnels, over black canals which Sheridan never knew existed in Brichester, under bridges which thundered with passing trains but which Sheridan—although he travelled frequently on the Brichester lines—could not place; down streets of lifeless houses, streets which, however devious, always at last attained the furtive store. Sheridan searched for landmarks along the route, but found none, not even the name of a street.

But other facts took shape for him as he carried away more books. That office door remained closed—even though he sometimes felt that life lurked in the room beyond; but if the owner were in there, why did he never come out? Particularly as his assistant displayed so little aptitude for his job. One Saturday night this shabby assistant undercharged Sheridan by more than a pound; the Saturday after that, he sent a pillar of books thudding to the dusty boards; always it was obvious that he wished to leave the shop as quickly as possible. Sheridan came almost to dread the man's fumbling among the piled volumes each weekend.

But habits are displaced by others. Sheridan had not known of the existence of an art film group, concealed in a college on Mercy Hill; but he was invited to join the group, before he missed the rare films they offered on Saturday evenings. One Thursday afternoon, when a grey sky menaced the flat office roofs, he accepted their invitation over the phone, felt a twinge of unease as he wondered how he would now tap his source of erotica. He walked out of the office at five o'clock and was caught up by the crowd, still wondering.

The man, whose name he never knew, was slinking through the crowd, eyes downcast. Sheridan's hand on his shoulder pulled his lips back in a snarl before he looked up.

"Look here," said Sheridan, "I can't make it this Saturday. I'm free now—can you take me to the shop?"

"I'm not supposed to," the other answered. "We can't go during the week."

The answer seemed a little obscure. "Well, if I don't get there tonight, I don't know when I can make it again."

For some reason, that aroused his listener. "All right, but we'll have to hurry. You'll look right if there's no books there when we get there." And with a whirl that flopped his long greasy hair against his blackened collar, the man flinched away through the hastening bodies.

This time the route soon dodged between two stores and down a long stone stairway; along a muddy alley where warehouses loomed above a railway cutting, then into a street whose patch of waste ground Sheridan thought he recognised. In his hurry, the man was taking less care than usual. Sheridan held back for a moment and scanned the house-fronts; and there, between two bedroom windows to the right, was the sign, letters black on white—Miller Street: 3. He hurried in pursuit of the round-shouldered figure, right across the waste patch, left up a desolate road, right up an alley where doors opened on overgrown yards and opaque windows, right again into another alley whose doors were locked. He knew already that this broke forth opposite the bookshop.

The man lingered as he brought forth his key from a torn pocket, dislodging newspaper cuttings and fluff. His steps down to the door seemed darkly contemplative. The lock grated and then Sheridan followed. "I don't know whether there is any," came a whisper through the drifting particles.

Only one book hid behind the journals on the table: *The Affairs of Hurstmonceaux and Faversham*. Sheridan grabbed it before it was smeared by the seller's fingers and flapped open his wallet. The other snatched the notes and crumpled them into his pocket; and at that moment there came an odd sound—like the very beginning of a cry, immediately choked off. There followed a muted scuffle which could be occurring only in the hidden office. Sheridan became aware of hands plucking at him and a voice muttering "Come on, come *on!*"; the assistant shoved him toward the exit. Sheridan managed a glimpse of the frosted glass as he was pushed out the door, and for the first time he saw evidence of life behind the store. A shadow passed across the pane. It must be the shopkeeper, and one gathered from his attitude that he was dragging something heavy; but some distorting quality of the glass, or perhaps the shop-keeper's preoccupied position, produced an horrible illusion—for in that instant Sheridan thought the man was headless.

Strangely disturbed, Sheridan ascended the steps; the assistant hurried after him. Below them a door burst open, and something scuttled across the boards. Teetering on a stair, the assistant lunged for the exit door and slammed it behind him, then urged Sheridan onto street level and back along the route they had recently taken.

The man was obviously unnerved; perhaps he had been ordered not to enter the shop unheralded, but this did not explain to his companion his unease near a group of silent and disused warehouses, nor his near-panic in the vicinity of a sluggish canal. His relief was patent when they found themselves on a main street. Derek Sheridan called through the engulfing crowd: "See you next Thursday, same place I met you today," but he was not sure that the call was heard.

He was even less sure when, a week later, the other had not arrived by five-thirty. Black clouds pressed overhead; the street lamps seemed threatened by night. The traffic stopped and ground forward, pedestrians ran and dodged; but the man did not approach or appear. Still, it didn't matter, Sheridan decided and levered himself away from an office wall. He could find his own way, although once one left the main streets the lights surrendered to darkness.

The urban throb faded behind him. At the end of an alley where white vapours boiled up from a railway cutting into which frowned warehouses, he found himself unsure of the correct turning. The rattle of a rusty pram attracted him to the mother who propelled it; "can you direct me to Miller Street?" he asked, and she looked at him oddly before pointing and elaborating.

Sleet dulled the pavements by the time he came abreast of the railings and lurking window. Belatedly shoving his sodden newspaper into his pocket, he negotiated the steps to the door.

He pushed the door; it creaked and opened onto the silence of piled books. Inside, Sheridan glanced around him. Nearby paper rustled, perhaps stirred by a rat behind the walls of books; otherwise the quiet released no sound. With unthinking stealth, he attained the table and lifted the magazines—the usual issues with possibly the usual dust coating them. Behind them the table top was bare. If this were not to be a wasted journey, Sheridan must make contact with the shopkeeper or his assistant.

The office door thudded open. A figure stood there, one side of its face impinged upon by the glare of a naked light bulb. From the twilight of the shop, Sheridan could make out few details of the newcomer; but even on that first sight he noticed that the tweed suit hung oddly on the body, and that the body itself never ceased a slight lateral swaying, as if restless for some movement. "Welcome to Roles' Bookshop," the figure said.

Sheridan was ushered into the compressed office. The unshaded bulb held the room in an adamant light; it equated the book-strewn desk, the papers and letters which littered the floor, a glass-fronted bookcase left of the door, but it could make nothing of the blackness which menaced beyond a gap in the right-hand wall, crudely shattered.

The room's occupant caught Sheridan's curious gaze. "Oh, that goes—down," he said, and seated himself behind the desk. "You couldn't see anything down there. Anyway, welcome. I'm sorry I haven't met you before—I probably wouldn't be speaking to you even now, but things have happened which have upset my routine. Sooner or later, I get to know all those who visit my place."

Sheridan glanced about for possible concealments of Ultimate Press books; the other continued: "Now you come here in search of erotica? I can understand your motives; the most significant knowledge is always that which is circulated underground—all through the ages the worthwhile existences have been subterranean. Your friends at the Ultimate Press understand this. Did you know they're aiming for publication of the banned Henricus Pott book next year?"

"Oh, they are?" Sheridan said, a little warily.

"Yes. I'm sure it would interest you, even though it's not the usual Ultimate book—would you say you had a thirst for forbidden knowledge? Of course. Well, this one's been suppressed for centuries; you understand that all the authorities thought it better that people didn't know of the black gulfs which opened under their feet—of the shapes which rose out of night . . . And I don't doubt that some people might be unnerved by the truths which are concealed in everything around them, might even go mad. I think you could read these books, though."

"Oh, yes, I think so. I feel that the written word, whatever it may be, shouldn't be represented as something more powerful."

"Well. I can't offer you Johannes Henricus, because it's well-nigh impossible to obtain his book at the moment; but I do have something just as interesting in that line." The shopkeeper stood up and moved to the bookcase with that peculiar undulant gait. He lifted down a shelf carrying nine bulky volumes, knocked books from the desk with his elbow and carefully set down the shelf in the cleared space. During this operation, Sheridan noticed something; and felt a faint surge of revulsion as he realised the man was deformed. The bookseller's hands were very large, at least as far as the palms were concerned; but his thick fingers were barely the length of a normal person's first joints. His thumbs seemed to grip the shelf with unusual strength.

"These were in a pile of Victorian encyclopaedias out there," said the shopkeeper. "I threw some rubbish—about accountancy, I think—out of this bookcase to make room for them. Imagine a bookseller not knowing he had such items in stock! Incredible, isn't it? Unless you suppose the idea was to hide them and try to forget they were there... Well, anyway. Have a glance through." He settled back in his chair.

The pages of the first volume were brittle under Sheridan's fingers. It fell open at what appeared to be a description of some subterranean route; but there were dark hints in the directions that one would not survive that route. There would be the sound of heavy, uneven footsteps, a swollen glowing figure when one turned to look, the sound of something vast heaving out of a nighted lake ahead. Sheridan glanced up to tap the room's reassuring light and found the other watching steadily from across the desk. He read on. Somewhere above the caverns was Brichester, but down here were only endless passages where unseen shapes hopped and scuttled in pursuit, grottos in whose depths great eyes awoke and peered, cave-cities of black towers where roads led still downward, a corridor blocked by a high stone wall beyond which lurked Y'golonac. Sheridan found the name Y'golonac underlined wherever it appeared.[8]

"What's the significance of this?" he asked, handing the open book to its owner.

"I assume you mean its present significance. Let me meander for a while. Y'golonac is currently of urgent importance because of a discovery made by a tramp. How does one become a tramp? I don't know; but months ago, this man was wandering the Brichester back streets in search of shelter—no money, no friends to give him refuge. It was raining, and he climbed under a canal bridge; and down there he found an archway, just above the water level. He managed to reach it and enter. There was a passage beyond; the deeper one went the better the shelter, he thought, and he lit his way downward with a box of matches, his only luxury. He would have

[8] On the left-hand page of the exercise book (left blank for comments and revisions) I later wrote "lead on to narration by speaker + include any effective detail".

expected to reach a storehouse of some sort, but the passage merely descended into the dark.

"He forged on so long that he lost track of time; finally one side of the passage fell away, into a gulf from which there came a dim luminescence, too slight to show him the contents of the abyss. But he thought he saw something gigantic, pulsing in the depths. As he turned to hurry back the way he had come, the matches fell out of his hand and clattered down the cliff—he never heard them strike bottom, but the throbbing down there seemed to intensify. He was suddenly afraid of the black corridor which had brought him there. There was another corridor leading away from the abyss, and he could see some distance along it by the light from the gulf—so he struck off that way. He didn't get far; he thought the corridor curved ahead of him, but in fact he came up against a wall which blocked the passage. He stood and looked at it, and wondered what to do.

"Then there came a deafening bass mutter from beyond the wall, and Y'golonac heaved up above it. His head and arms rose out of his body and reached toward the man, and the man went mad. The tramp's mind retreated into itself, away from the spongy face covered with eyes, the hands which tore from him one shriek of shocking horror. Can you imagine the feelings of someone when one of the Old Ones comes forth from the dark to peer at him? And can you imagine what passed through the mind of Y'golonac, if he has thoughts as you understand the word? After centuries of waiting in the dark beyond that wall, where only the tottering eyeless things of the dark came to worship him, came a messenger from the surface world—a planet of life still waiting to be cleared off. The messenger was quite docile now, quite coherent—but he would never be able to sleep at night again, nor perhaps ever. He could be allowed to return to the surface with perfect safety—but he would not go alone.

"So the tramp returned through the corridors, but this time there was a vast slithering behind him, a giant bulk towering over him. And when he drew near the surface—by another exit; there are countless openings into the depths from every town—he became aware of some process commencing behind him; there was a suffocating tension behind him. He never turned to look, and by this restraint he must have saved whatever sanity remained to him. For to come out on the surface, Y'golonac had to change shape. There were portions of his real body which would not metamorphose, and all the time he was on the surface his form was straining to return to its old shape, as it had been on Tond and nearer the rim; but by the time they came forth into a street, one could look at him and stay sane.

"He killed a man and took his place, and settled down to accustom himself to the environment. He could have burst forth and destroyed the earth as you know it, and left it desolate and haunted—but he must wait until the others were ready. He could wait—for what is time to the Old Ones? So he kept the tramp as his priest, and the tramp performed the elder rites before him and called down the demons of the stars, and brought victims to him to strengthen Y'golonac for the long wait. And when he wasn't worshipping Y'golonac, the man clung to shreds of his earlier life and kept to crowded places—the cinemas, public houses—as if for protection. As if there were protection anywhere on this planet, when even on this town's streets there are things fluttering, unseen, unheard, waiting for night. And one day he did something which displeased Y'golonac, and he became a victim, leaving Y'golonac free on the surface."

For the first time the speaker paused. Sheridan shifted and searched for some remark; he was frankly uneasy. But the other, having allowed him to assimilate the story, went on.

"That's why Y'golonac has become so important. Do you realise that when the time comes—and it will come—mankind will crumble before the powers that pour in from space? If you were to worship Y'golonac, you might survive. If you were to become his priest, you would live on through the eons of change which are to come. You say you're in pursuit of forbidden knowledge. Will you serve Y'golonac and see the cosmic pits which even the *Revelations of Glaaki* there never mentions?"

Sheridan replied as calmly as he could. "No, I don't think I can do that. It'd make too many demands on my life." He glanced over his shoulder at the door behind him and discovered that, sometime while he had listened to the bookseller, that door had closed and locked.

The voice said behind him: "Have you already guessed that I am Y'golonac?"

He turned. The figure behind the desk had risen, and he seemed to loom above Sheridan, to be on the point of bloating and filling the room. The voice muttered on. "There is an opening from the tunnels below very near here, and when that tramp—I never knew his name; I think he must have forgotten it down there at the wall—brought me forth I came in here and fed on the shopkeeper, Roles, and took his place. I've been here on the surface since then. That man brought victims, however he could lure them here—but when you came—there were vibrations about you—I felt you might be a fitting successor to that tramp . . . And he committed suicide when he brought you here last time, on a night he'd been told to stay away; I was feeding . . . I killed him."

Sheridan's back was to the wall. He glanced at the door again; there was no key in the lock.

"You don't believe me?" came an accusing mutter. "Look at that paper you have in your pocket!"

Sheridan automatically drew out the *Weekly News* and saw at once the shouted headlines: **BRICHESTER POLICE WARNING—MANIAC LOOSE!**—followed by a description of the latest of a series of atrocities; the body of a tramp had been discovered half-submerged in a canal—"portions of the body had been hacked away so as to suggest on first sight that they had been eaten". The Brichester police were puzzled.

"Now you realise the truth," the other insisted. "What other life can there be for you? You will do what is necessary to strengthen me, until at last the black cities rise from the depths—Cthulhu walks again—Glaaki climbs forth from the lake—Daoloth rends the barriers to free those which claw for entry . . . All this you will see as it once was—that tramp was nothing; I would never have let him see the ultimate, but to you I will reveal the black gulf beyond the rim, and what stirs there out of the light—and when you have been instructed, you will see me as Y'golonac . . . Can you still refuse?"

"I'm sorry, but I must," Sheridan replied. "And I've got an appointment to keep. I'm afraid you'll have to let me go now."

"What must I do to convince you? If you refuse to be my priest, you will never leave here."

Sheridan's voice rose. "I insist that you let me out! How dare you!" He suddenly became aware of the emptiness of the room; there was nothing with which he could threaten this madman. Unless the other opened the door for him, he was trapped. Then—he grabbed the first book of the *Revelations of Glaaki* and held it open in both hands. "If you don't unlock that door, I shall rip this apart! Page by page!"

But this time there came no answer. The figure was approaching around the desk, cutting off the jagged hole in the wall which too late appeared as an avenue of escape. Sheridan tore out one page, then another, then ripped away one board. The slow swaying approach continued—and Sheridan stopped appalled, his hands wrenching the binding apart in reaction. For the tweed suit was falling from what he had taken to be a man, and a naked shape was stepping forth toward him.

His mind virtually gave way at that point, as his whole being rushed inward in an attempt to escape that sight. The face was already twitching into quite another shape when the head sank out of sight between the shoulders with a dreadful wet sound. Derek Sheridan backed away, trying to throw out a scream which would express the revulsion and pure horror which gripped him. Yet as the headless thing swayed closer, a marginal thought comforted him; the object could not see, nor could it do any real harm, deformed as it was—unless he went insane when those swollen hands found him. Now it had backed him into a corner. Behind it, unattainable, he saw the locked door with its pane of frosted glass. The naked, white-shelled form came closer, and Sheridan managed at last to scream—but it was only the beginning of a shriek, immediately cut off, as the hands descended toward his face and the moist red mouths opened in their palms.

THE FRANKLYN PARAGRAPHS

(First Draft)

HE PUSHED THE BUTTON A THIRD TIME, BUT THE INDICATOR did not blink. The elevator must be on some upper floor, listening for a summons; but to Harvey Shea it seemed as if the machine were holding back, laughing at him down the shaft. Irate, he grabbed the tubular banister and stumped up the stairs.

He had been fuming long before he entered under the white stone archway of the Parkinson Library and surrendered his brief-case to a bored doorman in exchange for a numbered tag. On the bus, for example, he had been forced to sit with his back to the engine and nausea soon filled his mouth with a taste of stale egg; to make it worse, his fellow passengers' elbows forbade him to open the briefcase and distract himself with a little reading. One of these days, he vowed as he crossed the first-floor landing and continued upward past a labyrinthine mural map, he would buy a car. When he could afford it.

Of course, his annoyance could be traced farther back than the bus—to the previous day's wedding reception, in fact. To begin with, he disliked wedding receptions for their static artificiality; he had attended this one only because the bridegroom had been a school friend of his, someone he felt he would like to meet again.

But the invitation had manifestly been made out of a sense of duty; Shea hardly succeeded in speaking to his friend, whose eyes and endearments were all for the bride—a girl whom Shea immediately detested—and whose pleasantries only included a circle of boisterous bureaucrats with whom Shea found himself ill at ease. One young effeminate man whose purpose at the reception was not clear caught the bridegroom's remark that Shea was a writer. His enthusiasm turned sour, however, when he learned that Shea wrote ghost stories. To the man's question "Why do you write that sort of story?" Shea, sensing a lurking sarcasm, replied truthfully: "For the money." A young bystanding couple supposed that was intended to be funny, and laughed. If he had informed them that this was the truth Shea supposed they would take that to be funny. "But don't you have any purpose in writing?" the man persisted. "I mean, do you believe in the things you write about?" Shea immediately retorted: "Of course. All my work represents an attack on complacency," and made off for a further unsuccessful attempt to contact his friend.

He reached the library's fifth floor, passed through the entrance marked *Religion and Philosophy*. The clock above the librarian's desk proclaimed two o'clock. The long high room was almost empty, the seats at the reading-tables sat alone, the February sun through the rectangular panes held everything still. What nagged at him was a suspicion that the man at the reception had doubted his word; that the other presumed Shea to churn out his stories with no regard for meaning or implication. This was untrue. Surely Shea's very presence in this library proved so much. A hack writer would never visit libraries to check esoteric details—particularly not philosophical details, which Shea was pursuing now as he slipped free a book and carried it to the table.

He turned back the front board. As he had thought, the volume had not been out since his last reading; the darkening column of last year's datestamps was followed by a single virginal 1964 stamp, the date of his last visit. One could scarcely expect the book—*Magic, Legend and the Infinite Self*—to be popular considering the specialised subject and the hostility of the few reviews. Shea recalled one—was it the *Times Literary Supplement*?—"Beginning with concepts derived from Samuel Beckett, this work progresses in directions which one suspects are not clear even to the author. It does, however, provide me with my Cocktail Party Quote of the week: 'The being sometimes known as *God* is travelling at the speed of light (p. 114)". To Shea this seemed unfair. Certainly some of Franklyn's dicta dropped with dull thuds, but others had provided Shea with impressive chapter headings; for example, "Civilisation has changed nothing with regard to the supernatural. The greatest city of the world represents merely a façade behind which humanity hopes to lose the shapes which throb and crawl. If all the nights of a hemisphere were to fail one night, we would find ourselves no different from the caveman who cowered by his fire from colossi which lumbered and peered in the darkness"—if not: "If we accept that 'I think, therefore I am' we are surely in danger of either acknowledging intelligence in trees and stones or relegating such objects to the status of our own hallucinations. In the former case, what may be the intentions of our surroundings? In the latter, what may lie beyond our comforting delusions?—this is the basis of the Daoloth cycle."

Shea flipped onwards, past the dedication—"To Sebastian"—and came to the chapter he required. A glance at the clock placed him at ten past two. A girl in dark blue descended stairs in the distance of the room and threaded her way between the bookcases with a diminishing pile of books. Her heels clipped away on[1] the tiled floor and echoed along the tables. Shea began to copy passages into his notebook with a retractable pen whose nib retreated shyly into the barrel:

"Dreams, of course, are explicable in terms of the infinite self. We all, each of us, exist simultaneously in countless bodies and entities throughout the universe; and if we are conditioned by our surroundings to accept egotistically our human bodies as ourselves, let us not forget that our alien bodies have similarly accepted themselves as all, nor that all these entities are merely different facets of our ultimate personalities, imprisoned in their own place. It is not surprising, therefore, that fragments of experience filter from one facet to another in the form of dreams. Aware of the real nature of these nocturnal memories, I can reveal that I exist as a globular being covered with hair which rolls through catacombs on the planet Tond."

Shea flicked up the next page.

"Can't move—darkness—straining to move—closed in—wet

---

[1] "on" omitted in manuscript.

earth pressing me down from all sides—can't get out—trying to hold on to other places out in the light—dragged back in here—darkness pressing down—fingers won't move—"

Shea tossed the page back and attempted to separate the one he required from that to which he had clumsily turned. But his fingernail discovered no division. He had turned over correctly and found what, to say the least, seemed a non sequitur[2], and incoherent to boot. This was certainly not the continuation of Franklyn's argument, nor did he recall ever having passed it on his journeys through the book. He concentrated and attempted to make sense of the passage; but was met only by repetition of the words "page 192". Anything for relief; he returned as directed to the previous chapter.

"The death of the body represents in theory a step closer to our central self, since it means one personality less to distract the centre. It is obvious, of course, that we can never attain ourselves, for even should the universe end and with it all life, still each self would throw out spiritual messengers in an attempt to postpone the eternal imprisonment in knowledge and nothingness. But apart from this, the least violence at the moment of death, the least mental disturbance, or any tampering with the body or the possessions with which in life it was connected, and the personality is drawn back to earth as a revenant. It is less likely that a luxurious tomb retains its inhabitant, as the Egyptians supposed. Cremation is the only release; and even then, the revenant may be unable to free itself from its environment in life. Its mental struggles may be manifested as communications to the living; for example, a dead author may manifest himself through the print of his work—"

Shea stopped and looked up. He was remembering a paragraph in the *Brichester Weekly News*. He rarely paid attention to newspapers—his own world was complete enough without including anyone else's—but this news report he had read, understood, and mentally filed as of minor importance: the report of the death from heart failure of Roland Franklyn. It must have been a week ago. Shea stared ahead at the angled sheet of sunlight for some time; then a look of pleasant shock invaded his face. An elderly man in a thick black overcoat lowered himself into a seat at the next table, and Shea turned away and blocked his book from view with a crooked arm. Then he read on.

[2] "non sequitir" in manuscript.

At the top of the next page Franklyn spoke again, but with increasing hysteria. "Knew I wanted to be cremated—the bitch had me buried here—must escape in time—can feel someone reading this—someone aware— come here for God's sake and get me out— don't know where I am—can't see—save me for Christ's sake—"

It progressed down the lines of print, but increasingly blurred. Shea shut the book and stood up quickly, and the elderly man glanced at him with blank curiosity. Shea hurried to the bookcase and slammed the volume into place. How could he trace the source of these manifestations? A twinge of doubt at what he was pursuing passed through him, but he hastened to the librarian's desk to shake it off. This could change his writing completely; a confirmation of what he wrote—rather, of what he *believed*—certainly sufficient to confound any would-be critics he might meet in the future! Indeed, the fact that he had been chosen to receive this communication virtually proved the honesty of his occult writing.

The girl at the librarian's desk looked up through spectacles bought to acquire an intellectual air but merely suggesting myopia. "May I help you?" she enquired.

Mentally he checked through the file. The *Weekly News* had not mentioned Franklyn's funeral; it would therefore be pointless to adjourn to the reading room. "I was wondering about Roland Franklyn—the author of that book I was reading," he began. "He died recently, you know. Would you have any idea where he was buried?"

She regarded him sympathetically. "I'm very sorry, but I just don't know," she said. "You might try the reading room. Surely the newspapers will have something."

"Ah, yes. I'll do that, thank you. But perhaps you could tell me where he lived? Someone must still be in residence—wasn't he married?"

Her expression showed she was trying to understand. "He was, I believe, but I don't know precisely where the house was. You realise he came in here very seldom. When he did, he was always with a young man . . . " She glanced at the pen poised between her finger and thumb. Her gaze returned to him, and it was divided between kindness and determination. "Listen, I hope you won't mind if I speak personally, but you look so—well, as if you intend to rush off to his place. I shouldn't go just yet, not when the funeral will hardly be over. Because after all, his wife won't know you, will she? And I imagine she'd want to be alone at the moment. You could—send flowers, or something . . ."

She had interpreted his words in a way not clear to Shea. He hoped his real motives would impress her. "I think you've misunderstood me. I'm a writer," he revealed, a revelation he would make to few people besides librarians, since at school he had let it slip and a master had asked whether he had come to school in search of inspiration. Shea had been as misguided then as he apparently was now. Her sympathy faded and was replaced by an expression beyond his analysis. "Well, as I say, I'm afraid I can't direct you," she told him. "And I shouldn't think there'd be much at his house to interest you."

He slurred his feet outside *Religion and Philosophy*. He had certainly mishandled that encounter. But he refused to allow it to bother him. Similar incidents happened too often these days. Franklyn was more important—and where now? He clattered down the wide stone stairs, past the great mellow reading amphitheatre, and down a passage to slide his tag to the doorman and heft his briefcase into the sharp sunlit open air.

Once outside, he glanced about for inspiration and quickly grasped the promise made by a phone-box at his left. They could never have withdrawn Franklyn's number so soon—but had he been on the telephone? Shea ruffled the pages of the directory and his twin copied him beyond a smoke-stained mirror. He reached a page labelled FRAN. Someone had scribbled a number across the paper with a pen that expired on the final digit. Shea slid down the ladder of names: Franciscus, Dr Noel (that had a Gothic boom about it, he thought)—Franklinn, Col. W. H.—Franklyn, B. O.—Franklyn, Roland. 10 Fairview Terrace: MERcy Hill 2103. His hand fell to the receiver and drew away. His errand—the shifting vision he had of it—should not be accomplished by telephone. The address he had traced was certainly that of the writer, not that of some other Roland Franklyn, accountant or labourer. He must go there directly and question as delicately as possible whoever he found in that house.

After that its course planned itself. He made for the nearby terminus and boarded a bus for Mercy Hill. He was the only passenger on the upper deck, and the vehicle's crew were nowhere in sight. He took the front seat, placed his case between his feet and mused. A woman was peering in a display window ahead of him, while her two children punched each other behind her. On his right he could spy into an office; figures bent over desks, a girl stood up soundlessly to switch on a light. The driver approached below with his mate, threw away the remains of a cigarette and climbed into place. At last the bus shuddered[3] and moved forward lazily. Everything insisted that nothing could happen; this was to be a quiet, uneventful hour. But not, Shea thought, for him. Soon he would face proof that his suspicions of the supernatural were correct. The bus plunged across an intersection where traffic lights retained and released unaware of the deserted roads, and up Mercy Hill[4]. The conductor arrived and examined Shea's change while the latter named his destination. It was the next stop but one.

Fairview Terrace formed a step on the hill; the house he sought was on the higher side of the street, perched on a lawn reached by a steep stone flight between moist mossy brick walls. Shea struggled to the top, where unchecked grass marked off the progress of a flagged path to the door. Perhaps the building before him had been modern twenty years ago; it was impossible to decide, for the tenant's personality had conquered the architect's creation—a straight chimney had been clumsily built up into a frustum, a windowless wing had spread from the right, new red brick glared as it blocked a second-floor casement. Shea thought that the house looked perverse—distorted into a form which squatted evilly on the wet green grass. But this was to be expected from the dwelling of someone whose spirit diffused through the corridors of the universe. Shea strode forward and knocked on the door.

The woman revealed as the door swept inwards was dressed in black, which brooded against the dark red perspective of the hall—but her black was not the colour[5] of mourning. It clung too intimately to her body and large firm breasts. A head taller than Shea, she stared down from below waved bleached hair out of a face which powder had only blanched and imperfectly softened. She did not speak, neither did her unreadable expression.

"Is this the residence of Roland Franklyn?" he asked, and while he spoke realised his error.

"It was," she said without grief, "and I suppose you could say it still is . . . Who are you? One of his friends?"

Shea considered that his only course was to betray himself again.

---

[3] "shuddered" deleted in manuscript, but substitution is not extant.
[4] Altered to "Mercy Hill's" in manuscript, but addition is not extant.   [5] "colour" in manuscript.

"No, I'm a writer—occult literature and so forth, and I rather thought I might be able to—well, get at the deeper significance of what I write here—but I suppose this is hardly the best of times . . . "

But she was already ushering him in. "One has to be sure," she said[6] closing the door, "you could have been another Sebastian . . . What exactly was it you wanted?"

As he stared about the hall he hardly knew. The wallpaper looked flayed; it was as though he were standing in the raw intestine of some loathsome colossus. What added to the unreal and oppressive appearance of the tortured walls, whose unrelieved colour pressed heavily towards him, was the total absence of furniture; he surmised that the decorations had recently been evacuated. Her body had now turned from the door to agree with her inquisitive face. "I'm afraid—I'm afraid I don't even know how long it is since the funeral," he said, and when her face stayed enquiring continued: "I suppose Mr Franklyn has been buried?"

"Oh yes, I've had him buried right enough," and she led the way into a room on the left of the hall. Something in her hip-swinging walk under the low-backed dress Shea found unappetising. She indicated an armchair and continued: "Top of the hill. Mercy Cemetery, two days ago. Will you have something to drink?"

Shea accepted, if only in order to be alone and reconsider his line of attack in the light of this meeting with the actual Mrs Franklyn— a woman far different from the image of her he had contemplated on the bus. He gazed around the room. It was choked with furniture: two tables with coiling legs, any number of plump dark green armchairs, a sideboard carrying an army of dusty splintered cocktail glasses, a tightly rolled carpet showing its blackened reptilian underside. He noticed the telephone on a table just inside the door, presumably pulled in to the limit of its cord, still hanging on grimly with one hand on the skirting-board. The door opened and he switched his attention to the tinkling chandelier.

"So you've come to find the real thing?" she confirmed as she sat down opposite him, after setting down the tray of liquor and glasses on a low oval table lifted from behind a chair. "You believe in what you write, but you've never actually come up against it?"

"Exactly. I feel my work lacks conviction. One psychic experience would transmute it into something—meaningful."

---

[6] No comma in manuscript

"Listen," she said, leaning forward over the tray. "Let me tell you what your meaningful experience would be like if it was here you had it. You're expecting something that'll uplift you—enlighten you. Believe me, it wouldn't. Oh, it'd enlighten you if you want to put it like that—but it's loathsome and putrid. Listen what I have to put up with. Just this morning, when I was throwing his things out of the hall, the hatstand turned soft and wet as I lifted it and fat boneless things started pushing between my fingers. And later I was coming up the path and I saw that the flagstones were only a paper-thin covering over a black gulf where gigantic corpses were fumbling all over each other. And he returns in more direct ways—for the last two nights I've heard him flopping round the room next to mine pawing at the walls, and yesterday I looked out of the window and saw his face staring in at me—only it was eight feet across. He controls the whole house—almost."

"But—forgive me—why then don't you leave it?"

"Run, you mean? Not likely—not when I've got him where I want him at last. Twenty years I've been forced further and further back into a corner while his house took up all the room. Now he's dead. Heart failure, the doctor called it—but since he was one of them as well he knew it wasn't heart failure when my husband—" a look briefly crossed her face as though she had plunged her hand into something foul—"when *my husband* was found staring out of the window as if whatever he'd seen up in the sky had killed him. I suppose it had. Now the house is mine. I knew he'd come back and I'm just waiting to see how he'll appear next. Oh, you needn't look like that—" for Shea had involuntarily turned to the window as an indefinable shadow crossed it—"I think he'll have enough to occupy his mind at the moment. And when that's over, there's all the other forms in which he's crawling round the universe to contend with. He won't have time to bother me."

Some time ago Shea had commenced to question her warnings to him. "What strikes me is the fact that you've spent some nights here," he began. "Surely—"

"You expected I should be afraid? Not with the kind of mummery he's putting on. No, there was one good point about the way he tried to educate me when we were first married—students, we were—it toughened me up. Oh, I cried when he took me to Temphill and insisted that if I loved him I wouldn't look away from the things dancing on the graves there—but I could stand it by the

time he took me down the steps below the waste ground in
Clotton . . . And when he started to take over the house that used to
be ours, I wasn't intimidated. I knew what he was capable of doing,
though, so I pretended to shrink back and let him expand into all
the rooms. Almost all. It was my house as much as his, you can
appreciate that, but I was prepared to wait until I could make it all
mine." She tilted back her head to catch the last trickle of liquor in
her glass.

Shea had decided that he disliked this woman, and that he was
unlikely to learn anything further of interest from her. Besides, if
what he had deduced from the message in Franklyn's book were
correct, he was actually wasting time. But he was unwilling to leave
before he had tried for a peek at Franklyn's secrets. "I think you've
dissuaded me from actual psychic experience," he told her. "But
perhaps I could look through what your husband left behind? In his
rooms?"

She stood up and waited while he opened the door. "I suppose
upstairs will be what you want," she said from the inflamed hall,
"upstairs . . . My room is that way too, of course—my room—my
bed—which he didn't want anyway . . . Yes, come up. Take whatever interests you."

By now Shea had changed his mind. "Or—do I have the time?"
he mused aloud. "Look, one question first. I know your husband
was buried—but didn't he wish to be cremated?"

He was using his interpretation of part of Franklyn's cry for help
only as an evasive action, and had not prepared herself for his
response. She turned, one hand on the banister. "He did," she said.
"First, so what? And second, how did you find that out?"

"Oh, I heard. We writers, you know, must keep in touch . . . "

"Secret sources, eh? You gave yourself away that time, didn't
you?" She was approaching him, and the alluring smile on the stairs
had changed to a sneer. "Or was it anything except go upstairs? You
and Sebastian and the rest of his dirty admirers, you're all the
same . . . Don't know which is worse, that or your crawling for the
monsters you dig up . . . Yes, I had him buried, and he doesn't like
it, does he? He can feel the things waking up and pushing their way
up for him, can he? Nyarlathotep that he was always on about, he
doesn't like it when the minions come to claim him for
Nyarlathotep . . . Well, they should reach him any minute now, so
you go and be with him. Be with him at the end, you—"

Shea, having backed away as she spoke, finally swung round and ran down the molten passage out to the welcoming green lawn. The faded sunlit vistas below him failed to calm the formless rage he felt. However, he had learned what he had intended to learn: the burial-place of Roland Franklyn—the source of the paragraphs. He must climb to reach it. He circled the house, which was now ominously silent, and saw leading upward from the edge opposite his point of arrival an alley between angled walls. Beyond this, he plodded up a steep road past a school across whose yard children were chasing each other to plunge into a scrum at the bus-stop. He barely noticed them; he concentrated on his progress up the ramped streets and his fury at the woman in the house above Brichester, insulting him and drooling over her husband's helplessness in death like some fat black spider turning the sticky grey bundle which once was a fly.

The sun was setting when he reached the cemetery. The weed-grown walls were softened by its golden light, and the dead avenues diminished into a hazy distance. The graveyard was carved from the hill; far down the vague perspective the looming hospital floated above the blurred stones. The morose caretaker pointed away down one of the avenues[7], watched over by a frozen angel whose face was half white mutilation; over the caretaker's shoulder against the low wall Shea could see the mellow faces of the houses banked away towards the glittering river; just below on the hill tubes of scaffolding stood glinting dully on waste ground. Shea turned as the other limped away, and started for the misted avenue.

His feet swished through the wet grass as he pressed on, peering at the fallen pockmarked headstones, the paralysed broken-nosed angels yearning heavenwards, white with droppings[8]. He searched among the truncated spires which formed before him, the occasional shining lovingly-tended memorial, the perched urns like empty glasses left on a sideboard and forgotten, the tangled masses of rusty iron railing in the grass. As bedraggled spikes overcame the graves, he struck a balding path which crept on through the obscurity. Behind the retreating mist materialised the catacombs hollowed from the hillside behind dark flaking bars, some concealed by ivy—and ahead of him on the left he discovered a new stone. He

---

[7] "one of them" in manuscript, where the preceding sentence was subsequently inserted.
[8] The next three sentences deleted in manuscript: "The sun's shade was creeping towards him; he passed into it and his skin chilled. There was a new gravestone ahead on the left. He approached it across the greying grass and read the name: Roland Franklyn." .

approached and stood above it; at the head of the rectangle of new gravel he read the name—Roland Franklyn. Below it were the framing dates; nothing more.

He stood and waited, for what he did not know. The clean pebbles and marker betrayed nothing. Over him the sun drew its chilling shade. He considered what, precisely, did he expect to happen, and how could he force it? If he could communicate with the author of the paragraphs—He moved around the grave, and the pebbles stirred. A shudder took him before he realised that his shadow had shifted the gravel. He stooped towards the earth above the oppressed, imprisoning coffin, and opened his mouth to speak. Thus he stayed, reddening slightly at the thought of some mourner coming upon him speaking to a grave. Indeed, his speech would carry far across the cemetery through the silence caught in the swelling fog. No sample of the city's eternal hoot and hum filtered through the colourless blanket[9] below. In this contemplative quiet, his intentions seemed questionable. He could not see that anything was likely to transpire; he had the messages in the library, the confrontation on Fairview Terrace—it was enough. He straightened up.

The sound which he then heard in the sharpened silence came from a direction he could not locate. Distance, source, direction, identity, all were befogged among the fading avenues. It could have come from further down the hill, perhaps the building project he had noticed; it could have been a foreman shouting for finish over the thumping hammers and drills. This very uncertainty made it worse, spreading inexorably across Shea's future. For he was never sure that the sound was, or was not, that of a muffled bubbling voice crying out in terror as fists struggled into life at last and beat on the lid of a casket as it was dragged downwards, downwards . . .

He made himself turn deliberately and hurried back towards the gate, invisible at a remove from him he could not visualise. His hands shaking in his pockets, he persevered along the diseased path, a sickly half-buried caterpillar, between the black knotted trees and carvings marking unknown sights and truths. Grim spires loomed in the murk and menaced him. He passed under the iron-grilled entrance arch at last, but it was no better. Past the waiting metal tubes of the housing project he came upon the school, ominously

---

[9] "colorless" in manuscript.

crouching amid the vapours; and his shudder at its air of intelligent expectancy was intensified by the suspicion that before a day had passed it would be babbling with children, all watched and pawed by he knew not what unseen agents. From that point onward the secret windows of every house seemed on the point of revealing their festering life to him; one red-curtained window glowing above a deserted shopping street had a particular conviction of evil.

The lift which should carry him to his apartment did not work; for a moment he wondered what precise conjunction of forces had stopped it. Then he tried to smother his conjectures, but this proved futile. He did not bother to lock the door of his flat, nor did he glance at an unfinished page of his latest story, lying on his desk atop a fan of tales. Later, perhaps, he would destroy his manuscripts; as yet he could not grasp whatever future might be his. He pushed up the window and peered out into the night, as breaths of fog curled round him into the room. The aggressive neons of Brichester around him looked unreal, unsure of their own reality. It seemed that the sun would never arise over the haunted city. His greatest fear was that dawn, when it came, would prove to be no exorcism.

MUSHROOMS FROM MERSEYSIDE

It is not recommended to search
For the herd that feast under the church.
Their recherché cuisine
Would soon turn your face green
And would equally make your guts lurch.

Stay well clear of Byatis's face!
As a mug it's an utter disgrace.
It is bearded with worms,
Every one of which squirms.
If you're seized you're consumed without trace.

Take care by the river at Clotton!
It's not that the bridge there is rotten,
But that under the torrent,
And wholly abhorrent,
Lurk entities better forgotten.

Beware of the place of the cone!
For those insects won't leave you alone.
They will enter your head
And consume you with dread
As they merge with your flesh and your bone.

After Daoloth shows you what's real,
You'll find nothing has any appeal.
No use closing your eyes,
Because once you're made wise
Every sense will deliver the deal.

Any sounds that you hear on the plain
You'd do well to keep out of your brain.
"Every alien note"
(*Necronomicon* quote)
"Shapes a horror to drive you insane."

If you lodge in the house of the witch
You'll be tricked into rousing her lich
And performing a rite
In the depths of the night
That will waken a Thing in a niche.

The portal to Yuggoth's a tower
That offers an uncanny power.
If you climb to the peak
You'll be prompted to shriek
By vistas to make your mind cower.

Shortly after his death, Stanley Brooke
Reappeared as a species of spook.
A more accurate term
Would be some kind of worm
Not to mention an uncanny crook.

Never stay at the Goatswood hotel!
There's no telling what answers the bell.
And to finish your stay
You'll be carried away
By a creature too hellish for Hell.

You may think it's a bit of a swizz
That your visitor's only a phiz
That's suspended in air,
But you'd better beware—
The next face that flies off won't be his.

You shouldn't assume that he's rude,
Any fellow who's full of a brood.
You may feel more than ill
When his guts start to spill—
Just be grateful the chap isn't nude.

The ruler of Derd upon Tond
Had good reason to feel he'd been conned
When the globes that rotate
Sent him down to a fate
Of a kind of which none could be fond.

Despite his ambition to read,
Y'golonac yields to the need
To consume the bookseller
And then pass for the feller.
Librarians too should take heed.

If you find extra words in a book
Don't give them so much as a look.
For they've come from a grave,
And it's too late to save
The stiff who used them as a hook.

They should never have given me ink,
But not for the reason you think.
For along with my tales
My first amateur fails
Were drawings to make the sane blink.

To encourage the stars to come right,
Ghroth exerts all its mass and its might.
When the pattern takes shape
All observers will gape
As they witness the primeval night.

If you visit the place in the pines
You may burst into protests and whines,
Having learned that your kin
Occupy just one skin—
They did give you some ominous signs.

If you think that there's far too much light
In a village that's waiting for night,
Don't stick round to remark,
For what lives in the dark
Will turn you to a terrified mite.

If you're hearing a voice on the strand
Better pray that you don't understand.
There's no use to beseech
What looms over the beach,
Still less all the shapes in the sand.

The secret beneath Warrendown
Has made quite a few readers frown.
If you find your brow furrows,
Just ponder on burrows
And soon you may think of a noun.

Should Daoloth give you a name,
Don't imagine it's part of a game.
What you're called you'll become,
Which will leave your mind numb
And will earn you the wrong kind of fame.

One Cameron Thaddeus Nash
Thought Lovecraft a writer of trash,
And again and again
Nash would drone from his den
And believe that he wrote with panache.

Have a care near the tower of Selcouth!
For his creatures can prove he spoke sooth.
In the depths of the wood
They stay hungry for food
Although lifetimes have passed since their youth.

You'll find it's no use to cry "Pish!"
When your meal seems again to be fish.
Because once you're replete
You will be what you eat
And assume any shape that you wish.

Though the church may allege it's eternal,
The end of the world is its kernel,
Since its occult beliefs
Invoke ancient motifs
And forces far worse than infernal.

TWO POEMS BY
EDWARD PICKMAN DERBY

Azathot

That bubbling pool o
at the creation's ce
languishing mindlessl
Amorphous it is, of
Sightless and eyeless,
ceaselessly bubbling fo
which burst before
or form some cosm
the worlds, the bei
Once had it eyes,
of elder god had p

AZATHOTH

That bubbling pool daemonic elder slime
at the creation's centre, the universe's hub,
languishing mindlessly in the lightless void.
Amorphous it is, of blasphemous hue,
sightless and eyeless, featureless it is—
ceaselessly bubbling forth unspeakable things
which burst before the tinkling stars can
      crystallinely wink
or form some cosmic blight. From here proceeded
the worlds, the beings upon them.
Once had it eyes, but the blinding light
of elder god had put them out
before the first man stirred. Long will it exist
not live, not dead, but idiotically there.
And when at last that long-foreseen day comes
when the Old Ones will once more return
and stir from their foul darkness, it will come
to engulf all the universe, its elder counterpart
will also rise and blast forever
Azathoth into non-existence.

VISION OF A SHOGGOTH

Early one morning, before the sun had cast
its sanguinary rays upon my bedroom's wall,
I rose to walk in clime of early Fall.
I paced on paths where many feet had passed

and then, seeking I knew not what,
I left the places many feet had trod
and striking out across the grassy sward
came to a wood which I had often thought

resembled primeval forests. Into its shade I stole
as does a thief. I tried to find a mark
to prove that others had gone into the dark
between the trees. And soon, beside a bole

of hoary oak, printed in marshy ground
a mark I saw. Such as was never made
by earthy creature, but one from the shade
of cosmic shadows. Could I have turned around

I would have fled from that accursed spot;
but I was powerless, caught by spell hypnotical,
staring at this, this evidence of things fantastical
lying beyond life's veil, this blasphemous blot

from foot of revenant from elder world.
Shapeless it seemed, but symmetrical, abominably
as if it aped some idiot geometry.
Then while I stood, the last veil was then unfurled

and drawn away; and while my puny mind
fell into shards, and, gibbering, fled to hide,
the trees themselves were pushed aside
and from their shade a thing of nightmare oozed.

And as an odour of unspeakable must,
decay, corruption, rose to the sky,
the horror raised a liquid tentacle; and I
buried my face in adoration in the dust.

The Horror in the Crystal

(A Fragment)

IT WAS ON A DULL DAY, OF GREY SKY AND CEASELESS DRIZZLING
rain, that the small thing happened—that trivial event which set
off that chain of events which were to end in such hideous horror.

That day in November, I was standing under an awning to shelter
from the stinging drizzle, falling at an angle against the bitterly cold
wind. I had come down to London to see an exhibition of artwork
in the morbidly atmospheric style, possibly to purchase one or two
of the cheaper originals; I had, however, been hopelessly outbid over
the one painting that had interested me—a picture of yawning
graves and abominable figures feasting upon unnameable fare in a
moonlit cemetery. I stood, now, in this street under the awning;
above me, the sky was strangely grey, seeming to stretch into a void
for immeasureable distances. Uncertain of what to do, unwilling to
brave the icy rain once more, I stared across the roadway at the
opposite pavement. And it was then that the thing happened.

Across the street were great grim-appearing houses, of very
narrow frontage, and, I think, four storeys. On my side of the street
were dim-lit bookshops, of ancient awnings and windows grimed, it
seemed, with the dust of centuries—shops which could exist

nowhere but in this archaic side-street down which I had been cutting when the storm broke; but even these buildings were modern beside those which I now perceived across the dim street. These buildings were black, oblique-angled, seeming to lean sickeningly toward me. And, as I have mentioned, I was staring across at these alien-featured buildings, when a door opened in one of them, and a strange figure stepped out into the roadway.

My gaze was attracted to this individual at once. I could see little of him; his face was partly covered by his collar, upturned against the rain, and partly by his down-pulled soft hat. Thus I only glimpsed a little of the flesh of his face, but what I did perceive made me unaccountably uneasy. The face glistened and shone, as if it was covered with some liquid. Having stood under my awning for some little time, I knew that he had not entered the building during that period. Unless there was a second entrance to the place; and surely whatever rain might have touched him would have dried before now. Whence, then, this unaccountable wetness?

And this was not all. What had fixed my eyes upon him had not been this strange wetness, but rather his weird bearing. He moved out of that warped doorway in an undeniably furtive manner, peering up and down the street as if he were half-blind. Also, when he began to move away, he seemed to move with a vaguely frog-like half-hopping motion. And his hand was in the left pocket of his coat, which seemed to bulge as if it contained more than a hand. It could be some object less unnatural than a gun or weapon; but whatever it would be found to be, the strange creature obviously did not intend to relinquish it easily.

Rusty Links

I AM NOT A LOVECRAFT-HATER, I SHOULD SAY AT THE OUTSET, as Brunner or Knight. I am, I think, as great a fan of Lovecraft and the Cthulhu Mythos as any of those who have become known by their memoirs of HPL. But I also think that the Mythos is not the sort of thing which every writer is able to use convincingly in his work; and that is why I am disgusted by certain authors' feeble attempts to follow in HPL's footsteps. This article is an outpouring of my disgust at the revolting work of these various writers, who will be named in good time.

Before I begin, however, let me make clear that I don't consider HPL to be the only author who could write a good Cthulhu-Mythos story. The writers whose work nauseates me are, thank ghod, few. Such authors as CASmith, ZBBishop, FBLong, Kuttner, Howard[1], Hazel Heald, usually Bloch, and quite a number of others, could be relied upon to produce convincing and well-written Mythos work. And so we return to those who, unfortunately, could not . . .

The first author to come under dissection is one who, apparently, is acknowledged as a fitting successor to HPL by everyone but myself. This author is August Derleth. Derleth, in my opinion, suffers from over-exuberance in writing Mythos stories. He seems to have a Cecil B. de Mille love of the spectacular: if he has one deity in

---

[1] "Wandrei, Whitehead" erased in manuscript.

Rusty
Links...

by J.Ramsey Campbell..

I am not a Lovecraft-hater, I should say at the outset, as Brunner or Knight.

I am, I think, as great a fan of Lovecraft and the Cthulhu Mythos as any of those who have become known by their memoirs of HPL. But I also think that the Mythos is not the sort of thing which every writer is able to use convincingly in his work: and that is why I am disgusted by certain authors' feeble attempts to follow in HPL's footsteps. This article is an outpouring of my disgust at the revolting work of these various writers, who will be named in good time.

Before I begin, however, let me make clear that I don't consider HPL to be the only author who could write a good Cthulhu-Mythos story. The writers whose work nauseates me are, thank ghod, few. Such authors as CASmith, ZBBishop, FBLong, Kuttner, Howard, Wandrei, Whitehead, Hazel Heald, usually Bloch, and quite a number of others, could be relied upon to produce convincing and well-written Mythos work. And so we return to those who unfortunately, could not...

The first author to come under dissection is one who, apparently, is acknowledged as a fitting successor to HPL by everyone but myself. This author is August Derleth. Derleth, in my opinion, suffers from over-exuberance in writing Mythos stories. He seems to have a Cecil B. de a story, he appears to think it might be lonely in there, for he often throws in a couple more to keep it company.

More of this later, but first of all there is a similarity between a certain Derleth story and one of HPL's which seems to me to be too obvious to be coincidental. It seems very much to me that Derleth, unable to think of an original ending for *The Whippoorwills in the Hills*[2], merely lifted out the main parts of the last paragraph of *The Rats in the Walls* and made appropriate substitutions. For comparison, here are the relevant portions of each climax:

That is what they say I said when they found me in the blackness... crouching over the plump, half-eaten body of Capt Norrys, with my own cat... tearing at my throat. Now they have... shut me into this barred room at Hanwell... They must know that I did not do it. They must know it was the rats; the slithering scurrying rats whose scampering will never let me sleep: the rats they can never hear; the rats, the rats in the walls.

Now compare Derleth's:

That is what they say I was screaming when they found me crouching beside the body of poor Amelia Hutchins, tearing at her throat. And that is why they have locked me into this room with the bars at the window... I never raised mu hand against any human being... It was the whippoorwills; the incessantly calling whippoorwills; the damnable lurking whippoorwills waiting out there; the whippoorwills, the whippoorwills in the hills.

Apart from one or two minor differences, one can substitute "rats in the walls" in relevant places in the second quotation and have an approximately similar passage. The rest of the Derleth story is based very firmly on certain passages in *The Dunwich Horror*.

To refer to this phenomenon of *over-exuberance* as connected with Derleth, one might look up such tales as *The Return of Hastur* and *The Sandwin Compact*, in each of which no less than *three* deities put in an appearance. In the first, Cthulhu and Hastur, together with an unnamed Elder God, fight out the possession of a human body, while in the second, Cthulhu, Ithaqua and Lloigor take it in turns to dispose of Uncle Asa. Won't the story become a little cluttered after all this?

On the other hand, *The Black Island* seems equally as spectacular, and equally as phony, as a Hollywood movie. Surely it's going

---

[2] Short story titles italicised in manuscript.

a bit too far to drop atomic bombs on Cthulhu?—after which, it may be noticed, Derleth is careful to recompose the god. Rather like the interminable series of adventure novels, in which the villain always *just* escapes from the hero, to return and annoy him in the next thrilling sequel . . .

Just before leaving Derleth, *why* on earth do his stories almost invariably end on a paragraph which is completely italicised? Is it because the endings are so feeble that he feels that this italicisation shows the reader what kind of feverish terror he *should* be feeling? . . . And yet any mention of Derleth's Cthulhu-Mythos works in critical features invariably praise the stuff and elevate him as "capable of adding to the Cthulhu Mythos in a manner which would certainly have won him HPL's approval", to quote from the dust-wrapper of *The Mask of Cthulhu*. Myself, I like most of the tales in *The Survivor and Others*, *The Lurker at the Threshold* and *Lair of the Star-Spawn*, and not much else. To use the terminology of a popular programme, I think Derleth has more "misses" than "hits".

So, leaving Derleth's mutilated corpse to the night-gaunts, we come to a story by an author whose Mythos work I normally admire: Robert Bloch. It is, in fact, his too-long delayed sequel to *The Haunter of the Dark*, *The Shadow from the Steeple*. I say "too-long-delayed" because I feel that whatever inspired Bloch to think of a sequel to the HPL story (for Bloch thought of the idea in 1936 or thereabouts[3]) had gone dead by 1949, when the story was actually written[4]. The alien terror of the Mythos is ruined in this picture of the doctor whose face was luminous in the dark—a mere amateurish modernisation of HPL's sonnet about Nyarlathotep in the *Fungi from Yuggoth*: comparable with the spate of so-called science-fictional versions of the Adam-and-Eve legend, rife in the zines a few years ago.

The two Adolph de Castro stories, *The Last Test* and *The Electric Executioner*, are in no sense Cthulhu-Mythos: the references to the Mythos seem to have been included as afterthoughts, and it's obvious that these stories were originally intended to have nothing to do with HPL. As for *The Executioner*—however one looks at this, it is utterly ridiculous! A maniac goes around with a modified electric chair, expecting everyone to allow him to execute them, and

---

[3] I assume I was confusing this with "The Shambler from the Stars".
[4] I took the date of publication to be also the year it was written.

ends up finally by putting his own head in for no good reason and killing himself. Ultimately, it turns out that he was on the other side of the state at the time, participating in some kind of ritual, even though no reason whatsoever is given why he should feel this urge to teleport. Sorry, but it's crud as *any* sort of story!

Finally, I'd like to broadcast my aversion to a story which wasn't intended as a Mythos story, as far as I know—in fact, I'm damned if I can work out what it *was* intended as!—but does have some connection with HPL, since it's by his one-time wife, Sonia Greene or Davis. The story is *Four O'Clock*, and reminds me of Harvey Kurtzman parodying Poe. It concerns someone who is haunted by a man—though we never get to know *why*—who finally rises, out of the rotting earth of a graveyard, in the shape of a *clock*, no less! Surrealist, perhaps? . . .

So I end this dissection of my various hates in the Lovecraft Mythos: rusty links in the chain of stories of the HPL circle of authors. I've left quite a few authors in a much-mutilated state, and I've no doubt that my article will end up in the same state when you lot have finished with it: I await the letters. Confirmed HPL-haters need *not* write . . .

LOVECRAFT IN RETROSPECT

1969

I F I HADN'T BEEN ASKED TO WRITE SOME COMMENTS ON Lovecraft I should probably never have said all this. But I first began to doubt Lovecraft's stature on re-reading *The Haunter of the Dark*. Specifically, what could have led Lovecraft into the psychological absurdity of a death scene narrated by its frantically scribbling victim? The convention that one must demonstrate how a story could have reached its reader, of course; but adherence to a convention is no substitute for coherent creation. And the realization that this—one of his last and most respected tales—shows Lovecraft to have progressed at least in this aspect no further than the ludicrous melodrama of his distastefully sensationalist revision *The Loved Dead,* persuaded me to re-read and revalue his other "great" works. Which convinced me that although my own early writings—*The Inhabitant of the Lake* and so on—were wholehearted pastiches of Lovecraft, my subsequent work could not be other than a systematic rejection of Lovecraft's principles.

I cannot, for example, accept the principle that one must suppress characterization in order to throw the horror into clearer relief. There seems no doubt that Lovecraft conceived this as a method because his characterization was incompetent; but even if, for the sake of argument, we discuss the inherent validity of the principle, I don't see that it can be justified artistically unless the "horror" is shown to be somehow profoundly meaningful in itself. But Lovecraft wasn't Conrad or Kafka (or Hitchcock or Franju, for that matter) and the only "statement" his horror makes is that the universe is vast, hostile, *and inexorable.*

Inexorable—that was the point. I think even his admirers will admit that Lovecraft was a passive man, a victim of his own psychology and upbringing, and thus his concept of the universe could only be passive. Passive, too, was the way in which he accepted the conventional determinism and casual pessimism of the traditional horror tale. Where are the humanist tales of horror? These days, happily, some exist, but Lovecraft's one-dimensional characterization refused his characters the chance to develop or to try to control their own fate: which rendered his fatalism all the more facile.

His characters were almost all himself, of course, and in this sense he imagined the narrative happening to him. Yet the character lacked the depth one would have had every right to expect, and the cry of horror the stories should have uttered is never heard: because in story after story he was too concerned with communicating a sense of the infinitely horrible. Inevitably he failed: only mathematics can convey infinity. And he therefore fell back on telling us, time and again with progressive loss of power born of familiarity, what he was trying to communicate. I'd like to have gone along with him, but I can't become involved in the familiar fate of a musty Lovecraft bibliophile. Whatever impression he left on the genre as a whole has faded, except as preserved by a few faithful admirers, the last romantics. The sense of chaos and cosmic indifference has been powerfully conveyed by so many mainstream works that the horror tale must surely turn towards the more intimate, more personal and yet paradoxically more universal fear: Lovecraft's reticence (which never informed his style) might validly have left gaps to be filled in by our own externalized nightmares, but it needs a writer's imagination to spark off our own, while Lovecraft's either could not visualise his concepts or suffocated them in masses of biological detail. There remains *The Music* of *Erich Zann,* whose genuine reticence suggests a terror vague enough to haunt us all; and the Randolph Carter stories, where the neutral characterization is anything but fatal to the detachment of dream-fantasy. But on the whole, the dynamism of Robert E. Howard now seems more alive than the academic calculations of Lovecraft. In short, I no longer have night-mares, and I no longer have Lovecraft. Neither happens to me any more.

1994

What a prat I was! Perhaps nothing more need be said. Dave Sutton has asked me to put the above piece in context, however, so I shall. The most sinister spectre to haunt anyone may be their own youthful self; it rather seems so in my case. Those were the days when, with only a book of Lovecraft pastiches to my credit, I was trying to make a name for myself by being obnoxious in fanzines. I stomped on *King Kong* and was quite unfair, as Robert Aickman pointed out, to Kingsley Amis's *The Green Man*. I rate *Kong* and Amis much more highly now, but the scorn I spilled on them may catch the eye of some magpie anthologist when I'm no longer around to set the record straight, alas. I was confronted by the name I'd earned when the late Eric Bentcliffe asked me to read John W. Campbell's science fiction stories, which I had never read, so as to attack them in *Blazon,* the journal of The Knights of Saint Fantony. I attacked fandom instead.

Still, I'm not about to disown this piece on Lovecraft, much though I've grown to admire his work once again. Anything one writes is evidence of how one was at the time of writing. Having written a book based on Lovecraft's fears and visions I needed to move on to talk about my own, and writing the attack on his work appears to have been part, or more precisely a by-product, of that process. Once I'd got my reaction against him out of my system I was free to reevaluate him, and now he is one of the horror writers whose writing I return to most often, his letters included, and find something new each time. Without his influence on my stuff and on Fritz Leiber I might never have been heard of.

ON FOUR LOVECRAFT TALES

THE FATHERS OF THE MODERN HORROR STORY ARE POE IN America and Le Fanu in Britain, both of whom refined Gothic methods to produce seminal stories in the field. Nor should Hoffman's psychological fantasies be overlooked. If I take Lovecraft to be the most important single twentieth-century writer of tales of terror, it's because he unites the traditions that preceded him on both sides of the Atlantic and builds on their strengths. His *Supernatural Horror in Literature* is not only an appreciation of all that he found best in the genre and a critique of the flaws he saw, but also a statement of his own artistic ambitions. His fiction gives them life.

To an extent his reputation is the victim of his most famous creation, the Lovecraft Mythos. This took very gradual shape throughout most of his career, and involves inhuman beings from outer space or from other dimensions, creatures that are indifferent to man but often worshipped as gods or occult forces. He often cited references to them from the *Necronomicon*, his invented tome that took on such a life of its own that several versions by later writers have been published. The Mythos was conceived as an antidote to conventional Victorian occultism—as an attempt to reclaim the imaginative appeal of the unknown—and is only one of many ways his tales suggest worse, or greater, than they show. It is also just one of his means of reaching for a sense of wonder, the aim that produces the visionary horror of his finest work (by no means all of it belonging to the Mythos). His stories represent a search for the perfect form for the weird tale, a process in which he tried out all the forms and all the styles of prose he could.

Nevertheless the Mythos is his most visible bequest to the field, because it looks so easy to imitate or draw upon. As one of the first writers to copy Lovecraft without having known him, I must take some of the blame for the way his concept has been rendered over-explicit and over-explained, precisely the reverse of his intentions. Luckily his influence is far more profound. In his essays and letters he was able to preserve the notion of horror fiction as literature despite all the assaults pulp writing had made on its best qualities, a view that was especially fruitful in the case of Fritz Leiber, who followed his mentor's example of uniting the transatlantic traditions. Other correspondents such as Robert Bloch, Donald Wandrei and Henry Kuttner assimilated his vision into their own. More recently such diverse talents as T. E. D. Klein, Thomas Ligotti and Poppy Z. Brite have acknowledged Lovecraft's importance to their work, but who could accuse any of them of simple mimicry? His use of suggestion and allusion might seem beyond the reach of most filmmakers, but I submit *The Blair Witch Project* as the key Lovecraftian film, not least in the documentary realism he urged upon serious artists in the field and in the inexplicitness with which it conveys, to use his phrase, dread suspense.

Yet Lovecraft's achievement lies not so much in his influence as in the enduring qualities of his finest work. The field would be all the richer if more writers learned from both his care for structure and his larger principles. His yearning for the cosmic is the greatest strength of his best tales. He is one of the few masters of the tale of terror that reaches for, and often attains, awe. I'm going to examine in some detail the structures and use of language that he employed to this and other ends.

I want to start by looking at his earliest recognisably personal story, "Dagon". This was written in July 1917, and applies the principles he admired in Poe's tales of supernatural horror: " the maintenance of a single mood and achievement of a single impression in a tale, and the rigorous paring down of incidents to such as have a direct bearing on the plot and will figure prominently in the climax." Lovecraft wrote this in *Supernatural Horror in Literature*, where he analyses Poe's "The Fall of the House of Usher" as demonstrating "the essential details to emphasise, the precise incongruities and conceits to select as preliminaries or concomitants to horror, the exact incidents and allusions to throw out innocently in advance as symbols or prefigurings of each major step toward the hideous dénouement to come, the nice adjustments of cumulative force and the unerring accuracy in linkage of parts which make for faultless unity throughout and thunderous effectiveness at the climactic moment, the delicate nuances of scenic and landscape value to select in establishing and sustaining the desired mood and vitalising the desired illusion." It's worth remarking that when a writer analyses someone else's work they are often also talking about their own, and we shall see how he developed these methods in his own fiction.

August Derleth—prime mover of Arkham House, Lovecraft's first hardcover publisher—once summed up Lovecraft's structure thus: "Lovecraft got his effects by beginning soberly and with restraint, being careful to link his stories to reality, and proceeded with them with an air of doubt, as if the facts he chronicled could not mean what they did, so that the ultimate effect was all the more damning. . . . " We may observe that the opening tone is often restrained even when the material is Gothic; like Poe, Lovecraft was refining elements of the Gothic novel, focusing more closely on psychology and the supernatural. So "Dagon" opens with the lines "I am writing this under an appreciable mental strain, since by tonight I shall be no more. Penniless, and at the end of my supply of the drug which alone makes life endurable, I can bear the torture no longer; and shall cast myself from this garret window into the squalid street below." While this is undoubtedly melodramatic, it serves to warn the reader to examine the narrator's tale carefully, since it may be some extent delusional. The unreliable narrator is a favourite and certainly effective device of the genre, enriching many tales since Poe's "Tell-tale Heart" with ambiguity. It often means that the tale can be interpreted psychologically without losing its uncanny dimension. Sometimes (as in *Rosemary's Baby*, which can certainly be read as a study of prenatal paranoia) restricting the reader's view to a single consciousness works just as well.

Having established the background to the narrator's situation in just three paragraphs, Lovecraft immediately immerses us in it. "The change happened while I slept . . . " Like quite a few of his stories, "Dagon" is based on a nightmare and seems designed to convey the intensity of that experience. The sense of dislocation—of finding yourself somewhere you have no memory of reaching—will recur in later tales; it's surely a powerful symbol of psychological breakdown. The paragraphs describing the upheaved landscape recall the opening of Poe's "Usher" (itself an object lesson in setting the scene) in their oppressive vividness. Besides painting the scene in words, Lovecraft uses sound (or rather its absence) and smell to render it more immediate. There's also an early use of a technique that his detractors often seize upon—inexplicitness as a means of stimulating the reader's imagination. Here the reference to "other less describable things" that infest the mud is surely appropriate, implying that they're the remains of creatures carried up from depths so profound that the narrator can't identify the species (which a later reference suggests is prehistoric). At the same time the phrase seems intended to evoke disquiet, and it works that way for me.

The paragraphs describing the narrator's trek and its destination exemplify a style of prose Lovecraft often writes: realistic in detail—documentary, if you like—and yet incantatory in its choice of language. At times the language rises to a crescendo that includes poetic usages ("I know not why my dreams were so wild that night; but ere the waning and fantastically gibbous moon had risen far above the eastern plain, I was awake in a cold perspiration, determined to sleep no more") but just as important to its effect are the modulations that lead up to the linguistic climaxes, best represented by the paragraph that describes the pictorial carvings on the monolith. A rare lurch into cliché ("Then suddenly I saw it") betrays that this is an early tale. The story ends with what can only be a hallucination, which throws the rest of the narrative into question but doesn't, I think, lessen the power of its vision. That this vision meant a good deal to Lovecraft is clear from its recurrence and elaboration in his later work.

When writing horror it's important to be aware of the difference between this genre and that of magic realism. In "Notes on Writing Weird Fiction" (1937) Lovecraft writes "Never have a wonder taken for granted. Even when the characters are supposed to be accustomed to the wonder I try to weave an air of awe and impressiveness corresponding to what the reader should feel . . . Atmosphere, not action, is the great desideratum of weird fiction. Indeed, all that a wonder story can ever be is *a vivid picture of a certain type of human mood.*"

It's worth noting that in "Dagon" the narrator is entirely uncharacterised except by his behaviour; we never even learn what he was doing on the ship that was captured. There need be nothing wrong with this. Writers as different as Poe, Kafka and Samuel Beckett have conveyed terror by describing only a narrator's experiences, using them to illuminate his psychology. The American writer Steve Rasnic Tem has observed that the protagonist in a third-person tale of terror tends to be represented by a pronoun once they have been identified by name, so that they don't intervene too much between the narrative and our reading of their direct experience. In his essay "One View: Creating Character in Fantasy and Horror Fiction" he writes "all other objects in the story—the landscape, the other characters, the supernatural presence, even the individual events—represent some aspect of the protagonist (or victim)."

In "The Rats in the Walls" (written in August-September 1923) Lovecraft applies his documentary method to character, although the opening paragraphs are equally a chronicle of the location and an account of the tales told about it. By conflating these and the ancestry of the narrator he suggests how (again echoing Poe's "Usher") the place and its inhabitants share a common occult identity. It's also worth noting that the very first phrase establishes that the tale is set in what was then the present, adding to its immediacy. While effective tales of terror can still be set in the past—Susan Hill's *The Woman in Black*, for instance—modern work in the genre tends to use contemporary settings. Even if they've now been overtaken by nostalgia, writers such as M. R. James did at the time.

The narrator of "The Rats in the Walls" is de la Poer, the surname of a branch of Poe's ancestry. He's "a stolid Yankee" who has "merged into the greyness of Massachusetts business life". This justifies the sobriety of his narrative, but you may object that he hardly lives and breathes as a character; he isn't even allowed a first name. Even Lovecraft's most ardent admirers will admit that characterisation wasn't among his great strengths, but he developed a method that made this unnecessary, focusing on other aspects of the material. All the same, I'd argue that our narrator here is to some extent characterised by what he doesn't say. He expresses no grief over losing his injured son, and never even refers to the (deceased? estranged?) mother except to note her absence; we may conclude that he represses his emotions. Many manuals of composition recommend that writers should nurture every possible narrative skill; Stephen King's *On Writing* is a fine guide and more than that too—but you may also want to consider to what extent these skills enable you to convey and deal with your themes. Creative abilities aren't worth much if they're mechanically cultivated rather than growing organically out of the material.

The paragraphs that take us to Exham Priory maintain a light tone, the better to darken it later. The narrator's son is amused by the legends of the place, which is playfully portrayed as being "perched perilously upon a precipice", the kind of alliteration Lovecraft's apprentice Robert Bloch (later to write *Psycho* along with much else) would make central to his witty style. The son's friend Edward Norrys, who will become crucial to the tale, is said to be "a plump, amiable young man". One word in that phrase will come back to haunt the narrative, and planting this kind of almost subliminal hint can be a powerful device. The apparently superstitious villagers—not a cliché in themselves when "The Rats in the Walls" was written—regard the priory as "a haunt of fiends and werewolves". The hackneyed image both preserves the sense of rational disbelief that the accumulation of telling detail gradually undermines and prepares the way for darker revelations.

The mass of details in the next few paragraphs is artfully modulated; the subdued chronicle of the history of Exham is interspersed with hints about the family, which grow more evocative and sinister as they advance from indefinite "fireside tales" to ballads that seem disturbingly specific, and then to tales that Lovecraft makes the narrator call "hackneyed spectral lore". In fact not all of them are hackneyed, so that the phrase serves to emphasise their vivid strangeness and, in retrospect, their accuracy. It's surely a measure of Lovecraft's restraint that we are almost a third of the way through the story before he introduces the first reference to the rats of the title. The sober chronicle of the ancestor who fled to America is just ominous enough to foreshadow later events.

Having established the background, the story starts to build up telling details in the present. Note how the pet cat's restlessness is described as trite—again, a way of delaying acceptance of its significance. Similarly, the cat's later behaviour and that of its companions is presented as "picturesque" and accompanied by painterly images of architecture and lighting. By contrast, the narrator wakes into darkness from a nightmare rooted in the history of the place, and light shows him the first physical sign of the presence of the rats—or does it? Since nobody else has heard them, they could be a hallucination or proof that his senses are becoming bound up with his heritage.

As he and Norrys explore the sub-cellar they discover evidence of increasingly ancient practices; Lovecraft often uses such a progression to powerful effect. The two men keep a vigil in the cellar, and the narrator suffers a second nightmare whose climax and later significance is subtly hinted at: ". . . as I looked at these things they seemed nearer and more distinct—so distinct that I could almost observe their features. Then I did observe the flabby features of one of them—and awaked with such a scream that (. . .) Capt. Norrys, who had not slept, laughed considerably. Norrys might have laughed more—or perhaps less—had he known what it was that made me scream . . . " The alert reader may also note that Norrys is also described as "stouter" than his companion—another virtually subliminal detail that takes on a retrospective significance. During their vigil they learn that there is a vault below the sub-cellar. A progressive descent that reveals levels of new mystery is central to other Lovecraft tales—"The Mound" and "The Shadow out of Time", for instance.

Before the two men and a scientific party open the vault, the narrator has a third dream that sheds a sinister light on its predecessors without making the horror explicit. Lovecraft often allows the reader to anticipate on behalf of the protagonist, a method that can work just as well in horror as in tragedy, though it needs to be skilfully managed. Among the initial revelations is evidence that the passage to the vault was constructed from beneath the sub-cellar, a potently suggestive detail that's never explained. Does it imply that the de la Poer line was infiltrated by a subterranean race? In its inexplicability it helps the vault symbolise the narrator's subconscious—perhaps a hereditary one. At the sight of the contents of the vault Norrys appears to the narrator as "plump . . . utterly white and flabby" while de la Poer himself utters inarticulate sounds, images that prefigure the climax. Even now, despite the occasional rhetorical outburst—"Not Hoffmann or Huysmans could conceive a scene more wildly incredible, more frenetically repellent, or more Gothically grotesque than the twilit grotto through which we seven staggered"—most of the prose keeps its composure; that is, the narrator apparently keeps his. It's only when he ventures into the unlit gulf beneath the vault that he and his language regress, reverting like the layers of history through which the exploration has led him and fulfilling his identification with his house.

The reversion is preceded by several lines of the kind of prose that is popularly identified as Lovecraftian. "Then there came a sound from that inky, boundless, farther distance that I thought I knew; and I saw my old black cat dart past me like a winged Egyptian god, straight into the illimitable gulf of the unknown. But I was not far behind, for there was no doubt after another second. It was the eldritch scurrying of those fiend-born rats, always questing for new horrors, and determined to lead me on even unto those grinning caverns of earth's centre where Nyarlathotep, the mad faceless god, howls blindly to the piping of two amorphous idiot flute-players." I hope I've shown how carefully the culminating image here is prepared for, even within the paragraph; we may take the two Egyptian references as hinting at an occult correspondence between the horrors under Exham and ancient practices or legends elsewhere. In the dark he collides with "something soft and plump", and the reader hardly needs the final paragraph to confirm what the narrator refuses to admit. The final line rises to a crescendo as lyrical as it is horrific, and preserves the ambiguity of the narrative without lessening its cumulative power. It's as though all the narrator's repressions burst forth in the last few paragraphs, overtaking even his language before he regains some imperfect control.

The entire tale was "suggested by a very commonplace incident—the cracking of wallpaper late at night, and the chain of imaginings resulting from it." Such are the ways of fiction writing, which can transform the initial idea out of all recognition. "The Call of Cthulhu" (written in August or September 1926) was based on a dream, and Lovecraft recorded an element of the plot as early as 1919: "Man visits museum of antiquities—asks that it accept a bas-relief *he has* just made—*old* and learned curator laughs & says he cannot accept anything so modern. Man says that 'dreams are older than brooding Egypt or the contemplative Sphinx or garden-girdled Babylonia' & that he had fashioned the sculpture in his dreams. Curator bids him shew his product, and when he does so curator shews horror. Asks who the man may be. He tells modern name. 'No—*before that*' says curator. Man does not remember except in dreams. Then curator offers high price, but man fears he means to destroy sculpture. Asks fabulous price—curator will consult directors. Add good development and describe nature of bas-relief."

Before considering the tale, let me note how important the opening lines are to the effect of many of his stories (while the final line of each is crucial, but to be appreciated in context rather than quoted here). Here are a few of the openings:

"Cautious investigators will hesitate to challenge the common belief that Robert Blake was killed by lightning, or by some profound nervous shock derived from an electrical discharge" ("The Haunter of the Dark")

"You ask me to explain why I am afraid of a draught of cool air; why I shiver more than others upon entering a cold room, and seem nauseated and repelled when the chill of evening creeps through the heat of a mild autumn day" ("Cool Air")

"Bear in mind closely that I did not see any actual visual horror at the end" ("The Whisperer in Darkness")

"It is true that I have sent six bullets through the head of my best friend, and yet I hope to shew by this statement that I am not his murderer" ("The Thing on the Doorstep")

"I am forced into speech because men of science have refused to follow my advice without knowing why" (*At the Mountains of Madness*)

"From a private hospital for the insane near Providence, Rhode Island, there recently disappeared an exceedingly singular person" (*The Case of Charles Dexter Ward*)

"From even the greatest of horrors irony is seldom absent" ("The Shunned House")

Other tales begin by setting the geographical scene; we'll see this in "The Colour out of Space". As for "The Call of Cthulhu", it's one of those that begin with a statement of an aspect of Lovecraft's philosophy: "The most merciful thing in the world, I think, is the inability of the human mind to correlate all its contents." Mating science fiction and the occult, the tale is his first sustained essay in cosmic terror, founded in his sense of the indifference of the universe and of man's insignificance in space and time. Perhaps it's the scale of his theme that prompts him to make the narrative more persuasive by assembling documents that lead inexorably to the vast truth. The structure had already been used to lend conviction to fantastic and macabre tales; Wilkie Collins employed it in *The Moonstone*, and Stoker did in *Dracula*. While Lovecraft may have learned from at least the latter novel, the probable primary influence is Arthur Machen, who constructs "The Great God Pan" along those lines (and who is referred to by name in the second chapter of Lovecraft's story). In "The Call of Cthulhu" the method bears out the ominous vision of the opening paragraph.

Amid the sobriety of the first pages there are hints of menace, carefully restrained. The cause of Professor Angell's death is barely touched upon, but the reader is expected to pick it up. The nature of the bas-relief is lightly sketched to be developed later, though even so early there's a suggestion of wrongness. All the Providence and New Orleans locations are real, as is the earthquake, adding verisimilitude. The sculptor Wilcox's words to the professor are virtually identical to those Lovecraft told his correspondents that he spoke in his own original dream (one of the few details that figure unchanged in the tale). Given his wild dreams, the sculptor may seem to be a questionable witness of anything real, and the narrative withholds any endorsement of his account except by mentioning the professor's unusual interest in it. Lovecraft is reining his effects back, the better to release them where they'll be most telling, but he does include a hint of the size of the subject of Wilcox's dream. When the narrator begins to be swayed by the similarity of numerous other accounts, he's still inclined to blame some bias in the collection or interpretation of the data. By now, however, we're made to feel his skepticism may be unreasonable. It's an effective method of winning the reader over when used with skill, as here.

The second section of the narrative reveals the reasons for Angell's obsession, all the more effectively for their having been delayed. It begins with a detailed description of the monster Wilcox sculpted. Even here, however, it's a sculpture that's described, which prefigures the eventual manifestation and allows Lovecraft not to go into such detail at the climax. I believe he may have learned this approach from M. R. James's ghost story "Canon Alberic's Scrapbook", which Lovecraft had read in late 1925 and which uses the same technique; James also favoured complex structures, sometimes non-chronological, to achieve his effects. Early in this chapter Angell cites a further set of similarities, but these are more difficult to dismiss than the dreams, since they're authenticated by experts. Still, at this point they can be viewed merely as legends, the stuff of anthropology. Even the police inspector's account of the Louisiana ritual is challenged in a sense: the beliefs of the cultists are said to indicate "an astonishing degree of cosmic imagination" although they "might be least expected to possess it", a sentence in which skepticism is brought to bear and then subtly undermined.

It's worth examining the tone of Inspector Legrasse's account as given by the narrator. While the cult and its behaviour, together with the location, are described in evocative language, I don't think we're invited to assume that these are necessarily the policeman's words. (In "The Space-Eaters", an early and intermittently very effective example of Lovecraft's influence, Lovecraft's friend Frank Belknap Long makes a policeman use this sort of language in direct speech, inadvertently undermining the credibility of the characterisation.) As a contrast, the paragraphs setting out the cult's beliefs are in plain prose—more accurately, a naïve voice, an effective method of conveying more than it openly states (a child's voice can be especially powerful). The quotation from the *Necronomicon*—the forbidden book that is one of Lovecraft's most famous inventions—recalls a verse from his minor 1920 tale "Polaris", lines that refer to the Pole Star:

"Slumber, watcher, till the spheres
Six and twenty thousand years
Have revolv'd, and I return
To the spot where now I burn . . .
Only when my round is o'er
Shall the past disturb thy door."

"The Call of Cthulhu" develops this in terms of cosmic terror. I said earlier that his mythos was designed as an antidote to Victorian occultism, which he saw as excessively conventionalised and organised. Both the mythos and the *Necronomicon* were intended as partial glimpses of larger imaginative vistas, and it's regrettable that so many writers have sought to codify them.

The narrator's skeptical tone persists even in his visit to the sculptor Wilcox, but he can't entirely keep it up, given that he's aware of more than he has told us so far. As in "The Rats in the Walls", the tone is invaded by expressions of repressed material. The final chapter starts by introducing the first document to be quoted in full, the newspaper clipping. While the report exemplifies reticence, a couple of suggestive phrases lie low amid the sober journalism. The last and most damning item, the Norwegian sailor's reminiscence, is paraphrased, which allows Lovecraft to modulate the language, so that the circumstantial detail of the opening sentences soon gives way to lyrical evocations of terror. Some of the descriptions of the island strongly recall "Dagon", but in terms of the vision Lovecraft has now developed and expanded.

There's also a recurrence of one of his most potent effects—the vista or object that despite its ability to disturb only hints at greater and more terrible secrets hidden beyond or beneath. I'd suggest that part of the power of this image derives, as in "The Rats in the Walls", from symbolising the unconscious; in "The Call of Cthulhu", of course, it's actually the source of dreams. I should add that there's no need for Lovecraft to have intended the symbolism; sometimes in fiction the most eloquent material is partly unconscious, an unintended effect of telling the tale. The mythic echoes in the revelation of the monster are more conscious—certainly the references to the Cyclops, and the lethal effect of looking back is an equally resonant image from myth. The reference to an occurrence "that the chronicler would not put on paper" may seem typically Lovecraftian, but it has its origins in Kipling, who uses the technique twice in his horror story "The Mark of the Beast". Like "The Rats in the Walls", the present tale eventually but briefly bursts into delirious prose—"There is a sense of spectral whirling through liquid gulfs of infinity, of dizzying rides through reeling universes on a comet's tail, and of hysterical plunges from the pit to the moon and from the moon back again to the pit, all livened by a cachinnating chorus of the distorted, hilarious elder gods and the green, bat-winged mocking imps of Tartarus"—which is indeed a dream or a delirium. The last paragraphs do their best to recapture control, first in Johansen's coda and then the narrator's, but this can't overcome the cumulative effect of the tale, which may be said to employ conspiracy paranoia before the tendency became fashionable.

"The Colour out of Space" (written in March 1927) continues the evolution of Lovecraft's tales of terror towards science fiction. Later stories—"At the Mountains of Madness", "The Whisperer in Darkness", "The Shadow out of Time"—take this further, but in "Colour" he finds his single purest symbol of the otherness of the universe.

Hints of strangeness are woven into even the topographical realism of the opening paragraphs. The reference to "the hidden lore of old ocean, and all the mystery of primal earth" may resonate with readers of Lovecraft's earlier tales, but the images are delicate enough not to breach the understatement of the prose at this stage of the narrative. One way in which the scene-setting delays the full effect of the location is by holding it at a kind of aesthetic distance, with a theatrical reference ("the blasted heath") and a painterly one to Salvator Rosa. Just the same, there's a pronounced impression of wrongness, and the repetition of "the blasted heath" is followed by a description that reinvents the image. (As S. T. Joshi has pointed out, the phrase is both theatrical and poetic, having been used by Milton as well as Shakespeare.) The paragraph includes two images that will gather significance later: the "yawning black maw of an abandoned well whose stagnant vapours played strange tricks with the hues of the sunlight" and, more subtly, the "odd timidity about the deep skyey voids above" with which the place infects the unnamed narrator.

Like "The Call of Cthulhu" and other Lovecraft tales, the main text of "The Colour out of Space" is a story paraphrased by the narrator, which helps Lovecraft to control the tone and gives the reader the option of suspecting, at least to begin with, that the narrator's reconstruction of events may be unreliable. The meteorite and its effects are initially described in simple but evocative language (indeed, evocative because simple), which is followed by several paragraphs of scientific analysis that don't dissipate the sense of strangeness. A crucial event—the releasing of part of the contents of the meteorite—is shown with such reticence it's almost comical: "it burst with a nervous little pop". Again, the unnatural destruction of the meteorite is presented in purely scientific and meteorological terms, but all these details are being amassed towards conveying unease without acknowledging any reason for it. It's a case of letting the reader suspect worse than has been put into the words.

The first stages of the influence of the alien presence are very lightly conveyed. Nahum Gardner finds his work more tiring than formerly and blames his age. Lovecraft constructs many of his paragraphs towards a climactic sentence—in this case muted in its effect, but elsewhere (as in the lyrical passages I've quoted earlier) closer to classical musical structure. The new crop of fruit shows an "unwonted gloss", recalling the appearance of the meteorite. The alien taint begins to transform the wildlife, and despite the scientific reasons, the effects and the descriptions of them are oddly reminiscent of passages in George Macdonald's *The Princess and the Goblin*, a Victorian fairy tale in which animals have been mutated by magical influences; Lovecraft's increasing use of science in his fiction doesn't expunge the occult and fantastic but often embraces them, drawing on the imaginative strengths of both. The scientists who conducted the initial investigations of the meteorite now rationalise the effects around the Gardner farm, but the reader may well know better, although when the tale was written this dichotomy (between rationalists and some macabre truth) was less familiar in the genre. Employed skilfully, it can still work, and decades later Nigel Kneale made witty use of it in *Quatermass and the Pit*, a highly Lovecraftian piece.

The next few paragraphs grow oppressive with ominous details, psychological as well as physical. The first overt hints of something supernatural—the trees that move in no wind—are buried in the midst of paragraphs rather than dramatically placed at the end. Lovecraft may have learned this technique of unobtrusiveness in the layout of the material from M. R. James, who often uses this to startling effect (beware a recently edited edition of James that breaks down the paragraphs into shorter sections). Even when madness overtakes the Gardner family the language stays resolutely sober, except in the fragments of the mother's ravings. The hideous death of a family member is described by analogy with an earlier event, a reticent approach that I think adds to the horror.

The central section of the tale gives up detachment at last, with the informant Ammi Pierce's visit to the Gardner farm. The language only very gradually mounts to a pitch of physical horror, meanwhile subtly consolidating the hints of conscious alien activity around the farm (though even this is deftly qualified by the line "a buggy-wheel must have brushed the coping and knocked in a stone", which we're free to take at face value if we like, but not for long). The language reaches a crescendo with the scene of Nahum's death, particularly his monologue. In *On Writing* Stephen King describes Lovecraft as "a genius when it came to tales of the macabre, but a terrible dialogue writer," and cites this monologue as proof. Is it, though, when taken in context? After all, it's a report by the narrator of what Ammi Pierce (described at the outset as "rambling" with a mind that has "snapped a trifle") recalled nearly fifty years later. I think Lovecraft uses it as a way of modulating the tone of the narrative rather than as literal dialogue. Stephen objects that it consists of "carefully constructed elliptical bursts of information", but it reminds me oddly of the gasping voices we find in Samuel Beckett's later plays and prose. I can also report that I've read the whole story aloud to an audience and made Nahum's monologue work perfectly well.

As soon as Pierce flees the Gardner farm the prose reverts to sobriety, preparing for the final climax. Having progressed through understatement to gruesomeness, the story will reach for awe ("wonder and terror", as Fritz Leiber puts it). Unadorned prose and a scrap of rustic dialogue—more properly, another monologue—give way to ornate evocative language as the manifestations become unambiguous. Even so, just as in the previous two stories I've looked at here, delirious images are kept to a single sentence: "It was a monstrous constellation of unnatural light, like a glutted swarm of corpse-fed fireflies dancing hellish sarabands over an accursed marsh." The later passage that describes the "riot of luminous amorphousness" performed by the colour recalls Mrs Gardner's ravings, since the language consists very largely of verbs—a way of preserving suggestiveness while offering vividness.

To what extent may Lovecraft have been aware how Freudian some of the images of the well are? In 1921 he commented "We may not like to accept Freud, but I fear we shall have to do so." I suspect he would have repudiated any sexual reading of the investigation of the well, simply because it detracts from the sense of awe and terror he wants to convey. Such readings can be useful if they enrich a text, and for some readers they may do here. The disturbance of the well begins the upsurge of language and imagery that is rounded off by an ominous diminuendo, Pierce's glimpse of a trace of the colour that returns to the well. Form and content are one throughout the whole climactic scene. The extended coda sinks into language that is mostly plain, but of course this has gained resonance from the entire narrative—even such an unemphatic phrase as "the splotch of grey dust". However, Lovecraft uses one extraordinary verbal trick, repeating word for word the narrator's sentence about his own timidity from the opening scene. Some of the final lines might almost be trying to reduce the significance of the alien visitation, but the tale is surely proof against that. "It was just a colour out of space", but it epitomises Lovecraft's vision at least as powerfully as his mythos.

Since his death in 1937 he has emerged as one of the most important writers in the field, and a pervasive influence. He both drew on the strengths of the authors he most admired—Poe, Algernon Blackwood (whose tale "The Willows", with its evocation of absolute alienness, Lovecraft regarded as the greatest in the field), Arthur Machen, with his melding of Victorian science and the occult, and his sense of fairy tales and legends as metaphors for darker truths—and sought to improve on their limitations, as Lovecraft saw them. His ability in his best work to suggest terrors larger than he shows is as important as his attention to the power of language. While he wasn't averse to conveying "loathsome fright", his most lasting legacy is the sense of mingled wonder and dread. His influence has been celebrated by a remarkable variety of writers; besides those I named at the outset, consider Alan Moore, Jorge Luis Borges, Stephen King, Thomas Pynchon, Mark Samuels, Caitlín Kiernan, China Miéville, Laird Barron . . . Artists as different as H. R. Giger and John Coulthart have drawn inspiration from him, and directors such as Roger Corman, Sean Branney and Stuart Gordon have filmed his tales. His importance as a writer has been recognised by both the Library of America and Penguin Modern Classics, and the Penguin editions offer definitive restored texts. May his positive qualities continue to enrich literature! Horror fiction is much the better for them.

Let me end with a list of further recommendations. These stories demonstrate the considerable range of his best shorter work.

"The Outsider" (1921). Reminiscent of Poe's prose poems but original and personal; quite possibly an unconscious autobiographical metaphor.

"The Music of Erich Zann" (December 1921). Musical prose expressing a musical theme.

"The Festival" (1923). A delirious yet controlled tale that descends into the concealed antecedents of Christianity, and the first of his stories to cite a passage from the *Necronomicon* as background.

"Pickman's Model" (1926). Narrated in a conversational style, and exemplifying the dark humour (in this case deriving from Ambrose Bierce) that often figures in his work.

"The Thing on the Doorstep" (21-24 August 1933). Lovecraft's possession tale, reaching back through personality after personality to the possibly inhuman. As in "The Colour out of Space", there's an unemphasised poignancy about the characterisation and relationships.

"The Haunter of the Dark" (November 1935). Lovecraft's last major tale, suggested by an actual church in Providence and written as a wry tribute to his young correspondent Robert Bloch. A final melding of the occult and the astronomical, and an essay in the terrors of somnambulism.

AFTERWORD

I N ORDER TO GO FORWARD I MUST FIRST GO BACK. BEFORE
I wrote the tales that appear in *The Inhabitant of the Lake and
Other Unwelcome Tenants* (the PS edition, uniform with this
volume, and the only complete version), I'd already tried to engage
with the Lovecraftian. I'm afraid that by now I can only guess at the
chronology—I'd forgotten all about these sallies until very recently.
I had two goes at posing as Edward Pickman Derby, and my two
attempts at writing *Azathoth and Other Horrors* are here. This
must have been after I read "The Thing on the Doorstep" in Don
Wollheim's *Macabre Reader* (the Digit reprint, complete with Ed
Emsh cover) in, I believe, the summer of 1960. At this stage I hadn't
quite organised myself to attempt Mythos fiction, but it appears to
have been around the same time that I started a Lovecraftian tale,
"The Horror in the Crystal", the first item in an aborted collection,
The Creatures of the Shadow. About then I also read "Rusty
Chains", John Brunner's lambasting of Lovecraft in the March 1956
issue of *Inside and Science Fiction Advertiser*. My response was
"Rusty Links", which stomped on Lovecraftiana I found lacking,
not least some of Derleth's. With a prescience we may find
unnerving in retrospect, my mother persuaded me not to submit it
to whichever fanzine I had in mind, in case I antagonised the wrong
people. Though I fear she routinely went in for this kind of paranoia, in this case she was on the ball. The piece is plainly pitched at

fans—note the use of words like ghod and crud—but we're including it here for whatever historical significance it may contain. After that came my own first Mythos efforts, written perhaps in a bid to prove that I could do better than the work I denigrated.

I wrote "The Moon-Lens", the last story in *The Inhabitant of the Lake*, at the end of 1962, and set about revising it in January 1963. Meanwhile something else had happened: I'd discovered the fiction of Vladimir Nabokov. Reading Lovecraft in quantity—*Cry Horror*, the first collection of his work to appear in British paperback, and originally edited by Don Wollheim for Avon Books in 1947—had given me a model for my own attempts at fiction, and *Inhabitant* was the result. Now *Lolita* showed me how much more could be done with language, and before I'd finished the revision of "The Moon-Lens" I was inspired to give it a go. In fact, I was so fired up that I wrote the opening paragraphs of "The Stone on the Island" on a sheet of scrap paper at my desk in the Civil Service office where I worked.

Perhaps that's why the tale takes place there and even involves the name of a workmate on whom, in my embarrassingly delayed adolescence, I had an undeclared crush. The setting didn't please my correspondent J. Vernon Shea, although he approved of "The Church in High Street" as being appropriately Lovecraftian in its location. While several of the *Inhabitant* tales were based on entries in Lovecraft's Commonplace Book, "The Stone on the Island" pinched its idea from M. R. James—one of his "Stories I Have Tried to Write"—though I may well have rendered the source unrecognisable. For the record, here it is: "The man, for instance (naturally a man with *something* on his mind), who, sitting in his study one evening, was startled by a slight sound, turned hastily, and saw a certain dead face looking out from between the window curtains: a dead face, but with living eyes. He made a dash at the curtains and tore them apart. A pasteboard mask fell to the floor. But there was no one there, and the eyes of the mask were but eye-holes. What was to be done about that?" More than I managed, you might think. Kirby McCauley found the tale excessively sadistic, and now I do. On the other hand, when August Derleth read it he was enthusiastic, even though it announces my abandonment of his version of the Lovecraft mythos (after all, the five-pointed talisman proves to be useless). "I thought it stylistically a tremendous improvement over the first story of yours I read; you seem more sure of yourself, more firmly in control, and in general the story is very good."[46] I submitted it along with the final version of the *Inhabitant* collection, and I suspect he was a little disappointed in those stories by comparison with "The Stone on the Island", since they were written and rewritten earlier; it shows. Perhaps, as Shea felt, the combination of my own everyday experience and the Lovecraftian doesn't quite jell, but I would try it again in 1964, in "The Successor".

Successful it isn't. Bits of my life bob up in it without being properly subsumed. For instance, the film society Derek Sheridan frequents is based on the Merseyside Film Institute, based for decades in the Bluecoat Chambers in Liverpool. The ingratiating chap who takes him to the bookshop is a frankly unreasonable transformation of a Bluecoat regular, who did indeed espouse old films and dismiss newer ones regardless of quality. Given the titles of the books he reads, Sheridan seems pansexual if not (as I was in those days) rather detached from the whole business. I read banned books because they were banned, not out of any particular identification with the content. The present reader may need to be told that in those days all manner of books were forbidden in Britain—the works of de Sade and William Burroughs, among others. I made more of the link between the forbidden and the occult when I rewrote "The Successor" two years later. We're including the first draft here for comparison. "Let me meander for a while"! The author's inadvertent honesty went unnoticed by himself.

August 1964 finds me making another bid to combine the banal and the cosmic in "Before the Storm". A hint of William Burroughs creeps in, and I told him so ("Cthulhu meets Trak") during a very brief correspondence we had while he was in Tangier. In early 1965 I came up with the first draft of "The Franklyn Paragraphs", based on entry number 86 in Lovecraft's Commonplace Book: "To find something horrible in a (perhaps familiar) book, and not to be able to find it again." I'm visibly struggling with language and overwhelmed by irrelevant minutiae, and hadn't yet learned (as I did in the next tale I wrote, "The Cellars") to use an actual setting in closely observed detail. I hope I would have rewritten the story extensively before submitting it anywhere, but luckily it languished in manuscript while it awaited inclusion in *Demons by Daylight*, giving me time to write the tale afresh instead. The ominous vision of the schoolyard wasn't, as far as I recall, intended to suggest paedophilia.

I was equally dissatisfied with "Before the Storm", and hadn't sent it anywhere by 1967, when Derleth asked me to contribute a story to *Tales of the Cthulhu Mythos*. "BEFORE THE STORM is negligible," I told him, "and at the present I've no idea what do to improve it; THE FRANKLYN PARAGRAPHS contains only very minor Lovecraftian references, and the way I'm rewriting it at present it's likely to turn out more of a jeu d'esprit or a sort of elaborate literary joke."[47] Instead I sent him the new version of "The Successor", which I'd rewritten earlier that year.

I mean completely rewritten, as you'll see or have seen. I seem to have been as instinctive a writer then as I am now, and for several years my first drafts were riddled with misjudgements. I preferred to write a wholly new version of "The Successor" and several others rather than simply rework the first draft, of which there was too little worth salvaging. "Cold Print" does reuse a couple of images from the first version. Our protagonist Sam Strutt borrows characteristics from one of my Civil Service workmates (who did indeed look to me to lend him, as he called them, exciting books—Olympia Press titles, to be specific—and who found Jean Genet dull) and from a gym master at my old grammar school. Also lurking in the story is the influence of Robin Wood's seminal *Hitchcock's Films*, as revelatory to me in its way as reading Nabokov and still the single greatest work of film criticism I've ever read. I had in mind the moment in the diner scene in *The Birds* where, as Wood points out, the subjective viewpoint means that Doreen Lang accuses not just Tippi Hedren but the audience of having brought the birds. In both versions of the story the bookshop is based on the one my old friend John Roles ran. Unlike the Brichester shop, it was located downtown, but the cheerful chaos was authentic, believe me. Later he moved the whole stock to Waterloo outside Liverpool, where the shop grew more chaotic still and the books set about taking over his living space too. As I've written elsewhere, in 1999 he was murdered by a charity worker who was also a postcard collector. He and his death are apparently so insignificant that I can find almost no references to either online, and I was dismayed to read in the transcript of the perfunctory trial his killer received that John was said to have had few friends. He had many, quite a few of whom would have shown up at the trial if we'd known the date.

Forgive the digression. Perhaps it isn't wholly inappropriate to this book, since one element I've tried at times to bring to

Lovecraftian fiction is humanity. Let's get back to our book. The first version of "A Madness from the Vaults" was written at the end of 1962, and I was so dissatisfied with it that I didn't even mention it to Derleth, let alone including it in the typescript of *Inhabitant*. It languished in manuscript until Graham Hall, a penpal who was later to become an editor at Mike Moorcock's radical *New Worlds*, asked me for a contribution to his fanzine *Doubt*. I duly typed up "Madness", and it appeared in 1964, understandably offending some readers with its sadism. After that I was happy to let it be forgotten, and indeed to leave the Lovecraftian for several years once I'd finished "The Franklyn Paragraphs", until Meade and Penny Frierson approached me to contribute to their immense *HPL* anthology. By then I imagined I'd sloughed off Lovecraft's influence, though I'm happy now to say I was mistaken, and the only idea that occurred to me was to revamp "A Madness from the Vaults". I duly did, toning down the sadism and, I hope, telling a somewhat better tale.

I must return briefly to "The Franklyn Paragraphs", for the strangest anecdote in this afterword. Not many years ago I chanced upon an online reference to Errol Undercliffe. It took me to eBay, where a copy of a work by Undercliffe—*This Perverted Body*—was offered. Did I bid for it? Indeed, and I don't think anybody else did. It proved to be an A4 pamphlet, containing a typed two-page surrealist story and fifteen illustrated pages bearing a pair two surreal collages in the manner of Max Ernst, each with a caption ("The rattle made by vibrating teeth—the previous head of the convent faces half a dozen men of wisdom" is typically gnomic). While the pamphlet looks as if it could have been mimeographed, I've never heard of another copy, and I wonder if it might be unique—even designed for me to find. In that case, what occult effect may be intended? What may have taken hold of my mind?

In 1969 I'd written "Lovecraft in Retrospect" at the behest of David Sutton, who published it in his fanzine *Shadow*. I should explain that he didn't ask for an attack on Lovecraft, and I suspect he may have been taken aback by the diatribe but published it nonetheless. If I can put it into context, it was one of the reasons I gained a name (not one I'm proud of) for producing controversy on demand. I fear that to some extent it was provoked by an essay in *Shadow* on my tales by Eddy C. Bertin, not that I'm blaming him. Since he was writing a series of pieces about Lovecraftian authors, it's entirely understandable that his piece focused mainly on that aspect of my stories, but I felt that my more recently published stories showed I'd moved on and were insufficiently celebrated. By then I'd written all but one of the tales in *Demons by Daylight*, but the book wouldn't appear until 1973.

I did rediscover my Lovecraftian side in an odd way in 1973. I'd come upon a book of drawings I'd done at the age of fourteen or so, which derive not just from Lovecraft but from the covers of weird fifties paperbacks (Herbert van Thal's *Told in the Dark* for one) and of the British magazine *Phantom*, while the copulating creatures outside the cave are close relatives of those Matt Fox depicted on the front of the July 1949 *Weird Tales*. They're amateur, to put it mildly, but they do have a certain grotesque charm. Indeed, they so impressed Ray Bolger, the art master at St Edward's College, that he urged me to try painting, and the resultant daub (complete with a brief pretentious exegesis I wrote) hung on a corridor wall at my school for a while. Now, having attained twenty-seven and aided by a herbal stimulus, I did my best to put down in words what I saw. The resulting piece ("Among the pictures are these:") found a home in Harry O. Morris's magazine devoted as much to Lovecraft as surrealism.

Some way into 1974 Edward Berglund asked for a new tale for a Lovecraftian anthology he was editing for DAW Books. I'd been writing fulltime for about a year, and pretty well any commission would have been welcome. Alas, "The Tugging" is one more instance—the last, I hope—of my tendency to take ideas from Lovecraft's work and spoil them. Having managed in "The Insects from Shaggai" to misrepresent Azathoth and ruin the insect image I lifted from the Commonplace Book, in "The Tugging" I mangled the notion of the rightness of the stars, or at any rate reduced it to far less than it had been. I should have left the stars alone.

In April 1971 Derleth wrote to me "I am preparing a sequel to TALES OF THE CTHULHU MYTHOS. Will you consider doing a new Mythos tale for it?" Less than three months later he was dead. I believe years passed before I thought of trying to revive the anthology idea as a tribute to him. At the time I proposed it Donald Wandrei was in charge at Arkham House, but not long after it was commissioned James Turner took over. I met him in 1975, when I spent several pleasant days walking Derleth's walks and in general being made at home by the personnel of Arkham House. Jim had, shall we say, strong opinions, and perhaps felt the need to establish his editorial personality. During my stay we argued over my intention to include a new story by Karl Edward Wagner. Perhaps Jim felt he'd failed to make his point forcefully enough, since soon he sent me a letter warning that if I included fiction by (among other writers) Karl, the project would be killed (his words). He apparently felt Karl's "Sticks" wasn't up to Turner standards. Later he must have changed his mind about the tale, for he anthologised it himself.

In late 1975 I wrote "The Faces at Pine Dunes" for *New Tales of the Cthulhu Mythos.* It's one of two tales in the present volume that are based on the Freshfield area of Merseyside. I must have been working on it when I stayed in Chapel Hill, because I recall Manly Wade Wellman remarking that for him a caravan still bore the original Oriental meaning (and might for many Americans), which was why in the anthology version I referred to a caravan park. The tale—which, like "The Voice of the Beach", is set around Freshfield, where I had several seventies chemical experiences—could be categorised as acid horror.

"The Voice of the Beach" was written in 1977. This time I had no market in mind, but had regained enough of a sense of Lovecraft's achievement to make a bid at scaling those heights (forever out of reach for me, I fear). Like him, I think "The Colour out of Space" is his single finest tale, and I tried to do what it does—to convey a sense of cosmic terror without any explicit references to the mythos (his one or my imitation). Once it was written it seems to have wandered in search of a market for years. In time Lin Carter asked me "for old times' sake" to write a Mythos story for *Weird Tales,* and he looked at "The Voice of the Beach" but found it insufficiently Lovecraftian. In terms of the kind of Mythos tales Lin wrote, perhaps it was. I can't now recall whether it was in response to his comment that I made the tale even less Mythosish by removing a couple of scraps of alien language that, in the version he saw, the voice was heard to pronounce. The story found a home at last in *Fantasy Tales,* a magazine that captured for me at least as much of the feel of *Weird Tales* as Lin's revival of the title. I'd say that's where the tale belonged.

I felt I'd achieved as much as I could in tribute to Lovecraft for a while, and didn't try anything else of the kind—at least, not by intention—for nearly two decades. I did write "Blacked Out" in 1977 too, but the muffled echo of "The Haunter of the Dark" is inadvertent, and I included the story in the first edition of *Cold Print* only because Jeff Conner wanted to include an unpublished tale. Steve King was right to find Lovecraftian elements in *The Parasite*, and Everett Bleiler found some in *The Hungry Moon*—a "cut-price Cthulhu" was his phrase, as I recall. However, I didn't make another conscious attempt to be Lovecraftian until 1994.

Some years earlier Bob Weinberg had asked me to write a tale for a new Lovecraftian anthology. I had an idea but couldn't make it work. It wasn't until Scott David Aniolowski proposed to put together an anthology for Chaosium to celebrate my visit to the Necronomicon convention in Danvers that I returned to the idea and saw how it needed to be handled—exactly the same as any other story of a village with an inhuman secret. I read it at the convention, and later at the Preston Science Fiction Group, where Bryan Talbot—creator of the superb *Tale of One Bad Rat* and many other first-rate works—seemed amused. Had my Lovecraftian pottering revealed some hidden aspect to him?

In 1996 I began to look back at my old stuff. It seemed to me I'd had ideas that I wasn't sufficiently equipped to develop at the time, or that might benefit from additional exploration. "The Other Names" is a riff on the central theme of "The Render of the Veils"— if you like (and I hope some will) a domestication of a cosmic theme, which I meant it to throw into a different relief. At the turn of the century I took *The Case of Charles Dexter Ward* to some extent as a model for a novel of my own, *The Darkest Part of the Woods*, another attempt to conjure up the Lovecraftian without explicitly referring to the mythos. In the course of it I hope I did better by that Lovecraft dream I garbled in "The Insects of Shaggai". While *Creatures of the Pool* contains no overt references either, I've seen it argued that the novel makes Liverpool into a kind of British Innsmouth.

In 2009 it occurred to me to bring into print the letters Cameron Thaddeus Nash wrote to Lovecraft, since Arkham House had never published them. While they don't explain all the doubts Lovecraft had about his own worth as a writer, they seem to embody his feelings in an external human form. It's a pity that we lack his responses to the correspondence. Since then I've revisited "The Inhabitant of the Lake" in *The Last Revelation of Gla'aki*, which was my bid to clear away the clutter of the Mythos and return to Lovecraft's principles as they were before so much that came after him blurred them. I confess I was afraid that folk who liked my stuff would feel I'd reverted too far, while those who wanted me to return to my old ways might find the novella too affected by my present methods. Happily, I haven't seen any reactions along these lines, and so I'm attempting a trilogy, *The Three Births of Daoloth*. "That is not dead . . . " and all that, which certainly sums up the Mythos. I would like to think I'm learning to contribute to it rather than diminishing it with a surfeit of elaboration, and my recent close reading of several Lovecraft tales (for an essay included here) helped me to discover how much more there is to his work. Time—who can say how many years—will tell.

Ramsey Campbell
Wallasey, Merseyside
24 April 2015

ACKNOWLEDGEMENTS

"The Horror under Warrendown", copyright © 1995 by Ramsey Campbell. From *Made in Goatswood*, edited by Scott David Aniolowski.

"The Other Names", copyright © 1998 by Ramsey Campbell. From *Interzone* 137, November 1998, edited by David Pringle.

"The Correspondence of Cameron Thaddeus Nash", copyright © 2010 by Ramsey Campbell. From *Black Wings*, edited by S. T. Joshi.

The Last Revelation of Gla'aki, copyright © 2013 by Ramsey Campbell. Slightly revised for this Drugstore Indian Press edition.

"The Successor" (first draft of "Cold Print"), "The Franklyn Paragraphs" (first draft), "Mushrooms from Merseyside", "Two Poems by Edward Pickman Derby", "The Horror in the Crystal" (fragment), "Rusty Links", "Afterword", copyright 2015. Original to this volume.

"Lovecraft in Retrospect", copyright © 1969 by Ramsey Campbell. From *Shadow 7*, September 1969, edited by David A. Sutton. Further commentary copyright © 1994 by Ramsey Campbell. *From Voices From Shadow*.

"On Four Lovecraft Tales", copyright © 2013 by Ramsey Campbell. From *Morphologies: Short Story Writers on Short Story Writers*, edited by Ra Page.

"The Stone on the Island", copyright © 1964 by August Derleth. From *Over the Edge*.

"Before the Storm", copyright © 1980 by Ramsey Campbell. From *Fantasy Readers Guide* 2, March 1980.

"Cold Print", copyright © 1969 by August Derleth. From *Tales of The Cthulhu Mythos*.

"The Franklyn Paragraphs", copyright © 1973 by Ramsey Campbell. From *Demons by Daylight*.

"A Madness from the Vaults", copyright © 1972 by Meade and Penny Frierson. From *HPL*.

"The Tugging", copyright © 1976 by Edward P. Berglund. From *The Disciples of Cthulhu*.

"The Faces at Pine Dunes", copyright © 1980 by Arkham House Publishers, Inc. From *New Tales of the Cthulhu Mythos*.

"Blacked Out", copyright © 1985 by Ramsey Campbell.

"The Voice of the Beach", copyright © 1982 by Ramsey Campbell. From *Fantasy Tales* 10, Summer 1982.